全民英檢
中高級作文指南

The Brook
"I chatter over stony ways
In little sharps and trebles
I bubble into eddying bays
I babble on the pebbles."
- Tennyson

唐清世 著

序言

　　本書採取二個不同的角度來幫助讀者解開「全民英檢」中高級寫作能力測驗之謎。一方面從橫切面著手，依考試的範圍，有系統的從遣詞到成句來介紹中譯英，再由段落到章篇介紹各種不同的作文技巧，循序漸進的導引讀者進入英文作文的領域，透過對字、句、段、章的微觀了解到作文本身的宏觀掌握，來幫助讀者培養作文能力以達到扎實的程度。另一方面從縱切面落筆，依考試的題型及評分的標準，每節以習題切入，要讀者不斷練習來掌握作文技巧，用以增加讀者應試的能力來爭取高分。希望在理論及實用兩者並重的方法下，提供讀者一本真正具實效的自修指南。

　　中高級寫作能力的測驗部份，對翻譯及引導寫作的評分標準，要求著重在遣詞，妥切及靈活運用句構，並求內容切題，全文組織完整及連貫通順。根據這重點，本書第一章討論遣詞應注意的地方，以及如何從分析詞序的主從關係中求正確表達中、英文的意思。第二章討論英文句子的模式，提供讀者對英文句式的基本認識。在此基礎上，使用 x-bar 句法的理論，來分析英文句構各層次的構成要素，同時介紹如何使用「次元單位」的觀念來造句。為了提升讀者中譯英的應試能力起見，也另闢一節討論中譯英的基本智識。而這部份的習題，是配合「全民英檢」的題型供讀者練習中譯英的技巧。第三章以如何靈活使用句構為課題，先討論與此課題有密切關係的二個觀念，即「置換」及「省略」，然後再綜合討論各種靈活使用句構的方法，學習如何用不同的句法來表達相類似的文意。這一章將提供讀者在應試時，靠「法殊趣同」的方法來靈活使用句構以爭取高分。第四章討論段落及章篇的組合結構，著重介紹如何使用各種不同的方法，以求聯句及聯段的圓通以及章篇的形成，來使讀者了解各種求文意周密的技巧。而本章的習題，也配合「全民英檢」引導寫作部份的測驗題型，供讀者練習及掌握本章所介紹的技巧，來謀

求「全文組織完整及連貫通順」的要求。

本書習題的命題其內容是採用多元化的方式，諸如包括日常生活的流行話題，時事以及時常用到的抽象觀念。為配合讀者自修的需要起見，習題各部分的呈現方法包括下列幾個特點：每題提供「解析欄」，作重點解說，提示讀者應如何去做的線索，並適度提供重要的字彙、片語、字彙的搭配，以及應採用的句構，這些是以穿針引線的方法來協助讀者掌握用字、造句及作文的要領。同時每一習題另有「解答欄」，提供讀者隨做隨改的方便。英語的句法很多，假定讀者自己的解答與書中的解答有所不同時，也可透過比較來領悟不同的寫法。此外，有時更設「補充說明欄」，將非直接有關的資料提供讀者作參考，諸如文法上應注意的地方，或是其他可用的字彙及句構等。

本書有大量習題供讀者反複練習，讀者如能每天花一小時的時間，按步就班逐節去做，大概四個月到半年之間能全部做完，屆時，讀者英文作文的能力必達另一境界，對拿高分也更具信心。

本書內容雖然以「全民英檢」中高級應試生為主要對象，但由於書中所介紹的各種作文技巧，與一般英文作文的方法並沒有太多顯著的不同，因此本書也適合具大專英文程度的在校生及社會青年使用，您如果在準備類似的考試，例如特考及 TOFEL 等，這本書對提高您英文作文的能力必定也有很大的幫助。

本書對下列各出版商，允許我摘引其出版物的段落作例子使用，特此致謝：

1） The Economist Newspaper Limited, London.

2） The Global and Mail, Toronto.

3） The Ottawa Citizen, Ottawa.

4） Oxford University Press, London.

5） A.W. Sijthoff, Leyden, The Netherlands.

目 錄

第一章　字裡行間應注意出入

凡文「因字而生句，積句而成章」，因此在準備應考「全民英檢」寫作能力測驗的時候，第一步應從遣詞著手。我們不妨用下面二個例子來試試自己對遣詞有多少認識。第一個例子是 We need to face the fact that the need for/of doctors is increasing。在這一句中，need 之後究竟應該用系詞 for 還是 of？而同樣一個 need，其後跟 for 的意思與跟 of 的意思有何不同？這涉及到一字多義的問題。同時，同樣一個 need，在這句中出現二次，分別具有二種不同的詞性（parts of speech），這對我們字義的認識有什麼影響？這些問題與遣詞恰當與否有關。第二個例子是在 a senior U.S. official 片語中，詞序是將 senior 放在 U.S. 之前，但在 a U.S. counter-terrorism official 片語中，是將 U.S. 放在 counter-terrorism 之前，而不是放在後面，為什麼有這樣的區別？而這區別與句構變化有什麼關係？同時對正確表達中英文的意思有什麼影響？這些都牽涉到詞序的安排問題。

遣詞是否恰當，詞序是否合理，二者能影響我們駕馭字彙的能力，而懂得如何遣詞及安排詞序，在考試時可避免辭不達意的缺點。對如何遣詞及如何掌握詞序這二點，我們分別在下面逐節詳細討論。

1.1　遣詞需恰當

所謂遣詞恰當，一方面是指中、英文意思相切，另一方面是指英文字彙間的搭配恰當。例如，「士氣低落」可譯成 The morale is low. 這句中文的「士氣」與「低落」分別與英文的 morale 及 low 意思相切，同時在英文中，morale 與 low 在習慣上是相互搭配在一起使用

的，因此我們稱這句譯文符合了遣詞恰當的要求。需注意的是，遣詞的恰當與否在於選詞（diction），而不同的文體常使用不同的字眼。英文有二種不同的文體，一是正規文體（formal English，亦稱文言文體），一是通用文體（general English，亦稱口語體）[1]，前者用詞嚴謹，常使用在學術性的著作中，後者用詞通俗，是一般報章雜誌上常見的文體。「全民英檢」對中高級應試生似要求精熟通用文體，這可從其鼓勵學生多閱讀英文報紙及雜誌中看出。

由於不同的文體使用不同的字眼，因此遣詞恰當第一個需注意的地方是使用適合特定文體的字眼，例如： The above-mentioned information was conveyed to all students last week 在這一句中，above-mentioned 是屬正規文體的用法，通常用 above 即可。同時，convey 也是常在正規文體中出現的字眼，通常用 give 即可，因此原句在通用文體中可改寫成 The above information was given to all students last week.

遣詞恰當第二個需注意的地方是字無定義的現象。每一個字有其主要的直接意思及次要的間接意思。前者是一個字固定的本身內涵，後者是由變化而來的引申內涵。例如 senior 一字，其主要的意思是指 「老前輩」，這是可從字典中找到的直接意思，但 senior 一字與其他不同的字眼相搭配時，可間接引申出不同層次的意義，例如： a）資深的 （senior officer）, b）年長的 （senior citizen）及 c）高級的 （senior research fellow） 等三種特定的意思。需注意的是，有時一個間接引申的特定意思，本身也可演變成一個固有的直接意思。例如在「黑髮」、「青絲」及「芳華之年」三個詞組中，「黑

---

[1] 關於這二種文體的區別，請參第 4.3.3 節，習題一。英文另有一種「非正規文體」(informal English)，此種文體慣用俚語，且句構常常不拘文法，不屬常用的文體。

髮」是固有的直接意思，「青絲」是由「黑髮」引申出來的間接意思，雖然一黑、一青顏色有所不同，但其意思仍然相同，而「芳華之年」是由「青絲」引申出來的間接意思，在此，「青絲」本身既是「黑髮」的特定間接的引申意思，也是「芳華之年」的直接固有的意思。

　　通常，專有名詞及科學名詞其直接意思較固定，而其間接引申的意思較少，但一般其他字彙，尤其是代表抽象概念的用字，其直接固定的意思少，而間接引申的意思多。一般而言，字無定義的現象有二大類，一是一字多義（mutability of words），例如 save 可有下列不同的意思：

To save appearances	表保全體面的意思
To save one's breath	表緘默的意思
To save oneself	表偷懶的意思
To save one's face	表保全面子的意思
To save one's neck	表明哲保身的意思
To save one's trouble	表不必白費氣力的意思
To save the situation	表收拾時局的意思
To save the tide	表把握機會的意思
A fine save	表漂亮的救球的意思

在以上幾個例子中，save 一字因與不同字眼搭配而產生不同的意思。

　　另一種字無定義的現像是一字多詞性，例如：「我喜歡游泳」可翻成 I like swimming. 這裡 like 是動詞表「喜歡」的意思。而「有其父必有其子」可譯成 Like father like son. 這裡 like 是系詞表「有其」的意思。而 Like cases are to be decided alike. 在這一句中，like 是形容詞表「相同」的意思。再如：It looks like we are lost. 在這一句中，

like 是連接詞表「好像」的意思[2]。在這些例子中，like 一字的意義因詞性的不同而有所不同。明瞭字無定義的這個現象，能幫助我們在翻譯及作文時曉得如何採用適當的字眼及詞性。此外，在譯作時尚需注意「多字一義」的現象。例如描寫「酒醉」的字眼，除可用 drunk 外，另可用 fuddled, inebriated, intoxicated, jagged, juiced, loaded, sloshed, soused, stewed, stoned, tank-up, tie one on 及 tight。這現象也能影響我們在譯作時的遣詞。

須注意的是，一字多義的現象在翻譯時能產生「字無定譯」的結果。例如：「責任感薄弱」可譯成 The sense of responsibility is low. 在此例中 low 與 sense of responsibility 相搭配，表中文「薄弱」的意思，但我們在上文曉得，low 在與 morale 相搭配時，是表示「低落」的意思。這說明同樣一個字能譯出不同的意義。因此當我們在翻譯時，須針對不同的文意來選擇恰當的中、英文字眼，這樣才能達到遣詞恰當的要求。

遣詞恰當第三個需注意的地方是英文中有很多名詞，動詞，形容詞及系詞相互搭配，不同的搭配能產生不同的意思。例如 rest 一字當作名詞用時，可與動詞 take 搭配（take a rest）表示「休息」的意思，但與動詞 come 相搭配（come to a rest）時，則表示「停止」的意思，而與形容詞 eternal 相搭配（eternal rest）則表示「永息」（喻死亡）的意思，但當 rest 用作動詞時，如與系詞 on 相搭配（rest on）

---

[2]　Like 用作連接詞時，常與 feel, look, seem, sound 及 taste 等動詞共用，在其他場合下，不妨以 as 及 as if 來替代，例如: She arrived on time as (not like) we thought. 或 She talked to us as if (not like) we were her friends. 但需注意的是，like 的語氣較 as if 的語氣為重，例如: She treated us like we were her real friends 及 She treated us as if we were her real friends. 在這二例中，第二例含有並非是她的真正好朋友的意思。

則表示「依靠」的意思，而與系詞 with 相搭配時（rest with）則表示「全然」的意思。

　　根據以上的說明，如果社會上缺少醫生的情形愈來愈嚴重的時候，我們應該用 the need for doctors is increasing. 而如果是指醫生本身的需求愈來愈多的時候，我們應該用 the need of doctors is increasing.

　　綜合以上的說明，使我們不難理解平常在閱讀進修時，應多培養對字義的認識，因為這能影響我們譯作時的遣詞。例如「青絲成雪」可譯成 Snow-white hair was once silk-black. 也可譯成 Manhood's morning died while still touching noon. 前者是用髮色來描寫人生的過程，由青絲到白髮來喻人生的短暫，後者是用時間的流逝來描寫人生（manhood）在盛年之時（noon）就夭折，這二個例子在翻「青絲成雪」時對字義認識有所不同，因而產生不同的譯文，結果是使前者成為直譯，後者成為意譯。至於如何培養對字義的正確認識一點，這需要我們在平常閱讀進修的時候多查字典，尤其是查英文搭配字典，這樣在應試時，才能避免字裡行間因有錯誤的用詞而引起文意的混淆。

　　遣詞恰當另一個需注意的地方是用字需清晰（clarity），避免使用贅字，尤其是不必要的系詞及連接詞。例如：She failed to attend the meeting for the reason that she was not informed beforehand. 在這一句中，for the reason that 可用 because 來替代而將原句改寫成 She failed to attend the meeting because she was not informed beforehand. 這類贅字很多，下面列舉幾個常見的例子，供讀者平時參考。

全民英檢
中高級作文指南

不用	用
At this（that）point in time	Now（then）
Because of the fact that	Because
By means of	By
By reason of	Because of
By virtue of	By, under
Despite the fact that	Although, even though
During the time that ….	During, while
For the period of	For
For the purpose of	To
For the reason that	Because
From the point of view	From, for
In accordance with	By, under
In as much as	Since
In favor of	For
In order to	To
In relation to	About, concerning
In the area of	Roughly
In the event that	When, if
In the nature of	Like
In view of	Because
On the basis of	By, from
Prior to	Before
Subsequent to	After
Until such time as …	Until
With regard to	About, concerning
With respect to	On, about

　　除了應避免贅字之外，我們也應注意避免贅意，例如： In this paragraph, part of it consists of clauses that are joined by coordinate conjunctions and part of it consists of clauses that are joined by subordinate conjunctions. 在這一句中，使用了太多的字彙來表達一個簡單的文意，這句可簡化成 In this paragraph, part of it consists of compound sentences and part of it complex sentences.[3] 同樣：She withdrew into herself as a result of the fact that her husband had left her. 在這一句中可將 as a result of the fact that 用 because 來替代而改寫成 She withdrew into herself because her husband had left her. 這類贅意的例子也很多，下面我們列舉幾個常見的例子，供讀者平時參考。

不用	用
The fact that he had testified.	His testimony
He was aware of the fact that ….	He knew that …
In some instances students can ….	Sometimes students can ….
In the majority of instances students can ….	In most cases（usually） students can ….
There is no doubt that ….	Doubtless, no doubt
The question as to whether ….	Whether

　　一般來說，遣詞的不當可由使用直接固有的意思不當而引起，導致用字錯誤（incorrect word）而使措詞失靈。也可因援用間接引申的意思不當而引起，致使用字模稜兩可（fuzzy word）而使辭傷義，二者在譯作時應該盡量避免。在全文主旨允許的情形下，不妨考慮使用具體（concrete）及確切（specific）的字眼，少用抽象（abstract）

---

[3] 在此例中，我們也省略了第二個動詞 (consist)。有關省略的基本概念，請參第 3.2.1 節。

及籠統（general）的字眼，後者的情形常發生在涉及價值觀念的抽象名詞，由於此類字彙其間接引申意思多，往往一不小心，常使我們在譯作時，從一個內涵跳到另一個內涵而不自知。不論是措詞失靈或是用辭傷義，皆需我們更改字眼或者甚至修改上下文來糾正這種錯誤。

本節習題，前十五題練習字彙的搭配，後五題練習如何避免贅文。

習題一

將下句譯成英文。

成功不能憑空設想而出。

解析：

用片語 out of thin air 表「憑空而出」，用 conjure 與 up 相搭配表「設想」。

解答：

Success cannot be conjured up out of thin air.

習題二

將下句譯成英文。

風暴漸近，預示一個不穩定航行的壞兆。

解析：

用 bode 與 ill 相搭配表「預示壞兆」。注意 bode ill 之後常與系詞 for 相搭配。用 smooth 與 sail 相搭配表「穩定航行」。

解答：

The approaching storm bodes ill for a smooth sail.

習題三

a) 將下句翻成英文。

她一會兒就見您。

解析：

注意「一會兒」如何表達。

解答：

She will be with you in a moment.

b)　將下句翻成英文。

　　她在離開班公室前稍停了一會兒。

解析：

注意「停了一會兒」如何表達。

解答：

She paused for a moment before leaving her office.

補充說明：

這裡二個不同系詞的使用產生不同的意思，in a moment 表「即將」的意思，而 for a moment 表「有一會兒」的意思。

習題四

將下句翻成英文。

在伊拉克戰爭即將一觸即發的時候，很多回教徒遷往約旦居住。

解析：

注意「遷往 …居住」如何表達。用片語 in the walk-up to the war 表「戰爭即將一觸即發」。

解答：

In the walk-up to the war in Iraq, many Muslims immigrated to Jordan.

補充說明：

「戰爭即將一觸即發」也可用片語 in the run-up to the war 來表達。又，注意這裡「遷往 …居住」不能用 emigrate 來表達。二者的區別在於前者以目的地而言，而後者以出發地而言，本題是指遷往

15

約旦居住，而在 When Saddam Hussein was in power, many Iraqis emigrated 一例中，是指很多回教徒離開伊拉克。

習題五

將下句譯成英文。

他遠眺地平線處，那裡落陽襯映在彤雲中。

解析：

用 gaze 與系詞 out 相搭配表「遠眺」，以 setting 與 sun 相搭配表「落陽」，以 outline 與 against 相搭配表「襯映」，用 purple 與 sky 相搭配表「彤雲」。自結構言，「那裡 ...」句需用 where 子句使本句成一複合句。

解答：

He gazed out across the horizon where the setting sun was outlined against the purple sky.

補充說明：

此處 sun 另可分別與 waning, lowering, sinking, retiring, retreating 及 westering 諸形容詞相搭配表「落陽」的意思。有關複合句的用法，我們將在第 2.2.2 節中討論。又，注意中、英文不同的句構表達方法，亦即中文的二個句子用一個英文句子來表達。關於這一點，也請參第 2.2.2 節。

習題六

將下句譯成英文。

生還者努力追想所發生的事。

解析：

用片語 call to memory 表「追想」，注意其間必須與系詞 to 相搭配。

解答：

The survivors tried to call to memory what had happened.

補充說明：

注意動詞時式，「所發生的事」在「追想」之前發生，故用過去完成式。這裡我們也可用 recollect 或 remember 或 recall 來表「追想」，亦即 The survivors tried to recollect\remember\recall what had happened.

習題七

將下句翻成英文。

昨晚，約翰被一個醉漢開車給撞死了。

解析：

注意「醉漢」如何表達。

解答：

John was killed by a drunk driver last night.

補充說明：

Drunk driver 是法律用語，是指開車時飲酒量超過法定量，但尚未到喝醉的程度，這就是所謂的 impaired driving，如果這裡「醉漢」是指已到喝醉的地步，則需用 drunken driver，二者的區別是，凡 drunken driver 必定是一個 drunk driver，但 drunk driver 未必是一個 drunken driver。又，通常 drunk 用於動詞的後面，例如： Not all guests were drunk last night. 而 drunken 則用於名詞之前，例如： A drunken guest at the party ruined our night. 這裡不妨將 drunk driver 的用法視作一個例外。

習題八

將下句翻成英文。

讓我們知道你是否對投資感興趣。

解析：

注意「是否」如何表達。又，用動詞 interest 與 in 相搭配表「感興趣」。

解答：

Let us know whether you are interested in investment.

補充說明：

這裡不能用 if 來代替 whether，因為 Let us know if you are interested in investment 一句有二個可能的意思，一是指本題的意思，另一是指 If you are interested in investment, let us know. 這也就是說如果你對投資沒有興趣的話，則不必讓我們曉得，這與本題的意思不儘相同。If 與 whether 用在動詞 ask, doubt, know, learn 及 see 之後表不確定的意思時，常易引起這樣的誤解，宜注意。

習題九

將下句譯成英文。

條約的目的在於擺脫靠使用武力來成霸權。

解析：

用 wean 與 from 相搭配表「擺脫」，hegemony 表「霸權」，用 reliance 與 on 相搭配表「靠」。

解答：

The purpose of the treaty is to wean hegemony from its reliance on the use of force.

補充說明：

這裡 wean from 也可與 away 相搭配表「擺脫」的意思，而使本句翻成 The purpose of the treaty is to wean hegemony away from its reliance on the use of force.

習題十

將下句譯成英文。

警察冒生命危險來搭救落水的小孩。

解析：

用 put 與片語 on the line 相搭配表「冒 … 的危險」，用 drowning 與 child 相搭配表「落水的小孩」。

解答：

The policeman put his life on the line to rescue the drowning child.

習題十一

將下句譯成英文。

上星期我們在大賣場裡幾次與他邂逅。

解析：

用 fall 與 in 及 with 相搭配表「邂逅」。

解答：

We fell in with him several times in the shopping mall last week.

補充說明：

「邂逅」是指「偶然相遇」，因此也可用 cross one's path 而將這句翻成 We kept crossing his path several times in the shopping mall last week.

習題十二

將下句譯成英文。

我們學生的家長涉及全部社會各階層人士。

解析：

用 run 與片語 the whole gamut 相搭配表「涉及全部」，其後需跟系詞 from，用片語 walks of life 表「社會各階層」。

解答：

Parents of our students run the whole gamut of people from all walks of life.

習題十三

將下句譯成英文。

他因自己的桀錯而受害。

解析：

用 fall 與 victim 及 to 相搭配表「受害」，用 blunder 表「桀錯」。

解答：

He falls victim to his own blunder.

補充說明：

「他因自己的桀錯而受害」就是俗語所謂的「自食惡果」，諺語 What goes around comes around 有「因果得爽」或「自食其果」的意思，與這句話的意思很近。

習題十四

將下句譯成英文。

我哥哥與他前妻因她的瞻養費而引起衝突。

解析：

用 run 與 afoul 及 of 相搭配表「引起衝突」，用 maintenance 表「瞻養費」。

解答：

My brother ran afoul of his ex-wife over her maintenance.

補充說明：

「發生衝突」也可用 at odds with 或 at loggerheads with 來表達，例如： The premier was at odds with reporters 或 Tehran is at loggerheads with Washington over Iran's nuclear program. 注意這裡 odd 及 loggerhead 應用多數。

習題十五

將下句譯成英文。

選民期盼最近當選的總統立即讓經濟不景氣好轉。

解析：

用 turn 與 around 相搭配表「好轉」，用 recession 表「經濟不景氣」。

解答：

Voters expect the recently elected president to turn the recession around immediately.

補充說明：

「立即」也可用 on a dime 來表示，使本句改寫成 Voters expect the recently elected president to turn the recession around on a dime.

習題十六

將下句譯成英文。

發生車禍時，請即刻與保險公司連繫。

解析：

注意贅字，在此不用 in the event that 表「發生…時」，而用 when。用 contact（作動詞）表「連繫」。我們也可用 inform，雖然意思是指「通知」。

解答：

When there is a car accident, please contact your insurance company immediately.

補充說明：

Contact 用作動詞時，其後不跟系詞，但用作名詞時，其後常與系詞 with 相搭配，例如： His contact with the insurance company triggered a series of responses, including an immediate dispatch of a towing truck to the scene.

習題十七

將下句譯成英文。

在營業時間前，大賣場中幾乎沒有顧客。

解析：

注意贅字，在此不用 prior to 表「在 … 之前」，而用 before。用 business 與 hours 相搭配表「營業時間」。

解答：

Before the business hours, there are hardly any customers in shopping malls.

補充說明：

這裡 hardly 也可用 scarcely 來代替，但需注意的是 hardly 及 scarcely 常與 any 連用，如本題所示，也常與 at all 連用，例如： Before the business hours, one can hardly see customers at all in shopping malls. 同時 hardly 及 scarcely 二者，通常不允許與 not 與 none 使用，例如： Before the business hours, there aren't hardly any customers in shopping malls. 就不成文意。又，scarcely 之後如跟表時間的副句時，通常是用 when 或 before 子句，例如： The party had scarcely begun when（or before）it was called off. 此處需避免以 than 來替代 when 或 before, 即不用 The party had scarcely begun than it was called off. 此外需注意的是，如 hardly 或 scarcely 置於句首時，其後的主詞及動詞的位置需顛倒，例如： Hardly had I finished the meal when John arrived. 又，我們也可用 shoppers 來替代 customers, 但在此情形下，shoppers 與 shopping 鄰近使用唸來音調不諧和。

習題十八

將下句譯成英文。

有關車禍的詳情，警察問了好幾個問題。

解析：

注意贅字，在此不用 with respect to 表「有關」，而用 concerning。

解答：

The police asked several questions concerning the details of the car accident.

補充說明：

這裡也可用「交通事故」（traffic accident）來表「車禍」，同時本句也可用置換的方法改寫成 Concerning the details of the car accident the police asked several questions. 關於置換的用法，請參第 3.1 節。

習題十九

將下句譯成英文。

做父母親的必須得考慮孩子是否該受大學教育。

解析：

注意贅文，在此不用 the question as to whether 來表「是否該」，而用 whether。

解答：

Parents must consider whether their children should receive university education.

補充說明：

這裡也可用 have to 或 have got to 來表「必須」的意思，但二者的語氣比 must 更重，即 There has（has got）to be somebody at home 的語氣比 There must be somebody at home 為重。這裡另外有二點需注意，第一，have got to 祇用於現在式。第二，祇有 have to 能與 have 及 may 共用，因此我們可用 The city has had to rezone its commercial district. 但不能用 The city has had got to rezone its commercial district. 同理，我們可用 I may have to leave earlier. 但不能用 I may have got to leave earlier. 又，用 whether 的句子，雖有疑問的語氣但不加問號。例如： I am wondering whether you will be back for supper tonight. 這是因為 whether 用於 indirect question

的緣故。

習題二十

將下句譯成英文。

在大多數的情形下，算命是不科學的。

解析：

注意贅文，在此不用 in the majority of instances 來表「在大多數的情形下」，而用 usually。用 fortune-telling 表「算命」。

解答：

Usually fortune-telling is unscientific.

補充說明：

Unscientific 是由 not scientific 演變而來，後者表副詞的 not（解作「非」的意思）是由前者的 un- 來替代，這也就是說，在 unscientific 一字中，其副詞的意思是由 un- 來表達。此處 un 是用在形容詞之前，un 也能用在分詞之前，例如 unsatisfied 或 unbending。同樣，un 也能用在名詞之前，例如 unbelief。有時 un 用作「除去」或「喪失」的意思時，也可用在動詞之前，例如 untangle 或 unnerve。

1.2　詞序需合理

根據唐孟棨在《本事詩》中的記載，白居易家中有姬人稱樊素者善歌，有妓人稱小蠻者善舞。白氏在詩中曾有「櫻桃樊素口，楊柳小蠻腰」一聯，我們是否可將此聯寫成「樊素口櫻桃，小蠻腰楊柳」？要回答這問題，我們須從片語（phrase，亦稱短語）著手。字彙經搭配而成片語，而片語的使用首需注意其詞序的安排。本節從主從的觀點來討論中、英文的詞序問題。

我們將片語作為研究文句的出發點。每一片語由「主語」及「從語」二者構成，主語是著重點，而顧名思義從語是補充主語的意思，二者間的關係可用下面的構圖來表示其基本的型式[4]：

片語

/ ＼

主語 ＋ 從語

上面所稱的從語包括飾語（determiner 亦稱指定語）及形容詞。我們先從主語及從語二者的性質來討論主從關係。

主語及從語的關係可用 The young professor offers an analysis of grammar 一句來解釋。這句中有二個名詞片語，一是 the young professor，另一個是 an analysis of grammar，前者的主語為 professor，它的從語分別為 the（飾語，即冠詞）及 young（形容詞）。後者的主語為 analysis，它的從語分別為 an（飾語，即冠詞）及 of grammar（系詞片語用作形容詞）。

主語的使用決定何種特定從語的使用，例如：This internecine war was a judgment upon a sinful people. 在這一句中 a judgment upon

---

[4]　這就是英文造句中所謂的 x-bar syntax，其構圖像中文的「八」字，因此本書稱其為「八字構圖」。

a sinful people 是一個名詞片語，它的主語是 judgment（名詞），而它的從語除冠詞 a 外，另有一個系詞片語 upon a sinful people，在本句的文意內，使用其他系詞，諸如 of 或 for 都不成文意。同樣，在 They are out of luck 一句中的系詞片語 out of luck，其中系詞 out 是主語，它的從語為 of luck， 這裡祇能使用 of 而不能使用其他系詞。再如： He was personally considerate of other people. 在這一句中，有一個形容詞片語 considerate of other people，它的主語是形容詞 considerate，而從語是一個系詞片語 of other people，關於本句應該使用何種特定系詞一點，乃取決在主語 considerate。又如在 They are lunching at her house 一句中，lunching（動詞）是主語，它的從語是一個系詞片語 at her house，在此句的文意內，使用其他系詞也不成文意。瞭解主語對從語的影響，能幫助我們解釋為何英文中有的名詞、形容詞及動詞之後必須與一定的系詞相搭配，同時也可使我們在譯作時瞭解各種名詞、動詞及形容詞間應如何搭配來表達不同的文意[5]。

　　主從關係也是中文裡常見的現象。我們試用「霸王」與「王霸」來作說明。在「霸王」中，「王」為主，「霸」為從，用作名詞。在「王霸」中，「霸」為主，「王」為從，用作動詞。前者可用在「霸王妖姬」中，後者可用在「晉文公王霸天下」中。懂得這主從的區別，那末白居易一聯中的「樊素口」及「小蠻腰」皆為主語，「櫻桃」及「楊柳」分別為從語。此處主語是著重點，從語是補充主語的意思，二者的主從關係不能隨便顛倒。因此如使用「樊素口櫻桃，小蠻腰楊柳」，其重點就與原意有背。

　　應該注意的是，中、英文主從關係的表達方式不盡相同。例如

---

[5]　關於這一點，另參上節有關遣詞需注意的第三點。

英文 Room 705 是用中文「705 室」來表達，二者詞序完全不一樣。在英文裡 Room 在先，705 在後，而在中文裡 705 在先，「室」在後。這是中、英文二種語文的習慣用法無法解釋，但可從主從的觀念來理解，亦即在英文裡 Room 為從，705 為主，而在中文裡 705 為從，「室」為主。

　　片語的主從關係已如上述。這裡我們要進一步提出二個有關的問題，那就是主語及從語的種類問題，以及片語中主從關係的確認問題。前者涉及主從關係在文句結構中所扮演的角色，後者涉及精確表達中文與英文的文意問題。我們先討論主語及從語的種類，然後再討論主從關係的確認。

　　從上面幾個例子我們可以曉得，主語可為名詞，動詞，形容詞及系詞。我們再以下面幾個例子對主語及從語的種類作進一步的說明[6]。

A）John is a law teacher.

從片語 law teacher 而言，teacher（名詞）是主語，law（名詞）作其從語，而從文句結構言，此片語是用作主詞補語。

B）The criticism was made in a vicious language, little studied, much less understood.

從系詞片語 in a vicious language 本身而言，language（名詞）是主語，vicious（形容詞）乃其從語。從片語 little studied 及 much less understood 而言，二者多是過去分詞片語用作 language 的從語，而從文句結構言，in a vicious language 是一個修飾語，而 little studied 及 much less understood 是屬於形容 language（名詞）的補語。

---

[6]　有關下面各例所涉及的各種文句構成要素，諸如「述詞」,「補語」,「修飾語」及「主詞補語」等，請詳參第 2.1.3 各節。

C）The professor knows that her students are conscientious. [7]

從片語 knows that her students are conscientious 本身而言，主語是 knows（動詞），它的從語是一個 that 子句。從全句結構言，這個片語構成全句的述詞，而 that 子句是用作動詞的受詞。

D）Taxes were raised to carry on war.

從片語 were raised to carry on war 本身言，它的主語是 were raised（動詞片語），而它的從語是 to carry on war（不定詞片語）。而從文句結構言，這不定詞片語是用作修飾語。

E）Corporal punishment appears to be something going much out of fashion and rejected in liberal education as unnecessary.

從片語 to be something going much out of fashion 本身言，something 是主語，而 going much out of fashion 及 rejected

---

[7] 在通用文體中，that 子句在下列情形下可以考慮省略其中的 that：第一，that 子句的主詞與其前置詞不同時，例如在 The lab top that I am using belongs to my brother 一句中的 that 可省略而將這句改寫成 The lab top I am using belongs to my brother. 第二，當 that 子句用作某些動詞的受詞時，例如：The accused admitted that he had committed the crime 一句中的 that 可省略而將此句改寫成 The accused admitted he had committed the crime. 同樣上述 C)例也可寫成 The professor knows her students are conscientious. 除 admit 及 know 外，其他如 acknowledge，announce、believe、claim、confess、declare、find、insist、means、notice、seem、suggest 及 think 等動詞也適用此法。但需要注意的是，如 that 與其子句中的主詞間有修飾語存在時，則 that 不應省略，例如在 The accused admitted that under the influence of alcohol he had committed the crime 一句中的 that 如省略時即變成 The accused admitted under the influence of alcohol he had committed the crime 其文意就不清楚，因為修飾語 under the influence of alcohol 可解作形容 committed，也可解作形容 admitted. 在後者的情形，如寫成 The accused admitted, under the influence of alcohol, that he had committed the crime 意思就清楚了。

in liberal education as unnecessary 二者是其從語。從文句結構言，to be something 乃不定詞片語用作主詞補語，而 going much out of fashion 及 rejected in liberal education as unnecessary 是屬於形容 something 的補語，一是現在分詞片語，另一個是過去分詞片語。

F）They regard him as a hero.

從片語 him as a hero 本身言，him（代名詞）是主語，as a hero（系詞片語）是 him 的從語。從文句結構言，him 是受詞，而 as a hero 是一個受詞補語。

根據上面所舉的例子，我們不難發現，主語可為名詞、代名詞、動詞、形容詞、及系詞。而從語可為名詞、形容詞、現在及過去分詞片語、that 子句，不定詞片語及系詞片語。同時，從文句本身的結構而言，主從關係又反映在補語及修飾語的關係中。

瞭解主語及從語的種類以及它們在文句結構中的關係，能幫助我們明瞭句式結構的變化，例如下面一句：

(1) The witness proved that the defendant is innocent.

根據上述 C）例，這裡 that 子句是動詞 proved 的從語。

這句實際上可以改寫成下面二句[8]：

(2) The witness proved the defendant innocent.

這句的 defendant 是主語，形容詞 innocent 是它的從語。

(3) The witness proved the defendant to be innocent.

這句的 defendant 也是主語，而不定詞片語 to be innocent 是它的從語。.

---

[8]　此二句由省略而來。有關省略的方法，請參第 3.2.1 節。至於省略後之文句是否與原句文意相同一點，請參第 3.2.2 節。

以上三句意思相同，但我們可從不同的主從關係來曉得不同的句構變化，亦即 1）例屬 **SVO** 的模式，而 2）與 3）二例屬 **SVOCo** 的模式。同理，瞭解主語及從語的種類，另可協助我們從不同文意的句子中，來推究文句模式之來源，例如在下面幾個例子中主語及從語的種類雖然不同：

(4) They believe the broadcast（名詞作主語）to spread nothing but propaganda（不定詞片語作從語）.

(5) They heard the captain（名詞作主語）yelling（現在分詞作從語）.

(6) They saw the sun（名詞作主語）set（原形動詞作從語）.

(7) They watched the prisoners（名詞作主語）executed（過去分詞作從語）

但實際上我們如從文句結構的立場來仔細分析，不難發現從 4）到 7）各句雖然主語及從語變化多端，但多來自 **SVOCo** 的同一模式。因此在練習譯作時，主從關係的掌握能幫助我們明瞭文句的句構，進而增進我們英文的表達能力。

主從關係在句構中所扮演的角色已如上述，這裡我們要進一步討論主從關係的確認問題。中、英文主從關係的確認有時並不容易。例如：International non-governmental organization 一詞組，通常中文稱為「非政府的國際組織」，這稱謂將英文中的 international 及 non-governmental 的詞序給顛倒了，為什麼我們不稱「國際性的非政府組織」？所以有這樣的問題發生，是和中、英文主從關係的安排不一致有關。我們用下面二個例子來進一步說明。在 The Universal Declaration of Human Rights 中，declaration 是主語，universal（形容詞）及 of human rights（系詞片語）二者是其從語，次序是形容詞置前，系詞片語置後。而中文稱謂是「世界人權宣言」，與英文稱謂的

詞序相同，將「世界」置前，「人權」置後。但在 International Convention on Civil and Political Rights 的稱謂中，主語是 convention，從語分別是 international（形容詞）及 on civil and political rights（系詞片語），英文的詞序與 Universal Declaration of Human Rights 完全相同，但這個公約的中文稱謂是「公民權及政治權國際公約」，有趣的是其詞序與英文稱謂的詞序恰巧相反，將形容詞「國際」置後，系詞片語「公民權及政治權」置前。如果我們照「世界人權宣言」的用法，這公約的中文稱謂應該是「國際公民權及政治權公約」，而如果我們照「公民權及政治權國際公約」的用法，那末「世界人權宣言」應該稱為「人權世界宣言」。為什麼有這樣不一致的情形發生值得我們推敲。

主從關係的認識，能幫助我們瞭解在英文中，因名詞交換顛倒使用而可能引起的不同文意。例如：The implication that the media shelter the public from some news – or shelter that news from the public – is frustrating to journalists, in part because it's true. 這一句中有二個子句，分別是 the media shelter the public from some news 以及 [the media] shelter that news from the public. 在前句中，the public 是主語，from some news 是它的從語，而在後句中，news 是主語，from the public 是它的從語，第一個子句著重在 the public，而第二個子句著重在 news，這解釋了為什麼在後句中用 that news。根據這認識可使我們曉得，不論是受新聞蒙蔽的「大眾」，或是蒙蔽大眾的「新聞」，二者都令記者感到懊惱。

從這一點的瞭解，可使我們懂得英文中詞彙顛倒交換的不同用法。我們不妨用 offensive 及 conspicuous 二個字作例子來說明這一點。在 offensively conspicuous 中，conspicuous 為主，offensively 為從。而在 conspicuously offensive 中，offensive 為主，conspicuously 為從。根據這個瞭解，那末第一個片語的意思是指 blatant（公然的），

而第二個片語的意思是指 flagrant（罪惡昭彰的）。

　　從上面的討論使我們不難發現，中、英文的主從關係會影響二者文意的正確表達與否，在譯作時需確認主從關係，才能掌握如何妥善表達中、英文的意思，那末對如何妥善處理中、英文的主從關係，以正確的詞序來表達中、英文的文意，是在譯作時值得多多注意的一點，如此在應試時才不會犯詞序的錯誤。

習題一
將下面的片語翻成英文。

飛奔而來。

解析：

注意中、英文詞序不同的表達法，在中文裡「飛奔」置「而來」之前，但英文裡剛巧相反。

解答：

Come flying.

習題二
將下面的片語翻成英文。

裸奔

解析：

注意中、英文詞序不同的表達法，在中文裡「裸」置「奔」之前，但英文裡剛巧相反。

解答：

Running naked.

習題三
將下面的片語翻成英文。

跑著來

解析：

注意中、英文詞序不同的表達法，在中文裡「跑」置「來」之前，但英文裡剛巧相反。

解答：

Come running

習題四

將下面的片語翻成英文。

以往的好日子。

解析：

注意中、英文詞序不同的表達法，在中文裡「以往」置「好日子」之前，但英文裡剛巧相反。

解答：

Good old days.

習題五

將下句翻成英文。

學生離開時感到老師不體諒他們的苦處。

解析：

用 come 與 away 相搭配表「離開」，用 pains 表「苦處」，常與 share 相搭配來表「體諒苦處」（to share pains）。

解答：

Students come away feeling that their teacher does not share their pains.

補充說明：

這裡「離開」（come away）置於「感到」（feeling）之前，中、英文詞序相同。

習題六

將下句翻成英文。

納粹最重要戰犯之一被逮捕了。

解析：

注意 Nazi 與 war 的詞序。

解答：

One of the greatest Nazi war criminals was under arrest.

補充說明：

注意 Nazi 與 war 的詞序不能顛倒，如果翻成 war Nazi criminals 就不通了，這裡中、英文詞序相同。

習題七

將下句翻成英文。

咱們四人輕快地一起工作。

解析：

用 briskly 表「輕快地」。

解答：

The four of us worked briskly together.

補充說明：

這裡英文片語 the four of us 中，four 為主，of us 為從，與中文「咱們（從）四人（主）」詞序相同，但我們不能翻成 we（咱們）four（四人）來表達，這樣就不通了。

習題八

將下句翻成英文。

那是我昨天向你借的唯一的一本書。

解析：

注意「你唯一的一本書」在英文中的詞序，亦即 book 是主語，only 與 of yours 是形容 book 的補語，only 置 book 之前，而 of yours 置 book 之後，翻成 only book of yours。

解答：

That is the only book of yours that I borrowed yesterday.

補充說明：

注意，這裡詞序不能顛倒，如果寫成 That is your only book that I borrowed yesterday.文意就不通了。

習題九

1) 將下列片語譯成英文。

全盤否定過去

解析：

用 all-out 表「全盤」，用 negation 表「否定」作主語。

解答：

An all-out negation of the past.

補充說明：

注意這裡「否定」在中文是動詞，但在英文裡翻成名詞。這種詞性的轉譯屬翻譯的一種方法，平常在練習譯作時不妨可酌情使用。關於這一點，請詳參第 2.2.2 節。

2）比較上題中、英文的詞序有何不同。

解析：

需以主從關係來分析。

解答：

在中文裡，「過去」為主語，「全盤」及「否定」為從語，但在英文裡 negation 為主語，an、all-out 及系詞片語 of the past 皆為從語。

習題十

1) 將下列片語譯成英文。

歷史上難以抹滅的創傷

解析：

用 indelible 表「難以抹滅的」。注意何者作主語，何者作從語。

解答：

Indelible wounds in history

2) 比較上題中、英文之詞序有何不同。

解析：

需以主從關係來分析。

解答：

中、英文皆以「創傷」（wounds）作主語，但在中文裡，「歷史上」置於「難以抹滅」之前，這與英文的詞序恰好相反。

習題十一

1）將下句譯成英文。

旗子飄揚在藍天白雲裡。

解析：

將 float 表「飄揚」其後需與 against 相搭配。須從分別主從關係來做。

解答：

A flag is floating against the white clouds in blue sky.

2）分析以上英文句的主從關係。

解答：

White clouds 為主語置於 in blue sky（從語）之前，次序不能顛倒，否則 A flag is floating against the blue sky in white clouds. 就不成文意。

3）比較 1）與 2）句的詞序有何不同。

解析：

需以主從關係來分析。

解答：

英文 white clouds（主）置於 in blue sky（從）之前，但在中文裡，「藍

天」置於「白雲」之前，這與英文的詞序恰好相反。

習題十二

1) 將下句譯成英文。

最近該製造商收回成品。

解析：

用 recall 表「收回」。

解答：

Recently the manufacturer has recalled its products.

2) 將下句譯成英文。

這些報紙可回收。

解析：

用 recycle 表「回收」。

解答：

These papers could be recycled.

3) 分別比較中文的「收回」與「回收」與英文的 recall 及 recycle 的意思，說明其不同的由來。

解析：

需用主從關係來比較。

解答：

因為中文「收回」與「回收」的詞序相反意義不同因而影響我們英文的遣詞。

習題十三

1）將下句譯成英文。

和平促進文明的歷史進展。

解析：

用 evolution 表「進展」作主語，用 civilization 作從語, advance（作

動詞）表「促進」。

解答：

Peace advances the historical evolution of a civilization.

2）比較上題中、英文的詞序有何不同。

解析：

需以主從關係來分析。

解答：

中、英文皆以「進展」（evolution）作主語，但在中文裡，「文明」置於「歷史」之前，與英文的詞序恰好相反。

習題十四

1）將下句譯成英文。

　　亞洲的產業發展值得注意。

解析：

用 industrial development 表「產業發展」作主語，Asia 作從語，用 noticeable 表「值得注意」。

解答：

Asia's industrial development is noticeable.

2）將下句譯成英文。

　　亞洲產業的發展值得注意。

解析：

用 development 表「發展」作主語，用 Asia's industry 表「亞洲產業」作從語。

解答：

The development of Asia's industries is noticeable.

補充說明：

從以上二句的解答可知，英文中 development, industry 與 Asia 三者

因主從關係的不同安排可引起不同的中文意思。這也就是說，從中譯英的立場而言，需認識中、英文主從關係的不同，才能正確表達英文的意思。

習題十五

1）將下句譯成英文。

讓我們一起共享此光榮的一刻。

解析：

用 share 表「享」，glory 表「光榮」，this moment 表「此刻」作主語，glory 作從語。

解答：

Let us share this moment of glory together.

2）將下句譯成英文。

讓我們一起共享此刻的光榮。

解析：

用 glory 作主語，this moment 作從語。

解答：

Let us share the glory of this moment together.

補充說明：

從以上二句的解答可知，英文中 glory 與 this moment 因主從關係的不同安排可引起不同的中文意思。在此我們也可看出，在中譯英時，需認識中、英文主從關係的不同，才能正確表達英文的意思。

習題十六

1）將下句譯成英文。

罷工者公開宣稱堵塞市內交通。

解析：

用 striker 表「罷工者」，announce 表「宣稱」，block 表「堵塞」，city traffic 表「市內交通」，openly 表「公開」，句中需以 announce 為主語，openly 作從語。

解答：

The strikers openly announced to block the city traffic.

2）將下句譯成英文。

　　罷工者宣稱公開堵塞市內交通。

解析：

以 block 為主語，openly 作從語。

解答：

The strikers announced to block the city traffic openly.

補充說明：

從以上二句的解答可知，英文中用作從語的 openly 與不同主語相搭配可引起不同的中文意思。

習題十七

1）　將下句譯成英文。

　　警探立即決定偵查犯罪現場。

解析：

用 detective 表「警探」，investigate 表「偵查」，片語 crime scene 表「犯罪現場」，句中需以「決定」（作動詞）為主語，「立即」為從語。

解答：

The detective immediately decided to investigate the crime scene.

2）　將下句譯成英文。

　　警探決定立即偵查犯罪現場。

解析：

用「偵查」為主語，「立即」為從語。

解答：

The detective decided to immediately investigate the crime scene.

補充說明：

從以上二句的解答可知，英文中用作從語的 immediately 與不同主語相搭配可指不同的中文意思。

習題十八

1)　將下句譯成英文。

　　臺灣有野心成為全球華人「學習新世界」的網路中心。

解析：

用片語 a web-based hub 表「網路中心」。

解答：

Taiwan is ambitious to become a web-based hub for a new world of learning for Chinese people around the world.

2)　比較上句中「學習新世界」與 a new world of learning 有何不同。

解析：

需用主從關係來分析。

解答：

中、英文皆以「世界」為主語，而「學習」（of learning）與「新」（new）皆為從語，在中文裡從語「學習」放在「新」之前，但在英文裡，new 置 of learning 之前，而不用 a world of new learning。

習題十九

將下句翻成英文：

友誼該是情愛的泉源，不斷地衷心湧出。

解析：

用片語 a well of affection 表「情愛的泉源」，用 spring 與 up 相搭配

41

表「湧出」，用 perennial 表「不斷地」，用 warm 表「衷心」。

解答：

Friendship should be a well of affection springing up, perennially warm。

補充說明：

這裡中、英文詞序不同，中文的詞序是將「不斷地衷心」（perennial warm）置於「湧出」（springing up）之前，與英文的詞序恰巧相反。

習題二十

將下句譯成英文。

他是地方上一位顯貴的兒子。

解析：

用 local 表「地方上」，prominent 表「顯（要）」，aristocrat 表「貴（人）」。注意詞序。

解答：

He is the son of a prominent local aristocrat.

補充說明：

這裡中、英文詞序不同，中文的詞序是將「地方上」置於「顯（要）」之前，與英文的詞序恰巧相反。

第二章 句構以妥切運用為本

　　我們的母語是中文，通常在練習譯作時，必先有中文的意思，再有與中文相當的英文意思，然後透過合適的英文句式來造句。究竟我們對這三部曲有多少認識，不妨將下一句翻成英文，試試自己的英文表達能力：「我家後面有個山坡，坡上長滿著野花，野花嬌紅怒放」。這個句子是有三個不同的意思構成，即 1)「我家後面有個山坡」，2)「坡上長滿著野花」，3)「野花嬌紅怒放」，而每一個意思代表著文句中不同層次的一個單位，每一個層次的單位應有一個對等的英文意思，透過英文的句式，像疊積木似的來翻成一句而寫成 Behind my house lies a hillside which is teeming with wildflowers that are blooming in glittering scarlet. 這裡牽涉到很多中譯英的問題。例如，為什麼不翻成 Behind my house lies a hillside teeming with wildflowers blooming in glittering scarlet? 同時為什麼 behind my house 放在句前而不放在句後？這是牽涉到句式的問題。而在這第二個句式中，中文的三個子句為什麼用一個英文句子來表達？同時為什麼中英文裏有詞性轉譯的現象出現？（例如中文的形容詞"嬌紅"用英文的系詞片語 in glittering scarlet 來翻）。這些是與中譯英的技巧有關。在本章中，我們先從句子的立場來討論如何造句，再逐步從熟習英文的基本表達方法中，進入如何應用次元單位的觀念來中譯英造句，前者在第 2.1 節中討論，後者在第 2.2 節中討論。二者都是針對「全民英檢」中高級中譯英的測驗部分而設。

2.1 文句之模式

　　本節我們從文法的觀點，以提綱挈領的方式，來綜合說明文句

（sentence）的各種模式及其構成要數的位置，再進一步舉出各構成要數的基本種類。對文句的模式及其構成要數有一個清楚的認識，可以提供我們使用不同句式的必備知識，如此在應試時將有助于我們用妥切的句式來表達文意。

2.1.1 基本模式

　　文句是由子句（clause，亦稱分句）組成。子句的構成要素，原則上可分「主詞」（subject，亦稱「主語」，簡稱 "S"）及「述詞」（predicate，亦稱「謂語」）二大部分。在 The restaurant owner gave the beggar a piece of cake 一句中，The restaurant owner 屬主詞部分，gave the beggar a piece of cake 屬述詞部分。述詞部分的功用，是在闡明主詞的所作所為。

　　述詞部分也有其本身的構成要素，即 1）「動詞」（verb，亦即 predicator，又稱「述詞動詞」或「謂語動詞」，簡稱 "V"），2）「受詞」（object，亦稱「賓語」，簡稱 "O"），3）「補語」（complement，亦稱「定語」，簡稱 "C"）[1]，及 4）「修飾語」（adjunct，亦稱「狀語」，簡稱 "A"）[2]。根據以上所述，子句可有下列七種不同的基本模式。

1)　主詞 + 動詞 (SV)，例如：
　　The bell (S) is ringing (V).
　　這個基本模式可引申成下列三種不同的模式，每一種模式有三種不同的構成要素。

2)　主詞 + 動詞 + 補語（SVC），例如：
　　He (S) is（ V ）a priest (C).

---

[1]　有關補語的種類，請參第 2.1.3.4 節。

[2]　修飾語包括常用的副詞（adverb）及其他當作副詞用的詞類，諸如系詞片語等。有關修飾語的種類，請參第 2.1.3.5 節。

這句中的 a priest 用作形容主詞 he，故稱 「主詞補語」（subject complement，亦稱「主語補足語」，簡稱 （Cs））。

3) 主詞 + 動詞 + 修飾語 （SVA），例如：
It （S） is snowing （V） now （A）.

4) 主詞 + 動詞 + 受詞（SVO），例如：
The driver （S） injured （V） a pedestrian （O）.
這個模式又可演變成下列三種不同的模式，每一種模式有四種不同的構成要素。

5) 主詞 + 動詞 + 受詞 + 修飾語（SVOA），例如：
My neighbor（S）keeps（V）his snow blower（O）in his garage（A）.這 SVOA 模式另外有一個變格，即 SVOAC，例如：
The police （S） dragged （V） the winebibber （O） home （A） almost dead-drunk （C）。
在這個例子中，almost dead-drunk 是形容受詞 winebibber，因此稱「受詞補語」（object complement，亦稱「賓語補足語」，簡稱（Co））。

6) 主詞 + 動詞 + 受詞 + 補語（SVOC），例如：
The witness （S） proved （V） the defendant （O） innocent （C）.
在這個例子中，innocent 是形容受詞 defendant，因此也是「受詞補語」。

7) 主詞 + 動詞 + 受詞 + 受詞（SVOO），例如：
The police （S） gave （V） the driver （O） a parking ticket （O）.
這個例子中有二個受詞[3]，即 driver 及 parking ticket，前者稱「間接受詞」（indirect object，簡稱（O$_I$）），後者稱「直接

---

[3]　關於受詞的種類，請參第 2.1.3.3 節。

受詞」(direct object，簡稱(O_D))，因此這模式也可以 SVO_IO_D 來表示。而 SVO_IO_D 模式也有一個變格，即 SVO_IO_DC，例如：

Mr. Lee（S）gave（V）his friend（O_I）a generous loan（O_D）almost two million dollars（C）.

在這個例子中，almost two million dollars 是形容 loan，用作補語。

在上面前四種模式中，動詞的用法有所不同，在 SV 模式中，動詞不跟受詞，也沒有補語以及修飾語。在 SVC 的模式中，動詞之後跟補語。在 SVA 的模式中，動詞之後跟修飾語。而在 SVO 的模式中，動詞之後跟受詞，這就是及物動詞。

英文句子的結構，可根據上面各種基本模式，進一步演變成下例不同的模式，例如：

A) The travelers(S)carefully(A)packed(V)their belongings(O).
   這個例子是將上面第 5) 模式中的修飾語更改其位置而形成。

B) The veteran（S）was（V）previously（A）a guard（C）at an air force base（A）.

C) The divorcée（S）became（V）happier（C）finally（A）.
   這個例子可以視作上述第 2) 及第 3) 兩個例子的接合模式。

D) The wind（S）blew（V）relentlessly（A）last night（A）.

E) The professor（S）gave（V）her students（O_I）high praise（O_D）in class（A）.

F) The board of directors（S）appointed（V）George（O）professor emeritus（C）in last week's meeting（A）.
   這個例子是將上面第 5) 模式變格中的補語及修飾語，相互變更位置而成。

上面的例子，多是用單式主詞，受詞，補語及修飾語。如果用複式主詞，受詞，補語及修飾語時，那末句式又有另外三種不同的可能。

G) She（S）realized（V）that [she（S）was（V）alone（C）in the park（A）].

在這個例子中，that 子句是用作動詞的受詞，而本身另有主詞，受詞，補語及修飾語。

H) The rescue workers（S）became（V）disappointed（C）when [the victims（S）died（V）].

這個例子中的 when 子句是用作修飾語，而本身另有主詞及動詞。

I) That [the suspect（S）admitted（V）his crime（O）in court （A）] made（V）the case（O）more（A）sensational（C）.

在這個例子中，that 子句用作主詞，而本身另有主詞，動詞，受詞及修飾語。

此外，子句的各種基本模式，有時可互相轉換。例如： He is preaching.（SV）一句的文意包括 He is a priest.（SVCs）。再如：He is broke.（SVCs）一句的文意是指 He has no money.（SVO）。又如上面從 5）例到 7）例各模式，多可用被動語態來表達。曉得如何互相替換句式，能增加文句結構的變化，同時也可加強我們用不同文句表達的能力，這涉及如何靈活使用句式的問題，關于這一點，我們將于下章詳細討論。

為達到妥切運用句構的目的起見，本章各節習題，提供讀者很多練習各種句子模式的機會，希望讀者能耐心地逐節一一去做，如此也可為做以下其他各章的習題打下一個紮實的基礎。

習題一

1) 將下句譯成英文。

今晨天氣晴朗。

解析：

用 fine 表「晴朗」。

解答：

The weather was fine this morning.

補充說明：

如果上下文很清楚是在指氣候，那末這一句也可翻成 It was fine this morning. 又，「晴朗的天氣」除了用 a fine weather 外，也可以用 a clear\good weather，或者甚至用比較文雅一點的如 a grandly weather 或 an exquisite weather（「姣好的天氣」）。

2) 指出上句的模式。

The weather（S）was（V）fine（Cs）this morning（A）.

習題二

1) 將下句譯成英文。

他是一個本性和藹可親的人。

解析：

用 affable 表「和藹可親」。

解答：

He is a man of an affable nature.

2) 指出上句的模式。

He（S）is（V）a man of an affable nature（Cs）.

習題三

1) 將下句譯成英文。

他將時間花費在修閑消遣上（喻他磋跎光陰）。

解析：

用 spend 與 time 相搭配表「花費時間」，用 idle 與 pursuit 相搭配表「修閑消遣」，其前另需與 in 搭配。

解答：

He spent his time in idle pursuit.

2)　指出上句的模式。

　　He（S）spent（V）his time（O）in idle pursuit（A）.

補充說明：

這裡另外可用動詞 devote 或 pass 與 time 相搭配表「花費時間」。又，「蹉跎光陰」是指「浪費時間」的意思，可用 fritter, fool 及 trifle 與 time 相搭配來表達，但需注意的是其後皆需與 away 相搭配，例如：He fritters away his time.

習題四

1)　將下句譯成英文。

　　他勉強通過路試。

解析：

用片語 skin of his teeth 表「勉強」。

解答：

He passed his driving test by the skin of his teeth.

2)　指出上句的模式。

　　He（S）passed（V）his driving test（O）by the skin of his teeth（A）.

補充說明：

這裡另外可用動詞 squeeze 與 through 相搭配表「勉強通過」，而將這句翻成 He squeezed through his driving test.

習題五

1)　將下句譯成英文。

　　塔的高度是由其基面的寬度而定。

解析：

用 determine 表「決定」，base 表「基面」。注意，根據語氣，本句
需用被動語態。

解答：

The height of a pagoda is determined by the breadth of its base.

2)　指出上句的模式。

The height of a pagoda （S）is determined（V）by the breadth of its
base（A）.

補充說明：

關於什麼時候應該用被動語態，請參第 3.3.1 節。

習題六

1)　將下句譯成英文。

太多的工作堆給了約翰。

解析：

用 heap 與 on 相搭配表「堆給」。

解答：

Too many jobs have been heaped on John.

2)　指出上句的模式。

Too many jobs （S）have been heaped（V）on John（A）.

習題七

1)　將下句譯成英文。

今年所得的利潤是創記錄的。

解析：

用 all-time 與 high 相搭配表「創記錄」，其前另外需要用系詞 at
搭配，即 at all-time high.

解答：

This year's profits are at all-time high.

2) 指出上句的模式。

This year's profits（S）are（V）at all-time high（Cs）.

3) 補充說明：

我們也可用片語 at a record high 或 record-breaking 來表「創記錄」，使這句翻成 This year's profits are at a record high. 或 This year's profits are record-breaking.

習題八

1) 將下句譯成英文。

不久前聯考是升學機會的唯一方式。

解析：

用 joint entrance examination 表「聯考」，以 educational 與 advancement 相搭配表「升學機會」。

解答：

Not too long ago joint entrance examination was the only method for educational advancement.

2) 試指出上句的模式。

Not too long ago（A）joint entrance examination（S）was（V）the only method for educational advancement（Cs）.

習題九

1) 將下句譯成英文。

小說家的演講曲解了藝術及倫理的整個意義。

解析：

用 twist 表「曲解」，其後與 meaning 相搭配，用 art 表「藝術」，ethics 表「倫理」。

解答：

The novelist's speech twists the whole meaning of art and ethics.

補充說明：

此處 meaning 也可與 strain 相搭配表「曲解」的意思，使這一句譯成 The novelist's speech strains the whole meaning of art and ethics.

2) 指出上句的模式。

The novelist's speech（S）twists（V）the whole meaning of art and ethics（O）.

習題十

1) 將下句譯成英文。

我們希望一個沒有污染的城市將是一個無法捉摸的目標

解析：

用 elusive 與 target 相搭配表「無法捉摸的目標」的意思，

解答：

Our hope for a pollution-free city will be an elusive target.

2) 指出上句的模式。

Our hope for a pollution-free city（S）will be（V）an elusive target（Cs）.

補充說明：

這裡「無法捉摸的目標」與「無法達到的目的」的意思很近，因此也可以用 an unattainable goal 來取代。

2.1.2 文句各構成要素的位置

上節各種模式多是「直陳句」（declarative sentence），它們構成要素的位置基本上是主詞置於動詞之前，受詞及補語通常置於動詞之後，而修飾語的位置則不定，關於這一點，現在我們分別一一加

以說明[4]。

　　我們從上節知道，受詞有直接受詞及間接受詞二種。在上節 A）例中，belongings 是受詞，通常稱直接受詞，但在 E）例中有二個受詞，students 為間接受詞，praise 為直接受詞，通常間接受詞置於直接受詞之前。

　　同樣根據上節的介紹，我們曉得補語有述及主詞也有述及受詞的，前者稱主詞補語，後者稱受詞補語。例如，上節 B）例中的補語屬前者，亦即 veteran（主詞）從前是個 guard（補語）。此例屬單式主詞補語，而在 The fact is that she will never return 一句中，that 子句是形容主詞 fact，它本身另有主詞（she）以及述詞（will never return），因此屬複式主詞補語。而上節 F）例中的 professor emeritus 是屬後者，因為 professor emeritus 是受詞 George 的補語。

　　須注意的是，不論屬何種補語，它的位置應依照文意來安排，不能隨意變更。例如在上節 C）例中，照說補語述及名詞，具形容詞的性質，應放在它所形容的名詞之前，但這樣寫就不成句法（The happier divorcée became finally.）同樣，F）例基本上是屬於 SVOCA 的模式，其中受詞補語及受詞二者的位置也不宜隨意顛倒，因為如寫成 The board of directors appointed professor emeritus George in last week's meeting 這樣文意就不同。但在下例中，The witnesses（S）have proven（V）the conspiracy theory（O）wrong（C），如果將補語倒置，仍可保持原句的文意，亦即 The witnesses（S）have proven（V）wrong（C）the conspiracy theory（O）. 再需注意的是，通常受詞補語不宜置句前，例如將上節第 6）例改寫成 Innocent the witness

---

[4]　有關置換的觀念，請參第 3.1 節，而有關用置換來強調語氣的用法，請參第 3.3.6 節。

proved the defendant 就不成文句。

　　至于修飾語，它的位置並不固定，可置于主詞及動詞間，像上節 A）例所示，或動詞及補語間，像上節 B）例所示，或置於句後，像上節 C）及 D）二例所示。修飾語也可置句前，例如 Finally（A）the divorcée（S）became（V）happier（C）一句是由上節 C）例演變而來。

　　同樣，在上節 I)例中，可將修飾語 in court 的位置與受詞 his crime 互換而寫成 The suspect（S）admitted（V）in court（A）his crime（O）. 從文意及句子的平衡而言這句與原句相同。但是在下例中，修飾語位置的變更能影響文意。

A1） At midnight, Mary listens to the news and her children go to bed.

　　這句中的 at midnight 放在全句的前面，它的意思兼及前後二個子句。這是說 Mary 之聽新聞與孩子上床睡覺二者同時發生，這是因為將修飾語放在句首，是強調其意義特出的自然結果。但如將 at midnight 放在前子句之後，則失去它強調的程度，使它的意思僅及前子句而不兼顧後子句，像下例所示：

A2） Mary listens to the news at midnight and her children go to bed.

　　實際上，這一位置的變更影響後句的文意，因為在此 A2）句中，我們不清楚孩子是否也在子夜上床睡覺。那末在這裏如何避免因變更修飾語位置而引起文意的含糊？我們不妨在後子句中使用不同的修飾語使文意明確，像下例所示：

A3） Mary listens to the news at midnight and her children go to bed at nine o'clock.

　　在這句中，at midnight 及 at nine o'clock 分別述及它們本身之子句，而文意不及於另一子句。至于究竟修飾語在句中應放在何處一點，是取決于作者本人所欲表達的文意而定。

習題一

1) 將下句譯成英文。

他詭譎地譏笑我們。

解析：

用 laugh 表「譏笑」，其後需與 at 相搭配，用 cynically 表「詭譎地」。

解答：

He laughed at us cynically.

2) 將上句中修飾語的位置變更而改寫。

解析：

可將修飾語置于動詞之後。

解答：

He laughed cynically at us.

習題二

1) 將下句譯成英文。

她祇喝茶。

解析：

這一句與下一句要我們練習注意補語與修飾語位置的變更，能引起不同的文意一點。這裡 only 用作 tea 的補語。

解答：

She drinks only tea.

2) 將上句的 only 當修飾語用而改寫，並比較二句文意有何不同。

解析：

需變更 only 的位置來寫。

解答：

She only drinks tea. 在上句中，only 作形容 tea 的補語，重點在 tea，句謂「她祇喝茶」而不喝咖啡或其他飲料，但在這句中，only 作形容

drink 的修飾語，重點在 drink，句謂「她飲茶」而不是「啜茶」（She sips tea）。

習題三

1）將下句譯成英文。

　　喬治故意譏嗤珍妮。

解析：

用 sniff 表「譏嗤」，其後需與 at 相搭配。

解答：

George sniffed at Jean deliberately.

2）將上句中修飾語的位置變更而改寫。

解析：

可將修飾語置于動詞之後。

解答：

George sniffed deliberately at Jean.

習題四

1）　將下句譯成英文。

　　珍妮沒做對不起喬治的事。

解析：

注意「對不起的事」具有兩個否定的意思。

解答：

Jean did George nothing wrong.

2）　變更上句中直接及間接受詞的位置而改寫。

解析：

注意，直接受詞置間接受詞之前時，其後需用 to。

解答：

Jean did nothing wrong to George.

習題五

1) 將下句譯成英文。

在激辯落幕之後，理性應該抬頭（或取而代之）。

解析：

用 heated 與 argument 相搭配表「激辯」，用 fall 表「落」其後需與 on 相搭配，　用 rationality 表「理性」，及用 prevail 表「擡頭或取代」。

解答：

After the curtain falls on heated arguments, rationality should prevail.

2) 將上句中修飾語的位置變更而改寫。

解析：

可將修飾語置句後。

解答：

Rationality should prevail after the curtain falls on heated arguments.

補充說明：

注意，上句中的副句乃屬修飾語的性質。

習題六

1) 將下句譯成英文。

在我們成功之途中的無數黑暗時刻，信心是我們的導星。

解析：

用 dark 與 hours 相搭配表「黑暗時刻」，journey 表「（旅）途」，其後需與 to 相搭配。

解答：

Faith is our star in the numerous dark hours of our journey to success.

補充說明：

注意，此處是將中文二個子句由一個英文句子翻出，關于這一點請參

第 2.2.2.節。

2) 將上句中修飾語的位置變更而改寫。

解析：

可將修飾語置于句前。

解答：

In the numerous dark hours of our journey to success, faith is our star.

習題七

1) 將下句譯成英文。

老實說喬治沒拿到執照。

解析：

用 honestly 表「老實說」，license 表「執照」。

解答：

Honestly, Gorge didn't get the license.

2) 將上句中修飾語的位置變更而改寫。

解析：

可將修飾語置于句後。

解答：

George didn't get the license honestly.

3) 比較 1) 及 2) 二句的文意，並說明二者不同的原因。

解析：

本題是要我們注意修飾語位置的變更能影響文意一點。

解答：

2) 句的文意是喻喬治用不正當的方法拿到執照，與 1) 句意思不同的原因乃在于將修飾語 honestly 的位置變更而引起。注意，在 1) 句中 honestly 帶逗號，而在 2) 句中 honestly 不帶逗號。

習題八

1) 將下句譯成英文。

　　投資者需要足夠的市場規模來營利。

解析：

用 make 與 profit 相搭配表「營利」。

解答：

Investors need a market of a sufficient size to make a profit.

2) 指出上句的模式。

解析：

用上節所討論的方法來做。

解答：

Investors（S）need（V）a market of a sufficient size（O）to make a profit（A）.

3) 將上句中修飾語的位置變更而改寫。

解析：

可將修飾語置于句前。

解答：

To make a profit investors need a market of a sufficient size.

習題九

1) 將下句譯成英文。

　　病人每人有其自己的單人病房。

解析：

用片語 private room 表「單人病房」。

解答：

The patients each have their own private rooms.

補充說明：

注意，修飾語 each 的位置不同能引起動詞及代名詞的身與數的不同。這裡 each 置於複數主詞 patients 之後，在此情形下，動詞及代名詞的身與數不受 each 的影響，而取決於主詞，因此這裡動詞用複數（have）而代名詞亦用複數（their）。但主詞如是 we，而 each 置于動詞之後的情形下，代名詞可用單數也可用複數，如下面二例所示，We girls have each our own idea 或 We girls have each her own idea. 但比較上以第一例為通用。

2.1.3　各構成要素的種類

2.1.3.1　主詞

主詞可有不同的種類，有用名詞的，例如第 2.1.1 節中的 A）例。有用代名詞的，如第 2.1.1 節中的 G）例。有用系詞片語的，例如：Between eleven and noon suits me well for a lunch break.

主詞有用單式的，也有用複式的。複式主詞的種類可包括名詞片語，如第 2.1.1 節中的 F）例，或用 that clause 的，如第 2.1.1 節中的 I）例，或用不定詞片語的，例如：To do this exercise is difficult. 或用 wh- clause 的，例如 Who to ask for approval seems uncertain. 或 What made him say that is not clear. 有用動名詞的，例如：Walking on ice is dangerous. 有用副句作主詞的，例如：Because he is poor does not mean he could be despised. 甚至於有用名詞片語、that clause、系詞片語及形容詞共同表達的，例如：The new（形容詞）gas station（名詞片語）nearby the corner of the street（系詞片語）that was opened last week（that clause）offers an excellent service.

習題一

將下句譯成英文。

這本絕版書很貴。

解析：

用 out-of-print 表「絕版」，本句需用名詞片語作主詞。

解答：

This out-of-print book is very expensive.

習題二

1) 將下句譯成英文。

乞丐是餓了。

解析：

本句需用名詞作主詞。

解答：

The beggar is hungry.

2) 將下句譯成英文。

顯然的那乞丐是餓了。

解析：

用 obvious 表「顯然的」，本句需用 that 子句作主詞。

解答：

That the beggar is hungry is obvious.

習題三

將下句譯成英文。

什麼事令他如此生氣，實在使人費解。

解析：

用 unclear 表「使人費解」，本句需用 what 子句作主詞。

解答：

What makes him so mad is unclear.

補充說明：

注意，在用 what 子句作主詞時，其動詞的單複數需由全句動詞的單複數來決定。例如在 What most excites her is window-shopping 一句中，全句的動詞為單數（is），因此 what 子句的動詞亦為單數（excites），而在 What most interest him are family and career 一句中，全句的動詞為複數（are），因此 what 子句的動詞亦為複數（interest）。但在下例中，全句的動詞可用單數也可用複數，在此情形下，what 子句的動詞其單複數亦應作相對的調整，What truly command her respect are honesty and integrity. 這句視 honesty 及 integrity 分別為二個不同性質的行為，因此全句的動詞用複數（are），在此情形下，what 子句的動詞也應為複數（command），而在 What truly commands her respect is honesty and integrity 一句中視 honesty 及 integrity 為一個相同性質的行為，因此全句的動詞用單數（is），而 what 子句的動詞也因此為單數（commands）。此外，這裏也是將二個中文子句由一個英文句子翻出，關于這一點請參第 2.2.2 節。

習題四

將下句譯成英文。

玩冰滾球很有意思。

解析：

用 hockey 表「冰滾球」，本句需用動名詞作主詞。

解答：

Playing hockey is fun.

補充說明：

注意詞性轉譯的用法，這裏中文動詞（玩）用英文動名詞（playing）翻出。關於這一點請參第 2.2.2 節。

習題五

將下句譯成英文。

在市中心租屋會破費你很多。

解析：

用 cost 與 fortune 相搭配（cost a fortune）表「破費很多」，本句需用不定詞片語作主詞。

解答：

To rent a house in downtown will cost you a fortune.

補充說明：

注意詞性轉譯的用法，這裏中文動詞（租屋）用英文的不定詞（to rent）翻出。

習題六

將下句譯成英文。

在我記憶中老想起的事是媽媽的突然逝死。

解析：

用片語 memory dwells upon the most 表「在記憶中老想起的事」，本句需用 what 子句作主詞。

解答：

What my memory dwells upon the most is my mother's sudden death.

習題七

將下句譯成英文。

減少營業稅會推動企業起飛。

解析：

用 impetus 表「推動」，用 take 與 off 相搭配表「起飛」，本句需用不定詞片語作主詞。

解答：

To reduce sales tax will provide the impetus for the business to take off.

習題八

將下句譯成英文。

不祇因他人在公路上亂穿，就表示我也應該這樣開車。

解析：

用 zigzag 表「亂穿」，本句需用 simply because 子句作主詞。

解答：

Simply because other drivers are zigzagging on highway does not necessarily mean I should do the same.

習題九

將下句譯成英文。

相信法官可以沒有證據而判人罪是令人吃驚的想法。

解析：

用 staggering 與 thought 相搭配表「令人吃驚的想法」，本句需用不定詞片語作主詞。

解答：

To believe that a judge can convict a person without evidence is a staggering thought.

2.1.3.2 動詞

動詞有主動詞及助動詞，二者構成一個動詞片語。動詞隨它形式的不同可有「限定動詞」（finite verb）及「非限定動詞」（non-finite verb）二種。限定動詞是指動詞的字形受人稱、數、時式及語態的限制而有所變化。非限定動詞不受人稱，數及時式的變化，但仍具語態的變化。凡具限定動詞的子句稱「限定子句」（finite clause），而具非限定動詞的子句則稱「非限定子句」（non-finite clause）。例

如：He hopes that those paintings（S）will be removed（被動語態將來式）. 這句中的 that clause 本身有主詞，其中的動詞受時式及語態的變化，因此稱限定子句[5]。而在 He wouldn't let those paintings（O）be removed（non-finite verb in passive voice）一句中，those paintings 是受詞，動詞片語（be removed）無時式的變化但仍具語態的變化，因此稱非限定子句[6]。限定子句與非限定子句可以交互使用來變化句式，能增加我們英文的表達能力，關于這一點我們會在第 3.3.5 節中詳細討論。

非限定子句通常有下列四種不同的種類：

A）原形動詞（bare infinitive），例如：

We would rather leave than stay in such a circumstance.

B）不定詞片語，例如：

They went to shopping mall to buy groceries.

C）現在分詞片語，例如：

People saw their national flag flying at half staff over public buildings. 或者 The student body put forward a series of proposals demanding immediate reform.

D）過去分詞片語，例如：

Covered with deep snow the mountain is impassable. 或者 He turned down those applicants considered unqualified.

---

[5]　關於限定子句的省略，請參第 3.2 節。

[6]　關于非限定子句在文句中所扮演的角色，詳參第 2.1.3.4 及第 2.1.3.5 各節。

習題一

將下句譯成英文。

她急著回家準備晚餐。

解析：

仿效 B）例用不定詞片語成一非限定子句。

解答：

She hurried home to prepare supper.

補充說明：

注意詞性轉譯的用法，亦即中文動詞（準備）用英文的不定詞（to prepare）翻出。

習題二

將下句譯成英文。

他開車到附近的警察局去報告一件交通事故。

解析：

用 traffic 與 accident 相搭配表「交通事故」，仿效 B）例用不定詞片語成一非限定子句。

解答：

He drove to a nearby police station to report a traffic accident.

習題三

將下句譯成英文。

早在開賽前，觀眾已擠到體育館去搶座位。

解析：

用 long 與 before 相搭配表「早在」，用 flock 表「擠」其後須與 to 相搭配，用 snap 與 seat 相搭配表「搶座位」，注意 snap 之後另需與 up 相搭配，仿效 B）例用不定詞片語成一非限定子句。

解答：

Fans had flocked to the gymnasium to snap up seats long before the game started.

補充說明：

Seat 可與 find 或 get 相搭配表「找位子」，但語氣沒有「搶座位」強。此外，注意此處動詞的時式。這句述及一已發生的事情，故「開賽」用過去式，而「搶座位」發生在「開賽」之前，故用過去完成式。

習題四

將下句譯成英文。

一大塊冰塊從屋頂掉下來，落在她的腳旁碎成細塊。

解析：

用片語 a chunk of ice 表「一塊冰塊」，shatter 表「碎」需與 into 相搭配，依 C）例用現在分詞片語成一非限定子句。

解答：

A big chunk of ice falling from the roof shattered into pieces at her feet.

補充說明：

注意，「在她腳旁」須用系詞 at 而非 on，同時也注意將二個中文子句用一個英文句子來表達，以及中文的動詞（掉下）用英文的現在分詞（falling）翻出的詞性轉譯用法。

習題五

將下句譯成英文。

孔子的信條已是世代所遵守的道德標準。

解析：

用 generations 表「世代」，用 follow 表「遵守」，以 moral 與 standard 相搭配表「道德標準」，仿 D）例用過去分詞片語成一非限定子句。

解答：

Confucian dogma has been the moral standard followed by generations.

補充說明：

這裏也需注意中文的動詞（遵守）用英文的過去分詞（followed）翻出的詞性轉譯用法。

2.1.3.3 受詞

受詞可有下列幾種不同的種類：

A） 名詞片語，例如：

The thief broke the backyard door.

B） Who clause，例如：

The chairperson will decide who will be allowed to participate in the project.

C） That clause，例如：

The informant regrets that she contacted the police.

D） 動名詞，例如：

We all enjoy eating Chinese foods.

E） 不定詞片語，例如：

They consider to die for a just cause admirable.

至於間接受詞的種類較少，通常有名詞，例如第 2.1.1 節中的 E）例，有代名詞，如： John offered her his volunteer service. 也有使用關係代名詞子句的，例如：John offered whoever wanted to accept it his volunteer service.

習題一

將下句譯成英文。

他認為他的頂頭上司很公平。

解析：

用 immediate 與 superior 相搭配表「頂頭上司」作受詞。

解答：

He considers his immediate superior quite fair.

補充說明：

「公平」也有「合理」的意思，因此我們也可用 reasonable.

習題二

將下句譯成英文。

幸運對我們的心境常產生有益的影響。

解析：

用 luck 表「幸運」，以 salutary 與 effect 相搭配表「有益的影響」，而 effect 之後另需與 on 相搭配，用 spirits 表「心境」。將「我們心境有益的影響」用名詞片語表達作受詞。

解答：

Luck often produces a salutary effect on our spirits.

習題三

將下句譯成英文。

大家同意他所做的事十分有意義。

解析：

將「他做的事十分有意義」用 that 子句表達作受詞。

解答：

Everybody agrees that what he did is quite meaningful.

習題四

將下句譯成英文。

鄰居的朋友們保證我們經常在禮拜六晚上聚在一起玩橋牌。

解析：

用 make 與 sure 相搭配表「保證」，用 regularly 表「經常」。「保證…一起玩橋牌」要用 that 子句來表達作受詞。

解答：

Friends from our neighborhood make sure that we will regularly get together to play bridge Saturday night.

補充說明：

這裡也可用 gather together 來表「聚一起」。

習題五

將下句譯成英文。

經驗告訴我們運氣的意義並不太大。

解析：

將「運氣的意義並不太大」用 that 子句作直接受詞來表達。

解答：

Experience tells us that luck does not mean that much.

習題六

將下句譯成英文。

嫌疑犯承認犯了罪。

解析：

用 the accused 表「嫌疑犯」，用 commit 表「犯（罪）」。將「犯了罪」用動名詞表達作受詞。

解答：

The accused admitted committing the crime.

補充說明：

注意中文動詞（犯罪）用英文動名詞（committing）翻出的詞性轉譯用法。又，英文中有些動詞其後常跟動名詞，例如本題的 admit，習題七的 postpone，習題八的 enjoy 及習題九的 stop。其他常用的這些動詞另包括 avoid、can't help、consider、delay、finish、keep、mind 等。

習題七

將下句譯成英文。

我們再不能耽擱準備年會。

解析：

用 postpone 表「耽擱」，用 annual meeting 表「年會」。將「準備年會」用動名詞表達作受詞。

解答：

We should not postpone preparing the annual meeting any longer.

補充說明：

注意中文動詞（準備）用英文動名詞（preparing）翻出的詞性轉譯法。

習題八

將下句譯成英文。

喬治喜歡唸唐詩。

解析：

用片語 Tang poems 表「唐詩」。將「唸唐詩」用動名詞表達作受詞。

解答：

George enjoys reading Tang poems.

補充說明：

注意中文動詞（唸）用英文動名詞（reading）的詞性轉譯用法。

習題九

將下句譯成英文。

他們彼此該停止叫罵。

解析：

用 yell 表「叫罵」，其後需與 at 相搭配。將「彼此停止叫罵」用動名詞表達作受詞。

解答：

They should stop yelling at each other.

補充說明：

注意中文動詞（叫罵）用英文動名詞（yelling）翻出的詞性轉譯法。

習題十

將下句譯成英文。

他們計劃明天結束協商。

解析：

用 negotiation 表「協商」。將「明天結束協商」用不定詞片語表達作受詞。

解答：

They plan to finish the negotiation tomorrow.

2.1.3.4 補語

補語除可用名詞片語(如第 2.1.1 節 F)例中的 professor emeritus）及形容詞（如第 2.1.1 節 C）例中的 happier）外，尚可有下列幾種不同的種類：

A）不定詞片語，例如：

They believe the call-in program to convey nothing but biased views.（不定詞片語用作受詞補語）

B）過去分詞片語，例如：

In English grammar a direct object does not cause the event denoted by the verb.（過去分詞片語用作受詞補語）

C）現在分詞片語，例如：

They remember the effects of the earth-quake lasting for years. （現在分詞片語用作受詞補語）

D）動名詞，例如：

His hobby is playing tennis.（動名詞用作主詞補語）

E）Who clause，例如：

The professor who is from London gives high praise to her students.[7]（Who clause 用作主詞補語）

F）系詞片語，例如：

A friend in dire need is a friend who needs help.（系詞片語用作主詞補語，及 who clause 用作受詞補語）

G）That clause，例如：

They are preparing invitation cards that are for next week's reception.（That clause 用作受詞補語）

習題一

將下句譯成英文。

她一向回家很晚，有時高興有時心情低落。

解析：

用 used to 表「一向」，用 cheerful 表「高興」及 dejected 表「心情低落」，二者皆作補語。

---

[7]　本句是由一主句及副句連接成的複合句。有關子句的連接，請參第 2.2.1 節。本句另可用省略法改寫，詳參第 3.2 各節。

解答：

She used to come home very late, sometimes cheerful and at other times dejected.

補充說明：

注意 used to 與 to be used to 二者意思不同，前者指「過去一向如此」，但現在並不一定如此，而後者指「已習慣於」。在後者的情形，後面的動詞需用現在分詞，例如：John was used to borrowing money from his friends.

習題二

將下句譯成英文。

我們沒有理由懷疑他的誠意。

解析：

用 doubt 表「懷疑」與 sincerity（表「誠意」）二者相搭配，用不定詞片語來表達作受詞補語。

解答：

We have no reason to doubt his sincerity.

補充說明：

注意，中文動詞（懷疑）用英文不定詞（to doubt）翻出的詞性轉譯法。又，這裡也可用 question 來表「懷疑」，使這句翻成 We have no reason to question his sincerity.

習題三

將下句譯成英文。

此非應付問題的正當態度。

解析：

用 approach 表「態度」，以 tackle 與 problem 相搭配表「應付問題」，需用不定詞片語表達作補語。

解答：

This is not a proper approach to tackle the problem.

補充說明：

Approach 也可與 correct 相搭配表「正當態度」（correct approach），同時 settle 及 solve 也可與 problem 相搭配表「解決問題」，使本句翻成 This is not a correct approach to settle\solve the problem. 又，注意中文動詞（應付）用英文不定詞（to tackle）翻出的詞性轉譯法。

習題四

將下句譯成英文。

所有今天收到的貨物，會在一星期內遞交。

解析：

用 deliver 表「遞交」，「今天收到」用過去分詞片語表達作補語。

解答：

All the cargoes received today will be delivered within a week.

補充說明：

解答中的定冠詞 （the）不能忽略，因為是指今天收到的貨物，而非一般的貨物。又、本句是由 All the cargoes that are received today will be delivered within a week 省略而來。關於省略的用法，請參第 3.2 節.

習題五

將下句譯成英文。

他們正在討論顧問所提出的建議。

解析：

用 consultant 表「顧問」，suggest 表「提出」，以過去分詞片語表達作受詞補語。

解答：

They are discussing the proposal suggested by their consultant.

補充說明：

本句是由 They are discussing the proposal that was suggested by their consultant 省略而來。關於省略的用法，請參第 3.2 節.

習題六

將下句譯成英文。

我遇到我的鄰居在他的前院草地上工作。

解析：

用 front lawn 表「前院草地」，其前需與 on 相搭配。「工作」需以現在分詞片語表達作受詞補語。

解答：

I met my neighbor working on his front lawn.

補充說明：

本句是由 I met my neighbor who was working on his front lawn 省略而來。關於省略的用法，請參第 3.2 節.

習題七

將下句譯成英文。

祇有幾位學生在教室裡畫卡通。

解析：

用 a few 表「幾位」，「畫卡通」需以現在分詞片語表達作補語。

解答：

There are only a few students drawing cartoons in classroom.

補充說明：

本句是由 There are only a few students who are drawing cartoons in classroom 省略而來。關於省略的用法，請參第 3.2 節.

習題八

將下句譯成英文。

桌上的書每一頁都有圖片。

解析：

用 contain 表「（含）有」，「桌上」及「每一頁」皆需用系詞片語表達作補語。

解答：

The book on the table contains pictures on every page.

習題九

將下句譯成英文。

議院的法案招致選民的憤怒，認為該法案不合理。

解析：

用 legislature 表「議院」，用 attract 表「招致」，irrational 表「不合理」，用 regard 表「認為」。「（選民）認為議院的法案不合理」需用一 who clause 作選民的補語。

解答：

The legislature's bill attracts outrage from voters, who regard it as irrational.

補充說明：

原文是有二個文意構成，即「議院的法案招致選民的憤怒」（The legislature's bill attracts outrage from voters）及「選民認為議院的法案不合理」（Voters regard the legislature's bill as irrational.）解答是用複合句將二者連接在一起。關於子句的連接，請參第 2.2.1 節.

習題十

將下句譯成英文。

他喜愛的運動是游泳。

解析：

用 favorite 表「喜愛」，「游泳」用動名詞表達作主詞補語。

解答：

His favorite sport is swimming.

2.1.3.5 修飾語

修飾語由於種類很多，常常容易和補語相混，因此本節首先說明修飾語的各種不同的種類，然後再討論二者的區別。

修飾語可為副詞，例如第 2.1.1 節中 C）例的 finally，或屬系詞片語，如第 2.1.1 節中 F）例的 in last week's meeting。此外，名詞片語、原形動詞、不定詞片語、現在與過去分詞片語、無動詞式（verbless clause）[8]及副句，多可用作修飾語。我們分別舉例於下以便參考。

A） 名詞片語，例如：

His father passed away the year before last year.

B） 原形動詞，例如：

Rather than earn a regular salary, she prefers commission.

C） 不定詞片語，例如：

For John to pass the test, he should take a few more training lessons.

D） 現在分詞片語，例如：

George rushed to catch the bus, leaving his friends behind.

E） 過去分詞片語，例如：

He joined the team, convinced that his team could win the tournament.

F） 無動詞式，例如：

She went back to school again, her mind full of hope this time.

---

[8] Verbless clause 亦稱 small clause 或稱 fragmented clause，其結構與通常句子相似，但不帶動詞。關於無動詞式及與限定子句，非限定子句的互用，請參第 3.3.5 節。

G）　副句，例如：

He bid farewell to his former students because he got a new teaching position in Singapore.（這是表緣由的副句）[9]

　　修飾語的各種種類已如上述。這裏我們要進一步說明如何鑒別一句中的補語以及修飾語的問題。我們多習慣于中文的寫法，因此或許認為沒有必要鑒別何者是補語，何者是修飾語，因為凡屬前者我們用「的」，凡屬後者我們用「地」。但是在英文中，對這問題各家看法不同[10]。關於這一點，我們現在用 The police arrested a thief with a gun 一句來說明。這一句主要的意思是 The police arrested a thief，其中的述詞部份是由動詞（arrested）作主語，受詞（thief）用作從語，至于句中的系詞片語 with a gun 在句法結構上，究竟屬補語或修飾語有待進一步的說明。大凡構成文意的核心要素部份皆屬補語，否則屬修飾語。我們現在用 x-bar syntax（八字構圖）將上例分別用二種不同的方法來分析。

例1）

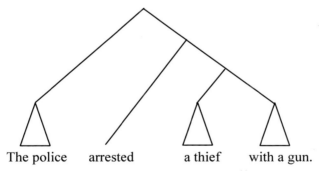

The police　arrested　　a thief　　with a gun.

在本例中，a thief 及 with a gun 互屬為鄰近要素[11]的關係。

---

[9]　有關副句的種類，請參第 2.2.1 節。

[10]　有關各學者對此點的主張，請參 P.H. Mathews, *Syntax* (London: Cambridge University Press, 1981), at 121-123, 124ff.

[11]　關于鄰近要素的觀念，請參第 2.2.1 節。

79

例 2）

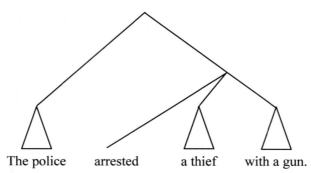

The police　　arrested　　a thief　　with a gun.

在本例中，a thief 及 with a gun 並不構成鄰近要素的關係，而 a thief，with a gun 與 arrested 三者卻構成鄰近要素的關係。

在上面二種不同的構圖中，with a gun 不論屬那一種解釋，皆可省略，其省略的結果，原句在文法上仍屬一完整的句子，亦即 The police arrested a thief.

因此 with a gun 是屬修飾語。至於如何決定句子的完整與否一點，則在於動詞的性質。例如在第 2.1.1 節的 I)例中（That the suspect admitted his crime in court made the case more sensational）made 為及物動詞，其後跟受詞 the case，如將 more 省略，在文法上並不妨害這句的完整(亦即 That the suspect admitted his crime in court made the case sensational)，但不能省略 sensational，否則就不成文句（亦即 That the suspect admitted his crime in court made the case more....）因此 more 屬修飾語，而 sensational 屬補語。瞭解這一點，對一句中補語及修飾語的鑒別就容易掌握。

習題一

將下句譯成英文。

落葉飄飛在秋風裏。

80

解析：

用 fallen 與 leaves 相搭配表「落葉」，用 fly 與 freely 相搭配表「飄飛」，以 autumn 與 wind 相搭配表「秋風」。本句需使用一系詞片語作修飾語來成句。

解答：

Fallen leaves are flying freely in the autumn wind.

補充說明：

這裡也可用 whirl 來表「飄飛」。

習題二

將下句譯成英文。

希望之火花在黑暗的時刻又復燃。

解析：

用 flame 與 hope 相搭配表「希望之火花」（the flame of hope），以 hope 與 rekindle 相搭配表「希望復燃」，用 hours 與 darkness 相搭配表「黑暗時刻」（hours of darkness）。本句需使用一系詞片語作修飾語來成句。

解答：

The flame of hope was rekindled in hours of darkness.

補充說明：

注意中、英文詞序的不同用法，在 the flame of hope 中，the flame 置於 of hope 之前，而不像中文「希望之火」中的詞序，將「希望」（the hope）置於「火」（of flame）之前。

習題三

將下句譯成英文。

他們提前一小時完成了他們的工作。

解析：

用 one hour earlier 表「提前一小時」。本句需使用名詞片語作修飾語來成句。

解答：

They finished their work one hour earlier.

補充說明：

本句也可以用 accomplish 或 complete 與 work 相搭配來表「完成工作」。注意此處中文動詞（提前）用英文副詞（earlier）來表達的詞性轉譯用法。習題六亦同。

習題四

將下句譯成英文。

一份報紙的社論必須建立在立場公正的基礎上。

解析：

用 editorial 與 newspaper（the editorial of a newspaper）相搭配表「一份報紙的社論」，用 impartial 與 stance 相搭配表「立場公正」。本句需使用系詞片語作修飾語來成句。

解答：

The editorial of a newspaper must be built on the basis of an impartial stance.

習題五

將下句譯成英文。

喬治不耐煩再多等。

解析：

用 impatient 表「不耐煩」。本句需使用不定詞片語作修飾語來成句。

解答：

George is impatient to wait any longer.

補充說明：

注意此處中文動詞（等）用英文不定詞（to wait）來表達。

習題六

將下句譯成英文。

火車提前離站，將幾位觀光客給擱下來了。

解析：

以 leave 與 behind 相搭配表「擱下」。本句需使用現在分詞片語作修飾語來成句。

解答：

The train left the station earlier, leaving a few tourists behind.

習題七

將下句譯成英文。

由於被能見度低所迫，駕駛員在馬尼拉機場作緊急降落。

解析：

以 poor 與 visibility 相搭配表「能見度低」，用 emergency landing 表「緊急降落」。本句需使用一過去分詞片語作修飾語來成句。

解答：

Forced by a poor visibility, the pilot made an emergency landing at the Manila airport.

習題八

將下句譯成英文。

自海外旅遊返回之後，這對年輕夫婦看來又相愛了。

解析：

以 journey 與 overseas 相搭配表「海外旅遊」。注意 journey 需與 to 相搭配。本句需使用一過去分詞片語作修飾語來成句。

解答：

Returned from a journey to overseas, the young couple seemed in love

again.

習題九

將下句譯成英文。

人們仍然懷疑，此種保證是否好得令人難以相信。

解析：

用 wonder 表「懷疑」，用片語 promise of this nature 表「此種保證」，用 too good...to 表「好得 …難以」。本句需使用一副句作修飾語來成句。

解答：

People still wonder if promises of this nature are too good to be true.

習題十

將下句譯成英文。

執政黨決定支援其獨立候選人。

解析：

用 stand 與 by（to stand by）相搭配表「支援」。本句需使用一不定詞片語作修飾語來成句。

解答：

The ruling party decided to stand by its independent candidates.

補充說明：

這裡也可用 prop up 表「支援」，將這句翻成 The ruling party decided to prop up its independent candidates.

2.2 句構應用與中譯英的基本認識

本節討論二個課題，一是使用 x-bar 句法的理論，來分析英文句構各層次的構成要素，進而介紹如何使用次元單位的觀念來造句。一是根據句構的觀點提供讀者對中譯英應具備的基本認識，前者在

第 2.2.1 節中討論，後者在第 2.2.2 節中討論。

2.2.1　次元單位與句構之關係

　　英文每一文句是由不同層次的語言單位連接而成，我們稱此語言單位為次元單位，而每一次元單位乃代表一種文意，在翻譯及作文時，我們可以從不同層次的次元單位中，根據其相依相契的關係來連綴文意。我們試用 Each student must submit two essays 一句的八字構圖（x-bar syntax）來說明這一點：

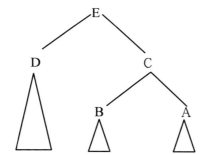

Each student must submit　two essays.

　　我們先就文法的觀點來分析本句中各單字的詞性。　在上圖中的第一層次上共有六個單字，其中有二個名詞（student 及 essay），一個助動詞（must），一個主動詞（submit），一個飾語（each）及一個形容詞（two）。我們在譯作時，對文句的結構須進一步注意各詞性間的相互隸屬關係。照上述的八字構圖，這六個單字分別構成不同的片語，而每一片語也可以次元單位的觀念來看待，這也就是說動詞片語 B）（must submit）及名詞片語 A）（two essays），在第二層次上分別成為二個二次元單位，這二個二次元單位，在第三層次上，共同隸屬于一個表第三次元單位的 C）。而 C）與另一名詞片語 D）（each student）在第四層次上，共同隸屬于代表全句的 E).

　　根據上述的八字構圖，各次元單位間相依相契的關係，可從幾個低次元單位相互組合成一個高次元單位得知，例如，B）與 A）組合成 C），而 C）與 D）組合成 E），而 E）本身乃代表全句的組合結構。其全部的組合結構關係可以進一步用下述八字構圖來表示。

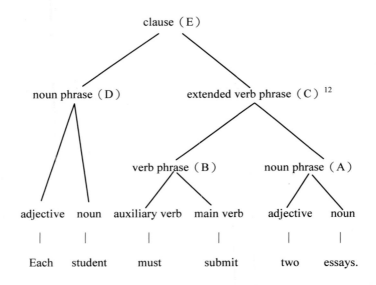

　　我們從上述八字構圖中可以曉得，全句 E）共有十種不同層次的次元單位組成，這包括六個表單字的第一層次的一次元單位，二個表片語的第二層次的二次元單位 B）及 A），以及另二個表片語的第三層次的三次元單位 C）及 D）。

12　此處所謂的 extended verb phrase（簡稱 EVP)是指 verb phrase 加上其受詞而言。有些討論造句的教材，將(B) 稱為 verb phrase$_1$ 而將 EVP 稱為 verb phrase$_2$。本書所採用的用語來自 R. Huddleston, *Introduction to the Grammar of English* (London: Cambridge University Press, 1984), at 6.

　　在上述八字構圖中，在第二層次上的 B）及 A）共同隸屬於 C），
因此稱此二者為 C）的構成要素。反之，在第三層次上，B）及 A）
雙具鄰近 C）的性質，故稱 B）及 A）為 C）的鄰近要素。同理，D）
不能稱為 C）的構成要素，因為 D）不屬於 C）。但 D）及 C）二者
共同隸屬於 E），故二者為 E）的鄰近要素，而 B）及 A）二者不能稱
為 E）的鄰近要素。要注意的是，唯有在八字所指之方向下才能視作
一組要素。例如，上圖中 submit 及 two 二者並無八字型的關係，因
此雙方不構成一組要素。此外，上述隸屬關係具雙向的特徵，從下而
上，呈現句中第一層次不同形式的詞性。從上而下，呈現句中四種不
同的結構，分由層次不同的次元單位所表達，例如 C），B）及 A）等。

　　次元單位的不同形式以及其隸屬關係已如上述，在此我們須進一
步說明各次元單位在造句上有何不同的功能。在文句的組合結構中，
每一次元單位在造句上皆有其一定的功能。例如在上述的八字構圖
中，第一組名詞片語作主詞，第二組名詞片語作受詞。動詞片語用作
述詞動詞（predicator）。我們可將上述的構圖，與該句的各造句功能，
合併列示于下以便參考。

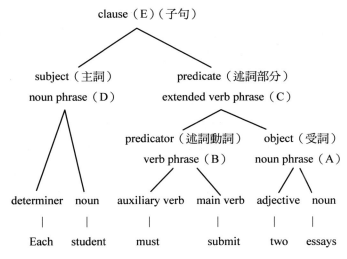

　　根據上面的說明，我們可用第 2.1.3.5 節中的二個八字構圖，進一步討論次元單位在造句上的功能。在例 1）中，因為 a thief 及 with a gun 互為鄰近要素，全句意為「警察逮捕持槍的小偷」。在例 2）中，a thief，with a gun 與 arrested 三者共同構成鄰近要素，a thief 是指「被捕者（小偷）」，with a gun 是指逮捕時所使用的工具，全句意為「警察持槍逮捕小偷」。

　　從上面二個例子可以曉得，同樣一個句子，因各次元單位的不同隸屬關係而產生二種不同的文意，分別為 The police arrested a thief who carried a gun（例 1）的文意）及 The police who carried a gun arrested a thief（例 2）的文意）。這二種不同的文意比原句 The police arrested a thief with a gun 的意思更為明確。從這裏我們不難發現，從次元單位的隸屬關係來討論文句的組合結構，能幫助我們正確地表達文意。此外，次元單位的隸屬關係與句式的變化亦有密切的關係。一方面，不論是何種詞性，在造句上可扮演不同的角色，例如在 The train arrived on time 一句中，train 及 time 皆屬名詞，前者屬名詞片語的次元單位（the train）乃用作主詞，後者屬系詞片語的受詞，而這個系詞片語本身乃用作修飾語，二者雖同屬名詞，但在造句的功用上有所不同。另一方面，不同文法上的詞性，可表達造句上相同的功用。例如，名詞片語的次元單位，固然可置句前用作主詞（如上例），而不定詞的次元單位，亦可置於句首用作主詞，例如：
To open a restaurant is her long-time dream.

　　以上我們用次元單位的觀念來剖解了英文的句構，說明何以「可以從不同層次的次元單位中，根據其相依相契的關係來連綴文意」的道理。下面我們用一個淺近的例子來解釋如何運用次元單位的觀念來造句。在「他正在林中獵兔」一句中，其核心的意思是「他正在打獵」（He is hunting），「林中」及「兔子」是二個不同的次元單

位，分別可用 in the forest 及 rabbits 來表達，這二個文意可用上述次元單位的隸屬關係加入核心意思上去而形成一句：He is hunting rabbits in the forest. 這是採用第 2.1.1 節中的第 5）模式來成句的。關於這一點，我們在下節討論如何中譯英時，會作更進一步的舉例說明。

　　這裡需附帶說明一點，「林中」（in the forest）在中文句構中放在句中，而在英文句構中置于句後，這是因為中、英文二者表達的方法有所不同而引起的。讀者或許會認為英文也可採用中文的句構而寫成：He is, in the forest, hunting rabbits. 這句構雖與中文的句構相同，但所表達的語氣却完全不一樣，英文句構採用了置換的方法將 in the forest 置句中來加強語氣，這是中文句構中沒有具備的語氣[13]。有關中、英文句構的不同與中譯英的關係，我們將於下節中詳細討論。

習題一

1) 將下句譯成英文。

　　他是位商人。

解析：

這一句表核心的意思。將用于下句讓我們練習用次元單位的觀念來造句。

解答：

He is a merchant.

2) 將下句譯成英文。

---

[13]有關加強語氣的用法，請參第 3.3.6 節.

他是位在加州的商人。

解析：

將「在加州」這一次元單位加在上句中來做。

He is a merchant in California.

習題二

1) 將下句譯成英文。

他聽到這不幸的消息。

解析：

以 tragic 與 news 相搭配表「不幸的消息」。

解答：

He heard the tragic news。

2) 將下句譯成英文。

他從電台廣播聽到這不幸的消息。

解析：

將片語 radio broadcast 表「電台廣播」，將這個次元單位加在上句中來做。

解答：

He heard the tragic news from a radio broadcast.

習題三

1) 將下句譯成英文。

此份投稿是篇佳作。

解析：

用 contribution 表「投稿」，gem 表「佳作」。

解答：

This contribution is a gem.

2) 將下句譯成英文。

此份投稿從頭到尾是篇佳作。

解析：

將片語 from first to last 表「從頭到尾」，將這個次元單位加在上句中來做。

解答：

This contribution is a gem from first to last.

習題四

1) 將下句譯成英文。

珍妮的毛衣搖來曳去。

解析：

用 dangle 表「搖曳」。

解答：

Jane's sweater is dangling.

2) 將下句譯成英文。

珍妮的毛衣搖曳到她的膝蓋處。

解析：

將片語 to her knees 表「到她的膝蓋處」，用這個次元單位加在上句中來做。

Jane's sweater is dangling to her knees.

習題五

將下句譯成英文。

青蔥的草地馳過我的眼前。

解析：

以 verdant 與 meads 相搭配表「青蔥的草地」，以 pass 表「馳過」。用次元單位的觀念來造句。

解答：

Verdant meads passed before my eyes.

補充說明：

注意，此處不能用 past 來替代 passed，因為 past 不是 pass 的過去式或過去分詞，而是副詞，例如：The minivan curls past the traffic light, smashing to a car making a left turn. Past 也用作形容詞，例如：It is always difficult to break with past habits. Past 也用作系詞，例如：Neighbors are straining to see past the hill, searching for an unidentified object flying in the sky. Past 也用作名詞，例如： Often it is a rewarding experience to recollect one's past.

習題六

1）將下句譯成英文。

　　保守黨幹得良好。

解析：

用 fare 表「幹」，用片語 very well 表「良好」。

解答：

The Conservative Party fares very well.

2）將下句譯成英文。

　　保守黨在上次選舉中幹得良好。

解析：

將 at the last election 表「上次選舉」，將這個次元單位加在上句中來做。

解答：

The Conservative Party fared very well at the last election.

補充說明：

與「保守黨在選舉中幹得良好」的相近意思有： a）「保守黨在上次選舉中獲勝」(The Conservative Party won the last election.)b）或者「幾

乎獲得全數席次」，在此情形可用 sweep the board 或 sweep the table，例如：The Conservative Party swept the board\table at the election（「保守黨幾乎獲得全數的席次」）。與「保守黨在選舉中幹得良好」相反的意思，可翻成 The Conservative Party fared poorly\badly at the election.

習題七

1) 將下句譯成英文。

　　示威者向警察屈服。

解析：

用片語 cave in 表「屈服」，其後另需與 to 相搭配。

解答：

The protesters caved in to the police.

補充說明：

這裡也可用 demonstrator 來表「示威者」。

2) 將下句譯成英文。

　　為了避免彼此對陣，示威者向警察屈服。

解析：

用片語 a pitched battle 表「對陣」，用 to avoid a pitched battle between them 表「為避免彼此對陣」。將這個次元單位加在上句中來做。

解答：

The protesters caved in to the police to avoid a pitched battle between them.

補充說明：

這裡我們不用…in order to avoid a pitched battle between them，因為 in order 是贅言。關於這一點請參第 1.1 節。

習題八

將下句譯成英文。

駕車技術多半是由重複的動作而構成。

解析：

用 driving 與 skill 相搭配表「駕車技術」，用 largely 表「多半」， 用 compose 表「構成」，其後需與 of 相搭配，而用 operation 表「動作」。試用次元單位的觀念來造句。

解答：

Driving skills are largely composed of repetitive operations.

習題九

1) 將下句譯成英文。

　　從鄰近的牧地裡，能聽到牛鈴的叮噹聲。

解析：

用 tinkling 與 cowbells 相搭配表「牛鈴的叮噹聲」（the tinkling of cowbells），用 neighboring 與 pasture 相搭配表「鄰近的牧地」。

解答：

The tinkling of cowbells could be heard from a neighboring pasture.

2) 將下句譯成英文。

　　從鄰近的牧地裡，能在不遠處聽到牛鈴的叮噹聲。

解析：

用片語 a short distance away 表「不遠處」。將「不遠處」這一次元單位加在上句中來做。

解答：

The tinkling of cowbells could be heard from a neighboring pasture a short distance away.

習題十

1）將下句譯成英文。

　　她躺伸在那裡。

解析：

用 stretch 表「伸」。

She lies stretched there.

補充說明：

這裡「躺」與「伸」的詞序，中、英文相同。

2）將下句譯成英文。

　她躺伸在那裡，微笑著休息。

解析：

用片語 in smiling repose 表「微笑著休息」。將「微笑著休息」這一次元單位加在上句中來做。

解答：

She lies stretched there, in smiling repose.

補充說明：

注意，中文的動詞（微笑）轉譯成英文的系詞片語（in smiling）。

2.2.2 句構與中譯英之關係

　　中高級「全民英檢」中譯英的測驗部分，雖不要求專業的翻譯技巧，但由於中、英文表達的方式有所不同，對如何翻成一段像樣的英文，是我們在準備考試前應具備的基本語文能力，因此本書特闢一節討論中譯英需具的基本智識，希望能有助于讀者對中譯英能力的培養，如此在應試時才能以道地的英文譯出中文的題意。

　　中、英文不同的表達方式來自二者文句結構的不同而引起，英文文句是有子句構成，各子句之間的關係可有「對等」（coordination）及「附屬」（subordination）之分。所謂對等，是指二者平行或反襯（contrast），前者如 and，both，both … and，not only … but also，後者如 but，or，either … or，neither … nor。所謂附屬，是指二者隸

屬。我們不妨用 a poor and old king 及 a poor old king 二個片語來說明這對等及附屬的觀念。在前者，poor 及 old 用 and 連接，二者皆為主語 king 的從語，因為 and 的使用使二者成為對等關係[14]。在後者的情形，poor 乃主語 old king 的從語，係隸屬於 old king，而與 old 並不形成對等的關係。這區別可用下述八字構圖來表達。

king	old king
poor = old	poor
對等關係	隸屬關係

　　我們如將這主從觀念用于子句間的相互關係時，則有對等句（coordinate sentence）及副句（subordinate sentence，亦稱「附屬句」或「從句」）之別。例如：

A） He has finished his assignments and（he）has left.

B） Because he has finished his assignments, he has left.

　　在上述 A）例中，「做完習題」與「離開」是用 and 來連接，二句意思平行成對等關係，由於二者皆可獨立成句，故稱「獨立子句」（independent clause）。而在上述 B）例中，由於用表緣由的「從屬連接詞」（subordinate conjunction）because 的緣故，使二句文意有先後因果的關係，這是說「做完習題」故而「離開」。因為「做完習題」在此必須依賴「離開」全句始成文意，故為副句。由對等句所組成的文句稱「并列句」（compound sentence，亦稱「合句」），而由一個主句及一個以上副句所組成的句子則稱「複合句」（complex sentence）。

　　在複合句中，主句與副句的隸屬，反映在它們相互間的邏輯關

---

[14] 在此情形，and 也可省略而用逗點取代另寫成 a poor, old king。

係上，這種邏輯關係可用不同的從屬連接詞來表達，現在我們列舉幾種常用的從屬連接詞，以便作平時練習造句的參考。

1) 表時間：after, as, as soon as, before, no sooner than, once, since, till, until, when, while。

2) 表場所：where, wherever。

3) 表條件：although, as long as, if, in case, even if, unless。

4) 表讓步：although, even if, even though, though, whether, while。

5) 表緣由：as, because, since。

6) 表結果：in order that, so that, such … that。

7) 表方式：as, as if, as though。

8) 表目的：in order that, so as to, so that, that。

9) 表比較：as, than, while。

這類副句，從句子的構成要素言，乃屬修飾語的性質。此外，關係代名詞 who、which、that 以及用 what、how、why 的子句也構成隸屬關係。我們試以下面幾個例子來說明如何用不同的隸屬關係來表達不同的句式。

B) The decline of the fundamental moralities of life comes over generations.

C) We always judge people by their distinction of achievements based on materialism.

這二句可用 and 相連接在一起表對等的并列句，而寫成：

D) The decline of the fundamental moralities of life comes over generations, and we always judge people by their distinction of achievements based on materialism.

我們也可用因果關係將 C）及 D）二句連接在一起表一複合句。這也

就是說將 D）視作 C）現象的緣由而寫成：

E) The decline of the fundamental moralities of life comes over generations, as we always judge people by their distinction of achievements based on materialism.

需注意的是，從句構來說，連接詞位置的不同有時可影響句中的文意，通常對等句中的子句，它們的次序可變更而不影響句中的文意。例如; It is six o'clock in the morning and（it）is raining. 這句可改寫成 It is raining and（it）is six o'clock in the morning 二者文意相同。但有時對等子句間具先後的關係時，則不宜變更其次序，否則句子的文意就不儘相同。例如： The suspect was shot and （he） was removed 一句如改寫成 The suspect was removed and （he） was shot 二者的文意就顯然不同。

從句構來說，通常連接詞置於其所連接的子句之前，例如在 George ordered two hot dogs, but his wife ordered a soft drink 一句中，but 是置于第二個子句之前，不能置于第二個子句之中而寫成 George ordered two hot dogs, his wife but ordered a soft drink 就不成文句。但有的連接詞如 though 及 as，在加重語氣時可置句中[15]。例如：

G1）Though she is pretty, she is slow. 可改寫成：

G2）Pretty though she is, she is slow. 用以加重 pretty 的語氣。又如：

H1）As he is unaware of a mechanical problem, he keeps driving his car. 可改寫成：

H2）Unaware as he is of a mechanical problem, he keeps driving his car. 用以加重 unaware 的語氣。

---

[15] 關於如何加重語氣的各種方法，詳參第 3.3.6 節.。

同時再從句構而言，英文副句的位置也能影響句式及文意。一般而言，副句在文句中的位置有前置、中置及尾置的不同，我們分別舉下面幾個例子來說明。

I1）　If it is convenient to you, we shall call a meeting tomorrow morning.（副句前置）

I2）　We shall call a meeting, if it is convenient to you, tomorrow morning.（副句中置）

I3）　We shall call a meeting tomorrow morning if it is convenient to you.（副句後置）

通常除加重語氣外，英文句式傾向于將副句置于主句之後，例如：

J1）　[1][2][That [3][if you could][3] you would come][2] will be a great surprise to her.][1]

在上例中，副句 if you could 乃插在另一副句 that 及 you would come 之間，二者皆置于句首作全句的主詞，而這一句又可改寫成下面的句式：

J2）　[1][It will be a great surprise to her [2][that you would come [3][if you could.][3]][2]][1]

在這句式中，二個副句皆置於句後。

比較 J1）及 J2）二句，有三點值得我們注意。第一，J2）句是採尾置法，唸來遠較 J1）句為平易順口，J1）句念來令人吃力，除在加重語氣的情形下，通常較少使用。第二，二句中副句本身的位置也有所不同，在 J1）句中，if you could 置於 you could come 之前，是屬前置的用法，而在 J2）句中，if you could 是置于 you could come 之後，是屬尾置的用法。第三，J1）句文意的展延是順 1、2、3 的次序，而 J2）句文意的展伸是屬 3、2、1 的次序，與 J1）句恰巧相反。

又須注意的是，在句構上主副句的位置需保持文意上的邏輯關

係，例如：While visiting his parents, George met his younger sister Jane. 在這句中，喬治訪親在先，遇到妹妹在後，此句如改寫成 While meeting his younger sister Jane, George visited his parents 就不成文意了。另須注意的是，副句的位置常易引起句式的含糊不清，我們試以下例來說明。

x[Common sense tells us] y[honesty is the best policy] and z[everybody should adopt such an attitude.]

根據文意，上句可用二種不同的句構來表達。第一種是將 Y 隸屬於 X，而視 Z 與 X 為對等的關係，這樣的句構可用下圖來表達。

第二種是將 Y 與 Z 視為對等，而共同隸屬於 X，這樣的句構可用下圖來表達。

照此二種不同的結構，原句的文意實際上可由下面二種不同的句式來表達：

Common sense tells us that honesty is the best policy, and everybody should adopt such an attitude. （第一種關係）

Common sense tells us that honesty is the best policy and that everybody should adopt such an attitude. （第二種關係）

我們對在英文中不同的結構，形成不同的句式代表著不同的文意一點已交待清楚。在中譯英時，講究將中文的意思以妥切的英文表達方式轉譯成英文的意思，如此才能「揣摩其意而造其語」而譯

出一句道地的英文。但中譯英並不是單純的文字搭配，而是需要我們掌握中、英文二種不同語文的表達能力，這不僅要求我們做到在第一章中所強調的遣詞需正確及詞序需合理，而且更要求中、英文句構搭配恰當。中譯英能力的培養與練毛筆字一樣，後者有入帖及出帖二個階段，而中譯英也有入句及出句二個步驟。首先我們需融會貫通中文的意思，深入瞭解一句的文意，如此來決定何者為核心意思，何者為次要意思，這入句的瞭解有助于在翻譯時達到傳神的要求。在譯成英文時，首先將主要的核心意思依英文句子的模式翻成一句基本句子，然後再將各次要的意思，依其與主要意思的關係，使用當作不同次元單位的補語及修飾語來插入這基本句中，翻成一句，達到出句的境界，然後再逐句推敲各句間的相互作用及邏輯關係，來譯出一段道地的英文。

　　中、英文表達的方法有所不同，例如「他往舊金山出差，完後，去拜訪住在聖地牙哥的親戚，剛剛才從加州返回」一句可譯成 He has just returned from California, where he visited his relatives living in San Diego, after making a business trip to San Francisco. 在此我們發現中、英文二句的意思雖皆以時間的推移為出發點，但二者所表達的邏輯關係並不一樣，中文將最後發生的事（返回）置句尾，而英文將最後發生的事置句前，二者表達的方法恰好相反。但須注意的是，中、英文表達的方法各具靈活的優點，例如在「昨天她因身體不舒服而告假一天在家」可翻成 She took a day off yesterday because she didn't feel well 也可翻成 Because she didn't feel well, she took a day off yesterday. 英文的句式是用上述副句置換的方法來變更，但中文不允許我們將原文用置換的方法來表達，因為「她告假一天在家，因昨天身體不舒服」的意思與原文不儘相同，原文僅指昨天告假一天在家，而此處指今天因昨天生病而告假一天，二相比較，英文表

達的方法較為靈活。但在 Let's try harder so that we can find the real cause of the problem 一例中，try harder 的意思與 find the real cause 的意思在英文裡不允許我們倒置，可是中文可用「讓我們再努力，以便找到問題的癥結」也可用「為了找到問題的癥結，讓我們再努力」來表達，在此中文的表達方法顯得比英文靈活。不論何者為靈活，需認識中、英文不同的表達方法，才能使我們在中譯英時不拘泥於一格。

中、英文不同的表達方法已如上述，這裏我們要進一步以次元單位的觀念來研究英文的表達方法。我們在第 2.2.1 節中曉得，在譯作時「可以從不同層次的次元單位中，根據其相依相契的關係來連綴文意」，這裏所指的次元單位分別可用不同的補語及修飾語[16]來表達。我們不妨用下面一個例子，來解釋英文句中各構成要素是如何緊密相扣在一起的。在 Multiple-track admissions have breathed new life into the liberal education taught at senior high schools in Taiwan 一句中，taught 為形容 liberal education 的補語，at senior high schools 是修飾語，形容 taught，而 in Taiwan 是另一個修飾語，用來形容 at senior high schools，這三個次元單位是依邏輯的關係緊銜在一起的，原因是 taught 形容 liberal education 因此放在 liberal education 之後，at senior high schools 是形容 taught 的，因此放在 taught 之後，而 in Taiwan 是形容 at senior high schools 的，因此放在 at senior high schools 之後，于是這三個次元單位遂相依相契，層層相扣而成 liberal education taught at senior high schools in Taiwan.

上面是一個淺顯的例子，這裏我們再舉一個看似複雜，但仍以同樣層層相扣的方法而寫成的一個句子。在下例中：

---

[16] 關于補語及修飾語的種類，請參第 2.1.3.4 及第 2.1.3.5 各節.

在一個特別令他感觸的時刻，索洛漂舟于月光中，回憶起兒時曾在此嬉遊。

這一句的基本文意是「索洛回憶起兒時曾在此嬉游」，可用一個基本子句來表示而翻成 Thoreau reflected on a boyhood adventure at that very place. 在這句中 at that very place 的次元單位，表中文的「曾在此」，而 a boyhood adventure 表中文的「兒時嬉遊」。此外，「在一個特別令他感觸的時刻」以及「漂舟於月光中」是點綴文中主旨的片語，分別可用 in a particularly revealing moment（修飾語）及 while adrift on the lake in the moonlight（修飾語）來表達。其中「漂舟」（adrift on the lake）及「月光中」（in the moonlight）是分別用不同的次元單位來表達。整個句子可將這些不同的次元單位，插在基本子句中而組合成下面一個整句：

In a particularly revealing moment Thoreau reflected, while adrift on the lake in the moonlight, on a boyhood adventure at that very place.

這句從句構來說，它的句式是將一個表修飾語的次元單位（in a particularly revealing moment）插在基本子句之前，另一個表修飾語的次元單位（while adrift on the lake in the moonlight）插在基本子句中的動詞之後。

根據上面二個例子，我們不難發現，次元單位好似音符，英文的句構好似五線譜，音符以不同的節奏跳躍在五線譜上能奏出一段悅耳的音樂，就像各次元單位靠靈活使用句構就能寫出「語不驚人死不休」的文意一樣。讀者平常如能本著這個觀念對英文的句構熟習應用，相信在應試時必能譯出一段道地的英文。

須注意的是，上例中文的「索洛漂舟於月光中」一句，在英文裡是用片語 while adrift on the lake in the moonlight 翻出，同時中文的動詞「回憶」雖用相當英文的動詞 reflect 來表達，但中文的動詞「嬉遊」卻是用英文的名詞 adventure 譯出，二者詞性不同。這種中、

英文詞性轉譯可在很多不同的情形下使用，關於這一點，我們用下面幾個例子來加以說明。

K) 我母親穿衣很樸素。可翻成 My mother is very domestic in her dress.

　　中文的動詞「穿衣」用英文的系詞片語 in her dress 翻出。

L) 他們沒有把握在午夜前到達目的地。可翻成 They are not sure to reach their destination before midnight.

　　中文的動詞「把握」用英文的形容詞 sure 翻出。

M) 他天才獨厚之處也恰是他缺陷之處。可翻成 His genius is rich exactly where he is poor.

　　中文的名詞「獨厚處」及「缺陷處」分別用英文的形容詞 rich 及 poor 翻出。

N) 堅毅是成功所必須的。可翻成 Persistency is a necessity for success.

　　中文的形容詞「必須的」用英文的名詞 necessity 翻出。

O) 她開車不小心，引起一樁嚴重的車禍。可翻成 Her careless driving resulted in a serious car accident.

　　中文的動詞「開車」用英文的動名詞 driving 翻出。此處更應注意的是中、英文不同的結構方法，那就是，中文用二句來表達英文一句的意思。

　　在應試時，如想不起中英文相當的詞性時，不妨考慮使用詞性轉譯的方法，這樣或許就比較容易翻。

　　不論中譯英，或英譯中，翻譯是門高度艱深的學問，在如何求「信」與「順」之間，其中有很多可講究的技巧。由於「全民英檢」對中高級的中譯英部分並未要求達到專業的程度，因此本書除提供讀者一些中譯英的基本智識外不擬作進一步的介紹。

　　我們在上節的習題中，有機會練習用次元單位的方法來造句，本節習題提供我們更多練習的機會。希望讀者能按著自己的興趣與程度盡量選擇來做，而且做得愈多愈好，這樣才能漸漸養成以次元單位來造句的習慣，以便利做以後各章的習題。

　　本節習題較多，共有二十七題，前二十五題分二大類，第一類是從對等及隸屬的關係來造句，第二類是練習中、英文詞性轉譯及不同的表達方法。習題一到習題十四屬第一類，習題十五到習題二十五屬第二類。在做第一類的習題時，讀者須先由二個子句間的關係來決定是用并列句或用複合句，而在使用複合句時，須進一步決定應該使用何種從屬連接詞。習題一是個示範題，幫助讀者瞭解如何去做其他十三題。在做第二類的習題時，注意解析欄中的提示。最後二題是綜合題。

習題一

1)　將下句譯成英文。

　　她工作努力。

解答：

She works hard.

2)　將下句譯成英文。

　　她窮。

解答：

She is poor.

3)　將 1）句及 2）句連成一整句。

解析：

用 and 來連接，表并列句。

解答：

She works hard and she is poor.　或

She is poor and she works hard.

補充說明：

在這一句中，二個子句的次序雖經變更，但仍不改變全句的文意。

4）將 1）句及 2）句連成一整句。

解析：

用 but 來連接，表并列句。

解答：

She works hard, but she is poor. 或

She is poor, but she works hard.

補充說明：

用 but 的并列句其前需用逗點。

5）將 1）句及 2）句連成一複合句。

解析：

用 although 來連接。

解答：

Although she works hard, she is poor. 或

She is poor though she works hard.

補充說明：

除在句首外，although 及 though 二者，以 though 為通用，如第二解答所示。

6）將 1）句及 2）句連成一複合句。

解析：

用 as if 來連接。

解答：

She works hard as if she is poor.

7）將 1）句及 2）句連成一複合句。

解析：

用 since 來連接。

解答：

Since she is poor, she works hard.或

She works hard since she is poor.

8)　將 1）句及 2）句連成一複合句。

解析：

用 even though　來連接。

解答：

She is poor even though she works hard.

習題二

1)　將下句譯成英文。

　　我們充滿自滿。

解析：

以 full 與 of 相搭配表「充滿」，用 self-satisfaction 表「自滿」。

解答：

We are full of self-satisfaction.

2)　將下句譯成英文。

　　我們絲毫沒有些許自得。

解析：

用片語 not the slightest bit 表「絲毫沒有些許」，注意 bit 之後需與 of 相搭配。用 self-complacency 表「自得」。

解答：

We are not the slightest bit of self-complacency.

3)　將 1）句及 2）句連成一整句表以下文意。

　　我們充滿自滿及絲毫沒有些許自得。

解析：

注意文中有「及」的意思，因此是用并列句。

解答：

We are full of self-satisfaction and（we are）not the slightest bit of self-complacency.

4) 將 1 ）句及 2 ）句連成一整句表以下文意。

我們充滿自滿，但絲毫沒有些許自得。

解析：

注意文中有「但」的意思，因此是用并列句。

解答：

We are full of self-satisfaction, but we are not the slightest bit of self-complacency.

5) 將 1 ）句及 2 ）句連成一整句表以下文意。

我們充滿自滿，雖然絲毫沒有些許自得。

解析：

注意文中有「雖然」的意思，因此是用複合句。

解答：

We are full of self-satisfaction though we are not the slightest bit of self-complacency.

習題三

1) 將下句譯成英文。

我們住在渥太華。

解析：

以 live 與 in 相搭配表「住在」，「渥太華」即 Ottawa.

解答：

We live in Ottawa.

2)　將下句譯成英文。

我們常到國立藝術館去。

解析：

用 National Arts Gallery 表「國立藝術館」。

解答：

We often go to the National Arts Gallery.

3)　將 1）句及 2）句連成一整句表以下文意。

我們住在渥太華的時候，常到國立藝術館去。

解析：

注意「我們住在 …的時候」是表時間的邏輯關係。本句應屬複合句。

解答：

When we lived in Ottawa, we often went to the National Arts Gallery.

補充說明：

本句述及以往的事情，故動詞用過去式。

習題四

1)　將下句譯成英文。

他們搬到本市。

解析：

用 move 與 to 相搭配表「搬到」。

解答：

They moved to this city.

2)　將下句譯成英文。

他們換了幾次工作。

解析：

用 change 與 job 相搭配表「換工作」。

解答：

全民英檢
中高級作文指南

They changed jobs several times.

3) 將 1）句及 2）句連成一整句表以下文意。

　　自從搬到本市以來，他們已換了幾次工作。

解析：

注意「自從 … 以來」是表時間的邏輯關係。本句應屬複合句。

解答：

Since they moved to this city, they have changed jobs several times.

補充說明：

注意動詞時式，副句中用過去式，主句中用現在完成式，表持續的狀況。

習題五

1) 將下句譯成英文。

　　學生沒有上網際網路的機會。

解析：

用片語 to go online 表「上網際網路」。

解答：

Students do not have chance to go online。

補充說明：

我們也可用 to gain access to Internet 表「上網際網路」。

2) 將下句譯成英文。

　　學生們變得懊惱。

解析：

用 become 與 frustrated 相搭配表「變得懊惱」。

解答：

Students become frustrated.

3) 將 1）及 2）二句連成一整句表以下文意。

當學生沒有機會上網際網路時，他們會變得懊惱。

解析：

注意「當…時」是表時間的邏輯關係。本句應屬複合句。

解答：

Students will become frustrated when they do not have the chance to go online.

4）　將1）及2）二句連成一整句表以下文意。

那些沒有機會上網際網路的學生會變得懊惱。

解析：

自句構言，用 who 子句來表達「沒有機會上網際網路的學生」。本句應屬複合句。

解答：

Those students who do not have the chance to go online will become frustrated.

習題六

1）　將下句譯成英文。

教育改革審議會從事了通盤評估本大學所需。

解析：

用 Evaluation Committee on Educational Reform 表「教育改革審議會」，用 conduct 表「從事」，以 overall 與 assessment 相搭配表「通盤評估」。

解答：

The Evaluation Committee on Educational Reform conducted an overall assessment of our university's needs.

2）　將下句譯成英文。

教育改革審議會向校董會提出一份八項即刻實行的優先事項。

解析：

用 Board of Directors 表「校董會」，submit 表「呈提」，用 priority 表「優先事項」，implementation 表「實行」。

解答：

The Evaluation Committee on Educational Reform submitted a list of eight priorities to the Board of Directors for immediate implementation.

3) 將 1）及 2）二句連成一整句表以下文意。

教育改革審議會從事了通盤評估本大學之所需，及向校董會提出一份八項即刻實行的優先事項。

解析：

注意此句中用「及」，故是一並列句。

解答：

The Evaluation Committee on Educational Reform conducted an overall assessment of our university's needs and submitted a list of eight priorities to the Board of Directors for immediate implementation.

4) 將 1）及 2）二句連成一整句表以下文意。

教育改革審議會從事了通盤評估本大學之所需之後，向校董會提出一份八項即刻實行的優先事項。

解析：

注意「之後」是表時間的邏輯關係。本句應屬複合句。

解答：

The Evaluation Committee on Educational Reform submitted a list of eight priorities to the Board of Directors for immediate implementation, after the Committee had conducted an overall assessment of our university's needs.或

112

After the Evaluation Committee on Educational Reform had conducted an overall assessment of our university's needs, it submitted a list of eight priorities to the Board of Directors for immediate implementation.

補充說明：

注意動詞時式。「提出即刻實行的事項」是一個過去的事，故用過去式，而「通盤評估」發生在「提出即刻實行的事項」之前，故用過去完成式。又本句另可依省略法改寫成 Having conducted an overall assessment of our university's needs, the Evaluation Committee on Educational Reform submitted a list of eight priorities to the Board of Directors for immediate implementation. 關於文句各種省略的方法，請參第 3.2 各節。

習題七

1) 將下句譯成英文。

一位無助的老婦人跪伏在路人前。

解析：

以 throw 與 on 相搭配表「跪伏」，用 passer-by 表「路人」。

解答：

A helpless old woman threw herself on the ground before passers-by.

補充說明：

注意此處的詞序，我們不用 old helpless woman，因為 old woman 為主，helpless 為從。同時注意 threw 之後用 herself.

2) 將下句譯成英文。

一位無助的老婦人為其生病的孫孩懇求一小掬食物。

解析：

用 implore 表「懇求」其後需與 for 相搭配，以 handful 表「一小掬」。

解答：

113

A helpless old woman implored a handful of foods for her sick grandchild.

3）將 1）及 2）二句連成一整句表以下文意。

　　一位無助的老婦人跪伏在路人前，為其生病的孫孩懇求一小掬食物。

解析：

根據文意，此句應為一并列句。

解答：

A helpless old woman threw herself on the ground before the passers-by and implored a handful of foods for her sick grandchild.

4）將 1）及 2）二句連成另一整句表以下文意。

　　一位跪伏在路人前的無助老婦人，為其生病的孫孩懇求一小掬食物。

解析：

自句構言，用 who 子句來表達「一位跪伏在路人前的老婦人」。本句應屬複合句。

解答：

A helpless old woman, who threw herself on the ground before the passers-by, implored a handful of foods for her sick grandchild.

習題八

1）將下句翻成英文。

　　他們辛苦工作。

解析：

用 hard 表「辛苦」。

解答：

They worked hard.

2）將下句翻成英文。

他們精疲力盡。

解析：

用片語 run out of steam 表「精疲力盡」。

解答：

They ran out of steam.

3）將 1）與 2）二句聯成一句，翻成英文表下面的文意。

他們辛苦工作到精疲力盡。

解析：

自句構言，這裡不妨用 so …that 來聯句，本句應屬複合句。

解答：

They worked so hard that they ran out of steam.

補充說明：

這裡「精疲力盡」也可用「疲憊不堪」（to a frazzle）來翻，即 They worked themselves to a frazzle（他們工作得疲憊不堪）。

習題九

1）將下句翻成英文。

他寫了一篇文章。

解析：

用 article 表「文章」。

解答：

He wrote an article。

2）將下句翻成英文。

他的文章嘲笑學校當局。

解析：

用 make 與 fun 相搭配表「嘲笑」，其後另需與 of 相搭配。

解答：

His article made fun of the school administration.

補充說明：

這裡也可用 poke 與 fun 相搭配表「嘲笑」，其後另需與 at 搭配，使本句翻成 His article poked fun at the school administration.

3）將1）與2）二句聯成一句，翻成英文表下面的文意。

他寫了一篇嘲笑學校當局的文章。

解析：

自句構言，用 that 子句來表達「一篇嘲笑學校當局的文章」。本句應屬複合句。

解答：

He wrote an article that made fun of the school administration.

習題十

1）將下句翻成英文。

百分之九十以上的公務員決定罷工。

解析：

用 take 與 strike 相搭配表「罷工」。

解答：

More than 90 percent of civil servants decided to take a strike.

2）將下句翻成英文。

這使他們完全不滿減薪一事達到高潮。

解析：

用 reach 與 acme 相搭配表「達到高潮」，用 salary 與 cut 相搭配表「減薪」。注意，此處的「這」是指1）句中的事，故用 it 為主詞。

解答：

It reached the acme of their total dissatisfaction at salary cut.

3）將1）與2）二句聯成一句，翻成英文表下面的文意。

當百分之九十以上的公務員決定罷工，這使他們完全不滿減薪一事達到高潮。

解析：

自句構言，本句應屬於用 when 子句來表達的複合句。

解答：

When more than 90 percent of civil servants decided to take a strike, it reached the acme of their total dissatisfaction at salary cut.

習題十一

將下句翻成英文。

我剛買到車票，車子就來了。

解析：

用連接詞 no sooner … than 來表「剛什麼…就什麼」。這是一句複合句。

解答：

I had no sooner bought the ticket than the bus arrived.

補充說明：

注意動詞時式，「買到票」發生在「車來」之前，故用過去完成式。

又，sooner 是比較級副詞，因此後面用 than 而不用 when。

習題十二

1) 將下句翻成英文。

我們詢問處平均一天收到近成千個電話之多。

解析：

用 information 與 center 相搭配表「詢問處」，用系詞片語 on average 表「平均」。

解答：

On average our information center receives close to one thousand calls a day.

2）將下句翻成英文。

我們詢問處從早晨八點開到下午五點，每星期五天。

解析：

用片語 open 8 a.m. to 5 p.m. 表「從早晨八點開到下午五點」，用名詞片語 five days a week 表「每星期五天」。注意，這名詞片語是當修飾語用。

解答：

Our information center is open 8 a.m. to 5 p.m., five days a week.

3）將 1）與 2）二句聯成一句，翻成英文表下面的文意。

我們平均一天收到近成千個電話之多的詢問處，從早晨八點開到下午五點，每星期五天。

解析：

自句構看，「我們平均一天收到近成千個電話之多的詢問處」需用 which-clause 來造句，因此全句是用複合句來成句。

解答：

Our information center, which receives close to one thousand calls a day, is open 8 a.m. to 5 p.m., five days a week.

習題十三

1）將下句翻成英文。

喬治利用約翰的無知而獲得巨利。

解析：

用 take 與 advantage 相搭配表「利用」，其後另需與 of 相搭配，用 enormous 與 profit 相搭配表「巨利」。

解答：

George took advantage of John's ignorance to make an enormous profit.

補充說明：

我們也可用 draw on 來表「利用」而將本句改翻成 George drew on John's ignorance to make an enormous profit.

2) 將下句翻成英文。

他們的商業關係不幸就變得更壞。

解析：

用 worsen 表「變得更壞」。

解答：

Their business relationship unfortunately worsened.

3) 將 1) 與 2) 二句聯成一句，翻成英文表下面的文意。

自從喬治利用約翰的無知而獲得巨利之後，他們的商業關係就不幸愈發變壞。

解析：

自句構來看，「自從喬治利用約翰的無知而獲得巨利之後」需用 since-clause 來造句，因此全句是用複合句來成句。

解答：

Since George took advantage of John's ignorance to make an enormous profit, their business relationship has been unfortunately worsened.

補充說明：

注意，副句中用過去式，主句中用現在完成式，表持續的狀況。又，這句也可用 ever since 來改寫成 Ever since George took advantage of John's ignorance to make an enormous profit, their relationship has been unfortunately worsened.這裡 ever since 一句的語氣要比 since 句子強。

習題十四

1) 將下句翻成英文。

約翰承擔起籌備同學會的差事。

解析：

用 take 與 on 相搭配表「承擔」，用 organize 表「籌備」，用 task 表「差事」。

解答：

John takes on the task of organizing a class reunion.

2) 將下句翻成英文。

約翰的努力沒有白費。

解析：

用 pay 與 off 相搭配表「沒有白費」。

解答：

John's effort pays off.

補充說明：

注意，pay off 通常意指「有好結果」或「取得成功」，這裡我們意譯成「沒有白費」。

3) 將 1）與 2）二句聯成一句，翻成英文表下面的文意。

約翰承擔起籌備同學會的差事，而他的努力沒有白費。

解析：

自句構看，這裡用「而」，因此本句是一個并列句。

解答：

John takes on the task of organizing a class reunion and his effort pays off.

習題十五

將下句譯成英文。

昨晚演出的演奏會非常成功。

解析：

中文的形容詞片語「非常成功」用英文名詞片語來轉譯。

解答：

The concert held last night was a great success.

補充說明：

上句是由 The concert that was held last night was a great success 省略而來。關於文句各種省略的方法，請參第 3.2 各節。

習題十六

將下句譯成英文。

不論動機何在，我們有義務誠懇對待朋友。

解析：

用 motive 表「動機」，oblige 以被動語態表「有義務」。注意，中文的形容詞「誠懇」用英文的不定詞來轉譯。

解答：

Whatever the motives, we are obliged to be frank with our friends.

習題十七

將下句譯成英文。

嫌疑犯的親友及一位關鍵證人被批准訪問監中的嫌疑犯。

解析：

用 the accused 表「嫌疑犯」，material witness 表「關鍵證人」。注意，中文的名詞「監中」用英文的系詞來轉譯。

解答：

The relatives of the accused and a material witness were permitted to visit the accused at the prison.

補充說明：

注意，在使用複數主詞時其動詞的身與數能影響文意，例如在 Eating banana and drinking ice water always upsets my stomach 一句中，動詞用單數，全句的意思是指同時吃香蕉及飲冰水能使我鬧肚子，但此句的動詞如用複數時（即 Eating banana and drinking ice water always upset

my stomach），全句的意思是指吃香蕉及飲冰水分別能使我鬧肚子。

習題十八

1) 將下句譯成英文。

她選用廣東話講。

解析：

用 Cantonese 表「廣東話」。注意，表某種語言的用詞，例如 Cantonese 或下句的 Mandarin，其前需與 in 相搭配，因此本句中文的動詞「用廣東話」須用英文的系詞來轉譯。

解答：

She chose to speak in Cantonese.

2) 將下句譯成英文。

她選用國語講。

解析：

用 Mandarin 表「國語」。 本句中文的動詞「用國語」也須用英文的系詞來轉譯。

解答：

She chose to speak in Mandarin.

3) 將下句譯成英文。

她選用國語而不用廣東話講。

解析：

根據文意，此句應為并列句。

解答：

（一）She chose to speak in Mandarin, but she chose not to speak in Cantonese. 或

（二）She chose to speak in Mandarin, but she chose to speak not in Cantonese. 或

（三）She chose not to speak in Cantonese, but she chose to speak in Mandarin. 或

（四）She chose to speak not in Cantonese, but she chose to speak in Mandarin

補充說明：

這裡有二點須要說明。第一，在（一）（三）及（二）（四）兩組解答中，各子句的次序雖經變更，但仍不改變其文意。第二，這幾個解答也可分別用省略的方法改寫如下：

（一）She chose to speak in Mandarin but not to speak in Cantonese. 或

（二）She chose to speak in Mandarin but not in Cantonese. 或

（三）She chose not to speak in Cantonese but in Mandarin. 或

（四）She chose to speak not in Cantonese but in Mandarin.

4）　上述解答中的 to speak not in Cantonese 與 not to speak in Cantonese 有何不同？

解析：

用主從的觀點來分別。

解答：

在 not in Cantonese 片語中，其主語為 in Cantonese，從語為 not，因此 not in Cantonese 意為「非廣東話」，而在 not to speak 片語中，其主語為 to speak，從語為 not，因此 not to speak 意為「不 … 講」，根據本題的意思，用 not to speak in Cantonese 為正確。

習題十九

將下句譯成英文。

他朝碼頭走去，左臂挾著一頂草帽，右肩扛著一對槳。

解析：

以 go 與 down 相搭配表「朝...走去」。本句中文的動詞「挾著」及

「扛著」皆須用英文的系詞來轉譯。

解答：

He went down the wharf with a straw hat in his left arm and a pair of oars on his right shoulder.

補充說明：

注意，此處中、英文不同的表達方法。在英文裡，本句另可用置換的方法改寫成： He went, with a straw hat in his left arm and a pair of oars on his right shoulder, down the wharf. 但中文不允許我們如此變化。又，pair 指「一對」時用單數動詞，例如： This pair of mittens is mine. 但如指「成雙」時用複數動詞，例如： The pair are now good friends. 而 pair 之前跟數字時，pair 本身可用單數或複數，但以用複數居多，例如： We bought eight pairs（or pair）of mittens.

習題二十

將下句譯成英文。

聽她唱歌，你必以為她是一位職業歌手。

解析：

以 take 與 for 相搭配表「以為」，professional singer 表「職業歌手」。本句中文的動詞「唱歌」用英文的動名詞來轉譯。

解答：

To hear her signing, you would take her for a professional singer.

補充說明：

注意，此處不定詞片語 to hear her signing 及習題六補充說明中的現在分詞片語（即 having conducted an overall assessment of the university's needs）二者的行為主體應為主句中的主詞，此處如寫成 To hear her signing, she makes you believe that she is a professional singer 就不成文意，因為 to hear her signing 的行為主體是作聽眾的你

第二章　句構以妥切運用為本

（you），而非歌唱者本人（she）。同理，在 Having conducted an overall assessment of our university's needs, a list of eight priorities was submitted to the Board of Directors for immediate implementation 一句中，其現在分詞片語的行為主體不明，也就是說誰做的通盤評估文中沒有交待，使全句文意含糊。在使用過去分詞片語時，也需要有這種考慮，例如在 Boiled or fried, one can make eggs a nutritious dish 一句中，文意也沒有交待清楚，因為 boiled 及 fried 是指 eggs 而非主詞 one，為了使文意清楚起見，這句應改寫成 Boiled or fried, eggs make a nutritious dish.

習題二十一

將下句譯成英文。

他們試了很多次，幫她找辦公室鑰匙，但無結果。

解析：

將中文的動詞「幫」用英文的不定詞轉譯，同時用一句英文來表達。

解答：

They tried several times to help her locate her office key without success.

習題二十二

將下句譯成英文。

今晚再度比賽，該顯出那一隊較棒。

解析：

用 rematch 表「再度比賽」，將中文的動詞「再度比賽」用英文的名詞來轉譯，同時用一句英文來表達。

解答：

A rematch tonight will show which team is better.

習題二十三

將下句譯成英文。

125

在我第一次到臺灣，曾有機會嘗到熱帶水果。

解析：

用 tropical fruit 表「熱帶水果」。本句中文的動詞「到」需用英文的系詞來轉譯。

解答：

On my first trip to Taiwan I had the opportunity to taste tropical fruits.

補充說明：

注意，中文的一個句子（在我第一次到臺灣），英文用系詞片語（on my first trip to Taiwan）來表達。

習題二十四

將下面的片語翻成英文。

從計程車過人行道到她公寓門口的幾步。

解析：

用 sidewalk 表「人行道」，用 taxicab 或 taxi 或 cab 表「計程車」。注意中、英文不同的表達方法。

解答：

…a few steps across the sidewalk from the taxicab to the entrance of her apartment.

補充說明：

這裏要注意中、英文不同的表達方法。這片語是由四個意思構成，即1)「從計程車」，2)「過人行道」，3)「到她公寓門口」，4)「幾步」。中文的意思是採取 1）2）3）4）的順序來表達，而英文的意思是採取 4）2）1）3）的順序來表達。

習題二十五

將下句翻成英文。

他小女兒也擅於電腦動畫，不足為奇。

解析：

用 computer 與 animation 相搭配表「電腦動畫」，用 not 與 surprisingly 相搭配表「不足為奇」。 注意中、英文結構不同的表達法。

解答：

Not surprisingly, his young daughter is good at computer animation as well.

補充說明：

注意，這裏中、英文結構不同的表達法，中文的「不足為奇」置句後，而英文的 not surprisingly 置句前。 此外，「擅於」也可用 be at home with 來表達而將這一句翻成 Not surprisingly, his young daughter is at home with computer animation as well. 同時也可以用 excel at 來表達而將這一句翻成 Not surprisingly, his young daughter excels at computer animation as well.

綜合習題之一

將下段譯成英文

1）這非洲小國總共有二家有線電視業，祇不過有十個電視頻道。2）有線電視祇傳達及百分之七的居民，為全非最低。3）該國的媒體產業幾不存在。4）該國僅有 15 家雜誌出版社，每年刊行 27 種雜誌。5）有三家主要書籍出版商，去年出版了超過四千本教科書。6）這幾乎與其全部在校入學生數量不相上下。

解析：

本題是根據「全民英檢」的題型，來練習中譯英。重點在根據以上二章所討論的方法翻成一段英文，這是說，在翻譯的過程中要講究字裏行間的用字，根據文意的相互邏輯關係，用妥善的句構來表達，以及使用中譯英的基本方法。在這裏不妨儘量考慮用次元單位的觀念來造句。以下我們一句一句來翻。

全民英檢
中高級作文指南

解答：

1）這非洲小國總共有二家有線電視業，祇不過有十個電視頻道。

解析：

用片語 cable TV company 表「有線電視業」，用 cable 與 channel 相搭配表「頻道」。

解答：

In this tiny African country there are a total of two cable TV companies with less than 10 cable channels.

補充說明：

注意，中、英文詞序不同的用法，在中文裏「非洲」置於「小」之前，而英文是將 African（非洲）置於 tiny（小）之後。中文的用法視「小國」為主，「非洲」為從，英文的用法視 African country 為主，tiny 為從。同時注意詞性轉譯的用法，中文的動詞「有」用英文的系詞 with 來表達，並且也注意中、英文句構的不同表達法，這裏中文的二個句子我們用一個英文句子來翻。

2）有線電視祇傳達及百分之七的居民，為全非最低。

解析：

用 reach 表「傳達及」。自句構來看，「為全非最低」是指「傳達及百分之七的居民」一事，故須用 which 子句來成句。

解答：

Cable TV reaches only 7 percent of the population, which is the lowest anywhere in Africa.

補充說明：

這裡 percent 之後可用單數動詞，也可用複數動詞，須視其後的名詞而定，在本題中 population 當一集體名詞使用，故其後用單數動詞（is）。再如在 Eighty percent of the legislature was in favor of the

128

resolution 一句中，動詞是用單數，原因是視 legislature 為一整體，但在 Eighty percent of the legislators were in favor of the resolution 一句中，動詞是用複數，原因是指百分之八十的立法委員。

3) 該國的媒體產業幾不存在。

解析：

用 media 與 industry 相搭配表「媒體產業」，用 non-existent 表「不存在」。

解答：

The media industry of this tiny African country is almost non-existent.

補充說明：

注意，medium 的複數有二，一是 mediums，一是 media，後者在新聞廣播用詞中，有時視作一個單數名詞來表示一特定新聞媒介方法，例如： The Internet is a useful media for entertainment. 雖然此處通常是用 medium，即 The Internet is a useful medium for entertainment. 而 media 也可與 the 相搭配（the media）成一集體名詞，表新聞廣播業界，在此情形下，如指集體名詞中各個體媒介時，其動詞用複數，例如： The media have covered the accident in detail. 但如指集體名詞本身時，則與 the press 的意思同，其動詞用單數，例如： The media has not shown much interest in space exploration these days. 在此意義下，不能用 medium 來替代 media, 即 The medium has not shown much interest in space exploration these days 即不成文意。

4) 該國僅有 15 家雜誌出版社，每年刊行 27 種雜誌。

解析：

用 magazine 與 publisher 相搭配表「雜誌出版社」，用 produce 表「刊行」。自句構言，「每年刊行 27 種雜誌」是指刊出這種雜誌的出版社，故須用 that 子句來成句。

解答：

This tiny African country has 15 magazine publishers that produce 27 titles annually.

補充說明：

我們也可用 print 表「刊行」。

5) 有三家主要書籍出版商，去年出版了超過四千本教科書。

解析：

用 book 與 publisher 相搭配表「書籍出版商」。自句構言，「出版了超過四千本教科書」是指印書總數的書商，故須用 that 子句來成句。

解答：

There are three major book publishers that published over 4000 textbooks last year.

補充說明：

這裏中文的二個句子我們用一個英文句子來翻。

6) 這幾乎與其全部在校入學生數量不相上下。

解析：

用片語 fall little short of 表「稍低於」（即喻「幾乎不相上下」），用 enroll 表「入學」。自句構言，「在校入學生」須用 who 子句來成句。

解答：

This is a figure that falls little short of its total number of students who were enrolled in schools.

補充說明：

這裡我們套用一字多義的原則，將 fall little short of 的本意（「稍低於」）引申為「幾乎不相上下」。

全段解答如下：

1)In this tiny African country there are a total of two cable TV companies

with less than 10 cable channels. 2）Cable TV reaches only 7 percent of the population, which is the lowest anywhere in Africa. 3）The media industry of this tiny African country is almost non-existent. 4）This tiny African country has 15 magazine publishers that produce 27 titles annually. 5）There are three major book publishers that published over 4000 textbooks last year. 6）This is a figure that falls little short of its total number of students who were enrolled in schools.

補充說明：

以上的解答，從句式的靈活使用及聯句的圓通各方面講多不理想。關於這幾點，我們將在以下二章中詳細討論。

綜合習題之二

將下段譯成英文。

1）警察在一場槍戰中射死了一位男嫌疑犯。2）一個男人從他車上跳下。3）一個男子試圖沿著公路而逃。4）一個男子用卡賓槍向其追捕者開火。5）此意外事故迫使其他開車的人們衝向儀表板下作掩護。6）此意外事故擴及二個郊區住宅區。7）此意外事故大約發生在下午五點，在六點左右結束。8）此意外事故使公路上留下滿地的子彈殼。

解析：

本題與綜合習題之一同，是練習中譯英。重點也是在講究用字，句構根據文意的妥善表達，以及使用中譯英的基本方法。在這裏也不妨儘量考慮用次元單位的觀念來造句。

解答：

1）警察在一場槍戰中射死了一位男嫌疑犯。

解析：

用 shootout 表「槍戰」，用 gun 與 down 相搭配表「射死」。

解答：

In a shootout police gunned down a male suspect.

2）一個男人從他車上跳下。

解析：

用 leap 與 from 相搭配表「從…跳下」。

解答：

A man leaped from his car.

3）一個男子試圖沿著公路而逃。

解析：

用 flee 與 along 相搭配表「沿…逃」。

解答：

A man tried to flee along a highway.

4）一個男子用卡賓槍向其追捕者開火。

解析：

用 pursuer 表「追捕者」，用 fire 表「開火」，用 carbine 表「卡賓槍」。

解答：

A man fired at his pursuers with a carbine.

補充說明：

注意，此處中、英文不同的表達方法，在中文的結構中，一般將「用卡賓槍」置於「追捕者」之前，而在英文的結構中，pursuers 置於 with a carbine 之前。

5）此意外事故迫使其他開車的人們衝向儀表板下作掩護。

解析：

用 send 表「迫使」，用 dashboard 表「儀表板」，用 cover 作名詞表「掩護」。

解答：

The incident sent other drivers diving under their dashboards for cover.

6）此意外事故擴及二個郊區住宅區。

解析：

用 span 表「擴及」，用片語 bedroom community 表「郊區住宅區」。

解答：

The incident spanned two bedroom communities.

7）此意外事故大約發生在下午五點，在六點左右結束。

解析：

用系詞 about 表「大約」，用 over 表「結束」。

解答：

The incident started about 5 p.m. and was over by 6 p.m.

補充說明：

注意詞性轉譯的用法，中文的動詞「結束」用英文的形容詞 over 來表達。

8）此意外事故使公路上留下滿地的子彈殼。

解析：

用 strewn 作形容詞表「滿地的」，用 bullet casing 表「子彈殼」。

解答：

The incident left the highway strewn with bullet casings.

全段解答如下：

1）In a shootout police gunned down a male suspect. 2）A man leaped from his car. 3）A man tried to flee along a highway. 4）A man fired at his pursuers with a carbine. 5）The incident sent other drivers diving under their dashboards for cover. 6）The incident spanned two bedroom communities. 7）The incident started about 5 p.m. and was over by 6 p.m. 8）The incident left the highway strewn with bullet casings.

補充說明：

　　同樣，以上的解答，從句式的靈活使用及聯句的圓通各方面講多不理想。關於這幾點，我們將在以下二章中詳細討論。

第三章　句構以靈活使用為上

我們在以上二章中做了很多習題，反覆練習了如何遣詞，以及透過次元單位的觀念，使用不同的英文句式來中翻英。在這基礎上，我們在本章中，進一步討論如何靈活使用句構。在此我們不妨想一想這一句1) All students must write a major essay before graduation, which is a policy that was adopted by this university not too long ago 能改寫成何種不同的句式？這一句可改寫成2) All students must write a major essay before graduation, which is a policy adopted by this university not too long ago. 這第2) 句刪除了1) 句中的 that was，祇是為何要如此省略？省略後的文意是否與原句有別？1) 句也可改寫成3) It is a policy adopted by this university not too long ago that all students must write a major essay before graduation. 這第3) 句是將1) 句中的主句位置前後顛倒變更而成，意思雖然二者相同，但為何要如此置換？置換後的語氣與原句是否相同？1) 句又可改寫成4) That all students must write a major essay before graduation is a policy adopted by this university not too long ago. 這第4) 句是將3) 句中的 that 子句置於句前，這也就是說，第4) 句用1) 句中的主句變成 that 子句作主詞，結果使 1) 句從一複合句變成一簡單句。我們不難發現，以上是透過置換及省略來變更原句的結構，使一個意思一共用了四種不同的句構，來達到表達相同或相似的文意的目的。曉得如何靈活使用句構，不但能增加文句的變化，同時也顯出我們作文的表達能力，這在應試時可幫助我們爭取理想的分數。本章先討論置換及省略的二個觀念，然後再逐節討論如何用各種不同的句式來表達相類似的文意。

3.1 置換的概念

　　所謂置換是指變更句中某一次元單位的正常位置而言。我們不妨用林肯的講稿作例子來說明這一點。林肯就任總統時的演講中有這樣一句 In your hands, my dissatisfied fellow countrymen, and not in mine, is the momentous issue of civil war. 這一句實際上是從 The momentous issue of civil war is in your hands, my dissatisfied fellow countrymen, and not in mine 一句演變而來。其中將主詞（the momentous issue of civil war）的位置倒裝以收強調語氣的效果。這種藉變更文句語序的用法即為本節所稱的置換。

　　以下我們分別從主詞，受詞，補語及修飾語來討論如何置換。

第一，主詞的置換

　　我們從第 2.1.3.1 節中討論主詞的種類時曉得，不定詞片語、系詞片語、that 子句及 wh- 子句皆可用作主詞。根據這理解，我們用下面幾個例子來說明如何置換主詞.

A1）**To utter such a word** is nonsense.

　　在這句中，我們可將真正的主詞（to utter such a word）移往句末而用 it 來作其形式上的主詞，使上句變成 it + predicate + subject 的模式來達到主詞尾置的目的。 在此 It 稱為「前導主詞」（anticipatory subject）。如此置換可將 A1）句改寫成：

A2）**It** is nonsense **to utter such a word**.

　　同樣的用法也可適用在下面二個例子：

B1）**For anyone to offer such a help** is considered generous.

B2）**It** is considered generous **for anyone to offer such a help.**

C1）**What people think of you** does not matter.

C2）**It** does not matter **what people think of you**.

　　在上面三個例子中，因置換而成的二種不同句式其文意相同，但比較上每例中的第二個模式是較常見的句式，且從語氣而言，第二句式的語氣較第一句式為強，因為強調部分是落在語尾的真正主詞上，例如就 C2）句而言，其重點落在 what 子句上。同理：

D1）**When we shall have a new director** is still unknown.

　　　也可用上述的方法改寫如下：

D2）**It** is still unknown **when we shall have a new director.**

　　但須注意的是，在此 D1）及 D2）二例中，when 子句的位置雖用置換的方法倒裝，但其語氣不因此而有所不同。我們不妨將此例視作一個例外。

第二，受詞的置換

　　置換的方法並不限於主詞，有時在 **SVOC** 的句式中，可用 it 來替代受詞而使真正的受詞置句末，例如在下面的 **SVOC** 句式中：

E1）　You may find making a living here exciting.

　　　這裡 making a living here 是用作動詞 find 的受詞，我們可依上法將其移置句末而將 E1）句改寫成：

E2）　You may find it exciting making a living here.

　　　此句中的 it 即指 making a living here。

　　　受詞的尾置有助於關係代名詞子句的連接，例如在下例中：

F1）　I gave a gift to my mother-in-law that I bought in New York.

　　　原則上關係代名詞子句應緊跟其先行詞之後，在上句中 that 子句遠離其先行詞 gift，為避免這種現象起見，不妨改變直接受詞的位置而將 F1）句改寫如下：

F2）　I gave my mother-in-law a gift that I bought in New York.

　　　上述 F1）及 F2）二句是變更主句中直接受詞及間接受詞的

正常位置，從 SVO_DO_I 變成 SVO_IO_D 的句式。同樣在下例中：

G1） We discovered the accident by chance that occurred last night.

這句的主句是屬於 SVOA 的摸式，可將其受詞的位置變更以便與 that 子句連接，如下例所示；

G2） We discovered by chance the accident that occurred last night.

在這句的主句中，非但受詞的尾置有助於 that 子句的連接，並且用作修飾語的系詞片語 by chance 臨接其所形容的動詞 discovered，使文意更密切。但需注意的是，通常間接受詞不宜單獨置句末，例如：

H1） Our teacher gave George a poor mark.

在此例中如將間接受詞 George 置句末改寫成：

H2） Our teacher gave a poor mark George.

就不成文句，在此情形下，唯一能成句的用法是在間接受詞前加一系詞 to，而將 H2）改寫成：

H3） Our teacher gave a poor mark to George.

受詞除可尾置外，也可移往句首，例如：

I1） I acknowledge that all cargoes were delivered.

在上句中，可將用作受詞的 that 子句前置，而改寫成：

I2） **That all cargoes were delivered** I acknowledge.

這是一種加強語氣的用法[1]。同理，不定詞的受詞，也可酌情前置，例如在下例中：

J1） I wish to complete the assignment on composition today, and the one on literature next week.

---

[1] 　關於其他各種加重語氣的用法，我們將在第 3.3.6 節中詳細討論

我們可將 to complete 的受詞 the assignment on composition 前置而寫成：

J2) **The assignment on composition** I wish to complete today, and the one on literature next week.

這也是一種強調語氣的用法。

第三，補語及修飾語的置換

置換也可從補語著手，例如在下例中：

K1) The shortage of oil supply is **more crucial.**

可將補語 more crucial 前置而改寫成：

K2) **More crucial** is the shortage of oil supply.

這也是加強語氣的寫法。至于修飾語的置換，我們可用下例來說明：

L1) A formation of enemy bombers appears over the horizon.

在這句中，可將用作修飾語的系詞片語 over the horizon 前置而改寫成：

L2) **Over the horizon** a formation of enemy bombers appears.

而在 L1) 例中，我們也可將修飾語前置及主詞尾置而改寫成：

L3) **Over the horizon** appears **a formation of enemy bombers**.

在 L2) 及 L3) 二例中，各主詞的強調程度有所不同。L2) 句將修飾語前置，使主詞介于修飾語與動詞之間，而 L3) 句將主詞尾置，二相比較以 L3) 句中的主詞較 L2) 句中的主詞為突出。

我們從置換在句中的各種適用情形可以知道，置換能影響語氣強調的程度及有便於子句的連接，在此另需討論的是置換時的語序

全民英檢
中高級作文指南

問題。片語中的主語及從語如屬鄰近要素的關係時[2]，二者應相置在一起不允隨便變更其語序。我們不妨用下面二個例子來說明。

M1）A gentleman with a bundle of roses in his hand appeared.

在這句中，系詞片語 with a bundle of roses in his hand 是當作形容 gentleman 的補語，而在下例中：

M2）A gentleman appeared with a bundle of roses in his hand.

系詞片語 with a bundle of roses in his hand 是當作形容動詞 appeared 時表情狀的修飾語。需注意的是，在 with a bundle of roses in his hand 的系詞片語中，a bundle of roses 為主語，in his hand 為其從語，二者屬鄰近要素的緊密關係，在置換時不允許隨意分開而變更其語序，因此如將 M2）例改寫成：

M3）A gentleman **with a bundle of roses** appeared **in his hand.**

文意就不通了。同樣 M2）例如改寫成：

M4）A gentleman **in his hand** appeared **with a bundle of roses**.

也不成文意。

變更句中某一次元單位的正常位置，其功用之一是在收強調語氣之效，而了解置換的使用，也有利於「法殊趣同」的應用，關於這一點，我們將在第 3.3 節中詳細討論。

習題一

1）　將下句譯成英文。

若干就業機會是與研究及發展密切有關。

解析：

用 employment 與 opportunity 相搭配表「就業機會」，用 related 表「有

---

[2]　關於鄰近要素一點，請參第 2.2.1 節.

140

關」，其後需與系詞 to 相搭配。

解答：

Some employment opportunities are closely related to research and development.

補充說明：

這裡也可用 job opportunity（工作機會）。假定同單位職位有空缺，則此類工作機會可用 job opening（職位空缺）來表達。

2)　將下句譯成英文。

昨天報紙登出若干就業機會。

解析：

用 advertise 表「登出」。

解答：

Some employment opportunities were advertised in yesterday's newspaper.

3)　將 1）及 2）二句連成一整句表以下文意。

昨天報紙登出若干與研究及發展密切有關的就業機會。

解析：

從句構看，「與研究及發展密切有關的就業機會」須用 that 子句，本句應屬一複合句。

解答：

Some employment opportunities that are closely related to research and development were advertised in yesterday's newspaper.

4)　將上句用本節所討論的置換方法改寫。

解析：

本題是練習主詞置換。

解答：

Advertised in yesterday's newspaper were some employment opportunities

全民英檢
中高級作文指南

that are closely related to research and development.

補充說明：

本句也可用省略法改寫成 Advertised in yesterday's newspaper were some employment opportunities closely related to research and development. 有關省略法的使用，請參第 3.2 各節。

習題二

1) 將下句用不定詞片語作主詞譯成英文。

自認罪愆是個德行。

解析：

用 confess 表「認錯」，sin 表「罪愆」，virtue 表「德行」。

解答：

To confess one's own sin is a virtue.

2) 將上句用本節所討論的置換方法改寫。

解析：

本題是練習主詞置換，參照 A1）例來做。

解答：

It is a virtue to confess one's own sin.

補充說明：

注意，這裏中文的動詞「認錯」用英文的不定詞 to confess 來翻的詞性轉譯用法。

習題三

1) 將下句用不定詞片語作主詞譯成英文。

犯這樣的錯誤是個罪愆。

解析：

以 commit 與 mistake 相搭配表「犯錯誤」。

解答：

To commit such a mistake is a sin.

補充說明：

我們也可用 make 與 mistake 相搭配表「犯錯誤」。

2)　將上句用本節所討論的置換方法改寫。

解析：

本題也是練習主詞置換，參照 A1）例來做。

It is a sin to commit such a mistake.

補充說明：

本題也用詞性轉譯的用法，將中文的動詞「犯」用英文的不定詞 to commit 來翻。

習題四

1)　將下句用 whether 子句作主詞譯成英文。

　　他是否會兌現一時仍是不明。

解析：

以 honor 與 promise 相搭配表「兌現」，用片語 for a while 表「一時」。

解答：

Whether he will honor his promise won't be known for a while.

2)　將上句用本節所討論的置換方法改寫。

解析：

本題是練習主詞置換，參照 C1）例來做。

解答：

It won't be known for a while whether he will honor his promise.

補充說明：

我們也可用 keep、redeem、respect、stand up to 與 promise 相搭配表「兌現」。例如： It won't be known for a while whether he will stand up to his promise.

習題五

1) 　將下句用 that 子句作主詞譯成英文。

　　她拒絕與她的父母親連繫，這令人感到荒唐。

解析：

句中的「這」是指「她拒絕與她的父母親連繫」一事，故需用 that 子句作主詞。用 contact（作動詞）表「連繫」，ridiculous 表「荒唐」。

解答：

That she refuses to contact her parents is ridiculous.

補充說明：

注意中文二句的意思用一句英文來表達。

2) 將上句用本節所討論的置換方法改寫。

解析：

本題是練習主詞置換。

解答：

It is ridiculous that she refuses to contact her parents.

習題六

1) 　將下句用 when 子句作主詞譯成英文。

　　利率何時降低仍是不明。

解析：

用 lower 表「降低」。

解答：

When the interest rate will be lowered is still unknown.

2) 　將上句用本節所討論的置換方法改寫。

解析：

本題是練習主詞置換，參照 D1）例來做。

It is still unknown when the interest rate will be lowered.

習題七

1) 　將下句用 when 子句作主詞譯成英文。

　　貨物何時遞送仍是不清楚。

解析：

用 deliver 表「遞送」。

解答：

When cargoes will be delivered is still unknown.

2) 　將上句用本節所討論的置換方法改寫。

解析：

本題也是練習主詞置換，參照 D1) 例來做。

解答：

It is still unknown when cargoes will be delivered.

習題八

1) 　將下句譯成英文。

　　你必定發現學習哲學是不容易的。

解析：

用 learning 表「學習」。

解答：

You must find learning philosophy difficult.

補充說明：

注意，這裏中文的「學習」（動詞）用英文的 learning（動名詞）來表達。

2) 　將上句用本節所討論的置換方法改寫。

解析：

本題是練習受詞置換，參照 E1) 例來做。

解答：

You must find it difficult learning philosophy.

習題九

1） 將下句譯成英文。

他們今晨討論了重要的問題。

解析：

以 important 與 issue 相搭配表「重要問題」。

解答：

They discussed the important issues this morning.

2） 將上句用本節所討論的置換方法改寫。

解析：

本題是練習受詞置換，仿照 I1）例來做。

解答：

The important issues they discussed this morning.

習題十

1） 將下句譯成英文。

昨天發生了一件慘事。

解析：

以 take 與 place 相搭配表「發生」，用 tragedy 表「慘事」。

解答：

A tragedy took place yesterday.

補充說明：

此處另可用 happen 或 occur 表「發生」。

2） 將下句譯成英文。

他們從一份報紙上曉得了這件慘事。

解析：

用 learn 表「曉得」其後需與 from 相搭配。

146

解答：

They learned the tragedy from a newspaper.

3）　將 1）及 2）二句連成一整句表以下文意。

　　他們從一份報紙上曉得昨天發生的慘事。

解析：

這裡「昨天發生的慘事」應用 that 子句，此句應屬一複合句。

解答：

They learned the tragedy from a newspaper that took place yesterday.

4）　將上句用本節所討論的置換方法改寫。

解析：

本題是練習受詞置換，仿照 G1）例來做。

解答：

They learned from a newspaper the tragedy that took place yesterday.

習題十一

1）　將下句譯成英文。

　　幾位至親陪他到非洲去。

解析：

以 close 與 relative 相搭配表「至親」，用 accompany 表「陪隨」，其後需與系詞 to 相搭配。

解答：

A few close relatives accompanied him to Africa.

2）　將下句譯成英文。

　　他將房地產分給幾位至親。

解析：

用 divide 表「分給」，estate 表「房地產」。

解答：

全民英檢
中高級作文指南

He divided his estate among a few close relatives.

3) 將 1）及 2）二句連成一整句表以下文意。

他將房地產分給幾位陪他到非洲去的至親。

解析：

這裡「陪他到非洲去的至親」應用 who 子句，此句應屬一複合句。

解答：

He divided his estate among a few close relatives who accompanied him to Africa.

4) 將上句用本節所討論的置換方法改寫。

解析：

本題是練習受詞置換，仿照 I1）例來做。

解答：

His estate he divided among a few close relatives who accompanied him to Africa.

習題十二

1) 將下句譯成英文。

他始終相信他的單位是有效率的。

解析：

用 department 表「單位」，efficient 表「有效率的」。

解答：

He always believes that his department is efficient.

2) 將下句譯成英文。

就我們所知，他衷心相信這一點。

解析：

用 as far as 表「就」，用 sincerity 表「衷心」，其前需與 with 相搭配。
注意，此處「這一點」是指上句他所相信的一點。

148

解答：

He believes it with sincerity as far as we know.

3) 將1）及2）二句連成一整句表以下文意。

他始終相信他的單位是有效率的，而就我們所知，他衷心相信這一點。

解析：

注意這裏用「而」，故需使用並列句。

解答：

He always believes that his department is efficient, and he believes it with sincerity as far as we know.

補充說明：

照說用 and 的并列句，其間不需用逗點，但此處二子句過長，因此用逗點隔開。

4) 將上句用本節所討論的置換方法改寫。

解析：

本題是練習受詞置換，須將當受詞的 that 子句尾置。

解答：

He always believes, and he believes it with sincerity as far as we know, that his department is efficient.

習題十三

1) 將下句譯成英文。

我要面試這三位申請人愈快愈好。

解析：

注意本句的語氣，「我要」用 I would like 來表達。用 applicant 表「申請人」，interview 表「面試」。

解答：

I would like to interview these three applicants as soon as possible.

2) 將下句譯成英文。

　　　其他申請人我要在下星期面試。

解析：

同樣，注意本句的語氣。

解答：

I would like to interview other applicants next week.

3) 將 1）及 2）二句連成一整句表以下文意。

　　　我要面試這三位申請人愈快愈好，而其他申請人可在下星期面試。

解析：

注意這裏用「而」，故需使用并列句。

解答：

I would like to interview these three applicants as soon as possible, and I would like to interview other applicants next week.

4) 將上句用本節所討論的置換方法改寫。

解析：

本題是練習置換 to interview 之後的受詞，仿照 J1）例來做。

解答：

These three applicants I would like to interview as soon as possible, and I would like to interview other applicants next week.

補充說明：

本句另可用省略法改寫成 These three applicants I would like to interview as soon as possible, and others next week. 有關省略法的用法請參第 3.2 節.

習題十四

1) 將下句譯成英文。

她請喬治明天去接她的母親。

解析：

以 pick 與 up 相搭配表「接」。

解答：

She asks George to pick up her mother tomorrow.

2)　將下句譯成英文。

她請喬治在下星期去接她的未婚夫。

解析：

用 fiancé 表「未婚夫」，注意拼音，fiancée 表「未婚妻」。

解答：

She asks George to pick up her fiancé next week.

3)　將 1）及 2）二句連成一整句表以下文意。

她請喬治明天去接她的母親，下星期去接她的未婚夫。

解析：

照文意本句需使用并列句。

解答：

She asks George to pick up her mother tomorrow, and she asks George to pick up her fiancé next week.

補充說明：

本句另可用省略法改寫成 She asks George to pick up her mother tomorrow, and her fiancé next week.

4)　將上述省略後的句子，用本節所討論的置換方法改寫。

解析：

本題是練習置換 to pick up 之後的受詞，仿照 J1）例來做。

Her mother she asks George to pick up tomorrow, and her fiancé next week.

習題十五

1) 將下句譯成英文。

　　一部轎車停在旅館的正前面。

解析：

用 limousine 表「轎車」，用片語 in front of 表「正前面」。

解答：

A limousine parked in front of a hotel.

補充說明：

這裡不宜用 before, 因為 before 是指「前面」而非「正前面」。

2) 將上句用本節所討論的置換方法改寫。

解析：

本題是練習修飾詞置換，仿照 L3) 例來做。

解答：

In front of the hotel parked a limousine.

習題十六

1) 將下句譯成英文。

　　連串的冰柱懸掛在屋簷處。

解析：

用片語 a string of icicles 表「一串冰柱」，用 eaves 表「屋簷」。

解答：

Strings of icicles hung from the eaves.

補充說明：

這裡動詞 hang 須與 from 相搭配。 注意 hung 是 hang 的過去式和過去分詞表「掛」的意思，hang 另一個過去式和過去分詞 hanged 是表「吊死」的意思。

2) 將上句用本節所討論的置換方法改寫。

解析：

本題是練習修飾詞置換，仿照 L3）例來做。

解答：

From the eaves hung strings of icicles.

習題十七

1）　將下句譯成英文。

　　一群狼出現在山的那一邊。

解析：

以 pack 與 wolves 相搭配（a pack of wolves）表「一群狼」。

解答：

A pack of wolves appeared over the mountain.

補充說明：

這裡動詞 appear 須與 over 相搭配。

2）　將上句用本節所討論的置換方法改寫。

解析：

本題是練習修飾詞置換，仿照 L3）例來做。

解答：

Over the mountain appeared a pack of wolves.

習題十八

1）　將下句譯成英文。

　　一個鬼站在暗處。

解析：

用 shadow 表「暗處」，其前須與 in 相搭配。

解答：

A ghost stood in the shadow.

2）　將上句用本節所討論的置換方法改寫。

解析：

153

本題是練習修飾詞置換，仿照 L3）例來做。

解答：

In the shadow stood a ghost.

習題十九

1) 將下句譯成英文。

　　這件事還沒有完成呢!

解析：

用片語 so far from 表「還沒有」。

解答：

It is so far from being completed!

2) 將上句用本節所討論的置換方法改寫。

解析：

本題是練習修飾詞置換。

解答：

So far is it from being completed!

補充說明：

注意，動詞（is）的位置在此用法中需置於主詞（it）之前。

習題二十

1) 將下句譯成英文。

　　貨物視作成交。

解析：

用 sold 表「成交」。根據語氣，本句需用被動式。

解答：

Commodities are considered sold.

補充說明：

這裡中文的名詞（成交）用英文的過去分詞（sold）來譯。

2)　將下句譯成英文。

　　貨物已交貨。

解析：

用 deliver 表「交貨」。根據語氣，本句也需用被動式。

解答：

Commodities are delivered.

3)　將 1）及 2）二句連成一整句表以下文意。

　　貨物一旦交貨即視作成交。

解析：

用 once 表「一旦」來連句。

解答：

Commodities are considered sold once they are delivered.

補充說明：

本句可用省略法改寫如下：

Commodities are considered sold once delivered.

4)　　將上述省略後的句子，用本節所討論的置換方法改寫。

解析：

本題是練習補語置換。

解答：

Commodities, once delivered, are considered sold.

補充說明：

本句也可改寫成 Once delivered, commodities are considered sold.

3.2 文句之省略

本節我們討論另一個與靈活使用句構有關的觀念，亦即文句的省略。我們先討論省略的基本概念（第 3.2.1 節），然後再討論省略模式的使用，以及省略對文意可能引起的侷限性問題（第 3.2.2 節）。

3.2.1 基本概念

由於副句允許我們在文句中連續使用，因此形成在副句中又插入副句的現象，產生非常複雜的句式。這種用法尤其在英文的正規文體中最為常見。例如：

An international law of communications **that** will be both rational and effective as law-in-action in an era **where** science and technology constantly move in advance of the society **that** they are supposed to serve may reasonably be expected to accord with the following policy objectives.[3]

但這種現象並非意謂著我們可在文句中無限制使用副句。實際上，副句的使用必須循主句的文意來漸次遞進的引申。我們不妨用上例作進一步的說明。

[1][An international law of communications [2][that will be both rational and effective as law-in-action in an era [3][where science and technology constantly move in advance of the society [4][that they are supposed to serve][4]][3] [2] may reasonably be expected to accord with the following policy objectives.][1]

---

[3]   摘自 *The International Law of Communications*, edited by E. McWhinney (Leyden, Sijthoff, 1971), at 11.

在上例中，第 4）子句隸屬於第 3）子句，第 3）子句隸屬於第 2）子句，而第 2）子句則隸屬於第 1）子句，分別在主詞片語 an international law of communications 及動詞片語 may ... be expected 間層層相疊，一方面使副句的文意依主句的主旨而衍生，另一方面使全句的文意隨副句的位置而變化，達到前顧後應的目的。但是，在複雜的文句中，文意難免有重複的地方，而省略的主要目的是在避免句中的贅文。那末如何識別文句中重複的部份？我們不妨從次元單位的觀念，用八字構圖來分析幫助瞭解。我們用 Mom will pay the invoice since Dad couldn't pay the invoice 一句來作說明。

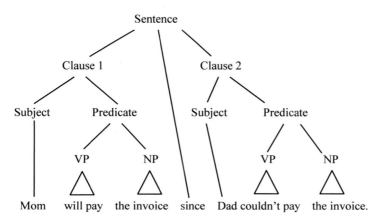

這是一句複合句，從八字構圖中可以發現，其重複部份落在平行的第三層次的次元單位上，這也是說落在述詞部分，因此其中之一可省略，但需注意的是，助動詞需保留。由是省略後的句式應為 Mom will pay the invoice since Dad couldn't.

　　一句中贅文的省略可在前句或後句選擇使用。原則上，後句的省略部分應在前句中保留，而前句的省略部分應在後句中保留。如何使用這「前後省略互補」的原則？我們不妨用下面的幾個例子來

說明。

A1）Shirley is pessimistic and Shirley will always be pessimistic.

在這句中，後句的主詞重複，故應省略，而前句的 pessimistic 因重複故也應省略而保留在後句中，如此省略後的句構為：

A2）Shirley is, and will always be, pessimistic.

須注意的是，此處 and will always be 及 pessimistic 之間，需用標點符號加以隔開以明省略。同理：

B1）George likes Chinese calligraphy, George admires Chinese calligraphy, and George practices Chinese calligraphy.

在這句中，主詞 George 在第一子句中使用，故可在第二及第三子句中刪除。至於第一及第二子句中的 Chinese calligraphy 可省略而保留在第三子句中，省略後的句式為：

B2）George likes, admires, and practices, Chinese calligraphy.

同理，在 admires、and practices 及 Chinese calligraphy 之間，需用標點符號加以分開。

在上面具三個子句的情形下（見 B1）句），如涉及助動詞時，則省略部分應落在第一及第三子句中。例如：

C1）They can visit their native country and they should visit their native country, but they won't visit their native country.

在這句中，visit their native country 是重複的部分，如照 B2）句的方式省略，則成下列的句式：

C2）They can and should, but won't, visit their native country.

這個句式不如下面的句式：

C3）They can and should visit their native country, but won't.

上句省略 C1）句中第一子句的 visit their native country 而保留助動詞 can，同時省略第三子句中的 they 及 visit their native country，但保留動詞片語 won't。至於在第二子句中

則省略 they 而保留述詞部分 should visit their native country。C3)句比 C2)句為佳。

須注意的是，并列句與複合句中的省略並不一致。在并列句中，有時主詞可省略。例如：

D1） They meant to apologize and they meant even to confess.

這句中的 they meant 為重複部分，可省略改寫如下：

D2） They meant to apologize, even to confess.

這句中，除後句的動詞被省略外，主詞也被省略，但在下面一個并列句中省略就不同：

E1） The teacher asked students to stop talking at once, but they wouldn't stop talking at once. 可省略而改寫成：

E2） The teacher asked students to stop talking at once, but they wouldn't.

在這例中，E1）句的第二個 stop talking at once 被省略，但 they 及 wouldn't 則被保留。

在複合句中，通常省略部分落在副句而不在主句，例如上面 Mom will pay the invoice since Dad couldn't 即為一例。但這句也可將副句前置，而改寫成 Since Dad couldn't, Mom will pay the invoice. 大凡在主句置於副句之後，而省略後的文意不難自副句中推知的情形下，省略亦可在主句中進行，因此本例也可改寫成 Since Dad couldn't pay the invoice, Mom will. 但副句中的主詞是否可以省略一點須視文意而定，例如在下例：

F1） John was not feeling well although he had taken some medication.

我們如將此例中副句的主詞省略而改寫成：

F2） John was not feeling well although had taken some

medication。

則就不成文意。

需注意的是，如主副句中的主詞相同，而副句的動詞為 verb to be 時，則副句中的主詞及動詞 verb to be 皆可省略。例如：

G1） George will not conduct the meeting if he is late.

此句可省略而改寫成：

G2） George will not conduct the meeting if late.

這種省略的用法，通常適用於帶 if、 once、though、unless、when 及 while 的副句中[4]。

省略的目的雖在避免句中的贅文，但省略後的文意如有含混之虞時，則不宜省略。例如：

H1） The president will meet the shareholders today and the vice-president tomorrow.

這句可有二種不同的意思，一是：

H2） The president will meet the shareholders today and he will meet the vice-president tomorrow.

根據本句的文意，H1）句乃將本句中代表主詞的 he 及動詞片語 will meet 省略。但 H1）句也可具下面的文意：

H3） The president will meet the shareholders today, and the vice-president will meet the shareholders tomorrow.

根據本句的文意，H1）句乃將本句中第二個 will meet the shareholders 省略。

從上面我們可以知道，二種不同的解釋，可使 H1）句產生二種不同的文意，這是因為不當省略而引起的混淆，在應試時不得不注意。

---

[4] 這是副句省略的方法之一，有關副句的各種省略的方法，詳參第 3.2.2 節.

習題一

1) 將下句譯成英文。

她將一切都責怪在她的父母親身上。

解析：

用 blame 表「責怪」，其後需與 on 相搭配。

解答：

She blames everything on her parents.

2) 將下句譯成英文。

她將一切都責怪在她的朋友身上。

解析：

與上句同。

解答：

She blames everything on her friends.

3) 將下句譯成英文。

她將一切甚至責怪在她的老師身上。

解析：

與上句同。

解答：

She blames everything even on her teachers.

4) 將 1)，2)及 3)三句用省略的基本概念改寫成一整句表以下文意。

她將一切都責怪在她的父母親身上，朋友身上，甚至老師身上。

解析：

使用前後省略互補的原則來做。

解答：

She blames everything on her parents, on her friends, and even on her

全民英檢
中高級作文指南

teachers.

習題二

將下句用省略的基本概念改寫成一整句表以下文意。

喬治洗了地板，擦乾了地板，同時在地板上打了蠟。

解析：

用 polish 表「打蠟」。注意，根據文意此句應屬並列句，可仿效 B2）例來做。

解答：

George has washed, dried, and polished, the floor.

習題三

1） 將下句譯成英文。

他但願能再訪校園。

解析：

用 campus 表「校園」。

解答：

He would like to visit the campus again.

2） 將下句譯成英文。

他但願能看看他從前的老師。

解析：

用 former 與 teacher 相搭配表「從前的老師」。

解答：

He would like to see his former teachers.

3） 將 1）及 2）二句連成一整句表以下文意。

他但願能再訪校園，能看看他從前的老師。

解析：

根據文意，本句應屬並列句。

解答：

He would like to visit the campus again and he would like to see his former teachers.

4）　將上句用省略的基本概念改寫。

解析：

仿效 D1）例來做。

解答：

He would like to visit the campus again and to see his former teachers.

習題四

1）　將下句譯成英文。

我常買貴的衣服。

解析：

以 expensive 與 clothes 相搭配表「貴的衣服」。

解答：

I often buy expensive clothes.

2）　將下句譯成英文。

這種衣服我的太太做得更好。

解析：

用 make 與 clothes 相搭配表「做衣服」。注意，本句需用被動語態。

解答：

Such clothes could be better made by my wife.

3）　將 1）及 2）二句連成一整句表以下文意。

我常買貴的衣服，這種衣服我的太太做得更好。

解析：

自句構言，「這種衣服我的太太做得更好」需用 that 子句，本句應屬一複合句。

全民英檢
中高級作文指南

解答：

I often buy expensive clothes that can be better made by my wife.

4）　將下句譯成英文。

　　　這種衣服我的太太能做得更便宜。

解析：

用 cheap 表「便宜」，注意此處是用比較級。

解答：

Such clothes could be made by my wife much cheaper.

5）　將 3）及 4）二句連成一整句表以下文意。

　　　我常買貴的衣服，而這種衣服我的太太做得更好，更便宜。

解析：

根據文意，此二句屬對等關係，故使用并列句。

解答：

I often buy expensive clothes that could be better made by my wife, and I often buy expensive clothes that could be made by my wife much cheaper.

6）　將上句用省略的基本概念改寫。

解析：

可參照 A1）例來做。

解答：

I often buy expensive clothes that could be better made by my wife and much cheaper.

習題五

1）　將下句譯成英文。

　　　秉信自省並非是懦怯的行為。

解析：

用 trust 表「秉信」，其後需與 in 相搭配，self-criticism 表「自省」，以

164

act 與 cowardice 相搭配表「懦怯的行為」（an act of cowardice）。

解答：

Trust in self-criticism is not an act of cowardice.

2）　將下句譯成英文。

　　秉信自省是誠實的行為。

解析：

以 act 與 honesty 相搭配表「誠實的行為」（an act of honesty）。

解答：

Trust in self-criticism is an act of honesty.

補充說明：

這裡中文的形容詞（誠實的）用英文的系詞片語（of honesty）來譯。

3）　將 1）及 2）二句連成一整句表以下文意。

　　秉信自省並非是懦怯的行為，反而秉信自省是誠實的行為。

解析：

注意句構，根據文意，用 but 表「反而」，因此本句應屬並列句。

解答：

Trust in self-criticism is not an act of cowardice, but trust in self-criticism is an act of honesty.

4）　將上句依省略的基本概念改寫。

解析：

可仿效 A1）例來做。

解答：

Trust in self-criticism is not an act of cowardice but an act of honesty.

補充說明：

本句另可用置換的方法將 not 置於第一個 an act 之後，照此寫法，須將第二個 an act 省略，使全句改寫成 Trust in self-criticism is an act not

習題六

1) 將下句譯成英文。

我們必須認定什麼是最破費的方法來達到我們的目標。

解析：

用 identify 表「認定」，expensive 表「破費」，以 achieve 與 goal 相搭配表「達到目標」。從句構看，須用 what 子句作受詞來表達「什麼是最破費的方法來達到我們的目標」。

解答：

We must identify what are the most expensive means to achieve our goals.

補充說明：

我們另可用 attain, carry out 及 reach 與 goal 相搭配表「達到目標」。又，means 如指一特定方法時，應用單數動詞，例如： The best means of achieving consensus is to appeal to reason. 但當 means 指若干特定方法時則具複數的意思，需用複數動詞 are，如本例，或如： The most effective means for reaching our goals are to be identified. 。而 means 也可解作「財源」（financial resources）其後需跟複數動詞，例如： Their means are far less adequate.

2) 將下句譯成英文。

我們必須認定什麼是最不破費的方法來達到我們的目標。

解析：

參照上句的解析。

解答：

We must identify what are the least expensive means to achieve our goals.

3) 將 1) 及 2) 二句連成一整句表以下文意。

我們必須認定什麼是最破費的方法來達到我們的目標以及必須

　　認定什麼是最不破費的方法來達到我們的目標。

解析：

根據文意本句應屬并列句。

解答：

We must identify what are the most expensive means to achieve our goals, and we must identify what are the least expensive means to achieve our goals.

4）　將上句依省略的基本概念改寫，表以下文意。

　　我們必須認定什麼是最破費，什麼是最不破費的方法來達到我們的目標。

解析：

用前後省略互補的方法來做。

解答：

We must identify what are the most, and the least, expensive means to achieve our goals.

補充說明：

注意此處二個逗點之使用。

習題七

1）　將下句譯成英文。

　　愛滋病感染率的急速成長與當今世界人口的主要威脅有關。

解析：

用 fast-rising 表「急速成長的」，用 AIDS-infection rate 表「愛滋病感染率」，以 associate 與 with 相搭配表「與…有關」，用 threat 表「威脅」，其後需與 to 相搭配。

解答：

The fast-rising AIDS-infection rate is associated with the major threat to

the contemporary world population.

2)　將下句譯成英文。

　　愛滋病感染率的急速成長已促成當今世界人口的主要威脅。

解析：

用 instrumental in causing 表「促成」。注意動詞時式，文中用「已促成」，故須用現在完成式。

解答：

The fast-rising AIDS-infection rate has been instrumental in cauaing a major threat to the contemporary world population.

3)　將 1）及 2）二句連成一整句表以下文意。

　　愛滋病感染率的急速成長與當今世界人口的主要威脅有關，且已促成當今世界人口的主要威脅。

解析：

根據文意，本句用「且」故應屬並列句。

解答：

The fast-rising AIDS-infection rate is associated with the major threat to contemporary world population and has been instrumental in cauaing a major threat to the contemporary world population.

4)　將上句依省略的基本概念改寫。

解析：

參照 A1）例來做。

解答：

The fast-rising AIDS-infection rate is associated with, and has been instrumental in cauaing, a major threat to the contemporary world population.

習題八

下句來自第 2.2.2 節，習題二第 5)句的解答：

We are full of self-satisfaction though we are not the slightest bit of self-complacency.

將上句依省略的基本概念改寫。

解析：

可仿效 G1）例來做。

解答：

We are full of self-satisfaction though not the slightest bit of self-complacency.

習題九

1)　將下句譯成英文。

　　他在洗澡時聽到有人按門鈴。

解析：

以 ring 與 doorbell 相搭配表「按門鈴」，以 take 與 bath 相搭配表「洗澡」。從句構看，此句應屬複合句。

解答：

He heard someone ring the doorbell when he was taking a bath.

補充說明：

注意，此處副句動詞時式用過去進行式，表示聽到按鈴時，正在洗澡。

2)　將上句依省略的基本概念改寫。

解析：

可依 G1）例來做。

解答：

He heard someone ring the doorbell when taking a bath.

補充說明：

全民英檢
中高級作文指南

有些動詞如 feel、hear 及 see 其後除能用原形動詞外，也可用現在分詞，在此情形下，二者意思不盡相同，前者指整個過程，後者指完全或一部過程。例如在 I saw the thief **running away** 一句中，其文意是指「我看到小偷逃跑的完全或一部過程」。但在 I saw the thief **run away** 一句中，是指「我看到小偷逃跑的整個過程」。

習題十

1）　將下句譯成英文。

　　他目睹一件車禍。

解析：

用 witness（作動詞）表「目睹」。

解答：

He witnessed a car accident.

2）　將下句譯成英文。

　　他昨夜開車回家。

解析：

注意，drive 本身已有「開車」的意思，因此「開車回家」不必用 to drive a car home。

解答：

He drove home last night.

3）　將 1）及 2）二句連成一整句表以下文意。

　　他昨夜開車回家時目睹一件車禍。

解析：

根據文意，從句構看，本句應屬複合句。同時注意動詞的時式。

解答：

He witnessed a car accident while he was driving home last night.

4）　將上句依省略的基本概念改寫。

解析：

可依 G1）例來做。

解答：

He witnessed a car accident while driving home last night.

補充說明：

此處副句動詞時式用過去進行式，表示目睹車禍時，正在開車回家。

3.2.2 基本模式及應用

　　根據上節所介紹的省略基本概念，我們現在進一步來分析子句中次元單位的省略所具的通用模式。省略的通用模式可有下列八種。

I ）　省略副句中的主詞及其動詞 verb to be，使成一非限定子句。例如：

A1）　Although they were exhausted, they kept marching.

A2）　**Although exhausted**, they kept marching.

　　　有時此種句式亦可省略從屬連接詞。例如：

B1）　Since she was annoyed, she decided to leave the meeting earlier.

B2）　**Annoyed**, she decided to leave the meeting earlier.

　　　此例不妨視作上例的變格[5]。

II ）　省略副句中的主詞，而將動詞變成現在或過去分詞片語。例如下面二例所示：

C1）　Although he lived in a remote city, he did come to attend the funeral.

C2）　**Although living in a remote city,** he did come to attend the

---

[5]　這裡已涉及從限定子句改寫成非限定子句的用法。關於這一點，請詳參第 3.3.5 節.

funeral.

D1） He is told not to leave the county unless it is authorized.

D2） He is told not to leave the country unless **authorized.**

III） 省略副句中的主詞及動詞，使成一無動詞式。例如：

E1） While he was in the army, he was active in community work as well.

E2） **While in the army,** he was active in community work as well.

IV） 省略關係代名詞子句使成一現在分詞片語。例如：

F1） Any driver who parked illegally will be fined for violation of traffic regulation.

F2） Any driver **parking** illegally will be fined for violation of traffic regulation.

V） 省略關係代名詞子句使成一不定詞片語 。例如：

G1） The place where you should visit is the Disneyland.

G2） The place **to visit** is the Disneyland.

這類句式有時也可插入不定詞的主詞，例如：

G3） The place **for you** to visit is the Disneyland.

此處需注意的是，在 G2）句式中，如不定詞與 the first、the second、the last 等使用時，宜謹慎使用省略，以免引起文句意思的混淆。例如：

H1） He is the first survivor that we attended.

在這句中，如依本模式省略改寫成：

H2） He is the first survivor **to attend.**

其文意與 H1）就不儘相同，因為前者指「已受過我們照料的生還者」，後者指「將要受我們照料的生還者」。

VI）省略關係代名詞子句使成一同位語[6]。例如：

I1） He sent for George, who is the most experienced doctor in town.

I2） He sent for George, **the most experienced doctor in town**.

VII）省略關係代名詞及其動詞 verb to be，但仍保留其補語。例如：

J1） An infusion of rhetoric enters into his arguments, which is not so apparent in his other writings.

J2） An infusion of rhetoric enters into his arguments, **not so apparent in his other writings.**

VIII）省略關係代名詞子句，而用過去分詞片語。例如：

K1） Cars that are parked illegally around the hospital will be towed away at owners' expense.

K2） Cars **parked** illegally around the hospital will be towed away at owners' expense.

　　上面所列舉的各種模式皆有一個共同的現象，那就是省略後的句式，其意義與原文相似。因此透過省略，能使我們使用二種不同的句法來表達類似的文意，這就是本書所稱的「法殊趣同」的用法。使用法殊趣同的方法，可使我們靈活應用文句，關於這一點，我們將於第 3.3 各節中詳細討論。

　　此外，我們在上節討論句法省略的基本觀念時，曾提及應注意省略可引起文意混淆不清的問題。這裡我們要進一步說明子句在省略後其文意具偏限性的問題。我們先用下例來解釋。

L1） Those children who are lying on the floor are pre-schoolers.

　　　這句可根據第 IV）模式，將關係代名詞子句省略成現在分

6　有關同位語的用法，詳參第 4.2.2 節。

詞片語如下：

L2） Those children lying on the floor are pre-schoolers.

在此例中，實際上我們已從一限定子句（即 what 子句）改寫成一非限定子句（即現在分詞片語）[7]。同理，L1）句可仿效第 III）模式，改寫成一無動詞式如下：

L3） Those children on the floor are pre-schoolers.

如果我們仔細觀察上面三個例子，不難發現在 L3）例中其無動詞式（即系詞片語 on the floor）已不明顯表達 L2）句中動詞「躺」的意思，因為 on the floor 也可能是指「匍匐在地上」，或者甚至是指「滾在地上」。而 L2）句中的現在分詞片語，也並不明顯表示動詞屬那一種時式，因為它可表 who are lying 如 L1）句所示，也可表 who lay 的過去式，或者甚至表示 who lie 的現在式。從文意的明顯性而言，上述 L1）至 L3）各例中，我們可發現關係代名詞子句其文意最為完備明顯，現在分詞片語次之，而系詞片語則更次之。

過去分詞片語與現在分詞片語相同，在文句省略變化上也有其侷限性。我們試用下例來說明。

M1） The only room that was painted in color is the recreational room.

本句可根據第 VIII）模式，將關係代名詞子句省略成過去分詞片語如下：

M2） The only room painted in color is the recreational room.

這裡也是從一限定子句（即 that 子句）改寫成一非限定子句（即過去分詞片語）。同理，M1）句也可仿效第 III）模式改寫成一無動詞式如下：

M3） The only room in color is the recreational room.

---

[7]　有關限定子句與非限定子句的互用，請參第 3.3.5 節.

在 M3）例中的無動詞式（即系詞片語 in color）與 M2）句相較，並不明顯表達「粉刷」的意思，因為 in color 或許是指「裝飾」（decorated）的結果而言。而 M2）與 M1）二句相比較，其過去分詞片語也無法明顯表達動詞屬那一種時式，因為除能表 M1）句中的過去式外，也可表現在式 that is painted。從文意的明顯性而言，上述 M1）至 M3）各例中，我們也可發現關係代名詞子句其文意最為完備明顯，過去分詞片語次之，而系詞片語則更次之。

不定詞片語也具上述侷限性的現象。 我們不妨從其主詞及動詞的時式來分別討論。我們先從主詞的角度來說明。

N1） The next flight to book is from London.

在上例中，不定詞 to book 的主詞不明。實際上這句分別可得意謂下面二種不同的文意：

N2） The next flight that can be booked is from London.或

N3） The next flight for you to book is from London.

這也就是說，N1）句的原句是 N2）句，其主詞為 the next flight，而在 N3）句中其主詞為 you，二句文意並不相同。

不定詞片語除其主詞能引起文意的不同外，其動詞的時式也可引起不同的文意。例如：

O1） The method to apply is difficult.

這句中 to apply 可指下例各句所代表的不同時式，亦即：

O2） The method that will be applied is difficult.或

O3） The method that should be applied is difficult. 或

O4） The method that must be applied is difficult.

因此，我們從上面 N1）至 O4）各例可以曉得，不定詞片語省略後其文意也具侷限性。

　　根據以上的討論，省略法的使用可導致句式文意的侷限性，當我們在綜合使用句法時不得不注意這一點。在應試時，我們需根據一己所欲表達的文意，來決定採取何種改寫的句式。

習題一

1)　將下句譯成英文。

　　在沿著河堤慢跑的時候，珍妮看到一頭狗在追一個小孩。

解析：

用 riverbank 表「河堤」，jog 表「慢跑」，以 chase 與 after 相搭配表「追趕」。從結構看，因為句中用「在…的時候」，故本句應使用表時間的從屬連接詞，是一個複合句。

解答：

While Jane was jogging along a riverbank, she saw a dog that was chasing after a little boy.

2)　將上句用省略法改寫，並指出屬何種模式。

解析：

While 子句仿效 A1) 例來做，而 that 子句仿效 F1) 例來做。

解答：

While jogging along a riverbank, Jane saw a dog chasing after a little boy. While 子句成一非限定子句故屬 I) 模式，而 that 子句成一現在分詞片語，故屬 IV) 模式。

補充說明：

注意，while 句中的主詞（Jane）被省略，故需替代主句中的 she。而本解答另可省略從屬連接詞(while)而改寫成 Jogging along a riverbank, Jane saw a dog chasing after a little boy. 這種用法僅限于主副句主詞相同，且表達同時的二個動作的情形下使用，因此如在 Since I am

176

seventy-five years old, my daughter does not allow me to do house chores
一句中，主副句主詞不同，如照上述的方法將此句改寫成 Being
seventy-five years old, my daughter does not allow me to do house chores
時文意就不通了，因為這裏 being seventy-five years old 變成是形容 my
daughter，而不是形容其真正的行為主體「我」（I）。因此本句如改寫
成 Being seventy-five years old, I am not allowed to do house chores 文意
就通了。

習題二

1)　將下句譯成英文。

在未禁止之前，學生可繼續免費使用網路服務。

解析：

用 Internet service 表「網路服務」。從結構看，因為句中用「在…之前」，
故本句應使用表時間的從屬連接詞，是一個複合句。

解答：

Students may continue to use free Internet service until it is forbidden.

2)　將上句用省略法改寫，並指出屬何種模式。

解析：

仿效 D1）例來做。

解答：

Students may continue to use free Internet service until forbidden. 副句
中的主詞被省略，而動詞變成過去分詞，故屬 II）模式。

補充說明：

注意，有些動詞之後，可用不定詞片語，也可用現在分詞片語（如
本例 continue），但二者文意稍有出入。現在分詞含有「已在」
（actuality）的意思，而不定詞含有「即將」（non-actuality）的意
思。例如在 They begin planning their itinerary 及 They begin to plan

their itinerary 二句中，前者謂「他們已在開始計畫行程表」，後者謂「他們開始即將計畫行程表」。前者「已在開始」，則目前已開始計畫。後者「即將計畫」，則目前尚未開始計畫。常用的這類動詞除 continue 及 begin 外，另有 cease、forget、like 及 start 等。根據這區別，我們另需注意的是有些動詞之後其文意祇能跟不定詞。例如： George longed to become a doctor. 這一句如改寫成 George longed becoming a doctor.其文意就不通了。而有些動詞之後其文意祇能跟現在分詞。例如將 They enjoy going to theatre together 一句改寫成 They enjoy to go to theatre together 其文意也同樣不通了。

習題三

1) 將下句譯成英文。

他在巴西時結識了一位半導體製造商。

解析：

以 make 與 acquaintance 相搭配表「結識」， acquaintance 之後另需與 with 相搭配，用 semi-conductor 表「半導體」。從結構看，因為句中用「在 ...時」，故本句應使用表時間的從屬連接詞，是屬一個複合句。

解答：

He made acquaintance with a semi-conductor manufacturer while he was in Brazil.

2) 將上句用省略法改寫，並指出屬何種模式。

解析：

仿效 E1）例來做。

解答：

He made acquaintance with a semi-conductor manufacturer while in Brazil. 省略後成一無動詞式，故屬 III）模式。

習題四

1）　將下句譯成英文。

　　使用毒品的學生會被勒令退學。

解析：

用 take 與 drug 相搭配表「使用毒品」。從結構看，「使用毒品的學生」需用 who 子句來成句，故本句是屬一個複合句。

解答：

Students who take drugs will be expelled from school.

補充說明：

動詞 expel 需與 from 相搭配。

2）　將上句用省略法改寫，並指出屬何種模式。

解析：

仿效 F1）例來做。

解答：

Students taking drugs will be expelled from school. 關係代名詞子句變成一現在分詞片語，故屬 IV）模式。

習題五

1）　將下句譯成英文。

　　他們答應會履行契約。

解析：

用 perform 表「履行」。從結構看，文中「會履行契約」需用 that 子句作受詞來成句。

解答：

They promise that they will perform the contract.

2）　將上句用省略法改寫，並指出屬何種模式。

解析：

仿效 G1）例來做。

解答：

They promise to perform the contract. 關係代名詞子句變成一不定詞片語，故屬 V）模式。

習題六

1）　將下句譯成英文。

　　我的母親是位護士，現在一家牙科診所工作。

解析：

用片語 dental clinic 表「牙科診所」。 從結構看，「我的母親是位護士」需用 who 子句來成句，本句是一個複合句。

解答：

My mother, who is a nurse, now works for a dental clinic.

2）　將上句用省略法改寫，並指出屬何種模式。

解析：

仿效 I1）例來做。

解答：

My mother, a nurse, now works for a dental clinic. 關係代名詞子句變成一同位語，故屬 VI）模式。

習題七

1）　將下句譯成英文。

　　那些曾受鼓勵參加課外活動的學生現在為考試而努力用功。

解析：

用 participate 表「參加」，其後需與 in 相搭配，用 extracurricular 與 activity 相搭配表「課外活動」。從結構看，「曾受鼓勵參加課外活動的學生」需用 who 子句來成句，故本句屬一個複合句。

解答：

Those students who were encouraged to participate in extracurricular activities are now studying hard for exams.

2） 將上句用省略法改寫，並指出屬何種模式。

解析：

仿效 K1）例來做。

解答：

Those students encouraged to participate in extracurricular activities are now studying hard for exams. 關係代名詞子句變成一過去分詞片語，故屬 VIII）模式。

習題八

1） 將下句譯成英文。

一位與本案有密切關連的罪嫌犯以極度有力的論點為自己辯護。

解析：

用 attached 表「關連」，以 extraordinary 與 force 相搭配表「極度有力」，用 argument 表「論點」，以 speak 與片語 in one's own defense 相搭配表「為自己辯護」。注意，在「一位與本案有密切關連的罪嫌犯」中，「罪嫌犯」為主詞，在句構上用 who 子句來成句，本句是屬一個複合句。

解答：

A suspect who is strongly attached to the case speaks in his own defense with extraordinary force of arguments.

2） 將上句用省略法改寫。

解析：

參照第 VIII）模式來改寫。

解答：

A suspect strongly attached to the case speaks in his own defense with

extraordinary force of arguments.

3) 說明 1）及 2）二句文意有何不同。

解析：

用子句省略後之侷限性的觀念來分析。

解答：

2）句中的文意不能完全代表 1）句中 who 子句的動詞時式，因為它也可代表 A suspect who was strongly attached to the case speaks in his own defense with extraordinary force of arguments.

習題九

1) 將下句譯成英文。

國會議員同意將臨時動議擱置。

解析：

用片語 members of parliament 表「國會議員」，用 motion（作名詞）表「臨時動議」，用 dismiss 表「擱置」。

解答：

Members of parliament agreed to dismiss the motion.

2) 將下句譯成英文。

國會議員同意議長將臨時動議擱置。

解析：

用 the speaker 表「議長」。

解答：

Members of parliament agreed for the speaker to dismiss the motion.

3) 說明 1）及 2）二句文意有何不同。

解析：

這題是討論不定詞片語的侷限性。

解答：

1）句中的主詞是 members of parliament，而 2）句中的主詞是 the speaker。

習題十

1）　將下句譯成英文。

　　觀光客訪問博物館。

解析：

用 visit 表「訪問」。

解答：

Tourists visit the museum.

2）　將下句譯成英文。

　　觀光客常被諭知不允在博物館內拍照。

解析：

用 take 與 photo 相搭配表「拍照」。本句照語氣需用被動式。

解答：

Tourists are often told not to take photos inside the museum.

3）　將 1）與 2）二句連接成一整句表以下文意。

　　觀光客訪問博物館時，常被諭知不允在博物館內拍照。

解析：

從結構看，「觀光客訪問博物館時」需用 when 子句來成句，本句是屬一個複合句。

解答：

When tourists visit the museum, they are often told not to take photos inside.

補充說明：

這裡主句中的 museum 是重複，因此省略。

4）　將 3）句用省略法改寫，並指出屬何種模式。

解析：

仿效 C1）例來做。

解答：

When visiting the museum, tourists are often told not to take photos inside.

副句中的主詞被省略，動詞變成現在分詞，故屬 II）模式。

補充說明：

這裡副句中的主詞（tourists）被省略，因此主句中的代名詞（they）需被 tourists 取代。

3.3　法殊趣同之各種方法

我們在上節中曉得，所謂法殊趣同是指用不同的句法來表達類似的文意，目的在求句式的靈活變化，用來表達我們作文的能力，好在應試時爭取高分。在謀求法殊趣同的過程中，我們要求做到「異句相從，文意相應」。如何做到這一點？我們不妨用主語及從語的觀念來解釋，例如：

A)　They count him their best friend.

B)　They count him as their best friend.

在上面二個例子中，從片語立場言，受詞 him 皆用作主語，在 A）例中，their best friend（名詞片語）是其從語，在 B）例中，as their best friend（系詞片語）為其從語。從句子的結構言，不論是 A）句或 B）句，這二個不同句子基本上多用 **SVOC。** 的模式來表達相同的文意。從這角度看，這二句達到異句相從，文意相應的要求。

法殊趣同的方法很多，本節將逐一介紹幾種常用的方法供讀者平時練習使用。

3.3.1 自動與被動語態之互用

　　根據英文文法，在一個含及物動詞的文句中，我們可依下面的原則來變更其語態，第一，將自動語句中的主詞（主事者 performer）與系詞 by 共用，變成被動語句中的受詞（受事者 receiver），第二，將自動語句中的受詞變成被動語句中的主詞，以及第三，將動詞從自動語態變成被動語態。但需注意的是，並非每一個及物動詞皆能根據以上的原則，從自動語態變成被動語態，同時 by 也不是唯一用在被動語句中的系詞。關于前者，我們用下面幾個動詞所作成的文句來作證明。

C)　They have a beautiful garden.

D)　This job does not fit her.

E)　His teammates lack the will power to win.

F)　This dress does not suit you.

在上面幾個例子中，如依英文文法來變成被動語態時皆不成文句。關於後者，除 by 外，其他系詞如 about, at, over, to 及 with 等也可用在被動語態中，我們這裏舉二個例子以作參考。

G1）Her health worries me.

上例可用被動語態改寫如下：

G2）I am worried **about** her health.

同理在下句：

H1）The setback surprised the coach.

也可用被動語態改寫如下：

H2）The coach was surprised **at** the setback.

　　如何用語態的變化來達到法殊趣同的目的？我們不妨從「被動的程度」及「被動的關係」二方面來討論。第一，從被動的程度來

說，被動的意義在被動語句中其程度有所不同。例如在 My mother made the cake 一句中，我們可依上述文法原則改寫成 The cake was made by my mother. 我們一看就清楚這是一個被動語句，因為句中使用 by 的緣故。但在 I was surprised to know that George refused to accept the offer 一句中，其被動語氣的程度不像使用 by 的句式那末明顯，但仍可看出具被動的意思，因為本句是由 To know that George refused to accept the offer surprised me.一句演變而來。第二，從被動的關係來說，我們可用不同的重點來表達被動的關係。例如：

I1) The public believe the court to have delivered a wrong decision.

在這一句中，我們可用二種不同的被動關係來改寫。第一種方法是著重在 the public 及 the court 之間的關係，而將 I1) 句改寫成：

I2) The court is believed by the public to have delivered a wrong decision.

第二種方法是著重在 the court 及 a wrong decision 之間的關係，而將 I1) 句改寫成：

I3) The public believe a wrong decision to have been delivered by the court.

在 I2) 及 I3) 二例中的被動語態，可由動詞語態的變化看出，在 I2) 例中動詞變成 is believed，而在 I3) 例中 to have delivered 變成 to have been delivered。

須注意的是，通常我們多用自動語態，而傾向少用被動語態，原因是被動語態的句式含字多讀來死板，但在下述情形下常以被動語態來表達，因此在使用本法時，切忌機械式地將自動與被動語態互換。

　　第一，當動詞的主事者不明時，例如： We had hoped to publish the results of our experiments, but the data was stolen not too long ago. 此例中偷資料者是誰不明。第二，當主事者不重要時，例如： Payments are now made twice a month. 此例著重在每月支付的次數，而非支付者是誰。第三，當用作加重副詞的語氣時，例如： The entire passage could certainly be made shorter with deletion of redundancy, but the shortened text would hardly be more inspiring. 這句式加重了 certainly 的語氣。第四，在醫學及自然科學的文章中，常用被動語態以表客觀，例如： A tsunami is caused by a vertical disturbance in the ocean, such as volcanic eruption or earthquake.

習題一

1) 將下句譯成英文。

　　他的分數不令他滿意。

解析：

照英文文法用自動語態表達。用 satisfy 表「滿意」。

解答：

His marks do not satisfy him.

2) 將上句用被動語態改寫表以下文意。

　　他對他的分數不滿意。

解析：

照英文文法用被動語態表達。

解答：

He is not satisfied with his marks.

補充說明：

此處動詞 satisfy 需與 with 相搭配。

3) 指出上句是用何種系詞表被動語態。

解析：

這題幫助我們瞭解被動的程度，這是說除用 by 來表達之外，其他系詞也可表被動語態。

解答：

上句是用 with 表被動語態。

習題二

1) 將下句譯成英文。

　　動物學家不瞭解這種哺乳動物的種類。

解析：

用 zoologist 表「動物學家」，mammal 表「哺乳動物」，species 表「種類」。照英文文法用自動語態表達。

解答：

Zoologists do not know this species of mammal.

2) 將上句用被動語句改寫。

解析：

照英文文法用被動語態表達。

解答：

This species of mammal is not known to zoologists.

3) 指出上句是用何種系詞表被動語態。

解析：

這題幫助我們瞭解被動的程度，這是說除用 by 來表達之外，其他系詞也可表被動語態。

解答：

上句是用 to 表被動語態。

習題三

1)　將下句譯成英文。

　　她建議部長減低通貨膨脹率。

解析：

用 minister 表「部長」，以 inflation 與 rate 相搭配表「通貨膨脹率」。

解答：

She advised the minister to reduce the inflation rate.

2)　將上句著重「部長」與「通貨膨脹率」間的關係用被動語態改寫。

解析：

依照 I2）或 I3）例來改寫。

解答：

She advised that the inflation rate should be reduced by the minister.

3)　將 1）句著重「部長」與「她」間的關係用被動語態改寫。

解析：

也依照 I2）或 I3）例來改寫。

解答：

The minister was advised by her to reduce the inflation rate.

習題四

1)　將下句譯成英文。

　　實驗室技工促學校行政單位替換所有的舊儀器。

解析：

用 laboratory 與 technician 相搭配表「實驗室技工」，以 school 與 administration 相搭配表「學校行政單位」，用 instrument 表「儀器」。

解答：

The laboratory technician urged the school administration to replace all the old instruments.

2)　將上句著重「學校行政單位」與「實驗室技工」間的關係用被動

　　語態改寫。

解析：

依照 I2）或 I3）例來改寫。

解答：

The school administration was urged by the laboratory technician to replace all the old instruments.

3)　將 1）句著重「學校行政單位」與「所有的舊儀器」間的關係用被動語態改寫。

解析：

依照 I2）或 I3）例來改寫。

解答：

The laboratory technician urged that all the old instruments should be replaced by the school administration.

補充說明：

注意，此句因具命令式的語氣故應改寫如下：

The laboratory technician urged that all the old instruments **be** replaced by the school administration.

習題五

1)　將下句譯成英文。

　　警察令綁架者釋放人質。

解析：

用 kidnapper 表「綁架者」，用 release 表「釋放」，用 hostage 表「人質」。

解答：

The police ordered the kidnapper to release the hostage.

2)　將上句著重「警察」與「綁架者」間的關係用被動語態改寫。

解析：

依照 I2）或 I3）例來改寫。

解答：

The kidnapper was ordered by the police to release the hostage.

3）　將 1）句著重「人質」與「綁架者」間的關係用被動語態改寫。

解析：

依照 I2）或 I3）例來改寫。

解答：

The police ordered that the hostage should be released by the kidnapper.

補充說明：

注意，此句也具命令式的語氣故應改寫如下：

The police ordered that the hostage **be** released by the kidnapper.

習題六

1）　將下句譯成英文。

　　學校當局採取高壓手段。

解析：

用 high-handed measure 表「高壓手段」。

解答：

The school administration adopted high-handed measures.

2）　將下句譯成英文。

　　高壓手段使學生憤怒。

解析：

用 drive ... mad 表「使...憤怒」。

解答：

The high-handed measures have driven students mad.

3）　將 1）與 2）二句連接成一整句表以下的文意。

　　由學校當局所採取的高壓手段使學生憤怒。

解析：

從句構看，「由學校當局所採取的高壓手段」須用 that 子句，本句應屬一複合句。

解答：

The high-handed measures that were adopted by the school administration have driven students mad.

4) 將上句用省略法改寫，並指出屬何種模式。

解析：

仿效第 3.2.2 節中的 K1）例來做。

解答：

The high-handed measures adopted by the school administration have driven students mad. 省略關係代名詞及其動詞 verb to be，但仍保留用作補語的系詞片語，故屬 VII）模式。

5) 將 4）句著重「學生」與「高壓手段」間的關係用被動語態改寫。

解析：

依照 I2）或 I3）例來改寫。

解答：

Students have been driven mad by the high-handed measures adopted by the school administration.

3.3.2 That 子句與不定詞之互用

有些動詞常用 that 子句作其受詞，例如：

A1）George believes that the custom officer is fussy.

在這種句式中，that 子句常可用不定詞來替代，使上例可改寫成：

A2）George believes the custom officer to be fussy.

上句實際上是採用動詞（believe）+ 受詞（即 that 子句的

主詞 custom officer）＋ 不定詞（to be fussy）的格式而成。
同理在：

B1） John considers that his brother is a nut.

一句中，我們也可用上述的方法改寫如下：

B2） John considers his brother to be a nut.

而 B2）句也可另外改寫成：

B3） John considers his brother a nut.

須注意的是，在 A1）及 B1）這類句式中，如 that 子句使用人稱代名詞（personal pronoun）作主詞時，在改寫時文法上應作適當的調整。例如：

C1） Marry believes that he is honest.

此句照上述方法改寫時，that 子句中的主詞 he 應改寫成 him，使 C1）句改寫成：

C2） Mary believes him to be honest.

這種用法的動詞很多，除上述 consider、believe 及 think 外，另有 advise、convince、demand、expect、hate、hope、know、love、persuade、prefer、suppose 及 wish 等。在本節的習題中，我們將使用幾個常用的這類動詞作練習此種句法的變換。

不定詞式常可用形式主詞 it 子句來替代。例如在 The best way would be to tell the truth 一句中，我們可用 It is best to tell the truth 來表達。與此模式相仿的用法是用 it … that 的句式來代替。例如：

D1） The debate turned out to be lengthy.

此句可改寫成：

D2） It turned out that the debate was lengthy.

須注意的是，在改寫時應酌情將動詞的時式作適當的調整，因此在上面 D1）例中，to be 應改寫成 D2）句中的 was。

全民英檢
中高級作文指南

習題一

1) 將下句譯成英文。

我們希望下次能通過測驗。.

解析：

用 wish 表「希望」，用 that 子句作受詞。

解答：

We wish that we would pass the test next time.

補充說明：

注意，用於 wish 之後的 that 子句是表假設語氣，與現在事實相反，故本句動詞用 would pass。

2) 將上句用本節所介紹的方改寫。

解析：

將 that 子句改寫成不定詞式。

解答：

We wish to pass the test next time.

補充說明：

這類的句式常涉及詞性轉譯的方法，例如在本句中，中文的動詞（通過）用英文的不定詞（to pass）來譯。此外，在非正式文體中（informal style），這裡也可用 want 來取代 wish。

習題二

1) 將下句譯成英文。

他們曉得全部努力將被糟蹋了。

解析：

用 know 表「曉得」，用 ruined 表「被糟蹋了」，用 that 子句作受詞。

解答：

They know that all their efforts will be ruined.

194

補充說明：

我們也可用 nullify 與 efforts 相搭配表「徒勞無功」，而將這句翻成 They know that all their efforts will be nullified.

2）　將上句用本節所介紹的方法改寫。

解析：

仿照 C2）例來做。

解答：

They know all their efforts to be ruined.

習題三

1）　將下句譯成英文。

　　他們期盼籃球賽會非常精彩。

解析：

用 expect 表「期盼」，用 basketball game 表「籃球賽」，用 that 子句作受詞。

解答：

They expect that the basketball game will be quite exciting.

2）　將上句用本節所介紹的方法改寫。

解析：

仿照 C2）例來做。

解答：

They expect the basketball game to be quite exciting.

習題四

1）　將下句譯成英文。

　　他希望他的傭金不久會轉存到他銀行的帳號上。

解析：

用 hope 表「希望」，commission 表「傭金」，bank account 表「銀行帳

號」，用 that 子句作受詞。

解答：

He hopes that his commission will be transferred to his bank account soon.

2） 將上句用本節所介紹的方法改寫。

解析：

仿照 C2）例來做。

解答：

He hopes his commission to be transferred to his bank account soon.

習題五

1） 將下句譯成英文。

他寧願實驗室新儀器由空運寄送。

解析：

用 prefer 表「寧願」，以 laboratory 與 instrument 相搭配表「實驗室儀器」，用 airfreight 表「空運」，用 that 子句作受詞。

解答：

He prefers that new laboratory instruments will be shipped by airfreight.

2） 將上句用本節所介紹的方法改寫。

解析：

仿照 C2）例來做。

解答：

He prefers new laboratory instruments to be shipped by airfreight.

習題六

1） 將下句譯成英文。

約翰曾勸瑪麗該接受這新職位。

解析：

196

用 persuade 表「勸」，以 new 與 appointment 相搭配表「新職位」，用 that 子句作受詞。

解答：

John persuaded Mary that she should accept the new appointment.

2）　將上句用本節所介紹的方法改寫。

解析：

仿照 C2）例來做。

解答：

John persuaded Mary to accept the new appointment.

習題七

1）　將下句譯成英文。

　　我的家庭醫生建議我去做一次驗血。

解析：

用 advise 表「建議」，family doctor 表「家庭醫生」，blood test 表「驗血」，用 that 子句作受詞。

解答：

My family doctor advised me that I should take a blood test.

2）　將上句用本節所介紹的方法改寫。

解析：

仿照 C2）例來做。

解答：

My family doctor advised me to take a blood test.

習題八

1）　將下句譯成英文。

　　我不經意地在學校裡碰到我的父親。

解析：

用片語 happen to meet 表「不經意地」。

解答：

I happened to meet my father at school.

2）　將上句用本節所討論的方法改寫。

解析：

仿照 D2）例來做。

解答：

It happened that I met my father at school.

習題九

1）　將下句譯成英文。

她看來一向健康不佳。

解析：

用 poor 與 health 相搭配表「健康不佳」，其前需與 in 相搭配。

解答：

She seems to have been in poor health.

2）　將上句用本節所討論的方法改寫。

解析：

仿照 D2）例來做。

解答：

It seems that she has been in poor health.

補充說明：

注意動詞時式，句中用「一向」，故我們用現在完成式。

習題十

1）　將下句譯成英文。

我湊巧曉得她的父親。

解析：

用 happen 表「湊巧」。

解答：

I happen to know her father.

2） 將上句用本節所討論的方法改寫。

解析：

仿照 D2）例來做。

解答：

It happens that I know her father.

3.3.3 詞類之互用

我們在第 2.2.2 節中曾討論過詞性轉譯的用法，這與本節所討論的詞類互用有所不同。詞性轉譯是指中、英文的詞性在翻譯時可轉變使用，這裏的詞類互用是指英文本身各詞類可互相交換使用。

英文中詞類互用常見的情形是名詞及動詞相互轉換使用。例如 lecture 一詞既可當名詞用也可當動詞用。大凡一個名詞，通常如另有一個相對的動詞存在時，我們可利用其動詞而改寫成另一相似的文句。例如在 their insistence on payment 一片語中，insistence 是名詞可換成動詞使此片語改寫成 They insist on payment 一句。同樣在 her realization that golden days were all gone 一片語中，也可依這個方法改寫成 She realizes that golden days were all gone.

這種詞類互用的方法也可適用於其他不同的情形。例如下面二句是將動詞用現在分詞改寫：

A1） A group of new recruits **arrived** at the training center yesterday.

這句可改寫如下：

A2） Arriving at the training center yesterday were a group of new recruits.

詞類的互用也可適用於名詞及不定詞之間。例如在：

B1） He pressed successfully for the creation of an ad hoc committee on curriculum planning.

一句中，creation 是名詞，我們也可根據上面的觀念將這句改寫成：

B2） He pressed successfully to create an ad hoc committee on curriculum planning.

同理，詞類的互用也可適用於現在分詞及動名詞之間。例如：

C1） Connie is fond of driving dangerously.

這例子中的現在分詞 driving 是屬動詞的性質，這可從其後跟副詞看出。

這一句可根據詞類互用的方法改寫如下：

C2） Connie is fond of dangerous driving.

在這個例子中，driving 是屬動名詞的性質，這可從其前跟一形容詞 dangerous 看出。我們從 C1）及 C2）二個例子可以曉得，具動詞性質的現在分詞可改寫成具名詞性質的動名詞，而動名詞有時又可用 that 或 it is...子句來改寫。例如：

D1） Her being an intelligent writer is well known.

這一句可用 that 子句改寫成下面一句：

D2） That she is an intelligent writer is well known.

或用 it is 子句來改寫成：

D3） It is well known that she is an intelligent writer.

這 D3）句實際上是屬裂句的形式，英文中常使用這種句式來表加重語氣。其加重語氣的部分（focus）落在 verb to be 之後（亦即此句中的 well known）[8]。

詞類的互用並不僅限於上述各種情形，實際上詞類的互用也可

---

[8]　有關裂句的使用，請參第 3.3.6 節.

適用在名詞及形容詞等其他情形。在本節習題中我們會有機會練習更多其他詞類互換的用法。

習題一

1) 將下句譯成英文。

　　房子受損壞到不可能再出售的程度。

解析：

用 so much … that 表「到 … 程度」， damage（作動詞）表「損壞」，resale 表「再售」。

解答：

The house was so much damaged that it made resale impossible.

補充說明：

注意，本句中文的動詞（再出售）用英文名詞（resale）來譯。

2) 將上句用詞類互用的方法改寫。

解析：

這習題練習名詞及動詞的互用，須將上句中作動詞用的 damage 在這句中改作名詞用，而上句中作名詞用的 resale 在這句中改用動詞 resell，同時將上句中的 so much … that 改用 such as 來表達損壞的程度。

解答：

The damage of the house was such as to make it impossible to resell.

補充說明：

此處 to resell 指 it。注意，damage 作名詞表「損害」時，是屬不可數名詞，不能用複數。用複數時表「賠償」的意思，二者文意不同。

習題二

1) 將下句譯成英文。

她為其所作的桀錯作衷心的道歉。

解析：

用 apology（作動詞）表「道歉」，其後需與 for 相搭配，blunder 表「桀錯」，sincerely 表「衷心地」。

解答：

She apologized sincerely for the blunder she made.

補充說明：

我們也可用 commit 與 blunder 相搭配表「犯桀錯」。

2) 將上句用詞類互用的方法改寫。

解析：

這習題練習名詞及動詞，以及副詞與形容詞的互用。須將上句中作動詞的 apology 在這句中改作名詞用，而上句中作副詞的 sincerely 在這句中改作形容詞用。

解答：

Her sincere apology was for the blunder she made.

習題三

1) 將下句譯成英文。

一位帶著厚講義本的老教授站在講台前。

解析：

用 thick 與 notebook 相搭配表「厚講義本」，podium 表「講台」。從句構看，「一位帶著厚講義本的老教授」需用 who 子句來成句。

解答：

An old professor who carried a thick notebook stood in front of the podium.

2) 將上句用省略法改寫。

解析：

試用第 IV）模式來做。

解答：

An old professor carrying a thick notebook stood in front of the podium.

3）　將上句用詞類互用的方法改寫。

解析：

這一題是練習動詞與現在分詞的互用，須將上句中作動詞的 stood，在這句中改作現在分詞，不妨參照 A2）例來做。注意，主詞位置的變更是因為加重語氣的原因。

解答：

Standing in front of the podium was an old professor carrying a thick notebook.

補充說明：

注意，本句中文的動詞（帶著），在英文中由用作形容詞的現在分詞（carrying）來譯。

習題四

1）　將下句譯成英文。

　　老闆打算審閱其經理所作的工作考核。

解析：

用 owner 表「老闆」，plan 表「打算」，review（作名詞）表「審閱」，以 job 與 evaluation 相搭配表「工作考核」。

解答：

The owner planned a review of his manager's job evaluations.

補充說明：

注意，此句將中文的動詞（審閱）用英文的名詞（review）來譯。

2）　將上句用詞類互用的方法改寫。

解析：

全民英檢
中高級作文指南

這一題是練習名詞與不定詞的互用。須將上句中作名詞的 review，在這句中改作不定詞。不妨參照 B1）例來做。

解答：

The owner planned to review his manager's job evaluations.

補充說明：

注意，此句將中文的動詞 （審閱）用英文的不定詞 （to review）來譯。

習題五

1） 將下句譯成英文。

喬治有豪飲的習慣。

解析：

用 drinking（現在分詞）表「飲」，用 heavily（副詞）表「過量地」。

解答：

George has the habit of drinking heavily.

補充說明：

此處也可用 excessively（副詞）表「過量地」。

2） 將上句用詞類互用的方法改寫。

解析：

這一題是練習現在分詞與動名詞，以及副詞與形容詞的互用。須將上句中作現在分詞的 drinking，在這句中改作動名詞。同時，上句中作副詞的 heavily 在這句中改作形容詞。不妨參照 C1）例來改寫。

解答：

George has the habit of heavy drinking.

補充說明：

本句也可將上句的副詞（excessively）變成形容詞（excessive）改

204

寫成 George has the habit of excessive drinking.

習題六

1）　將下句譯成英文。

　　她之成為激進份子令人遺憾。

解析：

用 radical 表「激進份子」，regrettable 表「遺憾」。仿效 D1）例來造句。

解答：

Her being a radical is regrettable.

2）　將上句用本節所討論的方法改寫。

解析：

本題練習動名詞與 that 子句的互用。依 D2）例來造句。

解答：

That she is a radical is regrettable.

3）　將 1）句用本節所討論的方法改寫。

解析：

本題練習動名詞與 it is 子句的互用。不妨依 D3）例來造句。

解答：

It is regrettable that she is a radical.

下面幾個習題另舉幾種在本節中沒有介紹過的詞類互用的方法來練習。

習題七

1）　將下句譯成英文。

　　截期可因正當理由而更改。

解析：

用 deadline 表「截期」，change（作動詞）表「更改」。

解答：

全民英檢
中高級作文指南

Deadline may be changed with a good reason.

2) 將上句用詞類互用的方法改寫。

解析：

這一題是練習動詞與形容詞的互用。須將上句中作動詞的 change，在這句中改作形容詞。

解答：

Deadline is changeable with a good reason.

習題八

1) 將下句譯成英文。

　珍妮喜歡在晚上看書。

解析：

用片語 reading at night 表「晚上看書」。

解答：

Jane likes reading at night.

2) 將上句用詞類互用的方法改寫。

解析：

這個習題練習名詞與形容詞的互用，須將上句中作名詞的 night，在這句中改作形容詞。

解答：

Jane likes night reading.

補充說明：

注意，此句將中文的動詞（看書），在英文中用表名詞的動名詞（reading）來譯。

習題九

1) 將下句譯成英文。

　僱主希望在本週解決勞工糾紛。

206

解析：

用 resolve（用不定詞）表「解決」，以 labor 與 dispute 相搭配表「勞工糾紛」。

解答：

The employer wants to resolve the labor dispute this week.

補充說明：

這句也可用 settle 來表「解決」。此外，這句將中文的動詞 （解決）用英文的不定詞 （to resolve）來譯。這裡 want 解作「想要」的意思，其後緊跟不定詞片語，在此情行下需注意二點。第一，如 want 之後沒有緊跟不定詞片語時，其後可跟系詞 for，例如： The employer wants very much for the employees to resolve the labor dispute this week. 第二，如 want 之後緊跟受詞時，則不能跟系詞 for，例如將 The employer wants the employees to resolve the labor dispute this week 這一句改寫成 The employer wants for the employees to resolve the labor dispute this week 就不成文意。 但當 want 解作「需要」的意思時，則其後需用系詞 for，例如： He does not want for extra money.（意謂他有的是錢）。

2)　將上句用詞類互用的方法改寫。

解析：

這個習題練習不定詞與過去分詞的互用，須將上句中作不定詞的 to resolve 在這句中改作過去分詞。

解答：

The employer wants the labor dispute resolved this week.

補充說明：

此句將中文的動詞（解決）用英文的過去分詞（resolved）來譯。

習題十

1)　將下句譯成英文。

他們嫉妒地為更好的職位而競爭。

解析：

用 compete 表「競爭」，其後需與 for 相搭配，用 jealously 表「嫉妒地」。

解答：

They compete jealously for a better position.

2）　將上句用詞類互用的方法改寫。

解析：

這個習題練習副詞與名詞的互用，須將上句中作副詞的 jealously 在這句中改作名詞。

解答：

They compete with jealousy for a better position.

3.3.4　比較句之互用

比較句式中通常有二個子句構成，用比較字眼諸如 more 或 less 與連接詞 than 共同構成一整句，使句中有主句及副句的分別。例如在 This exercise is more tedious to do than those we did before 一句中，主句是 This exercise is tedious to do. 其比較字眼 more 落在主句中，而副句是 Those we did before，二子句用 than 連接成一整句。

通常所謂比較有「正比」（comparison of equality），「反比」（comparison of inequality）及「尺度比」（scalar comparison）三種情形。所謂正比是指將同類事物在句中相比。所謂反比是指用正反相對的方法來襯現不同事物的意義。至于尺度比是介于正比及反比之間，是用一定的基準來比異同，這基準通常用在二種不同差異的情形，即 more ... than 及 less ... than。下面分別舉數例以便說明。

A）　正比

He is **as** rich **as** his father.

The second edition of this book is almost **the same as** its first edition.

The layout of this office building is similar **to** the one across the street.

B） 反比

His reasoning is different from yours.

C） 尺度比

This election campaign is **more successful than** the last one.[9]

Our new boss is **less demanding than** his predecessor.

在此有幾點須注意的。第一，通常比較字眼本身屬副詞性質（例如 as … as 中的第一個 as 或 more or less … than 中的 more 及 less），因此，除可與形容詞同用外，另可與副詞及限定詞同用，例如：

D1） I will contact her **as soon**（副詞）**as** I can.

D2） They worked with **as much**（限定詞）enthusiasm **as** they always do.

D3） She is **a great deal\even\far\much**（副詞）**more serious**（形容詞）**than** her sister.

須注意的是，有時比較字眼本身除屬副詞外，另可當作形容詞使用，例如：Nowadays, dietitians provide **more** advice on healthy foods **than** doctors. 此句中的 more 用作形容詞來形容受詞 advice。

第二，在尺度比中，通常是以句中的形容部份作基準來比較，

例如上述 C）例中分別以 successful 及 demanding 二個形容詞作基準，再用比較字眼來比其程度的高低。此基準有時也可用副詞來表達，例如在 Snails move more **slowly** than turtles do. 第三，上面從 A）到 C）各例是用省略法改寫而成。例如： He is as rich as his father 一句是從 He is as rich as his father is 改寫而成。但在比較句中行使省略時，也須注意因省略而可得引起文意上的混淆一點。例如：

E1） She likes Chinese foods more than her husband likes Chinese foods.

　　在這一句中，我們不難發現文意的重複部分落在述詞上，因此可將此句使用省略的方法改寫成：

E2） She likes Chinese foods more than her husband.

　　但需注意的是，E2）句除有 E1）句的文意外，另可解釋為：

E3） She likes Chinese foods more than she likes her husband.

　　為了避免此種混淆起見，不妨將 E2）句改寫成：

E4） She likes Chinese foods more than her husband does.

　　如此，文意才無混淆之虞。

通常我們可變更比較句中的隸屬關係及使用相反的比較字眼來表達相同的文意。我們用下面幾個例子來說明。

F1） In average my wife makes **more** phone calls **than** I do.

　　這句可更換主句及副句的位置來變更其隸屬關係，同時將 more …than 改用 less … than 來改寫如下：

F2） In average I make **less** phone calls **than** my wife does.

　　而 less … than 也可用 fewer … than 來替代。因此 F2）句又可改寫如下：

F3） In average I make **fewer** phone calls **than** my wife does.

我們也可用第 3.2 節所討論的省略法，來討論比較句中法殊趣

同的表達方法。例如：

G1） There are animals that are **more** intelligent **than** dogs.

這句中的 that 子句，可參照第 3.2.2 節的第 VII）模式改寫如下：

G2） There are animals **more** intelligent **than** dogs.

這句又可依置換的方法，將 more intelligent 置 animals 之前，改寫成下面另一文意相同的文句：

G3） There are **more intelligent** animals **than** dogs.

這裏透過省略及置換，我們用了三種不同的句式來表達了同一文意。

我們再用具比較意義的 so … that 及 such … that 的副句作例子，來討論法殊趣同的用法。通常用 so … that 及 such … that 的副句，分別可用 enough 及 too 來改寫。例如：

H1） The punch is **so** powerful **that** it knocks him down completely.

這句可用 enough 來替代 so …that 而改寫成：

H2） The punch is powerful **enough** to knock him down completely.

而使用 so … that 的副句也可用 so … as to 來替代。例如：

H3） The car is **so** much damaged **that** it is impossible to repair.

可改寫成：

H4） The car is **so** much damaged **as to** make repairs impossible.

同理，我們可用 too 來替代使用 such … that 的句子。例如：

I1） It is **such** a good lesson **that** we must not forget.

這句可用 too 來替代 such … that 而改寫成：

I2） It is **too** good a lesson for us to forget.

而上句又可省略不定詞的主詞而改寫如下：

I3） It is **too** good a lesson to forget.

而 such … that 的副句也可用 such … as to 來替代。例如：

J1） It is **such** a damaged car **that** repair is impossible.

可改寫成：

J2） It is **such** a damaged car **as to** make repairs impossible.

在上面 J1）例中，我們另可用詞類互換的方法來改寫如下：

J3） The **damage** of the car is such that repair is impossible.

這裡我們將一個動詞（damaged）變成一個名詞（damage）來改寫。同時 such that 又可用 such as to 來改寫如下：

J4） The damage of the car is **such as to** make repairs impossible.

以上我們用了四種不同的句法來表示相同的文意。

有時比較句亦可用不定詞或動名詞作主詞來改寫。例如：

K1） It is **more** expensive to buy gasoline **than** to buy diesel.

這句可用不定詞作主詞而改寫成：

K2） **To buy** gasoline is more expensive than to buy diesel.

K1）句另可用動名詞作主詞而改寫成：

K3） **Buying** gasoline is more expensive than buying diesel.

需注意的是，通常以不定詞作主詞時，是表一般的陳述，如 K2）句所示，而以動名詞作主詞，表一特定的「買」的行為，如 K3）句所示。

此外，在用 so … that 及 such … that 的副句中，不妨將主句中的比較部分置於句前而達加重語氣的目的。例如上面 H1）句可改寫成：

H5） **So powerful** is the punch that it knocks him down completely.

注意在這種用法時，主詞（the punch）及動詞（is）的位置也需變更。

同樣，I1）句也可改寫成：

I4） **Such a good lesson** is it that we must not forget.

習題一

1)　將下句譯成英文。

　　母親永遠是位具同情心的人物，而父親是位同情心少於母親的
　　人物。

解析：

以 sympathetic 與 figure 相搭配表「具同情心的人物」。仿效尺度比的
例子來做。

解答：

Mother is always a sympathetic figure, and father is a less sympathetic
figure than mother is.

2)　將上句用本節所介紹的方法改寫。

解析：

將上句中的重複部分刪除改寫。仿效 E1) 例來做。

解答：

Mother is always a sympathetic figure, and father less so.

習題二

1)　將下句譯成英文。

　　這些學生不像高年級生那般用功。

解析：

以 senior 與 class 相搭配表「高年級」，conscientious 表「用功」。仿效
尺度比的例子來做。從句構看，「不像高年級生那般用功的學生」需
用 who 子句來成句。

解答：

These are the students who are less conscientious than those in senior
class.

2)　將上句用省略法改寫。

用省略法的第 VII）模式來做。

解答：

These are the students less conscientious than those in senior class.

習題三

1）　將下句譯成英文。

家庭教育對成功的重要猶如色彩對油畫的重要一樣。

解析：

用片語 family education 表「家庭教育」，用 essential 表「重要」，其後需與 to 相搭配，用 oil painting 表「油畫」。用正比的方法來做。

解答：

Family education is as essential to success as colors are essential to oil painting.

2）　將上句用本節所介紹的方法改寫。

解析：

刪除上句中的重複部分，仿效 E1）例來做。

解答：

Family education is as essential to success as colors to oil painting.

習題四

1）　將下句譯成英文。

對抗看來不如協商有效。

解析：

用 confrontation 表「對抗」，effective 表「有效」，仿效尺度比的例子來做。

解答：

Confrontation seems to be less effective than negotiation.

2)　將上句用本節所介紹的方法改寫。

解析：

這一題幫助我們練習變更隸屬關係及使用反比字眼來變化，可參照F1）例來改寫。

解答：

Negotiation seems to be more effective than confrontation.

習題五

1)　將下句譯成英文。

　　理念較事物更具令人信服的價值。

解析：

用 idea 表「理念」，convincing 表「令人信服」，value 表「價值」，thing 表「事物」。仿效尺度比的例子來做。

解答：

Ideas have much more convincing values than things.

2)　將上句用本節所介紹的方法改寫。

解析：

這一題幫助我們練習變更隸屬關係及使用反比字眼來變化，可參照F1）例來改寫。

解答：

Things have much less convincing values than ideas.

習題六

1)　將下句譯成英文。

　　至理比勸戒更令人信服。

解析：

用 truth 表「至理」。仿效尺度比的例子來做。

解答：

Truth is much more convincing than persuasion.

2） 將上句之意思改譯成：

勸戒遠沒有至理那般更令人信服。

解析：

這一題幫助我們練習變更隸屬關係及使用反比字眼來變化。可參照
F1）例來做。

解答：

Persuasion is much less convincing than truth.

習題七

1） 將下句譯成英文。

體驗生活遠較賺大錢為重要。

解析：

用片語 to experience life 表「體驗生活」，to earn big money 表「賺大
錢」。可參照 K1）例來做。

解答：

It is far more important to experience life than to earn big money.

2） 將上句用本節所介紹的方法改寫。

解析：

本題需用變更隸屬關係及使用相反比較字眼來改寫。可參照 F1）例來
做。

解答：

It is far less important to earn big money than to experience life.

3） 另將 2）句用本節所介紹的方法改寫。

解析：

用 K2）例來改寫。

解答：

To earn big money is far less important than to experience life.

4）　另將 2）句用本節所介紹的方法改寫。

解析：

用 K3）例來改寫。

解答：

Earning big money is far less important than experiencing life.

補充說明：

注意，本題 3）、4）二解答的中文動詞（「體驗」及「賺」）分別用英文的不定詞及動名詞來譯。

習題八

1）　將下句譯成英文。

責備人與歪曲事實同樣有害。

解析：

用 twist 與 fact 相搭配表「歪曲事實」。用正比的方法參照 K1）例來做。

解答：

It is as harmful to blame a person as to twist the fact.

補充說明：

我們也可以 belie 或 misrepresent 與 fact 相搭配表「歪曲事實」。

2）　將上句用本節所介紹的方法改寫。

解析：

用 K2）例來改寫。

解答：

To blame a person is as harmful as to twist the fact.

3）　將 1）句另用本節所介紹的方法改寫。

解析：

用 K3）例來改寫。

解答：

Blaming a person is as harmful as twisting the fact.

補充說明：

本題 2）及 3）的解答中的中文動詞（「責備」及「歪曲」）分別是用
英文的不定詞及動名詞來譯。

習題九

1）將下句譯成英文。

　　他認為接受邀請比拒絕邀請為佳。

解析：

參照 K1）例來做。

解答：

He thinks that it is nicer to accept the invitation than to refuse it.

2）將上句用本節所介紹的方法改寫。

解析：

仿效 K2）例來做。

解答：

He thinks that to accept the invitation is nicer than to refuse it.

3）　將 1）句另用本節所介紹的方法改寫。

解析：

仿效 K3）例來做。

解答：

He thinks that accepting the invitation is nicer than refusing it.

補充說明：

注意，本題 2）及 3）的二個解答也使用詞性轉譯法，將中文的動詞

（「接受」及「拒絕」）分別用英文的不定詞及動名詞來譯。

習題十

1）　將下句譯成英文。

　　這是一個如此荒謬的理論致使沒有人爭論其推理。

解析：

用 absurd 與 theory 相搭配表「荒謬的理論」，reasoning 表「推理」，such … that 表「如此 … 致使」。參照 I1）例來做。

解答：

It is such an absurd theory that nobody argues its reasoning.

2）　將上句用第 3.1 節所介紹的方法改寫。

解析：

仿效該節第 I2）例來改寫。

解答：

Such an absurd theory is it that nobody argues its reasoning.

3）　將 1）句另用本節所介紹的方法改寫。

解析：

仿效 I2）例來改寫。

解答：

It is too absurd a theory for anybody to argue its reasoning.

4）　將 1）句另用本節所介紹的方法改寫。

解析：

仿效 J2）例來改寫。

解答：

It is such an absurd theory as to make nobody argue its reasoning.

3.3.5　限定子句，非限定子句及無動詞式之互用

　　我們在第 2.1.3.2 節中曉得，凡具限定動詞的子句稱為限定子

句，而具非限定動詞的子句稱為非限定子句。本節根據省略的基本概念，我們進一步討論如何使這類子句與無動詞式交換使用，來達到法殊趣同的目的。

我們在第 2.1.3.5 節中也曉得，現在分詞可用作修飾語，該節中所舉的例子是 George got off the train station, **leaving his luggage unattended.** 這一個非限定子句實際上是由下面一個限定子句簡化而來的，George got off the train station and left his luggage unattended. 這是限定子句與非限定子句互換的一例。

通常限定子句可與表時間，地點，條件等的從屬連接詞相接成一副句。根據第 2.2.2 節的討論，常用表時間的從屬連接詞有 after、as、before、since、when 及 while 等。常用表地點的從屬連接詞有 where 及 wherever 等，而常用表條件的從屬連接詞有 if 及 unless 等。我們分別用下面幾個例子來說明。

A1） **As we were approaching the city**, we encountered heavy traffic.

這個副句是一個表時間的限定子句。

B1） Students, **after they had finished their final exams,** started to leave campus for good.

這副句也是一個表時間的限定子句。

C1） **Wherever it is located,** such cancerous lump can be removed.

這副句是一個表地點的限定子句。

D1） **Unless it is forbidden by library regulations,** students may borrow reference books for a period of two days.

這副句是一個表條件的限定子句。

以上表時間，地點及條件的各副句，可依第 3.2.2 節的第 I）模式，分別省略改寫成下列不同的句式：

A2） **As approaching the city**, we encountered heavy traffic.

B2） Students, **having finished their final exams,** started to leave campus for good.

C2） **Wherever located**, such cancerous lump can be removed.

D2） **Unless forbidden by library regulations**, students may borrow reference books for a period of two days.

這上面四個句子有二個共同現象，第一，都是包括一主句及副句的複合句，及第二，都用省略法從限定子句改寫成非限定子句。

這裡我們對非限定子句的省略應作進一步的說明，大凡用現在分詞及過去分詞所構成的非限定子句，有時另可酌情省略其從屬連接詞，例如在上述 A2）例中表時間的從屬連接詞 as 可省略而使原句改寫成 **Approaching the city**, we encountered heavy traffic. 這句是一個採用現在分詞而成的非限定子句，但無從屬連接詞。同樣的方法也可適用於由過去分詞所構成的非限定子句。例如： **If it is explained in detail,** this project could become a meaningful undertaking. 這一個副句是表條件的限定子句，根據上面所介紹的方法可改寫成下面一個非限定子句，**If explained in detail**, this project could become a meaningful undertaking. 而這用過去分詞所構成的非限定子句，又可省略其從屬連接詞 if 而改寫成 **Explained in detail,** this project could become a meaningful undertaking.

另須注意的是，根據第 2.1.2 節的討論，上面 B2）例中的非限定子句可中置也可前置，而改寫成：

B3） **Having finished their final exams**, students started to leave campus for good.

這裡，從 B1）到 B3）各例，是經由省略及置換而成的三種不同的句構，但仍表一個相同的文意。根據句式，用現在分詞所

221

構成的非限定子句也可尾置。但需注意因此而可得引起的不同文意。例如： **Shopping in downtown,** I met my wife 與 I met my wife **shopping in downtown** 二者意思完全不同，前者是用作修飾語形容「我碰到我太太」，意思是指「我在市中心買東西的時候碰到我太太」，而後者乃用作 wife 的補語，意思是指「我碰到我太太在市中心買東西」。

用過去分詞所構成的非限定子句也可中置或前置，我們用下面的例子來說明：

E1） The design, **when it is completed,** will serve as a model for us to follow.

這副句是表時間的限定子句，依上面討論的方法可省略改寫如下：

E2） The design, **once completed**, will serve as a model for us to follow.

這表時間的非限定子句係中置，但也可前置改寫如下：

E3） **Once completed,** the design will serve as a model for us to follow.

以上三個例子，也是經由省略及置換而成的三種不同的句構，但仍是表一個相同的文意。

此外，我們在第 3.2.2 節中曾從省略的觀點提出八種不同的基本模式，我們如果用本節所討論的觀點作出發點，則不難發現除表時間，地點，條件的副句外，尚有其他從屬連接詞，諸如 while（表對照 contrast），though 或 even though（表讓步 concession）及 since（表緣由 cause），也可酌情用法殊趣同的方法來改寫。例如第 3.2.2 節中第 I）模式的 B2）例，是將使用表「緣由」的副句，從限定子句變為非限定子句的例子。此外，下例 F1）及 F2）二句說明如何用 wh-

子句將一限定子句改寫為一非限定子句。

從限定子句變成非限定子句的用法已如上述，我們再進一步分析如何從非限定子句變成一無動詞式。我們舉下面幾個例子來說明。

F1） Suddenly, a mother bear rears up on its hind legs, **whose body is in dark black** and **whose mouth is wide open,** and starts to roar.

這句中二個副句皆為 **SVC$_s$** 模式的限定子句，可用省略法將其改寫成一非限定子句如下：

F2） Suddenly, a mother bear rears up on its hind legs, **its body being in dark black** and **mouth being wide open**, and starts to roar.

本句中二個副句的句式已分別改變成一非限定子句，而這二個非限定子句本身又可用省略法改寫成一無動詞式如下：

F3） Suddenly, a mother bear rears up on its hind legs, **its body in dark black** and **mouth wide open,** and starts to roar.

這句式是英文散文中常見的結構，這裡我們透過法殊趣同的方法說明這種句法變化的由來。

又須注意的是，用上面的方法改寫成的無動詞式，有時尚可作進一步的簡化，我們分別舉下面幾個例子來說明。

G1） The announcement **that the chairperson made** is misleading.

根據第 3.3.1 節所討論的方法，上句也可用被動語態改寫如下：

G2） The announcement **that was made by the chairperson** is misleading.

而根據從限定子句變成非限定子句的用法，上句又可用省

略法的第 VIII）模式改寫成一非限定子句：

G3） The announcement **made by the chairperson** is misleading.

這 G3）例又可進一步簡化成一無動詞式如下：

G4） The announcement **of the chairperson** is misleading. 或者

G5） The **chairperson's announcement** is misleading.

上面 G4）及 G5）二句中的主詞皆屬片語，其主語皆為 announcement 但其從語有所不同，G4）例使用系詞片語（of the chairperson）置主語之後，而 G5）句使用所有格（chairperson's）置於主語之前。在本例中，我們使用了五種不同的句式來表達一類似的文意。

省略後的句式有時另可用置換的方法來增加句式的變化，例如：

H1） Those meals **that are easiest to prepare** are fast foods.

這是一個限定子句，可依省略的第 VII）模式而改寫成：

H2） Those meals **easiest to prepare** are fast foods.

而 easiest to prepare 乃形容主詞 meals 的補語，不妨將其中的 easiest 改置於 meals 之前，使 H2）句改寫成：

H3） The **easiest** meals to prepare are fast foods.

在本例中，我們透過省略及置換的方法，使用了三種不同的句式來表達一類似的文意。

在此另外須注意的一點是，省略部份的置換與文意的關係一點。我們用下例來作說明。

I1） The militiamen **who were in uniforms of different ranks** were well received by professional soldiers.

在這類型的句中，如用關係代名詞子句來限制主詞的意義時，不應用標點符號與其主句分開（如本句所示），這種副句稱為「限制性子句」（restrictive clause），其所以具限制主

詞的性質，乃因僅指「那些穿不同階級的軍裝的民兵」，但如果副句並不限制主詞的意義時，則應用標點符號與其主句分開，像下面的例子所示：

I2）The militiamen, **who were in uniforms of different ranks,** were well received by professional soldiers.

這種副句稱為「非限制性子句」（non-restrictive clause）[10]。但不論屬何種句式，關係代名詞子句的位置皆置於其先行詞（militiamen）之後，並無其他選擇。上面二個句子可分別用省略的第 VII）模式而改寫成：

I3）The militiamen **in uniforms of different ranks** were well received by professional soldiers, 及

I4）The militiamen, **in uniforms of different ranks,** were well received by professional soldiers.

在 I3）句中的系詞片語（in uniforms of different ranks）表明屬

---

[10] 關於 that 及 which 用於限制性子句及非限制性子句的問題，通常 that 是用在限制性子句，且其前不用逗點，而在使用非限制性子句時則用 which，同時其前需用逗點，例如: In average, each month she spends $200 on groceries and $50 for utilities and insurance, which add up to $3,000 annually. 但需注意的是，在下列二個限制性子句的情形下，應用 which 而非 that。第一，當二個限制性子句用 and 或 or 連句時，例如: This is a statement in which you will find the number of goods delivered and which you may regard as a notice for payment. 這裡用 that 就不成文意。第二，當限制性子句前已用 that 的情形時，例如: We want to promote only that model which will be made available on the market next month. 此外，含 that 限制性的句子，如以 whatever 或 whichever 起句時，通常 that 宜省略，例如: Whatever the manuscript you wish to write will be accepted by this publisher 而非 Whatever the manuscript that you wish to write will be accepted by this publisher. 同理，Whichever trip suits you is fine with me 而非 Whichever trip that suits you is fine with me.

何種 militiamen，具有限制主詞的性質已如上述，而 I4）句中的系詞片語縱使刪除，其原句的文意仍能成立，亦即 The militiamen were well received by professional soldiers. 因此具非限制性子句的性質，這系詞片語用于非限制性子句時（即 I4）例）可有二種不同的解釋，第一，這系詞片語除能看成形容主詞的補語外，另可看成形容動詞的修飾語，這是說，「穿不同軍裝」也與「受歡迎的行為」有關。當用作補語時，該系詞片語宜置于其所形容的名詞 （militiamen）之後（如 I4）例所示），但當用作修飾語時，除能置于動詞之前外（如 I4）例所示）尚可置於句前而寫成：

I5） **In uniforms of different ranks,** the militiamen were well received by professional soldiers.

從上面各例不難看出，在非限制性子句的情形下，有二點值得注意。第一，無動詞式的位置其變動性遠較關係代名詞子句為大，這是因為無動詞式可中置也可前置（試比較 I4），I5）及 I2）各句自明）。第二，無動詞式的主語乃係全句的主詞 （militiamen），這與關係代名詞子句的性質有所不同，因為後者的主詞並不一定用作全句的主詞，例如：

I6） The militiamen were well received by professional soldiers, **who were in uniforms of different ranks.**

在這例中，關係代名詞子句的主詞是其先行詞 professional soldiers，而 professional soldiers 並非是全句的主詞。

本節不厭其煩的列舉了很多限定子句，非限定子句及無動詞式的例子來說明三者的互用。瞭解這種句法上的變化，可增進我們作文的表達能力，達到靈活使用句式的目的。

習題一

1) 將下句譯成英文。

孔子思想深植于我們的家庭生活。

解析：

用片語 Confucian thinking 表「孔子思想」，以 deeply 與 rooted 相搭配表「深植」。

解答：

Confucian thinking is deeply rooted in our family life.

補充說明：

我們也可用 firmly 與 rooted 相搭配表「深植」。

2) 將下句譯成英文。

孔子思想在各方面指引我們的思想及行為。

解析：

用 guide 表「指引」，以片語 in every respect 表「各方面」。

解答：

Confucian thinking guides our thought and behavior in every respect.

3) 將上述 1）及 2）二句連成一并列句。

解析：

將 1）及 2）二句用 and 連接，並注意用省略法刪除重複的部分。

解答：

Confucian thinking is deeply rooted in our family education and guides our thought and behavior in every respect.

4) 將 3）句用本節所介紹的方法改寫。

解析：

照本節開始所舉限定子句與非限定子句互換的一例來做，那也是說，從第二子句著手用現在分詞子句來改寫。

解答：

Confucian thinking is deeply rooted in our family education, guiding our thought and behavior in every respect.

習題二

1）將下句翻成英文。

　辯護律師盡力向陪審團解釋凶殺案背後的真正動機。

解析：

用 take 與 pains 相搭配表「盡力」，注意此處 pain 需用多數，用 the jury 表「陪審團」，注意 jury 之前必需用 the，用 murder 與 case 相搭配表「凶殺案」。

解答：

The defense lawyer takes pains to explain to the jury the true motivation behind the murder case.

補充說明：

這裡也可用 at pains 表「盡力」而將這句翻成 The defense lawyer is at pains to explain to the jury the true motivation behind the murder case. 同時我們也可用 go out of one's way 來表「盡力」，而將這一句改翻成 The defense lawyer goes out of his way to explain to the jury the true motivation behind the murder case.

2）將下句翻成英文。

　辯護律師希望陪審團能發現凶手的光明的一面。

解析：

用 bright 與 side 相搭配表「光明的一面」。

解答：

The defense lawyer hopes that the jury will find the bright side of the murderer.

3） 將下句翻成英文。

辯護律師盡力向陪審團解釋凶殺案背後的真正動機，而希望陪審團能發現凶手的光明的一面。

解析：

注意句中用「而」，故本句需用一并列句來成句。

解答：

The defense lawyer takes pains to explain to the jury the true motivation behind the murder case and hopes that the jury will find the bright side of the murderer.

4） 用法殊趣同的方法將上句改寫。

解析：

照本節開始所舉限定子句與非限定子句互換的一例來做，那也是說從第二子句著手用現在分詞子句來改寫。

The defense lawyer takes pains to explain to the jury the true motivation behind the murder case, hoping that the jury will find the bright side of the murderer.

習題三

1） 將下句翻成英文。

首相為全國做好作戰準備。

解析：

用 brace 與 for 相搭配表「準備好」。

解答：

The prime minister braces the whole nation for war.

2） 將下句翻成英文。

首相重申他預備下臺，如果國會退縮。

解析：

用 reiterate 表「重申」，用 resign 表「下臺」，用 back 與 off 相搭配表「退縮」。從句構看，因用 if clause，故屬一複合句。

解答：

The prime minister reiterates that he is prepared to resign if the parliament backs off.

3）將 1）與 2）二句連接成一整句表以下文意。

首相為全國做好作戰準備，而重申他預備下臺，如果國會退縮。

解析：

從句構看，因用「而」，故屬一并列句。

解答：

The prime minister braces the whole nation for war and reiterates that he is prepared to resign if the parliament backs off.

4）用法殊趣同的方法將上句改寫。

解析：

照本節開始所舉限定子句與非限定子句互換的一例來做，那也是說從第二子句著手用現在分詞子句來改寫。

解答：

The prime minister braces the whole nation for war, reiterating that he is prepared to resign if the parliament backs off.

習題四

1）將下句翻成英文。

自然環境的變更使天然資源隨之衰退。

解析：

用 accompany 與 by 相搭配表「隨之」，用 decline 表「衰退」，本題需用被動式來表示。

解答：

Environmental changes are accompanied by the decline of natural resources.

2) 將下句翻成英文。

天然資源隨之衰退已接近消耗量超過資源利用的限度。

解析：

用 amount 與 consumption 相搭配表「消耗量」(the amount of consumption)，用 availability 與 resources 相搭配表「資源利用」，用 outstrip 表「超過」，用 limit 表「限度」。從結構看，「消耗量超過資源利用的限度」需用 which 子句來成句。

解答：

The decline of natural resources has approached the limit at which the amount of consumption outstrips the availability of resources.

3) 將 1) 與 2) 二句連接成一整句表以下文意。

自然環境的變更使天然資源隨之衰退到已接近消耗量超過資源利用的極限。

解析：

注意，這裏「資源隨之衰退到...的極限」需用一非限制性的 which 子句來表達。

解答：

Environmental changes are accompanied by the decline of natural resources, which has approached the limit at which the amount of consumption outstrips the availability of resources.

4) 用法殊趣同的方法將上句改寫。

解析：

本題須將上句中的限定子句變成一非限定子句，仿效省略法的第 IV) 模式來改寫。

解答：

Environmental changes are accompanied by the decline of natural resources, approaching the limit at which the amount of consumption outstrips the availability of resources.

習題五

1) 將下句譯成英文。

背著背包的老師碰到一個學生。

解析：

用 sack 表「背包」。注意，從句構看，「背著背包的老師」需用 who 子句來成句。本句宜用限制性子句來表達。

解答：

The teacher who carries a sack meets a student.

2) 將 1) 句用本節所介紹的方法改寫。

解析：

本題須將上句中的限定子句變成非限定子句，這也是說需將 who 子句用省略法第 IV) 模式來改寫成一現在分詞片語。

解答：

The teacher carrying a sack meets a student.

3) 討論 2) 句中的現在分詞片語能否前置。

解析：

比較 I3) 及 I4) 二例的解釋來做。

解答：

不能，因為 1) 句中的 who 子句屬限制性子句。但如果 1) 句是用非限制性子句，那麼 2) 句可改寫成 Carrying a sack, the teacher meets a student. 注意此處須用逗號。

4) 將下句譯成英文。

老師與背著背包的學生碰面。

解析：

注意，從句構看，「背著背包的學生」需用 who 子句來成句。本句宜用限制性子句來表達。

解答：

The teacher meets a student who carries a sack.

5） 將 4）句用本節所介紹的方法改寫。

解析：

本題須將上句中的限定子句變成非限定子句，也是說需將 who 子句用省略法的第 IV）模式來改寫成一現在分詞片語。

解答：

The teacher meets a student carrying a sack.

6) 討論 5）句中的現在分詞片語能否前置。

解析：

比較 I3）及 I4）二例的解釋來做。

解答：

不能，因為 5）句中的 who 子句屬限制性子句，同時如前置，這現在分詞片語不再形容 student。

習題六

1) 將下句譯成英文。

從董事會打電話來的那位女士是董事會的董事長。

解析：

用片語 board of directors 表「董事會」。用 chairperson 表「董事長」，而不用「chairman」。注意，從句構看，「從董事會打電話來的那位女士」需用 who 子句來成句。本句宜用限制性子句來表達。

解答：

全民英檢
中高級作文指南

The lady who called from the board of directors is its chairperson.

2）　將上句用本節所介紹的方法改寫。

解析：

本題須將上句中的限定子句變成非限定子句，也就是將 who 子句用省略法的第 IV）模式來改寫成一現在分詞片語。

解答：

The lady calling from the board of directors is its chairperson.

3）　將 2）句用本節所介紹的方法改寫。

解析：

本題須將上句中的非限定子句變成一無動詞式，仿效省略法的第 VII）模式來改寫。

解答：

The lady from the board of directors is its chairperson.

補充說明：

這句中的 from the board of directors 是一個補語，形容主詞 lady。此外，從子句省略後的侷限性而言，這第 3）句的文意不能完全代表 1）句中 who 子句的意思，因為它也可表 The lady who **came** from the board of directors is its chairperson 的意思。

習題七

1）　將下句譯成英文。

　　嫌疑犯今春被捕，他因犯謀殺罪而受審。

解析：

用 suspect 表「嫌疑犯」，其前需與 the 相搭配，以 put 與 trial 相搭配表「受審」，注意，trial 之前需與 on 相搭配，用 commit 表「犯罪」。本題須用并列句來表達。

解答：

The suspect was captured this spring and was put on trial for committing murder.

補充說明：

我們也可用 arrest 表「被捕」。

2）　將下句譯成英文。

　　今春被捕的嫌疑犯因犯謀殺罪而受審。

解析：

注意，從句構看，「今春被捕的嫌疑犯」需用 who 子句來成句。本句宜用非限制性子句來表達。

解答：

The suspect, who was captured this spring, was put on trial for committing murder.

3）　將2）句用本節所介紹的方法改寫。

解析：

本題須將上句中的限定子句變成非限定子句，用省略法的第 VIII）模式將 who 子句改寫成一過去分詞片語。

解答：

The suspect, captured this spring, was put on trial for committing murder.

4）　將3）句用置換方法改寫。

解析：

參照 I5）例來做。

解答：

Captured this spring, the suspect was put on trial for committing murder.

5）　說明何以4）句可用置換方法改寫。

解答：

因為2）句中使用非限制性子句的緣故。這裏我們透過省略及置換，

使用了四種不同的句法來表達一個相同的文意。

習題八

1） 將下句譯成英文。

那位在朋友中素有畢卡索第二之稱的年輕畫家是一位印象派畫家。

解析：

用 known 與 as 相搭配表「素有 …之稱」，用 impressionist 表「印象派畫家」，Picasso II 表「畢卡索第二」。 注意，從句構看，「素有畢卡索第二之稱的年輕畫家」需用 who 子句來成句。本句宜用非限制性子句來表達。

解答：

The young painter, who is known among his friends as Picasso II, is an impressionist.

2） 將 1）句用本節所介紹的方法改寫。

解析：

本題須將上句中的限定子句變成非限定子句，用省略法的第 VIII）模式將 1）句來改寫成一過去分詞片語。

解答：

The young painter, known among his friends as Picasso II, is an impressionist.

3） 將 2）句用置換方法改寫。

解析：

參照 I5）例來做。

解答：

Known among his friends as Picasso II, the young painter is an impressionist.

4） 說明何以 3）句可用置換方法改寫。

解答：

因為 2）句中使用非限制性子句的緣故。這裏我們透過省略及置換，使用了三種不同的句法來表達一個相同的文意。

習題九

1） 將下句譯成英文。

那位非常直言不諱的工會領袖向聚集的工會成員致辭。

解析：

用 outspoken 表「直言不諱」，用 assemble 表「聚集」，用片語 union members 表「工會成員」。 注意，從句構看，「那位非常直言不諱的工會領袖」需用 who 子句來成句。本句宜用非限制性子句來表達。

解答：

The union leader, who is quite outspoken, addressed the assembled union members.

2） 將 1）句用本節所介紹的方法改寫。

解析：

本題須將上句中的限定子句變成一無動詞式，仿效省略法的第 VII）模式來改寫。

解答：

The union leader, quite outspoken, addressed the assembled union members.

補充說明：

此句中的 quite outspoken 是補語，形容主詞 the union leader。

3） 將 2）句用置換方法改寫。

解析：

參照 I5）例來做。

解答：

Quite outspoken, the union leader addressed the assembled union members.

4)　說明何以 3）句可用置換方法改寫。

解答：

因為 1）句中使用非限制性子句的緣故。這裏我們也透過省略及置換，使用了三種不同的句法來表達一個相同的文意。

習題十

1)　將下句譯成英文。

　　急著成交的珍妮，毫不猶豫地接受了這份交易。

解析：

用 anxious 與 deal 相搭配表「急著成交」，其中 anxious 之後另需與 for 相搭配，用 hesitation 表「猶豫」。注意，從句構看，「急著成交的珍妮」需用 who 子句來成句。本句宜用非限制性子句來表達。

解答：

Jane, who was anxious for a deal, accepted the contract without hesitation.

2)　將 1）句用本節所介紹的方法改寫。

解析：

本題須將上句中的限定子句變成一無動詞式，仿照省略法的第 VII）模式來改寫。

解答：

Jane, anxious for a deal, accepted the contract without hesitation.

補充說明：

這句中的 anxious for a deal 是補語，形容主詞 Jane。

3)　將 2）句用置換方法改寫。

解析：

參照 I5）例來做。

解答：

Anxious for a deal, Jane accepted the contract without hesitation.

4）　說明何以 3）句可用置換方法改寫。

解答：

因為 1）句中使用非限制性子句的緣故。這裏我們透過省略及置換，使用了三種不同的句法來表達一個相同的文意。

習題十一

1）　將下句翻成英文。

他堅持一己的立場。

解析：

用 unbudged 與 from 相搭配表「堅持」。

解答：

He is unbudged from his position.

2）　將下句翻成英文。

他向對手作最後攤牌的挑戰。

解析：

用片語 throw down the gauntlet 與 to 相搭配表「挑戰」，用 showdown 表「攤牌」。

解答：

He throws down the gauntlet to his opponent for a final showdown.

3）　將 1）與 2）二句連接成一整句表以下文意。

由於他堅持一己的立場，他向對手作最後攤牌的挑戰。

解析：

從結構看，「由於…」需用 because 子句來表達，這是一句複合句。

解答：

Because he was unbudged from his position, he threw down the gauntlet to his opponent for a final showdown.

補充說明：

這裏我們用過去式來表達。

4）　用法殊趣同的方法將上句改寫。

解析：

本題須將上句作副句的限定子句變成一非限定子句，可仿效 If explained in detail…的例子來改寫。

解答：

Unbudged from his position, he threw down the gauntlet to his opponent for a final showdown.

習題十二

1）將下句翻成英文。

　　約翰在 1989 年開始經營他的商店。

解析：

用 run 與 shop 相搭配表「經營…商店」。

解答：

John started to run his shop in 1989.

2）將下句翻成英文。

　　他收藏的古董是本地區最廣的。

解析：

用 collection 表「收藏」，用 region 表「地區」。

解答：

His collection of antiques is the region's largest.

補充說明：

這裡「最廣的」是用 largest 而不用 biggest，原因是通常 large 表範圍（scope or range），而 big 表大小（size）。

3）將 1）與 2）二句連接成一整句表以下文意。

約翰在 1989 年開始經營他的店，而他收藏的古董是本地區最廣的。

解析：

從結構看，因句中用「而」，故需用一并列句成句。

解答：

John started to run his shop in 1989 and his collection of antiques is the region's largest.

4）將下句翻成英文。

約翰是本地區收藏古董最廣的所有人，他在 1989 年開始經營他的店。

解析：

從結構看，本句也用一并列句成句。

解答：

John is the owner of the region's largest collection of antiques and he started to run his shop in 1989.

5）將 4）句用無動詞式的方法改寫。

解析：

我們在第 2.1.3.4 節中曉得名詞片語可用作補語，因此這理不妨將第一個子句改成無動詞式來做。

解答：

Owner of the region's largest collection of antiques, John started to run his shop in 1989.

習題十三

1）將下句翻成英文。

　　高雄是臺灣南部的一個城市。

解析：

用片語 southern part of Taiwan 表「臺灣南部」。

解答：

Kaohsiung is a city in the southern part of Taiwan.

2）將下句翻成英文。

　　他出生在高雄。

解析：

注意，出生是用被動式。

解答：

He was born in Kaohsiung.

3）將下句翻成英文。

　　自他離開高雄以來已有五十年之久了。

解析：

從結構看，「自...以來」需用 since 子句來成句，故屬一複合句。

解答：

It has been 50 years since he left Kaohsiung,

4）將下句翻成英文。

　　他離開他出生在臺灣南部的高雄以來已有五十年之久了。

解析：

這裡「他離開他出生在臺灣南部的高雄」需用 which 子句來成句，故屬一複合句。

解答：

It has been 50 years since he left Kaohsiung, which is a city in the southern part of Taiwan where he was born.

補充說明：

注意中、英文不同結構的表達方法，如照英文句式，中文的意思是「他離開高雄已有五十年之久，高雄是臺灣南部的一個都市，他在那兒出生」，這不是道地的中文。

5）　將4）句用無動詞式的方法改寫。

解析：

這理需將 which 子句依省略第 VII）模式改成一無動詞式來做。

解答：

It has been 50 years since he left Kaohsiung, a city in the southern part of Taiwan where he was born.

習題十四

這個習題看似複雜，但實際上並不難。仍是用省略法將限定子句變成非限定子句，然後再用置換的方法表相同的文意。請讀者依各項題解逐步去做。

1）　將下句譯成英文。

　　教宗的靈柩是用杉木做成的。

解析：

用 coffin 表「靈柩」，用 cedarwood 表「杉木」，　用 make 與 of 相搭配表「做成」，這句文意需用被動語態來表達。

解答：

The Pope's coffin was made of cedarwood.

2）　將下句譯成英文。

　　教宗的靈柩上有一個十字架的標誌。

解析：

用 mark 表「標誌」，其後需與 with 相搭配。這句文意也需用被動語態

來表達。

解答：

The Pope's coffin was marked with a cross.

補充說明：

這裡中文名詞「標誌」是用英文動詞（mark）轉譯。

3） 將上述1）及2）二句連成一並列句。

解析：

將1）及2）二句用 and 連接，並注意用省略法刪除重複的部分。

解答：

The Pope's coffin was made of cedarwood and was marked with a cross.

4） 將上述1）及2）二句連成一複合句表以下文意。

用杉木做成的教宗靈柩上，有一個十字架的標誌。

解析：

從結構看，「用杉木做成的教宗靈柩」需用 which 成句，本句宜以非限制性子句來表達。

解答：

The Pope's coffin, which was made of cedarwood, was marked with a cross.

5） 將4）句用本節所介紹的方法改寫。

解析：

本題須將副句中的限定子句變成非限定子句，可用省略法的第 VIII）模式來改寫。

解答：

The Pope's coffin, made of cedarwood, was marked with a cross.

6） 將5）句用置換方法改寫。

解析：

參照 I5）例來做。

解答：

Made of cedarwood, the Pope's coffin was marked with a cross.

7） 將上述 1）及 2）二句連成一複合句表以下文意。

　　上面有一個十字架標誌的教宗靈柩是用杉木做成的。

解析：

從結構看，「上面有一個十字架標誌的教宗靈柩」需用 which 成句，本句宜以非限制性子句來表達。

解答：

The Pope's coffin, which was marked with a cross, was made of cedarwood.

8） 將 7）句用本節所介紹的方法改寫。

解析：

本題須將副句中的限定子句變成非限定子句，可用省略法的第 VIII）模式來改寫。

解答：

The Pope's coffin, marked with a cross, was made of cedarwood.

9） 將 8）句用置換方法改寫。

解析：

參照 I5）例來做。

解答：

Marked with a cross, the Pope's coffin was made of cedarwood.

10） 將下句譯成英文。

　　成千萬的人們擠入聖彼得廣場。

解析：

用 crowd 與 into 相搭配表「擠入」，用 St. Peter's Square 表「聖彼得廣

場」。

解答：

Thousands of people crowded into the St. Peter's Square.

11） 將下句譯成英文。

擠入聖彼得廣場的成千萬人們來朝見教宗的靈柩。

解析：

用 pilgrim 表「朝見」。從結構看，「擠入聖彼得廣場的成千萬人們」需用 who 成句，本句宜以非限制性子句來表達，同時主句宜用被動語態來表達。

解答：

The Pope's coffin was pilgrimmed by thousands of people who crowded into the St. Peter's Square.

12） 將 11）句用本節所介紹的方法改寫。

解析：

本題須將副句中的限定子句變成非限定子句，可用省略法的第 VIII）模式來改寫。

解答：

The Pope's coffin was pilgrimmed by thousands of people crowded into the St. Peter's Square.

13） 將上述 1）及 12）各句連成一整句表以下文意。

成千萬的人們擠入聖彼得廣場來朝見用杉木做成的教宗靈柩。

解析：

本句需仿效 11）句，用被動語態來表達。

解答：

The Pope's coffin was made of cedarwood and was pilgrimmed by thousands of people crowded into the St. Peter's Square.

14）將上述 2）及 12）各句連成一整句表以下文意。

成千萬的人們擠入聖彼得廣場來朝見上面有一個十字架標誌的教宗靈柩。

解析：

本句需仿效 11）句，用被動語態來表達。

解答：

The Pope's coffin was marked with a cross and was pilgrimmed by thousands of people crowded into the St. Peter's Square.

15）將上述 2）、6）及 11）各句連成一整句表以下文意。

成千萬的人們擠入聖彼得廣場來朝見教宗的靈柩，靈柩是用杉木做成的，上面有一個十字架標誌。

解析：

這個題目讓我們用省略的觀念及置換的方式來練習換句的技巧。下面二個解答皆是使用本節所介紹的方法來表達相同的文意。

解答：

第一， Made of cedarwood, the Pope's coffin was marked with a cross and was pilgrimmed by thousands of people crowded into the St. Peter's Square.

第二， Marked with a cross, the Pope's coffin was made of cedarwood and was pilgrimmed by thousands of people crowded into the St. Peter's Square.

習題十五

將下面的中文譯成一句英文整句。

（1）沙發是從國外進口的，（2）是用紅檜木做成，（3）被放在二個落地燈之間，（4）它的座墊套是由具東方風格的繡花做成。

解析：

我們在習題十四的第 15）題解中，逐步練習了如何用二種不同的英文句法來表達同一個中文意思。這裡我們用同樣的方法來熟練這種增加句式變化的技巧。中文原意有四組文意構成（如編號所示）。第一組需用 couch 表「沙發」，overseas 表「國外」。第二組用片語 mahogany wood 表「紅檜木」。第三組用片語 floor lamp 表「落地燈」。第四組用 cushion-cover 表「座墊套」，embroider 表「繡花」，片語 oriental style 表「具東方風格」，其前需與 in 相搭配。這四組意思分別可用下面四個基本句子來表達：

a） The couch was imported from overseas.

b） The couch was made of mahogany wood.

c） The couch was placed between two floor lamps.

d） Its cushion-cover was embroidered in oriental style.

這四個句子可用一個最原始的文句來表達如下：

The couch was imported from overseas and was made of mahogany wood; it was placed between two floor lamps and its cushion-cover was embroidered in oriental style.

這原始文句是用分號將四個基本句子連接成一整句。文法及句構皆可行，但句式缺少變化。我們可參照習題十四的第 15）題的方法以及 F1）例來分別改寫成下列三種最顯著的不同句式。

解答：

第一， Imported from overseas, the couch was made of mahogany wood and was placed between two floor lamps, its cushion-cover embroidered in oriental style.

第二， Made of mahogany wood, the couch was imported from overseas and was placed between two floor lamps, its cushion-cover embroidered in oriental style.

第三，Placed between two floor lamps, the couch was made of mahogany wood and was imported from overseas, its cushion-cover embroidered in oriental style.

上面三個解答是用省略的方法，將限定子句變成非限定子句，然後再用置換的方式而寫成。如果我們再將非限定子句變成無動詞式的話，那末可仿效 F3）例的用法，將第三個解答進一步改寫如下：

第四，Placed between two floor lamps, the couch was made of mahogany wood and was imported from overseas, its cushion-cover in oriental style.

上面第一及第二的解答也可用此法再進一步改寫。讀者不妨自行模仿去做。這裡我們如用這四個句法與上述原始句式相比，不難發現這幾句的句法變化要巧妙得多。

　　在此我們也須注意子句省略後的侷限性問題，我們如比較 its cushion-cover in oriental style 與 its cushion-cover embroidered in oriental style 不難發現二者意義並不完全相同，原因是 its cushion-cover in oriental style（座墊套具東方風格）的文意較 its cushion-cover embroidered in oriental style（座墊套具東方風格的繡花）為廣，因為「座墊套具東方風格」可指設計花樣，格式，或所用的質料等，而並不僅限於繡花。

補充說明：

關於 among 及 between 的區別，通常 between 用於二個個體間的關係，如本例所示，而 among 是用於二個以上的個體關係，例如：They divided the bonus among themselves. 但這並不意謂 between 不能用於二個以上的個體關係，例如在下列情形下仍應用 between：

　　第一，當各個體表空間關係時，例如： Iraq lies between Turkey, Iran, Jordan, Kuwait, Saudi Arabia, and Syria. 第二，當各個體表時間

及範圍時,例如: The accident occurred between Monday and Wednesday of last week. 這是指從上星期一到上星期三這三天的一段期間,再如在 The spacecraft crashed between the creek, the rocks, and the woods 一句中,這是指太空船墜毀在小溪,岩石及叢林中的一段地帶(range)的意思,但在 The spacecraft crashed among the creek, the rocks, and the woods 一句中,這是指小溪,岩石及叢林是太空船墜毀失事的地點(location)的意思。第三,當突顯各個體時,例如在 a free trade agreement between the U.S., Canada and Mexico 一例中,表示每一個國家對其他二個國家分別受特定的條約的拘束,而 among 指一個個體包括在集體中的意思,例如在 John is among the best of our players 一句中,John 是包括在 best players 中,從這二例可知,between 有排外性(exclusiveness)而 among 有包含性(inclusiveness),根據這區別,Diplomatic negotiation between nations is desirable 一句具有每一個國家對其他國家分別作外交協商的意思,而 Diplomatic negotiation among nations is desirable 一句則具有若干國家相互形成集團互相協商的意思。

3.3.6 加強語氣之方法

在作文時,我們常使用不同的方法來變更句中的節奏以收強調語氣的效果。在第 3.1 節中我們曉得用置換來加強語氣,這裡我們進一步介紹其他各種加強語氣的方法。

最簡單的方法是使用字型來加強語氣,例如在 This is **not** a drill 一句中,是用粗體字來表達加強語氣。有時也可用斜體字或引號(quotation marks)來替代粗體字。其次是使用命令式的動詞(should 及 must)來加強語氣,例如:All borrowed equipments **must be returned** immediately. 或用命令口吻來表達加強語氣,例如:**Come** back at once. 這句實際上是 You come back at once 的縮寫。我們也可用標點符號來加強語氣,例如:What a marvelous performance! 是用驚嘆號來加強語氣,而下面二個例子是分別用逗點及破折號(dash)[11] 使句中的音節停頓來轉變語調。例如: This is, **however**, by no means true 一句乃用逗點使音節停頓來強調 however,而 Of course, there is a better way to bargain – **swapping** 這一句是使用破折號來強調 swapping。再如在下面二個例子中:

A1) Correcting assignments, term papers, and exams is so demanding that teachers must constantly take recreational activities to make themselves fit for the job.

A2) Correcting assignments and term papers and exams is very demanding – so demanding that teachers must constantly take recreational activities to make themselves fit for the job.

在以上二個例子中,A2)句的語氣遠較 A1)句為重,因為句首將 assignments,term papers 及 exams 三者用二個 and 來連接表加重語氣,同時又使用一破折號使語調停頓以收強調的效果。讀者不妨吟讀比較這二句,就不難體會出其中的區別。

文句的強調也可用 there 句來表達。我們在第 2.1.1 節中曉得,子句是由主詞及述詞二者構成,例如: subject + verb to be + predication 句式即為一例。此類句式可用「導引詞」there 來改寫表達強調語氣,其方法是將 there 置於句前,而將原句中的真正主詞置於 verb to be 之後,使成 there + verb to be + subject(focus) + predication 的模式。採此種模式的句子,使讀者對真正的主詞由於後置的關係而產生停頓的感受,以收強調的效果。我們用下面幾個

---

[11] 有關破折號用于同位語的句式,請參第 4.2.2 節。

例子分別來說明這種用法。

A) No one was talking.

There was **no one** talking.

這是從 **SV** 的模式來改寫成 there 句。

B) No one is here.

There is **no one** here.

這是從 **SVA** 的模式來改寫成 there 句。

C) Nothing is free.

There is **nothing** free.

這是從 **SVC** 的模式來改寫成 there 句。

D) Many people are giving blood.

There are **many people** giving blood.

這是從 **SVO** 的模式來改寫成 there 句。

E) A sales person is pushing the deal through.

There is **a sales person** pushing the deal through.

這是從 **SVOA** 的模式來改寫成 there 句。

F) Something is giving her trouble.

There is **something** giving her trouble.

這是從 **SVO$_I$O$_D$** 的模式來改寫成 there 句。

在這裏我們須注意幾點。第一，there 在上面幾個例子中屬文法上的主詞（grammatical subject），但在觀念上原句的主詞仍應視作 there 句的真正主詞，如 D）例中的 many people 及 E）例中的 sales person，因此稱觀念主詞（notational subject）。因為這個緣故，there 句中動詞的單複數是取決于觀念主詞，如第 D）及第 E）二個例子所示。而當觀念主詞是有二個單數主詞構成時，其動詞可用單數也

可用數複，例如：In each lunch box there is（are）a sandwich and a drink. 同理，當觀念主詞的第一個主詞是單數，而第二個主詞是複數時，動詞也可用單數或用數複，例如： In each lunch box there is（are）a sandwich and two drinks. 第二，there 句實際上另可用 wh- 及 that 子句來改寫。例如第 D）例可用 There are many people who are giving blood 來表達，或如上述第 F）例可用 There is something that is giving her trouble 來表示。從另外一個角度來看，這是第 3.2.2 節中省略的第 IV）模式的復原。第三，通常是在原句帶 verb to be 的情形下使用 there 子句，如上面幾個例子所示。但也有例外，我們不妨用下面幾個例子來說明這一點。

G1） Something **keeps** giving her trouble.

這個句子是用動詞 keep 而非 verb to be，但仍允許我們用 there 句來改寫如下：

G2） There is something that **keeps** giving her trouble.

同理，下例的動詞是 rose 而非 verb to be，但如將主詞及動詞的位置互換後，仍可使用 there 句。

H1） A hopeful prospect of a new future **rose** in her mind.

這個句子可用 there 句來表達，其中將主詞及動詞的位置更換而改寫成：

H2） There **rose** in her mind **a hopeful prospect of a new future.**

There 句雖是常用的加重語氣方法之一，但如果從與其原句可得互用一點而言，也可視作法殊趣同的方法之一。

強調語氣的另一個方法是使用裂句（clef sentence）。所以稱裂句是因為這種句式是將原句一分為二的緣故。大多數裂句是用 it + verb to be 作起句，其後跟所欲加重的部分及一 that 子句，使裂句成為 it + verb to be + focus + that …的模式。假定加重部分是人稱名詞

時，則用 who 來替代 that，如下面例 I2）句所示。

從加重語氣的部分來說，裂句可有不同的變化，我們用下例來說明。

I1）　Shirley drove a sports car to school yesterday.

　　　這個句子可有下列各種不同加重語氣的可能：

I2）　加重語氣落在主詞上。

　　　It was **Shirley** who drove a sports car to school yesterday.

I3）　加重語氣落在受詞上。

　　　It was **a sports car** that Shirley drove to school yesterday.

I4）　加重語氣落在表時間的副詞上。

　　　It was **yesterday** that Shirley drove a sports car to school.

I5）　加重語氣落在表目的地的副詞上。

　　　It was **to school** that Shirley drove a sports car yesterday.

從上面幾個例子可以曉得，專有名詞（Shirley），名詞片語（sports car），副詞（yesterday）及系詞片語（to school）皆可用作加重語氣的部分。此外，副句也可用作加重語氣的部分。例如：It was **because the semester was over** that students started hunting for summer jobs. 須注意的是，在裂句的模式中，通常動詞是不能用作加重語氣的部分，因此如將 I1）句改寫成 It was **drove** that Shirley a sports car to school yesterday 就不成文句。又須注意的是，裂句中的 that 子句其動詞的單複數取決於著重的部分。例如在 It is Shirley's parents who **give** her a sports car 一句中其著重的部分是 parents，故 who 子句中動詞用複數。而在 It is **Shirley's boy friend** who **gives** her a sports car 一句中其著重的部分是 boy friend，因此 who 子句中的動詞用單數。

有時裂句中的非著重部分的位置可以變動，我們不妨用下面一個例子來說明：

J1） It was **actually** Shirley who drove a sports car to school yesterday.

這句中的 actually 可移往 who 子句而將上句改寫如下：

J2） It was Shirley who **actually** drove a sports car to school yesterday.

需注意的是，裂句中的否定語氣應該用二種不同的方法來表達。第一種方法是在加重部分置 not。例如：It was **not** Shirley who drove a sports car to school yesterday. 第二種方法是增加一個新的著重部分用以比較。例如在上面從 I2）到 I5）各例子中，可用下面從 K2）到 K5）所示的方法來分別表達：

K2） It was **not Jane but Shirley** who drove a sports car to school yesterday.

K3） It was **not a mini van** but a sports car that Shirley drove to school yesterday.

K4） It was **not last week but yesterday** that Shirley drove a sports car to school yesterday.

K5） It was **not to a shopping center but to school** that Shirley drove a sports car yesterday.

上面幾個例子，另可酌情以置換的方法來改寫。例如 K2）句可改寫成 It was Shirley, **but not Jane**, who drove a sports car to school yesterday. 其他各例亦同。

裂句也可用疑問句來表達，其方法與通常疑問句的使用法相同，是將動詞移置句前而在句後加一問號。因此上面 I2）例的疑問句為 **Was** it Shirley who drove a sports car to school yesterday? 同理，裂句也可用驚嘆句來表達，方法是在句前用 what 且將原句中的著重部分移往 what 之後，再在句末加驚嘆號而成。因此上面 I3）句可表達成 **What a sports car** it was that Shirley drove to school yesterday!

上面 I3）句另外也可用假裂句來表達。假裂句實際上衍自裂句，是將裂句中的 that 子句變成 what 子句而置於句首，其加重語氣的部分仍置於動詞 verb to be 之後，這可用 what + ... + verb to be + focus 的模式來表示。因此，如果加重部分落在 sports car 時，上面的 I3）句可改寫如下：

I6） What Shirley drove to school yesterday was **a sports car.**
實際上這是一個 **SVC** 的句式，其中將主詞及補語互相倒置改寫而成，如下例所示：

I7） A sports car was what Shirley drove to school yesterday.

假裂句中的著重部分可用名詞來表達，如上面 I6）例所示（a sports car）。也可用限定子句來表達，例如： What we know was **that Shirley drove a sports car to school yesterday.** 此外動名詞及不定詞片語也可用作加重部分，如下面各例所示：

L） **What** they were doing to their boss was **pulling his leg**.

M） **What** the chairperson did was **to weigh the pros and cons.**

須注意的是在上面 M）例中，如 what 子句的動詞 do 為現在進行式時，其加重部分的動詞時式須與其相當，如下例所示：

M1） **What** the chairperson is **doing** is **weighing** the pros and cons. 上面的例子介紹了如何用裂句及假裂句來加重語氣及其各種變化，我們可從此二者能互換使用中不難推知這也是法殊趣同的方法之一。

習題一

1） 將下句譯成英文。
電子郵件方便，快，簡單，同時便宜。

解析：

用 easy 表「方便」。

解答：

E-mail is easy, fast, simple, and cheap.

2）　將上句用本節所介紹的方法，使加重語氣落在「便宜」上。

解析：

用破折號來改寫。

解答：

E-mail is easy, fast, simple – and cheap.

習題二

1）　將下句譯成英文。

　　　以不當理由將副本送給太多的人。

解析：

用片語 far too many people 表「太多的人」。

解答：

Copies were sent to far too many people for the wrong reason.

2）　將上句用本節所介紹的方法，使加重語氣落在「不當理由」上。

解析：

用破折號來改寫。

解答：

Copies were sent to far too many people – for the wrong reason.

習題三

1）　將下句譯成英文。

　　　寬容比批評有價值。

解析：

用 outweigh 表「比...有價值」。

解答：

Tolerance outweighs criticism.

2) 　將下句譯成英文。

　　批評往往很多。

解析：

用 plenty 與 of 相搭配表「很多」。

解答：

There is often plenty of criticism.

3) 　將 1)與 2)二句連接成一整句表以下文意。

　　寬容比批評更有價值，而批評往往很多。

解析：

從句構看，因為用「而」，故本句應是一并列句。

解答：

Tolerance outweighs criticism and there is often plenty of criticism.

4) 　將上句用本節所介紹的方法，使加重語氣落在「批評往往很多」

　　上。

解析：

用破折號來改寫。

解答：

Tolerance outweighs criticism – and there is often plenty of criticism.

補充說明：

這加重語氣的意思是說，因批評很多故需更多的容忍。

習題四

1) 　將下句譯成英文。

　　對缺少興趣一事，行政單位顯出仍無體認的迹象。

解析：

用 the administration 表「行政單位」，用 awareness 表「體認」。從句構

看，所謂「行政單位顯出無體認的迹象」是指「缺少興趣一事」，因此需用 that 子句來成句。

解答：

A lack of interest is something that the administration has shown no sign of awareness.

補充說明：

注意，中文的動詞（體認）用英文的名詞（awareness）來轉譯。

2) 將下句譯成英文。

缺少興趣是問題的癥結。

解析：

以 heart 與 problem 相搭配表「問題的癥結」。

解答：

A lack of interest is the heart of the problem.

補充說明：

我們也可以 core 與 problem 相搭配表「問題的癥結」。

3) 將 1）及 2）二句連成一整句表以下文意。

對缺少興趣一事，行政單位顯出仍無體認的迹象，而缺少興趣是問題的癥結。

解析：

注意句中用「而」故需用并列句成句。

解答：

A lack of interest is something the administration has shown no sign of awareness and it is the heart of the problem.

4) 將上句用加重語氣表以下文意。

對缺少興趣一事，行政單位顯出仍無體認的迹象，而就是這缺少興趣一點是問題的癥結。

解析：

使加重語氣落在「就是這缺少興趣一點是問題的癥結」上，用破折號來改寫。

解答：

A lack of interest – and it is the heart of the problem – is something the administration has shown no sign of awareness.

習題五

1） 將下句譯成英文。

這二個候選人仍在爭論問題。

解析：

以 debate 與 issue 相搭配表「爭論問題」。

解答：

The two candidates are still debating the issue.

2） 將上句用 there 子句改寫。

解析：

仿效 D）例來做。

解答：

There are two candidates still debating the issue.

3） 將上句用 who 子句改寫。

解析：

參照有關 D）例的第二注意點來做。

解答：

There are two candidates who are still debating the issue.

補充說明：

這裏我們用了三個不同的句子，來表達一個相似的文意。

260

習題六

1）　將下句譯成英文。

　　公園裡突然發生併發爆炸。

解析：

以 burst 與 explosion 相搭配表「併發爆炸」，用 occur 表「發生」。

解答：

A burst of explosions suddenly occurred in the park.

2）　將上句用 there 句改寫。

解析：

套用 there 模式來做。

解答：

There occurred suddenly a burst of explosions in the park.

補充說明：

照 there 句的模式，這句應寫成 There occurred a burst of explosions suddenly in the park. 但 suddenly（副詞）是形容 occurred（動詞）故二者放在一起。

習題七

1）　將下句譯成英文。

　　二對夫婦在車禍中喪生。

解析：

用 a couple 表「一對夫婦」。

解答：

Two couples were killed in a car accident.

2）　將上句用 there 句改寫。

解析：

套用 there 模式來做。

解答:

There were two couples killed in a car accident.

3) 將上句用 who 子句改寫。

解析:

參照有關 D) 例的第二注意點來做。

解答:

There were two couples who were killed in a car accident.

習題八

1) 將下句譯成英文。

經常運動能增進我們的健康。

解析:

以 regular 與 exercise 相搭配表「經常運動」,以 improve 與 health 相搭配表「增進健康」。

解答:

Regular exercise can improve our health.

補充說明:

我們也可以 benefit 與 health 相搭配表「有利於健康」。

2) 將上句中的「經常運動」表加重語氣。

解析:

用裂句的模式來做。

解答:

It is regular exercise that can improve our health.

習題九

1) 將下句譯成英文。

他聲稱他的長兄沒有涉及販毒。

解析:

用 claim 表「聲稱」，用片語 elder brother 表「長兄」，以 drug 與 trafficking 相搭配表「販毒」。從結構看，用 that 子句作受詞來表「他的長兄沒有涉及販毒」。

解答：

He claimed that his elder brother was not involved in drug trafficking.

補充說明：

注意，involve 其後需與 in 相搭配。

2）將上句中之「長兄」表加重語氣。

解析：

在 that 子句中用裂句模式來做。

解答：

He claimed that it was not his elder brother who was involved in drug trafficking.

習題十

1）將下句譯成英文。

她用限時專送寄給她頂頭上司一封辭職信。

解析：

以 immediate 與 supervisor 相搭配表「頂頭上司」，用 special 與 delivery 相搭配表「限時專送」。

解答：

She sent a letter of resignation to her immediate supervisor by special delivery.

2）將上句中的「辭職信」表加重語氣。

解析：

仿效 I3）例來做。

解答：

It was a letter of resignation that she sent to her immediate supervisor by special delivery.

3) 將 1 ）句中的「她的頂頭上司」表加重語氣。

解析：

仿效 I3）例來做。

解答：

It was to her immediate supervisor that she sent a letter of resignation by special delivery.

4) 將 1 ）句中的「限時專送」表加重語氣。

解析：

這是將強調置于副詞上，可仿效 I4）或 I5）例來做。

解答：

It was by special delivery that she sent a letter of resignation to her immediate supervisor.

5) 將 4 ）句中的「辭職信」表加重語氣。

解析：

使用假裂句模式來做。

解答：

What she sent to her immediate supervisor by special delivery was a letter of resignation.

習題十一

1) 將下句譯成英文。

　　我們正在學習英文文法。

解析：

用 study 或 learn 表「學習」。

解答：

We are studying English grammar.

2） 將上句中的「英文文法」表加重語氣。

解析：

用裂句模式來做。

解答：

It is English grammar that we are studying.

3） 將下句譯成英文。

我們正在學習英文句法。

解析：

用 syntax 表「句法」。

解答：

We are studying English syntax.

4） 將上句中的「英文句法」表加重語氣。

解析：

用裂句模式來做。

解答：

It is English syntax that we are studying.

5） 將2）及4）二句用否定語氣連成一句表以下文意。

我們正在學習的是英文句法而非英文文法。

解析：

照 K4）例及置換的方法來做。

解答：

It is not English grammar but English syntax that we are studying. Or

It is English syntax, but not English grammar, that we are studying.

6） 將2）及4）二句用否定語氣連成一句表以下文意。

我們正在學習的是英文文法而非英文句法。

解析：

照 K4）例及置換的方法來做。

解答：

It is not English syntax but English grammar that we are studying. Or

It is English grammar, but not English syntax, that we are studying.

7） 將 2）句表加重語氣。

解析：

用假裂句的模式來做。

解答：

What we are studying is English grammar.

8） 將 3）句表加重語氣。

解析：

用假裂句的模式來做。

解答：

What we are studying is English syntax.

9） 將 5）句用表加重語氣。

解析：

用假裂句的模式來做。

解答：

What we are studying is not English grammar but English syntax. Or

What we are studying is English syntax but not English grammar.

10） 將 6）句表加重語氣。

解析：

用假裂句的模式來做。

解答：

What we are studying is not English syntax but English grammar. Or

What we are studying is English grammar but not English syntax.

習題十二

1）　將下句譯成英文。

市場競爭影響商品的價格

解析：

以 market 與 competition 相搭配表「市場競爭」，以 commodity 表「商品」。

解答：

Market competition affects the price of a commodity.

2）　將上句中的「市場競爭」表加重語氣。

解析：

用裂句模式來做。

解答：

It is market competition that affects the price of a commodity.

補充說明：

注意動詞（affect）用單數，因為著重部分 market competition 是單數。

3）　將下句譯成英文。

投資成本影響商品的價格。

解析：

以 investment 與 cost 相搭配表「投資成本」。

解答：

Investment costs affect the price of a commodity.

4）　將上句中的「投資成本」表加重語氣。

解析：

用裂句模式來做。

解答：

It is investment costs that affect the price of a commodity.

補充說明：

注意動詞用複數，因為著重部分 investment costs 是複數。

5） 將 1）及 4）二句用否定語氣連成一句表以下文意。

影響商品價格的是市場競爭而非投資成本。

解析：

仿效 K4）例及置換的方法來做。

解答：

It is not investment costs but market competition that affects the price of a commodity. Or

It is market competition, but not investment costs, that affects the price of a commodity.

6） 將 1）及 4）二句用否定語氣連成一句表以下文意。

影響商品價格的是投資成本而非市場競爭。

解析：

仿效 K4）例及置換的方法來做。

解答：

It is not market competition but investment costs that affect the price of a commodity. Or

It is investment costs, but not market competition, that affect the price of a commodity.

7） 將 4）句表加重語氣。

解析：

用假裂句模式來做。

解答：

What affects the price of a commodity is investment costs.

8）　將5）句表加重語氣。

解析：

用假裂句模式來做。

解答：

What affects the price of a commodity is market competition but not investment costs.

9）　將6）句表加重語氣。

解析：

用假裂句模式來做。

解答：

What affects the price of a commodity is investment costs but not market competition.

習題十三

1）將下句譯成英文。

　　繫爭的是事實問題。

解析：

用 issue 表「繫爭」，其前需與 at 相搭配。

解答：

A question of fact is at issue.

補充說明：

注意中文的動詞（繫爭）用英文的系詞片語（at issue）來轉譯。同時注意，從主從關係言，中、英文皆以「問題」（question）為主語，「事實」（fact 與系詞 of 連用）為從語，但中、英文的詞序表達有所不同，在中文裏，「事實」置於「問題」之前，而在英文中，question 置於 fact 之前。

2）將上句中的「事實問題」表加重語氣。

全民英檢
中高級作文指南

解析：

用裂句模式來做。

解答：

It is a question of fact that is at issue.

3）將下句譯成英文。

　　繫爭的是邏輯推理。

解析：

以 logic 與 reasoning 相搭配表「邏輯推理」。

解答：

The logic of reasoning is at issue.

補充說明：

注意詞序問題，在中文裏，「推理」為主語，「邏輯」為從語（即「邏輯的推理」），而在英文中，logic 是主語，reasoning 與系詞 of 連用為從語。

4）將上句中的「邏輯推理」表加重語氣。

解析：

用裂句模式來做。

解答：

It is the logic of reasoning that is at issue.

5）將2）及4）二句用否定語氣連成一句表以下文意：

　　所繫爭的是邏輯推理而非事實問題。

解析：

仿效 K4）例及置換的方法來做。

解答：

It is not a question of fact but the logic of reasoning that is at issue. Or

It is the logic of reasoning, but not a question of fact, that is at issue.

270

6）將 2）及 4）二句用否定語氣連成一句表以下文意。

　　所繫爭的是事實問題而非邏輯推理。

解析：

用裂句模式來做。

解答：

It is not the logic of reasoning but a question of fact that is at issue. Or

It is a question of fact, but not the logic of reasoning, that is at issue.

7）將 2）句表加重語氣。

解析：

用假裂句模式來做。

解答：

What is at issue is a question of fact.

8）將 4）句表加重語氣。

解析：

用假裂句模式來做。

解答：

What is at issue is the logic of reasoning.

9）將 5）句表加重語氣。

解析：

用假裂句模式來做。

解答：

What is at issue is not a question of fact but the logic of reasoning. Or

What is at issue is the logic of reasoning but not a question of fact.

10）將 6）句表加重語氣。

解析：

用假裂句模式來做。

解答：

What is at issue is not the logic of reasoning but a question of fact. Or

What is at issue is a question of fact but not the logic of reasoning.

習題十四

1）將下句翻成英文。

　　在中東及南亞各處，民族主義從歷史上得到啟示。

解析：

用 take 與 cue 相搭配表「得到啟示」，注意其後需與系詞 from 相搭配。

解答：

Elsewhere in the Middle East and in South Asia, nationalism took its cue from history.

2）將下句翻成英文。

　　在中東及南亞各處，民族主義再度強力激起。

解析：

用 flare 與 up 相搭配表「激起」，用 intensity 表「強力」，注意其前需與系詞 with 相搭配。

解答：

Elsewhere in the Middle East and in South Asia, nationalism flared up again with new intensity.

3）將下句翻成英文。

　　在中東及南亞各處，民族主義從歷史上得到啟示而再度強力激起。

解析：

句中用「而」，故需用并列句成句。

解答：

Elsewhere in the Middle East and in South Asia, nationalism took its cue from history and flared up again with new intensity.

4）將下句翻成英文。

在中東及南亞各處，民族主義猶如從歷史上得到啟示而再度強力激起。

解析：

注意句中用「猶如」。從句構看，本句需用表條件的副句。本句是一個複合句。

解答：

Elsewhere in the Middle East and in South Asia, nationalism flared up again with new intensity as if it took its cue from history.

5）將上句用省略法改寫。

解析：

仿效省略第 II）模式來寫。

解答：

Elsewhere in the Middle East and in South Asia, nationalism flared up again with new intensity as if taking its cue from history.

6）將上句的副句用置換方式改寫。

解析：

我們在第 2.1.3.5 節中曉得副句也可用作修飾語，因此我們可根據第 3.1 節中有關修飾語置換的討論來改寫，將修飾語放于動詞 flared 之前。

解答：

Elsewhere in the Middle East and in South Asia, nationalism, as if taking its cue from history, flared up again with new intensity.

7）將上句的 in the Middle East 及 in South Asia 用加重語氣改寫。

解析：

這裏我們可用破折號來加重語氣。

解答：

Elsewhere - in the Middle East and in South Asia – nationalism, as if taking its cue from history, flared up with new intensity.

補充說明：

這裡從 4）到 7）各題，我們使用以上各章節所討論的方法，用四種不同的句構來表達一個相同的意思。

習題十五

1) 將下句翻成英文。

婚姻與事業二者皆重要。

解析：

用 both … and 表「二者皆」。

解答：

Both marriage and career are important.

補充說明：

在使用 both … and 的時候，句構需保持對稱平行，例如本句 both …and 之後皆用二個平行的名詞，再如在 Basketball is a popular sport both in North America and in Europe 一句中，both …and 之後用二個平行的系詞片語，而此句不應寫成 Basketball is a popular sport both in North America and Europe 因為 both 之後是用系詞片語，而 and 之後是用名詞，二者不對稱平行。同樣 either …or，neither … nor 及 not only … but also 也如此用法。

2) 將下句翻成英文。

目前他並不像擔心教育那樣來擔心婚姻與事業。

解析：

用片語 right now 表「目前」，用 concern 表「擔心」其後需與 about 相搭配。注意，此句意謂婚姻與事業沒有如教育一般那麼重要，因此

用 as …as 來表「並不像…那樣」來成句。

解答：

Right now he is not as concerned about marriage and career as he is concerned about education.

補充說明：

上面這一句可以用省略的方法將第二個 concerned 刪除而改寫成 Right now he is not as concerned about marriage and career as he is about education.

3) 　將 1）及 2）二句翻成英文表以下的文意。

　　雖然婚姻與事業二者皆重要，但目前他並不像擔心教育那樣來擔心婚姻與事業。

解析：

從句構看，因句中用「雖然」，故需用複合句成句。

解答：

Although both marriage and career are important, right now he is not as concerned about them as he is about education.

補充說明：

這裡我們將主句中的 marriage 及 career 用代名詞 them 來取代。

4) 　將 3）句的語氣加重在「婚姻與事業」上改寫。

解析：

本題需用置換及破折號的方法來做。先將副句中置而放在破折號中，同時將副句中的 marriage 及 career 用 both 取代，而將主句中的 them 還原成 marriage 及 career。

解答：

Right now he is not as concerned about marriage and career – although both are important – as he is about education.

第四章　段落之聯句合趣與章篇之結構

　　我們在以上三章中，分別從字（彙）及文句的立場來討論如何妥善及靈活使用句構。在這基礎上，我們在本章中進一步討論句與句之間如何連貫以求通順，以及一段內容如何求完整，前者涉及聯句的圓通，後者涉及合趣的周密。我們不妨用下面一段來試試自己對這二個課題有多少認識。為便於說明起見，原文各句皆加編號。

1）Any organization – a company, a government ministry, a charity, the local golf club – tends to become inward-looking if there is too little external discipline. 2）Reams of academic literature have been produced to show how civil servants, however good-hearted, naturally act in their own interests, boosting their budgets, protecting their power, resisting outside scrutiny. 3）So it is in private companies, except that managers there face discipline from competition with other firms, from the need to satisfy customers and from the demands of shareholders. 4）Competition and pressure from customers have both become a lot more intense in most industries in the past two decades, all over the world, with beneficial effects on productivity and innovation. 5）Pressure from shareholders, however, has not.

"Beyond Shareholder Value" in *A Survey of Capitalism and Democracy* （*The Economist,* June 28th - July 4th, 2003, at 9）

　　我們如果分析本段的內容，不禁要問，本文是用什麼鋪陳敘寫的方法來展開文意？我們發現作者極攻起調，將全段的文眼放在段首，提出不論是公家或私人機構，如果沒有外來的掣肘（external discipline）就會變成故步自封（inward looking）作其主旨來層層向前推展。第 2）句作者將公務員的所作所為（例如 protecting their power 及 resisting outside scrutiny 等）作為故步自封的例子，使文意與第 1）句的主題句（topic sentence）相連結。第 3）句作者以私人公司所面臨的問題（competition, customers' satisfaction 及 demands of shareholders）作為外來掣肘的例子，通過跳接之筆與第 1）句文意遙相應接，而第 2）句與第 3）句之間，作者則用了一個轉折詞 so 作承上起下的過渡，使這二句銜接在一起。第 4）句是第 3）句的引申，作者使用與第 3）句中的同義字（competition 及 pressure from customers）使二者文意前後照應。第 5）句的手法與第 4）句相同，作者視 pressure from shareholders 與第 3）句中的 demands of shareholders 字義相通來貫穿始終，各句間作者是靠這幾個往復回環的方法來求相互間文意的自然流衍。再從整段而言，作者將第 1）句主題句視作總綱，其他各句視作引申總綱的細節，用演繹的方法，通過直線型的段形，由上而下使內容周密，全段給人的印象是層次井然，首尾照應，承轉圓熟，且結構嚴密。

從以上概略的分析，使我們曉得作者用何種通篇造語的方法來導引我們了解內容，便於我們接受作者的論點。因此在應試作文時，懂得如何使用聯句圓通及合趣周密的各種方法，能便於閱卷老師了解我們謀篇佈局的層次及脈絡，有利於我們取得理想的分數。

那末如何謀篇佈局？我們不妨將段落視作句子的化身來討論。段落也具主詞及述詞二大部分。但其主詞乃指表達一段主旨的主題句，亦即一段的文眼，而其述詞部分是指鋪陳排比的細節，以不同的句式來舉證例示，比照類推及闡明解釋。本章先討論段落的形式，然而逐節討論如何求段落的連貫通順及組織完整，再以討論章篇的結構作收章。

4.1 段落之型式

段落的聯句合趣有其一定的形式，通常表文眼的主題句是起句，或置於接近一段的開端處，雖然有時主題句也出現在一段的中間甚至段尾。一個好的主題句需具備簡潔（concision）、分明（clarity）及切題（relevance）三個要件。

主題句有其不同的形式。通常皆以直陳句來表達，但有時為了引起讀者的注意，段落有用疑問句來起段的，例如下面有關美國及歐洲太空總署（European Space Agency）火星探險一段，就是以這種方法起段的。

For all their sophistication, the rovers won't be especially good at addressing the question people ask most： Is there now, or might there ever have been, life on Mars? The devices can make inferences, looking for evidence of water or iron. And if the microscopic imager sent back a picture of a microbial fossil that would settle the question. But even NASA acknowledges that when it comes to searching for life, the Europeans have the edge this time.

（J. Kluger, "Destination Mars, " *TIME Europe Magazine*（Jun. 16, 2003）. 摘自 http：//www.time.com/time/europe/magazine/article）

有時也用驚嘆句作主題句的，例如 Nathaniel Hawthorne 在 *The Haunted Mind* 中即採這種方法起段。

What a singular moment is the first one, when you have hardly begun to recollect yourself, after starting from midnight slumber! By unclosing your eyes so suddenly, you seem to have surprised the personages of your dream in full convocation round your bed, and catch one broad glance at them before they can flit into obscurity….

有時甚至採用驚嘆句及疑問句連用的方式來起段的，例如：

That man! What man? That man of whom I said that this magnificent countenance exhibited the noblest tragic woe. He was not of European blood. He was handsome, but not of European beauty. His face white – not a Northern whiteness; his eyes protruding somewhat, and rolling in their grief ….

William Makepeace Thackeray, *Autour de mon Chapeau*

這種起段的方法比用直陳句作起句更易引起讀者的注意，不妨酌情使用，但切忌濫用以免流於形式。

須注意的是，有時段落的起調並非是主題句。例如：

In almost no time the typhoon grew to its greatest height. The heads of the raging waves hurled up high in the air, roaring with the thunder of the wind. Rollers from the storm were creaming along the beach, making a steady boiling noise. The gale scoured the beach. Flowerbeds nearby the beach were adorned with flowers bending to the wind. By dawn the wind was moderating, when a shaft of twilight first appeared in the tinted sky.

本段沒有顯著的主題句，但從文意可知，從第一句開始，每句皆與一隱藏的主題有關，即描寫颱風過境的情景。

從形式言，不同的讀者及課題涉及段落字數的多寡及其複雜的程度。段落的字數不宜過多也不宜過少，通常在 120 字到 150 字左右是可以接受的數字，雖然有時偶爾可發現以二三句成段的。至於段落的複雜程度與不同領域的課題有關，例如報章雜誌上看到的文章，文意較純學術性的文章為通俗。此外自形式言，每一段落須有結語。結語須因前面的鋪陳而與主題句遙相呼應，使全段文意一氣呵成。

　　段落的聯句合趣有其一定的造型，這種造型是我們在作文時對段落外表所勾勒出的輪廓，這與下面第 4.3 節中所討論的各種文意周密的方法有所不同。此處是指段落外形的呈現方法，而後者是指段落實質內容的呈現方法。

　　基本上，段落聯句合趣的造型有直線型，分枝型及回環型三種。直線型的方式是在一系列的有關思維中，從一個相似的觀點逐一伸展到另一個相同的觀點，在整個呈現的過程中，一氣蟬聯而下，既不迂迴也不回環。我們不妨用下段來作說明。

1）Words, therefore, as well as things, claim the care of an author. 2）Indeed of many authors – and those not useless or contemptible – words are almost the only care： many make it their study not so much to strike out new sentiments as to recommend those which are already known to more favourable notice by fairer decorations. 3）But every men, whether he copies or invents, whether he delivers his own thoughts or those of another, has often found himself deficient in the power of expression, big with ideas which he could not utter, obliged to ransack his memory for terms adequate to his conceptions, and at last unable to impress upon his reader the image existing in his own mind.

Samuel Johnson, *The Pains of Composition*

　　這一段是在表達「情物交融」之難。1）句是作者的主張（assertion），就「詞彙」與其所代表的「物象」相提並論，將心生的文辭視作情（即文中的 sentiments），這與中文裡講究「辭以情發，情以物遷」的道理相似。基此出發點，文中將「辭物相稱」視作一個作家「巧言切狀」的看家本領，在這觀點下，作者在 2）句引申（development）練字之難，就像中文裡對字義講究在「義訓古今」

上下功夫，追求文字古今有別，興廢殊用的道理，用以避免詞旨失調。3）句結語（conclusion）認為不論創作或模仿，用字之難常無法達到「物與神遊」的境界。全文一百多字將文字工作者對咬文嚼字之苦發揮得淋漓盡致。整段的文意呈現可用下圖來表達。

1）句（assertion）

↓

2）句（development）

↓

3）句（conclusion）

分枝型的方法是將一系列有關的思維，循不同的方向伸展，但仍相互拘攣補綴，使整段具雙重結構，我們用下段來說明。

> And this is how I see the East. I have seen its secret places and have looked into its very soul; but now I see it always from a small boat, a high outline of mountains, blue and afar in the morning; like faint mist at noon; a jagged wall of purple at sunset. I have the feel of the oar in my hand, the vision of a scorching blue sea in my eyes. And I see a bay, a wide bay, smooth as glass and polished like ice, shimmering in the dark. A red light burns far off upon the gloom of the land, and the night is soft and warm. We drag at the oars with aching arms, and suddenly a puff of wind, a puff faint and tepid and laden with strange odours of blossoms, of aromatic wood, comes out of the still night – the first sight of the East on my face. That I can never forget. It was impalpable and enslaving, like a charm, like a whispered promise of mysterious delight.
>
> Joseph Conrad, *Youth*

這段的文眼置於最後的 That I can never forget 上，全文以此文眼

寫來，具體描寫如何令他難忘。作者在文中由細處著墨，透過視角的變化，由遠及近地逐一描寫，將其感受從無限（遠眺）變成有限（近觀），而漸漸地帶往高潮。祇見他移舟海上，遠遠望去，滔滔海水與陸相平，漫漫無邊的一色山水，早晚景色不一：湛藍渺邈的晨景，迷濛漂渺的午景及齒山彤霞的黃昏。灼熱的海面流躍在作者的眼前，灣中風平浪靜，水面清澈如鏡，粼波閃爍，江海凝光，在遠山近水划樂處，夕陽度西山，日暮生夜靜，暖風飄花香，這一幅山水晚靜圖令他難忘。整個一段上半部用遠體的畫面來襯托海的浩闊，使這無限的感受，在下半部用慢收近景的方法，一氣貫注地變成作者對黃昏幽雅的有限感受。全段透過遠近縱深的感受，以情對景，相合自然。作者在寥寥數句之中，將他陶醉而又無法言喻的喜悅，用輕宕的筆法先從無限見有限，再從有限歸無限地交替發展，使全段文意飄揚含茹的達到高潮。

　　這一段作者用圓轉清麗的文詞，精練流俐的句式及曼聲促節的音律來描寫他「遇思入詠」的感興，從靜悟中來表達意舒詞緩的風格，由景及意層層推進，充分利用了分枝法，使全段的雙重結構錯落有序地渾然成為一體，整段文意的呈現可用下圖來表達。

由遠眺及近觀描寫 That I can never forget.

從遠景描寫：移舟海上，　　　　從近景描寫：江海凝光，夕陽西度，
一色山水，早晚景色不一。　　　　一幅山水晚靜圖。

由遠體的畫面來襯托海的浩　　　由慢收近景的方法來描寫作者對
闊以表作者的無限感受。　　　　黃昏幽雅的有限感受

從無限見有限，再從有限歸無限的感受中使全文的情景宛轉繼承。

　　回環型的方法是將一系列有關的思維，用參差錯落的方法前後呼應，以開頭及結尾作突出的重點，使二者迭起融合，回旋往復。我們用下例來說明。

　　1）I was taking a walk in this place last night between the hours of nine and ten, and could not but fancy it one of the most proper scenes in the world for a ghost to appear in. 2）The ruins of the abbey are scattered up and down on every side, and half covered with ivy and elder-bushes, the harbours of several solitary birds which seldom make their appearance till the dusk of the evening. 3）The place was formerly a churchyard, and has still several marks in it of graves and burying-places. 4）There is such an echo among the old ruins and vaults, that if you stamp out a little louder than ordinary you hear the sound repeated. 5）At the same time the walk of elms, with the croaking of the ravens, which from time to time are heard from the tops of them, looks exceedingly solemn and venerable. 6）These objects naturally raise seriousness and attention;

7) and when night heightens the awfulness of the place, and pours out her supernumerary horrours upon every thing in it, I do not at all wonder that weak minds fill it with specters and apparitions.

Joseph Addison, *The Spectator, No. 110.*

　　這段的文眼在於描寫何以有人捕風捉影地認為古寺是個鬧鬼的地方。1）句開頭描寫夜景，使人感到此地有鬼的一幅畫面，為以下各句作張本。2）句照應前句，用寺院中的廢墟及傍晚才出現的烏鴉來點綴上句的景物，而 3）句指出古寺曾是墳場及還留下墓地的痕跡，這給讀者留下很多聯想的空間。既然曾是墳地，那末是夜或許鬼哭淒淒，既然留下墓地的痕跡，那末白骨露野亦未可知，這為 4）句從荊條盤紆的廢墟中傳出的腳步迴響，倍添寂冷陰森的感覺。在這裡作者已從前幾句描寫寂寥景物的「視覺形象」，進一步轉出蕭瑟的「聽覺感受」。此 4）句的「聲感」又為 5）句在陰森叢林中嘎然長鳴的烏鴉作墊筆。6）句承接以上各句的文意為 7）句作引申，同時以上各句皆屬長句，讀者一氣直下唸到此處已稍感吃力，而此 6）句是用短句，給讀者一個緩和語調的機會。7）句用一個轉折詞 and 來承上抒感，含蘊著上述各句的視感及聲感，再加上夜幕深沉對人產生的心理影響，難怪使人疑神疑鬼，這樣又連環雙綰地回到了第一句突出的畫面上。

　　全句作者除利用視感及聲感來增加此地的神秘外，又參差錯落地用了表「幽暗」的字眼來襯托與鬼的關係。例如「夜色蒼茫」，「古老寺院」，「夜半步聲」，甚至用烏鴉傳神地來代表黑色，使在聲感的背後又塗上一抹「色感」的輪廓，愈發有「聲」有「色」地道出令人疑神疑鬼的原因。

　　這一段，作者用省淨的辭語，流暢清新的筆調，將各句的文意，從突出開頭及結尾中，層次遞進的連貫在一起，使二者密不可分，

相接為用。整段的文意呈現可用下圖來表示。

1）句（古寺是使人捕風捉影的鬧鬼的地方）

視覺形象：　　　　　　　　7）句（類推重申疑神疑鬼的重點）

2）句（古寺的晚景及晚出
的烏鴉）及3）句（古寺曾是　　6）句（視覺形象及聽覺感受的
墳地）　　　　　　　　　　總結）

聽覺感受：
4）句（廢墟中的腳步聲）
及5）句（烏鴉鳴林中）

　　以上介紹了三種段落的型式，須注意的是，段落的型式是我們在作文時，對文意的伸展於有意無意中所勾勒出的輪廓，因此在作文時應由文意來帶動型式的採取，切忌先謀何種型式再求文意的伸展，以免窒礙文思。

習題一

A) 指出下列三句何者為主題句，同時將此三句，依主題句不同的型式重新組合成一段。

1) The sentence ought to be one, not merely of immediate arrest, but of severe punishment. 2) Ordinary criminal justice requires that innocence cannot be pleaded in answer to a charge of violence by terrorism. 3) If a person joins a terrorist movement and commits violence, it is no defense that he has done so for a political cause.

解析：

這題須先從內容分析來決定何者為主題句，何者為申述主旨的細節，然後再依主題句的形式重新組合成一段。從文意而言，因政治理念而參與恐怖主義所作的暴力行為不能構成無罪的藉口（3）句的意思），而法院對此種暴行的制裁應為立即逮捕及嚴重處罪（1）句的意思），所以能如此做，乃是循刑事制裁不視此種行為是無罪的原則（2）句的意思）。根據這文意，2）句是主題句，是用直陳句表達，而 1）與 3）兩句為細節。須注意的是，3）句是 1）句的前題，這是說凡從事此種暴行的人必須受法院的嚴屬制裁，因此應放在 1）句之前。根據這分析，這段可有二種不同的重組方式，那就是 2）3）1）或 3）1）2），前者是主題句前置，後者是主題句尾置。

解答：

2）Ordinary criminal justice requires that innocence cannot be pleaded in answer to a charge of violence by terrorism. 3）If a person joins a terrorist movement and commits violence, it is no defense that he has done so for a political cause. 1）The sentence ought to be one, not merely of immediate arrest, but of severe punishment. 或

3）If a person joins a terrorist movement and commits violence, it is no defense that he has done so for a political cause. 1）The sentence ought to be one, not merely of immediate arrest, but of severe punishment. 2）Ordinary criminal justice requires that innocence cannot be pleaded in answer to a charge of violence by terrorism.

B）指出本段是用何種型式來伸展文意。

解答：

根據上題的內容分析本段採用的型式是屬直線型。

習題二

1) 分析下段的內容，指出那一句是主題句，安置在何處，用何種方式表達。

A bizarre crime story has come to Canada, but we aren't allowed to tell you. On Monday, Newfoundland Judge Derek Green forbade the media to report on the extradition hearing of Dr. Shirley Turner, a pregnant physician accused of murdering her former lover, the suspected father of her baby. The publication ban is necessary, said the judge, to protect Dr. Turner's right to a fair trial if she is sent back to Pennsylvania, where the victim's body was found.

Does the judge think a Pennsylvania jury would read and be unduly influenced by a Newfoundland news report? Judge Green said that in the information age, anything is possible.

The information age was supposed to facilitate freedom of speech, not be used as an excuse to limit it.

"Muzzled," *Ottawa Citizen* (May 31, 2002), at A14.

解析：

這題也須依上題的方法先作內容分析，然後再來決定何者是主題句。

解答：

主題句是 The information age was supposed to facilitate freedom of speech, not be used as an excuse to limit it. 是尾置，以直陳句表達。

2) 指出本段是用何種型式來伸展文意。

解答：

本段的文意是一氣直寫而成，故屬直線型。

習題三

1）　分析下段的內容，指出那一句是主題句，安置在何處，用何種方
　　式表達。

> Perhaps Mr. Bean is among the organizers of the Jubilee Pageant
> that will parade past Buckingham Palace tomorrow to mark the
> Queen's 50 years on the throne. Certainly somebody must have a
> dark, bizarre sense of humour. How else to explain that the
> procession will be led by 50 Hells Angels?
>
> Murderers? Shippers of cocaine? Perish the thought. These are *nice*
> Hells Angels – respectable ones. Quite different from the scum
> found in Canada and Scandinavia, where scores of bikers have died
> in the Angels' turf wars over the years. This we know because the
> palace has been solemnly assured that none of the riders slated to
> rumble past has a criminal background. Rather, their gleaming
> Harley Davidsons will be a paean to Britain's "cultural diversity,"
> the Jubilee's theme. Right.
>
> And to think the British Monarchy is sometimes accused of being
> out of touch with reality. Preposterous. Too bad Charles Manson
> couldn't get parole for the day.
>
> "Born To Be Wild," *The Globe and Mail* (June 3, 2002), at 14.

解析：

這題也須依第一題的方法先作內容分析再來決定何者為主題句。

解答：

全文的文意在申述為何英女王五十年登基慶典上有 Hells Angels 帶頭
遊行的理由。因此主題句是屬第一段的最後一句，是尾置，用疑問句
表達。

2） 指出本段是用何種型式來伸展文意。

解答：

本段文意分別是用 nice Hells Angels 及 bad Hells Angels 雙重結構來伸展文意，故屬分枝型。

習題四

指出下段是用何種型式來伸展其文意。

1）Since the dawn of history, owls have been the pitiable victims of ignorance and superstition. 2）Hated, despised, and feared by many peoples, only their nocturnal habits have enabled them to survive in company with civilized man. 3）In the minds of mankind they have been leagued with witches and malignant evil spirits, or even have been believed to personify the Evil One. 4）They have been regarded as precursors of sorrow and death, and some savage tribes have been so fixed in the belief that a man will die if an owl alights on the roof of his dwelling and that, it is said, some Indians having actually seen the owl on the roof-tree have pined away and died. 5）Among all these eerie birds, the Barn Owl has been the victim of the greatest share of obloquy and persecution, owing to its sinister appearance, its weird night cries, its habit of haunting dismal swamps and dank quagmires, where an incautious step may precipitate the investigator into malodorous filth or sucking quicksands, and its tendency to frequent the neighborhood of man's dwellings, especially unoccupied buildings and ghostly ruins. 6）Doubtless the Barn Owl is responsible for some of the stories of haunted houses, which have been current through the centuries. 7）When divested by science of its atmosphere of malign mystery, however, this owl is seen to be not only harmless but a benefactor to mankind and a very interesting fowl that will well repay close study.

E.H. Forbush, *Birds of Massachusetts and Other New England States*

解析：

本段的 1）句是主題句，開宗明義指出貓頭鷹是人類無知及迷信的犧牲者。2）3）4）各句申述貓頭鷹之不受人歡迎甚至受到卑視的種種原因（第一號魔鬼的化身，死亡的先兆以及野蠻部族對貓頭鷹的迷信等），5）句另提出屬貓頭鷹同類的倉鴞何以不受歡迎的原因。6）句引申 5）句的文意，7）句說明倉鴞非但不是害鳥而且是益鳥，用反襯的方法與主題句遙相應接，全段的文意可用下圖來表達。

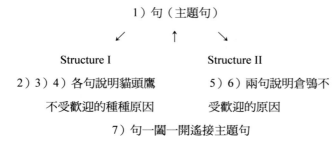

1）句（主題句）

Structure I　　　　　　　Structure II

2）3）4）各句說明貓頭鷹　　5）6）兩句說明倉鴞不
　不受歡迎的種種原因　　　　受歡迎的原因

7）句一闔一開遙接主題句

解答：

本段是用雙重結構來伸展文意，故屬分枝型。

習題五

A）下文來自第 2.2.2 節中的綜合習題一的解答。指出何者為主題句，同時將內容依主題句不同的型式重新組合成一段。

1）In this tiny African country there are a total of two cable TV companies with less than 10 cable channels. 2）Cable TV reaches only 7 percent of the population, which is the lowest anywhere in Africa. 3）The media industry of this tiny African country is almost

non-existent. 4）This tiny African country has 15 magazine publishers that produce 27 titles annually. 5）There are three major book publishers that published over 4000 textbooks last year. 6）This is a figure that falls little short of its total number of students who were enrolled in schools.

解析：

這題須先從內容分析來決定何者為主題句，何者為申述主旨的細節，然後再依主題句的形式重新組合成一段。從文意看，第3）句是主題句，是用直陳句表達，具備簡潔，分明，及切題的要件，而其他各句是申述主旨的細節。根據這分析，這段可有二種不同的重組方式，3）1）2）4）5）6）或 1）2）4）5）6）3），前者是主題句前置，後者是主題句尾置。

解答：

（一）用前置的方法，解答應為：3）The media industry of this tiny African country is almost non-existent. 1）In this tiny African country there are a total of two cable TV companies with less than 10 cable channels. 2）Cable TV reaches only 7 percent of the population, which is the lowest anywhere in Africa. 4）This tiny African country has 15 magazine publishers that produce 27 titles annually. 5）There are three major book publishers that published over 4000 textbooks last year. 6）This is a figure that falls little short of its total number of students who were enrolled in schools.

（二）用後置的方法，解答應為：1）In this tiny African country there are a total of two cable TV companies with less than 10 cable channels. 2）Cable TV reaches only 7 percent of the population, which is the lowest anywhere in Africa. 4）This tiny African country has 15 magazine publishers that produce 27 titles annually. 5）There are three major book publishers that published over 4000 textbooks last year. 6）This is a figure that falls little short of its total number of students who were enrolled in schools. 3）The media industry of this tiny African country is almost non-existent.

補充說明：

這裡尚可用 3.2 中所討論的省略方法使第 6）句變得靈活一些而改寫成 This is a figure that falls little short of its total number of students enrolled in schools. 須注意的是，這二個解答，在聯句的圓通方面尚可有改進的地方，關於這一點，我們將在第 4.2 各節中詳細討論。

B)　指出本段是用何種型式來伸展文意。

解答：

根據上題的內容分析，二個解答的型式多是直線型。

習題六

　　這裡我們要從事一項模擬測驗。選一個您平常感興趣的課題作為「英文引導寫作」的題目。

　　第一步，根據所選的題目，用中文意思寫下一段約 400 字左右的短文，然後根據中文的意思擬出一句全文的主題句，這主題句需符合簡潔，分明及切題的要求，但型式不拘，可採取您認為最恰當的型式來表達。在做下一步之前，請審閱一下全文的內容，凡與主旨無關的意思應予刪除，而意思不完備的地方應加以充實及改正，將這去蕪存菁的中文原稿作為做以下二個步驟的藍圖。

　　第二步，將此中文稿根據以上三章所討論的方法翻成英文，在

中譯英時需注意第一章所著重的遣詞需正確，詞語搭配需恰當及詞序的主從關係，同時每句中文需依第二章所討論的英文基本模式來表達，在這裡不妨儘量考慮使用簡單句（simple sentence），同時也儘量依次元單位的觀念來造句。

　　第三步，依子句連接的觀念，將全文的簡單句依其文意的相互邏輯關係，連接成并列句或複合句，同時在連接時，使用第三章所討論的各種方法來滋潤句子的結構，使句構靈活。

　　這一英文初稿，目前祇要求做到字裡行間用字注意出入，句構妥善及靈活使用的功夫，我們在本章討論完後，再使用各種方法使聯句圓通及文意周密，好使此稿成為一段文意連貫通順及組織完整的短文。

4.2　段落之聯句求圓通

　　根據上面一節，我們將段落看作句子的化身，曉得段落的述詞部分是指鋪陳排比的細節，以不同的句式來舉證例示，比照類推來闡明解釋其主旨。在這寫作過程中須注意的是，每一段的內容在求總義一體（unity）。這可從聯句的「圓通」（flow）及合趣的「周密」（coherence）二點來分析。「圓通」是要求句句相銜，使各句的排列組合相接為用，以求全段文意的連貫有序。「周密」是要求文意與主旨相切（relevance），文意的起承轉合需連貫通順，密不可分，如此才能使全段的結構嚴謹，成為一個完整的整體。我們在本節中先討論聯句的圓通，而合趣的周密將於下節討論。

　　從聯句的圓通而言，其相互排列在求各句的連貫，便於讀者循文生意。如何才能達到這個要求？我們可在文中安排使用各種不同的「路標」（sign posts）使各句承上啟下，鱗次為用。這種路標可通過詞彙的互用，文法上的方法及轉折詞來表達。本節將逐一詳細討論。

4.2.1 詞彙之互用

　　所謂詞彙的相互為用是指文中用意思相同或相通的字彙來組合文句，使上下文成一整體。這種「互文」的方法，通常以「頂針」的修辭法最為普遍。所謂「頂針」是指後句緊承前句，將前句句末的字彙像聯珠一樣當作後句句首的字彙，例如在「青青河邊草，綿綿思遠道，遠道不可思，夙昔夢見之」《古辭，飲馬長城窟行》中的「遠道」即為一例。在英文裡也有這種蟬聯句式的用法，例如在 The military build-up is threatening. The threat may not be alleviated in the near future 二句中的 threatening 及 threat 乃透過詞類的互用以頂針法寫成，使文意自然而又連貫。

　　詞彙的互用並不僅限於頂針的用法，我們另可在文中不同的地方使用詞彙互用來求聯句的圓通。我們不妨再用下段來說明這一點。

1）I was taking a walk in this place last night between the hours of nine and ten, and could not but fancy it one of the most proper places in the world for a ghost to appear in. 2）The ruins of the abbey are scattered up and down on every side, and half covered with ivy and elder-bushes, the harbours of several solitary birds which seldom make their appearance till the dusk of the evening. 3）The place was formerly a churchyard, and has still several marks in it of graves and burying-places. 4）There is such an echo among the old ruins and vaults, that if you stamp out a little louder than ordinary you hear the sound repeated. 5）At the same time the walk of elms, with the croaking of the ravens which from time to time are heard from the tops of them, looks exceedingly solemn and venerable. 6）These objects naturally raise seriousness and attention; 7）and when

night heightens the awfulness of the place, and pours out the supernumerary horrours upon every thing in it, I do not at all wonder that weak minds fill it with spectres and apparitions.

Joseph Addison, The Spectator, No. 110

這一段採用很多詞彙互用的方法，例如表 place 的出現在 1）句及 7）句、2）句的 abbey 及 3）句的 churchyard，表 night 的字眼出現在 1）句及 7）句以及 2）句的 dusk of the evening，而表與 ghost 有關的字眼則分別出現在 1）句及 7）句的 spectres 與 apparitions. 須注意的是，這段包括二種不同的同義字，一是指字義相同，例如 churchyard 及 burying place，另一是指字義相通，例如 ghost, spectre 及 apparition，此三者通常皆指鬼魂，但意義並不完全相同，充其量祇能說字義相通 （spectre 指妖靈而 apparition 指陰靈）。由於每一個字所代表的意義其層次不盡相同，因此在使用同義字時，其意義有相同及相通的二種可能。

使用同義字的好處在於避免連續使用同一字彙，用以增加文中用字的變化，且可藉此來維持各句間的脈絡以求圓通。

詞彙本身意義可有相同及相通的區別外，另可根據所使用的文句來揣摩其意思是否相同。例如：The student representatives were quite vocal in yesterday's meeting. The radical elements on campus proposed a series of demands for immediate action. 在這一段中，第二句中的 the radical elements on campus 是影射第一句中的 student representatives。很明顯的，作者將此二個不同的詞組相提並論，使先後二句文意聯貫在一起。

習題一

下段摘自 R.W. Emerson 的 *English Traits* 一書，是該書第十一章描

寫英國貴族的起段。使用本節所討論的方法，指出此段中各句是
用何種方法相互銜接，使文意聯貫。

1）The feudal character of the English state, now that it is getting
obsolete, glares a little, in contrast with the democratic tendencies.
2）The inequality of power and property shocks republican nerves.
3）Palaces, halls, villas, walled parks, all over England, rival the
splendor of royal seats. 4）Many of the halls, like Haddon or
Kedleston, are beautiful desolations. 5）The proprietor never saw
them, or never lived in them. 6）Primogeniture built these sumptuous
piles, and I suppose it is the sentiment of every traveller, as it was
mine. 7）It was well to come ere these were gone. 8）Primogeniture
is a cardinal rule of English property and institutions. 9）Laws,
customs, manners, the very persons and faces, affirm it.

解析：
縱觀全文，本段2）句中的 inequality of power and property 是用字義
相通的方法述及1）句中的 feudal character。3）句述及各種不同的建
築與封建皇家建築相媲美。4）句舉二個 halls 與3）句相應，這二句
是用字義相同（halls）的方法相銜接。6）句述及由長子負責建造這
種建築物，承接3）4）各句的建築物，而為以下7）8）9）三句作張
本，這三句皆以 Primogeniture 與6）句相銜接，是字義相同的用法。
解答：
本段大致上是用詞彙互用的方法來求聯句的圓通。

習題二
使用本節所討論的方法，指出下段中各句是用何種方法相互銜接，使
文意聯貫。

1）That difficult poems are not popular. This is something that any reader or writer of difficult poems must face squarely. 2）There are no three ways about it. 3）But just because a poem is not popular doesn't mean it has no value! 4）Unpopular poems can still have meaningful readings and, after all, may not always be unpopular. 5）Even if the poem never becomes popular, it can still be special to you, the reader. 6）Maybe the poem's unpopularity will even bring you and the difficult poem closer. 7）After all, your own ability to have an intimate relation with the poem is not affected by the poem's popularity.

Charles Bersteine, "The Difficult Poem," *Harper's* (June 2003),

摘自 http：//epc.buffalo.edu/authors/bernstein/essays/difficult-poem.html

解析：

本段主旨在說明難懂的詩，所以不流行（unpopular）的原因，全段除 2）句外，其他各句皆直接以是否流行來相互銜接，亦即 1）、3）及 4）各句用 not popular 或 unpopular，5）句用 never becomes popular，6）句用 unpopularity，7）句雖用 popularity，但從全句的意思看仍是針對 unpopular 一點而言。

解答：

本段是用字義相同的方法來求文意的聯貫。

習題三

使用本節所討論的方法，指出第 4.2.3 節本文中第 11）例各句是用何種方法相互銜接，使文意聯貫。

解析：

這三句中，第 1）2）句中的 terrorism，2）及 3）句中的 national security 分別意思相同。

解答：

這三句是用字義相同的方法來求文意的聯貫。

習題四

斟酌第 4.1 節習題六的英文初稿，試用本節所討論的方法加以改進。

4.2.2 文法上之各種方法

在文法上有很多方法可使文句相互組合以求圓通，這些方法包括使用指定語（例如 this、these、that、those、the one、the other、the former 及 the latter），代名詞，關係代名詞子句來替代前句中所使用的名詞。例如下段是讚美福特的車子（即 1909 年出廠的 Model T），各句皆用 it 來相互組合。

It was the miracle God had wrought. And it was patently the sort of thing that could only happen once. Mechanically uncanny, it was like nothing that had ever come to the world before. Flourishing industries rose and fell with it. As a vehicle, it was hard-working, commonplace, heroic; and it often seemed to transmit those qualities to the persons who rode in it. My own generation identifies it with youth, with its gaudy, irretrievable excitements ….

Richard L. Strout, *Farewell to Model T*

此外也可用同位語（appositive）使文句組合。我們用下例來作說明。

The suspect, a Chinese American, was released yesterday by the police. The arrest of a Chinese American was a rebuke to members of his family, who called it a case of racial discrimination.

本段中 1）句的 the suspect 與 2）句的 a Chinese American 原屬二個意思完全不同的詞組，但經第一句的同位語的使用，使先後二句相提並論，文意相互呼應。同位語使用的前提是二者須相同或

包容。例如上述 the suspect 及 a Chinese American 二者是屬相同，而在 An out-of-print book, *The Life of Samuel Johnson,* is now available on the market 一句中，*The Life of Samuel Johnson* 是屬於絕版書的一例，因此二者是屬包容。

本書在前面二章中所討論的不同句法，有很多皆可用同位語的觀點來解釋其句構。我們可用下面幾個例子來作說明。

我們在第 3.2.2 節省略的第 VII）模式中曾使用：

A1）An infusion of rhetoric enters into his argument, which is not so apparent in his other writings. 一例來改寫成

A2）An infusion of rhetoric enters into his argument, not so apparent in his other writings.

這句中的 not so apparent in his other writings 是一形容詞片語，以同位語的方法將 A1）句簡化組合而成。而根據第 3.3.5 節的討論，本句是一個非限制性子句經省略而成的一同位語句式。再如在下例：

B1）A popular sport, which is called hunting, becomes his lifelong hobby. 此例可依省略法改寫成

B2）A popular sport, hunting, becomes his lifelong hobby.

這個例子中的 hunting 是使用動名詞以同位語的方法將原句 B1）簡化組合而成。此外，我們在第二章中曉得，關係代名詞子句可用作補語，例如：

C1）The maxim is not well-known that every inch of time has its merit.

　　這句中的 that 子句是用作補語來形容主詞 maxim。本句可用同位語的觀念來改寫如下：

C2）The maxim that every inch of time has its merit is not

well-known. 使原句改寫成一限制性子句的同位語句。

同理，受詞補語也可用同位語的觀念來解釋。例如：

D1）He made the suggestion that she should resign from her post.

這句中的 that 子句是用作受詞補語，實際上是具同位語的作用來表達。

同理，why 子句及不定詞作補語的用法，也可以同位語的觀念來解釋，如下面 E）及 F）兩例所示：

E）The other question, why she flunked the entire course, was not raised.

F）Their goal, to be the top team, has never been realized.

再如在下例中：

G1）The science-technology museum, which is financed by an overseas investor, represents the current state of arts. 我們可根據省略的方法改寫成：

G2）The science-technology museum, financed by an overseas investor, represents the current state of arts. 這句是將過去分詞用同位語的方法，將原句簡化再組而成。在使用這種句法時，不能忽略的是文意是否代表原句的全部意思，這涉及子句省略後的侷限性問題，我們已在 3.2.2 中詳細討論過，不再贅述。

而第 3.1 節中所討論的置換用法，也可以同位語的觀念來解釋句構。例如在上面 G2）例中，我們可將同位語前置來突出其位置，以收加重語氣的功效，如下句所示：

G3）Financed by an overseas investor, the science-technology museum represents the current state of arts.

再如在下例中：

H1）Dr. Smith, a distinguished scientist, will deliver a speech here tonight. 我們可將這句的同位語前置來突顯其文意，而改寫成

H2）A distinguished scientist, Dr. Smith will deliver a speech here tonight. 在此我們不能忽略的一點是，無動詞式其位置的變動性遠較關係代名詞子句為大的問題，關於這一點，我們已在第 3.3.5 節中詳細討論過，不再贅述。

此外，同位語有時也可用非造句的方法來表達，例如用 that is, namely 及破折號。我們下面分別舉二個例子供讀者參考。

I）Cross the street only when traffic permits, that is, traffic light turns green.

J）This bill is intended to legalize a moral code – the code of conduct of those who serve the public. 這裡的破折號是採取同位語的格式來引申解釋 moral code，與第 3.3.6 節中用破折號來加重語氣的用法有所不同。

我們使用了同位語的觀念來融會貫通以上二章所討論的若干句構，希望透過這樣的了解，不但能協助讀者懂得如何用同位語使文句圓通，同時也使讀者掌握各種句構的變化及其相互之間的關係，以利應試時表達靈活使用英文文句的能力。

習題一

將下面二句譯成英文。

二條受傷的鯨魚在水面上掙扎，這掙扎將會持續一會兒。

解析：

這二句是使用詞彙互用的方法來成段。用 struggle 表「掙扎」，在第一句中當動詞用，在第二句中當名詞用，用片語 for a while 表

「一會兒」。

解答：

Both wounded whales are struggling on the surface. The struggle will last for a while.

習題二

1) 將下句譯成英文。

文學院語文教授湯笙先生曾參與本校的改組計劃，他反對所提出的改革方案。

解析：

這一句實際上有三個基本意思構成，分別是 a）湯笙先生是文學院的語文教授，b）湯笙先生曾參與本校的改組，c）湯笙先生反對所提出的改革方案。在 a）句中用 Faculty of Arts 表「文學院」，用片語 language professor 表「語文教授」。在 b）句中用 participate 表「參與」，注意其後需與 in 相搭配。用片語 the planning of our university's reorganization 表「本校的改組計劃」。在 c）句中用 be opposed 表「反對」。注意 opposed 是形容詞非表被動語態，且其後需與 to 相搭配。用片語 a proposed reform policy 表「被提出的改革方案」。這三個基本意思可用三個簡單英文句來表達如下：

a) Mr. Thomson is a language professor of the Faculty of Arts.

b) Mr. Thomson once participated in the planning of our university's reorganization.

c) Mr. Thomson is opposed to the proposed reform policy.

解答：

這三句意思相關，故可根據子句連接的方法，用 who 子句改寫成一複合句如下：

Mr. Thomson, who is a language professor of the Faculty of Arts and who

once participated in the planning of our university's reorganization, is opposed to the proposed reform policy.

2) 將上句用同位語改寫。

解析：

將上句的 who is a language professor of the Faculty of Arts 用省略法改寫成一無動詞式作同位語用。

解答：

Mr. Thomson, a language professor of the Faculty of Arts, who once participated in the planning of our university's reorganization, is opposed to the proposed reform policy.

習題三

1) 將下句譯成英文。

湯笙是位學者，現年 60 歲，現在加州，曾肄業於一所由天主教教會所資助的大學。

解析：

這一句實際上是有五個基本意思構成，分別是 a）湯笙是位學者，b）湯笙現年 60 歲，c）湯笙現在加州，d）湯笙曾肄業於一所大學，及 e）該大學受天主教教會的資助。在 e）句中用 Catholic church 表「天主教教會」，用 fund 表「資助」，這裡 fund 當動詞用。這五個基本意思可用五個簡單英文句來表達如下：

a) Thomson is a scholar.

b) Thomson is now 60 years old.

c) Thomson is now in California.

d) Thomson was educated in a university.

e) The university is funded by a Catholic church.

解答：

這五個句子的意思相關，故可根據子句連接的方法，用 who 及 that 子句改寫成一複合句如下：

Thomson, who is now 60 years old and who is now in California, is a scholar who was educated in a university that is funded by a Catholic church.

2)　將上句用同位語改寫。

解析：

上句寫得很笨拙，我們可以將 who is now 60 years old and who is now in California 用省略法改寫成一無動詞式作同位語用，同時 who was educated 及 that is funded by a Catholic church 也可分別用省略法改寫。

解答：

Thomson, now 60 years old and in California, is a scholar educated in a university funded by a Catholic church.

習題四

1)　將下句譯成英文。

　　湯笙從前是位程式工程師，現在是位中學老師。

解析：

這一句實際上是有二個基本意思構成，分別是 a）湯笙從前是位程式工程師，及 b）湯笙現在是位中學老師。在 a）句中，用 programmer 表「程式工程師」。在 b）句中，用片語 high school teacher 表「中學老師」。這二個基本意思可用二個簡單英文句來表達如下：

a)　Thomson was previously a programmer.

b)　Thomson is now a high school teacher.

解答：

這二句意思相關，故可根據子句連接的方法，用 who 子句改寫成一複合句如下：

Thomson, who was previously a programmer, is now a high school teacher.

2) 將上句用同位語改寫。

解析：

將上句的 who 子句用省略法改寫成一無動詞式作同位語用。

解答：

Thomson, previously a programmer, is now a high school teacher.

習題五

1) 將下句譯成英文。

受選民排斥的湯笙移居國外，與一群環保者一起合作。

解析：

這一句實際上有三個基本意思構成，分別是 a）湯笙受選民的排斥，b）湯笙移居國外，及 c）湯笙與一群環保者一起合作。在 a）句中，用 reject 表「排斥」。在 b）句中，用 overseas 表「國外」。在 c）句中，用 environmentalist 表「環保者」，用 align 表「合作」，注意，其後須與 himself 及 with 相搭配。這三個基本意思可用三個簡單英文句來表達如下：

a) Thomson was rejected by the voters.

b) Thomson moved to overseas.

c) Thomson aligned himself with a group of environmentalists.

解答：

這三句意思相關，故可根據子句連接的方法，用 who 子句改寫成一複合句如下：

Thomson, who was rejected by the voters, moved to overseas and aligned himself with a group of environmentalists.

2) 將上句用同位語改寫。

解析：

將上句的 who 子句用省略法改寫成一無動詞式作同位語用。

解答：

Thomson, rejected by the voters, moved to overseas and aligned himself with a group of environmentalists.

3)　將上句用置換方法改寫。

解析：

參照 H2）例來做。

解答：

Rejected by the voters, Thomson moved to overseas and aligned himself with a group of environmentalists.

習題六

將下句譯成英文。

由於其燦爛的山河景色，臺灣曾被稱為 Formosa，一個美麗的島嶼。

解析：

本句需依 J）例用破折號來解釋 Formosa 一字的意思。用 lustrous 與 landscape 相搭配表「燦爛的山河景色」。

解答：

Due to its lustrous landscape Taiwan was once called Formosa – a beautiful island.

習題七

將下句譯成英文。

中國的詩淵遠流長溯自《詩經》。

解析：

本句需用破折號來解釋文中的「淵遠」乃指《詩經》。用 trace 表「溯自」，注意在此意思下，需與 back to 相搭配 （to trace back to），用

distant 與 origin 相搭配表「淵遠」，用片語 long course 表「流長」，用 The Book of Songs 表《詩經》。

解答：

Chinese poetry traces a long course back to a distant origin – The Book of Songs.

習題八

將下句譯成英文。

在病人的桌上有三束花，一束是他母親送的水仙花，一束是他太太送的鬱金香，另一束是他女兒送的紅玫瑰花。

解析：

本句需使用破折號來解釋三束屬那一類的花，可依 J) 例來做。用 atop 表「（桌）上」當系詞用，片語 a bouquet of flowers 表「一束花」，用 lily 表「水仙花」，用 tulip 表「鬱金香」。

解答：

There are three bouquets of flowers atop the patient's desk – lilies from his mother, tulips from his wife, and red roses from his daughter.

補充說明：

這裡破折號是用來解釋何種花束，為了使破折號與 bouquets of flowers 相近以便解釋起見，應用置換的方法將本句改寫成 Atop the patient's desk are three bouquets of flowers – lilies from his mother, tulips from his wife, and red roses from his daughter.

習題九

將下句譯成英文。

不僅家長對新政策有所質疑，即使在教育界第一線服務的老師也有所保留。

解析：

這一句實際上有二個基本意思構成，分別是 a）不僅家長對新政策有所質疑，及 b）即使在教育界第一線服務的老師也有所保留。在 a）句中，用 skeptical 表「質疑」，其後需與 about 相搭配。注意本句的語氣，「家長」是指對「新政策有所質疑」人士中的一部分，因此本句需用 who 子句成句。在 b）句中，用片語 on the front lines of education 表「在教育界第一線服務」。注意這裡「老師」是指在「教育界第一線服務」的工作者，用破折號來成句比較容易。用 reservation 表「保留」。這二個基本意思可用二個簡單英文句來表達如下：

a) Parents are not the only ones who are skeptical about the new policy.

b) Even those workers who are on the front lines of education – the teachers – have reservations as well.

解答：

這二句意思相關，故可根據子句連接的方法改寫成一并列句如下：

Parents are not the only ones who are skeptical about the new policy, and even those who are on the front lines of education – the teachers – have reservations as well.

補充說明：

這裡可使用省略法將本句另改寫成 Parents are not the only ones skeptical about the new policy, and even those on the front lines of education – the teachers – have reservations as well.

習題十

A) 下面一段來自第 2.2.2 節中綜合習題之二的解答，指出主題句何在及文意的伸展是採用何種方法。

1）In a shootout police gunned down a male suspect. 2）A male leaped from his car. 3）A man tried to flee along a highway. 4）A man

fired at his pursuers with a carbine. 5）The incident sent other drivers diving under their dashboards for cover. 6）The incident spanned two bedroom communities. 7）The incident started about 5 p.m. and was over by 6 p.m. 8）The incident left the highway strewn with bullet casings.

解析：

從文意及段落的型式來著手作內容分析。

解答：

在這一段中，每一句皆循著一個隱藏的主旨在那裡鋪陳描寫公路上的槍戰情景。其文意的伸展是採用直線型的方式，從警察射死男嫌疑犯開始，步步敘述槍戰的經過及結果。

B） 將上面一段用第 3.2 節及本節所討論的方法來改進。

解析：

第 1）至 4）句的意思是相連貫的，其中 2）至 4）句的意思是發生在 1）句之後，因此可置 after 於 1）句之後與 2）至 4）句相連結，而 2）至 4）句的「跳下」、「逃」及「開火」是三個連續的動作，我們可將這三句暫時用並列句合併如下， 1）In a shootout police gunned down a male suspect after 2）a man leaped from his car and 3）a man tried to flee along a highway and 4）a man fired at his pursuers with a carbine. 上句 2）句中的 a man 應用代名詞 he 來替代，同時 3）及 4）句中的 a man 應省略，使此句改寫成 1）In a shootout police gunned down a male suspect after 2）he leaped from his car and 3）tried to flee along a highway and 4）fired at his pursuers with a carbine. 這裡「開火」的動作是與「逃」同時發生的，故可用 while 子句來重寫成 1）In a shootout police gunned down a male suspect after 2）he leaped from his car and 3）tried to flee along a highway, 4）while he was firing at his pursuers with a carbine. 而

這句又可依省略第 II）模式改寫成 1）In a shootout police gunned down a male suspect after 2）he leaped from his car and 3）tried to flee along a highway, 4）while firing at his pursuers with a carbine. 同時也可以考慮用修飾語 at the same time 來加強表示「同時發生的意思」，使此句再改寫成 1）In a shootout police gunned down a male suspect after 2）he leaped from his car and 3）tried to flee along a highway, 4）while at the same time firing at his pursuers with a carbine. 同時 5）及 6）二單獨句可用 which 子句合併成一複合句，使改寫成 The incident, 5）which sent other drivers diving under their dashboards for cover, 6）spanned two bedroom communities. 同理，7）與 8）二句可合併成一句，並且將其中 8）句的 the incident 省略，改寫成 7）The incident started about 5 p.m. and was over by 6 p.m. 8）and left the highway strewn with bullet casings. 而此句又可依第 2.1.3.5 節的 D）例改寫，以及將主詞 incident 用代名詞 it 來替代，使全句改寫成 7）It started about 5 p.m. and was over by 6 p.m., 8）leaving the highway strewn with bullet casings.

修正後的全文應是：

1）In a shootout police gunned down a male suspect after 2）he leaped from his car and 3）tried to flee along a highway, 4）while at the same time firing at his pursuers with a carbine. The incident, 5）which sent other drivers diving under their dashboards for cover, 6）spanned two bedroom communities, 7）It started about 5 p.m. and was over by 6 p.m. , 8）leaving the highway strewn with bullet casings.

習題十一

斟酌第 4.1 節習題六的英文初稿，試用本節所討論的方法加以改進。

4.2.3 轉折詞之使用

　　英文中有很多副詞，常用在句首來轉折組合文句，使各句的相互連接顯得靈活及自然。這種轉折詞（亦稱承轉詞）具路標的功用，來導引讀者了解全文的內容使文意通順。下面我們分別列舉幾種常用的轉折詞及其用法，供讀者平時參考使用。

1) 表與前句有緣由（reason）的關係： after all, for.

　　例如： The very truth of his arguments is not quite true. After all every sophistry must face truth.

2) 表與前句有結果（consequence）的關係： accordingly, as a result, consequently, hence, so, therefore, thus.

　　例如： They were born in Taiwan and raised in North America. Hence, they are the descendants of Taiwanese migrants to North America.

3) 表與前句有相同（similarity）或相異（comparison）的關係：by comparison, by the same token, likewise, similarly.

　　例如： Parents are models for children at home. By the same token, teachers are exemplars for students in school.

4) 表與前句有對照（contrast）的關係：but, conversely, however, in contrast, instead, nevertheless, on the contrary, on the other hand, though, yet.

　　例如： Philosophers are seekers after truth. On the contrary, politicians are impatient of restraint by any creed.

5) 表與前句文意有限制（qualification）的關係：admittedly, certainly, no doubt, of course, obviously.

　　例如： A person's fortune is knowledge and virtue. Obviously,

wealth and credit are not signs of fortune.

6）　表與前句文意有引申（addition）的關係： also, and, besides, furthermore, in addition, moreover.

例如： Vanity enslaves us to pomposity. And it makes us contemptible to modesty.

7）　表與前句文意有重複（repetition）的關係：at any rate, in any case, in any event, in other words, in this sense.

例如： If discussed frankly, the question could be easily solved without difficulty. In this sense negotiation is better than confrontation.

8）　表與前句文意有總結（conclusion）的關係： finally, in brief, in conclusion, in short, in summary, lastly, to conclude, to sum up, then.

例如： Our goal was at last achieved through fearless sacrifice and countless dangers. Let's, then, remember the lessons learned.

9）　表與前句有時間（temporal relationship）的關係：at the same time, before, later on, meanwhile, presently, subsequently, till now.

例如： The court's decision is not binding on foreigners, At the same time, however, it might have a persuasive effect.

10）　表列舉（exemplification）的關係： as a case in point, for example, for instance.

例如：The new manager does not know his priorities. For example, he plans to write a user's manual first and a monthly report next.

11）　表與前句有一系列（series）的關係： finally/lastly, for one thing/for another（thing）, in the first place/in the second （place）/etc., the first/the second/etc., the former/the latter, the one/the

other.

例如： Why should states make war on terrorism? For one thing, terrorism could accomplish the destruction of ordinary communities that can fatally disturb the security of an entire nation. For another, national security is the means through which individual citizens achieve fundamental freedom.

12） 表回到原題（return to the point）的關係： at any rate, in any case, in any event.

例如： Her father has been in poor health for a while. At any rate she often prepares her sick father for the worst.

13） 表離題（digression）的關係： by the way, incidentally, now, so far, thus far, turning to.

例如： In the beginning of this century we witnessed the tragic destruction of the Twin Towers, shaking the City of New York to its core. Since then, messianic terrorists have become more powerful by their use of weapons of destruction, threatening the safety of every ordinary people all around the world. By the way Muslim extremists bent on self-sacrifice with a religious cause even become themselves suicide bombers.

　　須注意的是，轉折詞的使用應依文意而定，不宜濫用以免流於形式。求聯句圓通的幾種常用的方法已如上述，我們平常在作文時如能多注意練習，久而久之就能養成使用這種技巧的習慣，那末在應試時對如何求聯句圓通一點自能應付自如。

習題一
細讀下段原文，指出作者用何種方法使文句銜接。

1）'What is Truth?' said jesting Pilate; and would not stay for an answer. 2）Certainly there be that delight in giddiness, and count it a bondage to fix a belief; affecting free-will in thinking, as well as in acting. 3）And though the sects of philosophers of that kind be gone, yet there remain certain discoursing wits which are of the same veins, though there be not so much blood in them as was in those of the ancients. 4）But it is not only the difficulty and labour which men take in finding out of truth; nor again that when it is found it imposeth upon men's thoughts; that doth bring lies in favour; but a natural though corrupt love of the lie itself. 5）One of the later school of the Grecians examineth the matter, and is at a stand to think what should be in it, that men should love lies, where neither they make for pleasure, as with poets, nor for advantage, as with the merchant; but for the lie's sake. 6）But I cannot tell：this same truth is a naked and open daylight, that doth not shew the masks and mummeries and triumphs of the world, half so stately and daintily as candlelights.

Sir Francis Bacon, Of Truth

解答：

本段有四處用轉折詞來銜接文句，即 2）句用 certainly, 3）句用 and，4）句及 6）句用 but。

習題二

1）　將下句譯成英文。

政府原先打算五年內投入二十億美金設立一研究基金。

解析：

用 set 與 aside 相搭配表「投入」，用 set 與 up 相搭配表「設立」，用片語 research fund 表「研究基金」。

解答：

The government originally planned to set aside U.S. $2 billion over a period of five years to set up a research fund.

2） 將下句譯成英文。

今年預算祇編列了五千萬美金。

解析：

用 earmark 表「編列」。

解答：

Only U.S. $50 million has been earmarked for this year's budget.

補充說明：

這裡也可用 allocate 表「編列」。注意，英文的 one million 等於中文的一百萬，中文的一億是英文的 100 million, 而英文的 one billion（美制）等於中文的十億。此外，U.S. $50 million 是指一個整數故動詞用單數。

3） 將下句譯成英文。

這數目與原來所編列的數目相差有天壤之別。

解析：

用 far 與 cry 相搭配表「相差有天壤之別」，其後另需與 from 相搭配（a far cry from）。

解答：

This figure is a far cry from the amount originally allocated.

補充說明：

這裡也可用 far short of 表「相差有天壤之別」，而將這句翻成 This figure is far short of the amount originally allocated.

4） 將 2）及 3）二句連接成一句表以下文意。

今年預算祇編列了五千萬美金，這數目與原來所編列的數目相差有天壤之別。

解析：

從句構看，「這數目與原來所編列的數目…」需用 which 子句來成句，故本句屬一複合句。

解答：

Only U.S. $50 million has been earmarked for this year's budget, which is a far cry from the amount originally allocated.

5）　將上句用第 4.2.2 節中同位語的觀念來改寫。

解析：

仿傚該節 A1）例來做。

解答：

Only U.S. $50 million has been earmarked for this year's budget, a far cry from the amount originally allocated.

6）　將 1）及 5）二句用適當的轉折詞來銜接成一小段，表以下文意。政府原先打算五年內投入二十億美金設立一研究基金。但今年預算祇編列了五千萬美金，這數目與原來所編列的數目相差有天壤之別。

解析：

根據本節所列舉的各種轉折詞中，此處可用 however（表對照）來銜接。

解答：

The government originally planned to set aside U.S. $2 billion over a period of five years to set up a research fund. However, only U.S. $50 million has been earmarked for this year's budget, a far cry from the amount originally allocated.

補充說明：

這裡也可根據第 3.3.6 節中所討論的方法，用破折號來加重「這數目

與原來所編列的數目相差有天壤之別」的語氣，而將這段改翻成 The government originally planned to set aside U.S. $2 billion over a period of five years to set up a research fund. However, only U.S. $50 million has been earmarked for this year's budget – a far cry from the amount originally allocated.

習題三

1) 將下面二句分別譯成英文。

老師們永遠善盡其職責。老師們的確值得我們最高的推崇及衷心的感念。

解析：

在第一句中，用 fulfill 表「善盡」。 在第二句中，用 deserve 表「值得」，注意「的確值得」是加重語氣，因此需用 do deserve 來表達，用片語 highest praise 表「最高的推崇」，用 heartfelt 與 honor 相搭配表「衷心的感念」。

解答：

Teachers always fulfill their duties. Teachers do deserve our highest praise and heartfelt honor.

2) 將上述二句用適當的轉折詞來銜接成一小段。

解析：

根據本節所列舉的各種轉折詞中，此處可用 therefore（表結果）來銜接。

解答：

Teachers always fulfill their duties. Therefore they do deserve our highest praise and heartfelt honor.

補充說明：

這裡根據第 4.2.2 節的方法，以 they 取代 teachers.

習題四

1） 將下面三句分別譯成英文。

罷工者寧願與政府對抗而不願協商。到市中心的路被堵塞了。
警察驅散示威者，使該地區較前寧靜。

解析：

在第一句中，用 confront 表「對抗」，用 negotiate 表「協商」，其
後需與 with 相搭配，用 rather...than 表「寧願」。在第二句中，用
片語 leading to downtown 表「到市中心」。在第三句中，用 disperse
表「驅散」，用 demonstrator 表「示威者」。

解答：

The strikers would rather confront than negotiate with the government.
The road leading to downtown was blocked. The police dispersed the
demonstrators, making the area quieter.

2） 將上述三句用適當的轉折詞來銜接成一小段。

解析：

本段第二句是第一句的結果，在本節所列舉的各種轉折詞中，可選用
as a result, 而第三句在時間上較第二句為後，故可用 later on 來銜接。

解答：

The strikers would rather confront than negotiate with the government.
As a result, the road leading to downtown was blocked. Later on the
police dispersed the demonstrators, making the area quieter.

習題五

1） 將下面二句分別譯成英文。

幹行政的難題是在滿足不同的要求。而真正的考驗在於綜合不
同的意見。

解析：

中高級作文指南

在第一句中，以 difficult 與 issue 相搭配表「難題」。在第二句中，用 challenge 表「考驗」，用 synthesize 表「綜合」。二句不妨用動名詞作主詞補語來成句。

解答：

The difficult issue of an administrator is satisfying different demands. His real challenge is synthesizing different views.

補充說明：

此處「滿足...要求」也可用 meet 與 demand 相搭配，而將這句改翻成 The difficult issue of an administrator is meeting different demands。

2） 將上述二句用適當的轉折詞來銜接成一小段。

解析：

根據本節所列舉的各種轉折詞中，此處可用 however（表對照）來銜接。

解答：

The difficult issue of an administrator is satisfying different demands. However, his real challenge is synthesizing different views.

習題六

1） 將下面二句分別譯成英文。

孩子們雀躍的與他們的雙親重逢。孩子們從一門跑出又從另一門跑進。

解析：

在第一句中，用 jubilant 表「雀躍的」。 在第二句中，用片語 run out of 表「跑出」，用片語 run in through 表「跑進」。注意此處 run 與不同系詞搭配所表達的不同意思。

解答：

Children were jubilant to see their parents again. Children ran out of one door as they ran in through the other (door).

補充說明：

這裡「雀躍」也可用動詞 enthuse 來表達，其後須與系詞 over 相搭配，將這句改翻成 Children enthused over seeing their parents again. 此外，當 as 用作表時間的連接詞時，其前不加逗點，如本句所示，但當 as 用作表緣由的連接詞時，其前需加逗點，例如 John won't be here, as he wasn't invited.

2）　將上述二句用適當的轉折詞來銜接成一小段。

解析：

根據本節所列舉的各種轉折詞中，此處可用 meanwhile（表時間關係）來銜接。

解答：

Children were jubilant to see their parents again. Meanwhile, they ran out of one door as they ran in through the other (door).

補充說明：

這裡根據第 4.2.2 節的方法，以 they 取代 children。注意，meanwhile 與 meantime 意思同，但在用作修飾語時，通常 meanwhile 較常用，如本例所示。但當名詞用時，通常 meantime 較常用，例如： In the meantime let us pray for her safe return.

習題七

1）　將下面二句分別譯成英文。

一旦開始談判，就該表露你的意圖。一旦進入談判，你該表達和解的意願。

解析：

在第一句中，用 intention 表「意圖」。在第二句中，用 enter 表「進入」，注意其後需與 into 相搭配，用 compromise 表「和解」，用 willingness

表「意願」。

解答：

Once you start to negotiate, you should signal your intention. Once you enter into a negotiation, you should show your willingness to compromise.

2） 將上述二句用適當的轉折詞來銜接成一小段。

解析：

根據本節所列舉的各種轉折詞中，此處可用 in other words（表重複）來銜接。

解答：

Once you start to negotiate, you should signal your intention. In other words, once you enter into a negotiation, you should show your willingness to compromise.

習題八

1） 將下句翻成英文。

無奈近幾年來政府財政拮据。

解析：

用片語 to keep a tight hold on one's purse strings 表「財政拮据」。

解答：

Unfortunately, over the recent years the government has kept a tight hold on its purse strings.

2） 將下句翻成英文。

各研究機構所提出的新研究項目深受注意而鮮有實惠。

解析：

用片語 research project 表「研究項目」，用片語 little in the way of real benefits 表「鮮有實惠」。

解答：

New research projects proposed by research institutes have received plenty of attention but little in the way of real benefits.

3）　將 1）及 2）二句用適當的轉折詞來銜接成一小段，表以下文意。無奈幾近年來政府財政拮据。結果使各研究機構所提出的新研究項目深受注意而鮮有實惠。

解析：

根據本節所列舉的各種轉折詞中，此處可用 as a result（表結果）來銜接。

解答：

Unfortunately, over the recent years the government has kept a tight hold on its purse strings. As a result, new research projects proposed by research institutes have received plenty of attention but little in the way of real benefits.

習題九

1）　將下面二句分別譯成英文。

制定於 1913 年的德國公民法是基於血統。在加拿大出生及長大的孩子將不會有困難成為加拿大公民，縱使他們的雙親不是加拿大人。

解析：

在第一句中，用 enact 表「制定」，用片語 citizenship law 表「公民法」，用 base 表「基於」，其後需與 on 相搭配，用片語 blood ancestry 表「血統」。從句構看，「制定於 1913 年的德國公民法」需用 that 子句來成句。在第二句中，用 raise 表「長大」，從句構看，「在加拿大出生及長大的孩子」需用 who 子句來成句。

解答：

Germany's citizenship law that was enacted in 1913 was based on blood ancestry. Children who were born and raised in Canada will have no difficulty becoming Canadian citizens even if their parents are not Canadians.

補充說明：

注意，以上二句也可用省略法改寫成 Germany's citizenship law enacted in 1913 was based on blood ancestry. Children born and raised in Canada will have no difficulty becoming Canadian citizens even if their parents are not Canadians. 又，bear 的過去分詞有二，即 born 及 borne，前者僅用於被動式，指「出生」的意思，如本例所示。後者則使用在自動式，其意思不限於「出生」的意思，例如： She has borne four children（她已生育四個孩子）或 We have borne his insolence for a while （我們對他的無禮容忍已久）。

2） 將上述二句用適當的轉折詞來銜接成一小段。

解析：

根據本節所列舉的各種轉折詞中，此處可用 by comparison（表相異）來銜接。

解答：

Germany's citizenship law enacted in 1913 was based on blood ancestry. By comparison, children born and raised in Canada will have no difficulty becoming Canadian citizens even if their parents are not Canadians.

習題十

斟酌第 4.1 節習題六的英文初稿，試用本節所討論的方法加以改進。到此為止，英文初稿經使用各種聯句圓通的方法來改進，相信與初稿相比，這第二稿必定有很多改良的地方，讀者不妨朗讀此

兩稿的內容，相信不難發現那一稿比較通順易解，不過這第二稿尚需經過合趣周密的方法來改進才能定稿，關於這一點，我們將於下節討論。

4.3　段落之合趣求周密

我們在第 4.2 節起段中指出，周密是在求文意與主旨相切，且其轉承起合需連貫通順，密不可分。在本節中，我們進一步討論如何使用不同的周密方法來控引情理，使全段的文意脈絡貫通，構成一嚴謹的整體。

4.3.1　前因後果

段落闡明及解釋內容的方法很多，其中之一是從因果的觀點來伸展文意，這種觀點包括邏輯上的因果關係，時間先後的因果關係，以及不同重要性的因果關係。不論採用何種方式，皆本著「設問舉答」的態度來進行。我們用下段有關報導教宗對世界各地不安的看法來說明。

> Pope Benedict XVI, in analyzing what caused terrorism, said in the Vatican's annual review of world conflicts that "consideration should be given not only to its political and social causes, but also to its deeper cultural religious and ideological motivation." Pope Benedict also issued a warning about fundamentalism. "Religious fanaticism, today often labeled fundamentalism, can inspire and encourage terrorist thinking and activity," he said.
>
> *The Ottawa Citizen* (December 14, 2005), at A13.

這段短文提出導致恐怖主義的不同的原因，分別是政治、社會以及意識形態的動機，文意的細節是循不同的原因逐一安排成段。

習題一

指出下段中何者為因，何者為果，同時指出其前因後果是如何安排的。

　　It has been a tough year for car dealers in North America. Poor interior design, rising labor costs and soaring gasoline price all have made much more difficult to turn a car dealership into profit. In addition, foreign models have proven a tough competitor for potential buyers, and many of the well-known makes, such as GM Oldsmobile, have failed in the contest.

解析：

先從文意來分析何者為主題句，何者為細節，然後從這分析中找出何者為因何者為果。

解答：

本段起句是主題句表結果，其他各句是說明此結果的原因，各原因依相等重要性作平行的安排成段。

補充解釋：

Prove 的過去分詞有二，即 proved 及 proven，此處也能用 proved. 但在當形容詞用時，通常是用 proven 而不用 proved，例如： a proven authority on criminology.

習題二

將下段譯成英文，同時指出何者為因何者為果，以及前因後果是如何安排的。

1）2003 年四月二十三日，世界國際衛生組織頒佈了一份旅遊警示，這份旅遊警示要求人們除必要的旅行外，應避免 Toronto 市。2）這造成幾乎無法使大家前往 Toronto 旅遊，而夏季到 Toronto 的旅遊預約減少到百分之五十。3）該市失業的增加及航空交通的減少歸因於由「嚴重急性呼吸道症候群」所引起的經濟損失。4）幾家大航空公司

宣告幾項措施來應付被「嚴重急性呼吸道症候群」所猖肆的旅遊事業,差一點要宣佈破產。 5)這旅遊警示強調預防措施的重要,對加拿大的金融中心卻造成可怕的經濟損害。

解析:

本題應從二個步驟來做。先是中翻英,再從內容分析全段主旨是什麼,然後再從細節中分明何者為因何者為果,以及因果關係是如何安排的。

第一步 中翻英

1) 2003 年四月二十三日,世界國際衛生組織頒佈了一份旅遊警示,這份旅遊警示要求人們除必要的旅行外,應避免 Toronto 市。

解析:

用片語 travel advisory 表「旅遊警示」,片語 essential trip 表 「必要的旅行」,用片語 steer clear 表「避免」,注意其後需與 of 相搭配。從句構看、「這份旅遊警示」需用 that 子句來成句。

解答:

On April 23, 2003, the World Health Organization issued a travel advisory that warned people to steer clear of Toronto for all but essential trips.

2) 這造成幾乎無法使大家前往 Toronto 旅遊,而夏季到 Toronto 的旅遊預約減少到百分之五十。

解析:

用 booking 表「預約」,用 cut 表「減少」。從句構看,原句用「而」,故需用并列句來成句。

解答:

Getting people to travel to Toronto was made almost impossible and summer bookings for tourism to Toronto were cut by up to 50 percent.

補充說明：

這裡也可用 reduce 表「減少」。

3）該市失業的增加及航空交通的減少歸因於由「嚴重急性呼吸道症候群」所引起的經濟損失。

解析：

用片語 air traffic 表「航空交通」，用 blame 表「歸因」，用片語 severe acute respiratory syndrome （簡稱 SARS）表「嚴重急性呼吸道症候群」。

解答：

The SARS-induced economic loss in the city was blamed for the rise in unemployment and drop in air traffic.

4）幾家大航空公司宣告幾項措施來應付被「嚴重急性呼吸道症候群」所癱瘓的旅遊事業，差一點要宣佈破產。

解析：

用 combat 表「應付」，用 savage 表「癱瘓」，用片語 stop short 表「差一點」，其後需與 of 相搭配（stop short of）。從句構看，原句是由「航空公司宣告幾項措施…」以及「差一點宣佈破產」二個主要的意思構成。

解答：

A few major airlines announced several measures to combat the SARS-savaged tourism and stopped short of declaring bankruptcy.

5）這旅遊警示強調預防措施的重要，對加拿大的金融中心卻造成可怕的經濟損害。

解析：

用 underscore 表「強調」，用 preventive 與 measure 相搭配表「預防措施」，用 wreak 與 havoc 相搭配表「造成損害」。

解答：

The travel advisory underscored the importance of preventive measures and wreaked a dreadful economic havoc in Canada's financial capital.

補充說明：

這裡也可用 emphasize 表「強調」。此外，wreak havoc 偶而也可用 work havoc 來表達，但如用在過去式時，不應用 wrought havoc。

第二步　段意分析

根據第一步的譯文，全段初步解答如下：

1）On April 23, 2003, the World Health Organization issued a travel advisory that warned people to steer clear of Toronto for all but essential trips. 2）Getting people to travel to Toronto was made almost impossible and summer bookings for tourism to Toronto were cut by up to 50 percent. 3）The SARS-induced economic loss in the city was blamed for the rise in unemployment and drop in air traffic. 4）A few major airlines announced several measures to combat the SARS-savaged tourism and stopped short of declaring bankruptcy. 5）The travel advisory underscored the importance of preventive measures and wreaked a dreadful economic havoc in Canada's financial capital.

解答：

本段 5）句的[The travel advisory] wreaked a dreadful economic havoc in Canada's financial capital. 為全段的結果，起因是「世衛」的旅遊警示，因此對 Toronto 產生一連串的影響，諸如往 Toronto 旅遊銳減，失業的增加及航空交通的減少，導致觀光業及航空業的萎縮，這些皆是嚴重打擊 Toronto 經濟的原因。全段依時間的先後次序，用直線型的段落型式寫成。

上面初步的解答，另可從句構的靈活及聯句的圓通二方面來改善。1）

句可用省略的第 IV）模式改寫成 On April 23, 2003, the World Health Organization issued a travel advisory warning people to steer clear of Toronto for all but essential trips. 2）句是 1）句的結果之一，故可用轉折詞 as a result 使聯句圓通，而改寫成 As a result, getting people to travel to Toronto was made almost impossible and summer bookings for tourism to Toronto were cut by up to 50 percent. 4）句可使用省略法，將限定子句變成非限定子句而改寫成 A few major airlines, announcing several measures to combat the SARS-savaged tourism, stopped short of declaring bankruptcy. 5）句中的[The travel advisory] wreaked a dreadful economic havoc in Canada's financial capital 實際上是全段的結果，為特出此結果起見，不妨將此句改寫成一複合句，使此子句當作主句，而將 The travel advisory underscored the importance of preventive measures 當作副句。同時全段祇有這樣一個 travel advisory，因此不妨在此將其簡寫成 the advisory，由是，全句可改寫成 While the advisory underscored the importance of preventive measures, it wreaked a dreadful economic havoc in Canada's financial capital.

根據以上各點，修正後的解答應是：

1）On April 23, 2003, the World Health Organization issued a travel advisory warning people to steer clear of Toronto for all but essential trips. 2）As a result, getting people to travel to Toronto was made almost impossible and summer bookings for tourism to Toronto was cut by up to 50 percent. 3）The SARS-induced economic loss in the city was blamed for the rise in unemployment and drop in air traffic. 4）A few major airlines, announcing several measures to combat the SARS-savaged tourism, stopped short of declaring bankruptcy. 5）While the advisory underscored the importance of preventive measures, it wreaked a dreadful

330

economic havoc in Canada's financial capital.

習題三

將下段譯成英文，同時指出本段何者為因何者為果，以及根據前因後果的關係將本段重新安排。

1）資訊竊盜成為娛樂產業最頭痛的事。2）在資訊經濟中，盜印的猖獗使數位內容變得一文不值。3）盜印之所以猖獗是因為一個地下光碟工廠一年能大量生產上百萬的盜製光碟。4）據報導，任何一套熱賣遊戲皆淪為盜版的市場。5）這樣使原發行者的利潤大幅縮水。

解析：

本題應從二個步驟來做。先是中翻英，再從內容分析全段主旨何在，然後從細節中分別何者為因何者為果，最後再依因果關係重新安排文意。

第一步　中翻英

1）資訊竊盜成為娛樂產業最頭痛的事。

解析：

用 information 與 robbery 相搭配表「資訊竊盜」，entertainment 與 industry 相搭配表「娛樂產業」，用 nightmare 喻「頭痛的事」。

解答：

Information robbery becomes the entertainment industry's worst nightmare.

2）在資訊經濟中，盜印的猖獗使數位內容變得一文不值。

解析：

用 information 與 economy 相搭配表「資訊經濟」，用 digital 與 content 相搭配表「數位內容」，用 piracy 表「盜印」，用 rampant 表「猖獗」。

解答：

In information economy rampant piracy renders digital content worthless.

全民英檢
中高級作文指南

補充說明：

注意，中、英文詞序不同的用法，在中文裡「盜印」置於「猖獗」
之前，而英文是將 piracy（盜印）置於 rampant（猖獗）之後。中
文的用法視「猖獗」為主，「盜印」為從，英文的用法視 piracy 為
主，rampant 為從。

3）盜印之所以猖獗是因為一個地下光碟工廠一年能大量生產上百萬
的盜製光碟。

解析：

用 optical-disc 與 factory 相搭配表「光碟工廠」，用 churn 與 out 相搭
配表「大量生產」。從句構看，本句中有「因為」的意思，故應用複
合句來成句。

解答：

Rampant piracy is made possible because an underground optical-disc
factory is capable of churning out millions of pirated discs a year.

4）據報導，任何一套熱賣遊戲皆淪為盜版的市場。

解析：

用 best-selling 與 game 相搭配表「熱賣遊戲」，用 pirate 表「盜版」，「淪
為…的市場」是指「市場受…控制」的意思，故可用 dominate 來表
達。從句構看，本句中「任何一套熱賣遊戲皆淪為盜版的市場」是指
所報導的事實，故需用 that 子句作受詞來成句。

解答：

It was reported that pirates dominated the market of any best-selling
game.

5）這樣使原發行者的利潤大幅縮水。

解析：

用 reduce 表「縮水」，用 producer 表「發行者」。注意，句中的「這

樣」是指上句「淪為盜版的市場」的意思。

解答：

Such dominance greatly reduces the profits of the original producer.

補充說明：

這裡也可用 siphon 與 off 相搭配表「縮水」，亦即： Such dominance greatly siphons off the profits of the original producer.

第二步　段意分析

根據第一步的譯文，全段初步解答如下：

1）Information robbery becomes the entertainment industry's worst nightmare。2）In information economy rampant piracy renders digital content worthless. 3）Rampant piracy is made possible because an underground optical-disc factory is capable of churning out millions of pirated discs a year. 4）It was reported that pirates dominated the market of any best-selling game. 5）Such dominance greatly reduces the profits of the original producer.

解答：

本段根據文意分析，2）句應為主題句，領起下文，其中 3）4）5）各句應為細節，分別說明為什麼盜印猖獗的原因，各句緊接，推層遞進到 1）句作結論。因此全段文意應依 2）3）4）5）1）的次序來安排如下：

2）In information economy rampant piracy renders digital content worthless. 3）Rampant piracy is made possible because an underground optical-disc factory is capable of churning out millions of pirated discs a year. 4）It was reported that pirates dominated the market of any best-selling game. 5）Such dominance greatly reduces the profits of the original producer. 1）Information robbery becomes the entertainment

industry's worst nightmare.

上面的解答，另可從句構的靈活及聯句的圓通二方面來改善。

3）句的主詞（rampant piracy）與 2）句同，故可依第 4.2.2 節所討論的方法，用代名詞 it 來替代。4）及 5）二句意思緊密相關，故可用複合句改寫成 4）It was reported that pirates dominated the market of any best-selling game, 5）which greatly reduces the profits of the original producer. 而此複合句又可使用省略法，將限定子句變成非限定子句而改寫成 4）It was reported that pirates dominated the market of any best-selling game, 5）greatly reducing the profits of the original producer. 1）句是全段的結果，故可用轉折詞 as a result 使聯句圓通改寫成 As a result, information robbery becomes the entertainment industry's worst nightmare. 根據上面各點，修正後的解答應是：

2）In information economy rampant piracy renders digital content worthless. 3）It is made possible because an underground optical-disc factory is capable of churning out millions of pirated discs a year. 4）It was reported that pirates dominated the market of any best-selling game, 5）greatly reducing the profits of the original producer. 1）As a result, information robbery becomes the entertainment industry's worst nightmare.

習題四

斟酌第 4.1 節習題六的英文初稿，試用本節所討論的方法加以改進。

4.3.2 舉證例示

所謂舉證例示（illustration）是指以舉例來說明事理，這種方法的好處是在選擇事例使內容具體化，以便讀者了解。通常我們用 as a case in point, for example, for instance 等字眼來舉證例示。例如：

But of the intentionally consoling passages in the book, the most impressive to me was that in which he refers to instincts and adaptation such as those of the wasp, which writers on natural history subjects are accustomed to describe, in a way that seems quite just and natural, as *diabolical*. That, for example, of the young cuckoo ejecting its foster-brothers from the nest; of slave-making ants, and of the larvae of the Ichneumonidae feeding on the live tissues of the caterpillars in whose bodies they have been hatched. He said that it was not perhaps a logical conclusion, but it seemed to him more satisfactory to regard such things 'not as specially endowed or created instincts, but as small consequences of one general law' – the law of variation and the survival of the fittest.

W.H. Hudson, *Wasps*

這段以幼鳥爭巢，媒蠃捕螟蛉子來哺育其幼蟲等實例來舉證解釋黃蜂的兇殘，以說明「適者存」的道理。再如：

Even today, the disparity in anxiety level between the two sexes continues. In last week's Time/CNN poll, for instance, a healthy majority of men said they were more fearful about an economic downturn than another terrorist attack(56% to 37%); women, on the other hand, were marginally more worried about terrorism（57% to 43%）. And 59% of men said they are more concerned about national security than they were before 9/11, but 71% of women are. Among moms with children under 18, the figure is 76%.

K. Tumulty, "Goodbye, Soccer Mom. Hello, Security Mom," *Time* (June 2, 2003). 摘自 http：

//www.uvm.edu/~dguber/POLS125/articles/tumulty.htm.

　　這段除用 for instance 之外，另以各種統計數字來證明自 9/11 以來，在美國男性仍重視經濟問題，而女性則重視安全問題，是一個典型的舉證例示的用法。而在下例中：

> Foremost among these misconceptions is that we must balance the environment against human needs. That reasoning is exactly upside-down. Human needs and a healthy environment are not opposing claims that must be balanced; instead, they are inexorably linked by chains of cause and effect. We need a healthy environment because we need clean water, clean air, wood and food from the ocean, plus soil and sunlight to grow crops. We need functioning natural ecosystems, with their native species of earthworms, bees, plants, and microbes, to generate and aerate our soils, pollinate our crops, decompose our wastes, and produce our oxygen. We need to prevent toxic substances from accumulating in our water and air and soil. We need to prevent weeds, germs, and other pest species from becoming established in places where they aren't native and where they cause economic damage. Our strongest arguments for a healthy environment are selfish：we want it for ourselves, not for threatened species like snail darters, spotted owls, and Furbish louseworts.
>
> J. Diamond, "The Last Americans," *Harper's Magazine* （June 2003）, 摘自 http：
>
> //www.mindfully.org/Heritage/2003/Civilization-Collapse-EndJun03.htm

在這一段中，作者不用 for instance 等的字眼，也不用統計數字，而是用各種不同的具體實例來証明作者的立場，亦即我們不因環

保而環保，而是因人類本身的需要而環保。此外在下例中：

> Gypsies are still widely thought of in terms of crude stereotypes –
> as thieves, vagrants, and fortune-tellers – not as a distinct people
> who have preserved their own language and culture.

這裡，破折號中的三個例子，是作者用來解釋 crude stereotypes 的
意思，亦可視為舉證例示的一種方法。

習題一

指出下段主題句的形式何在，及用何種方法來伸展文意。

> Have the recent U.S. accounting scandals got you worried that too
> many executives are lying and cheating in the boardroom? You
> ought to see them on the golf course.
>
> A survey by Guidelines Research & Consulting Inc. of New York
> found that 82 per cent of American senior executives admit to
> cheating at golf, up from 55 per cent in 1993. The most popular
> transgressions include secretly moving the ball to a better position
> and taking shots over again without penalty. (No word on whether
> they ask their caddies to shift triple bogeys to off-balance-sheet
> entities.)
>
> If you think a bit of creative scorekeeping seems harmless enough,
> consider that 87 per cent of these same executives place wagers on
> their golf matches, typically in the hundreds of dollars. Furthermore,
> the bad habits don't end on the golf course：86 per cent of golfing
> executives admit they also cheat in business.
>
> You'd think that with all this cheating going on, executives would
> accept it as part of their slightly twisted version of the game, but not

so. Eighty-two per cent say they "hate" people who cheat them in a golf match.

It's clear that, in both golf and business, many executives have forgotten the rules of fair play. They've given a whole new meaning to the phrase "improving your lie."

The Globe and Mail (July 3, 2002), at A14.

解答：

此段主題句採取疑問句的形式，文中的內容是用各種統計數字來例舉而伸展文意。

習題二

1) 將下面三句譯成英文。

人們通常依其先祖的傳統方式來拜神。古老傳統有相當的價值。節儉是常理而非例外。

解析：

在第一句中，用片語 to worship god 表「拜神」，在第二句中，用 value 表「價值」，在第三句中，用 frugality 表「節儉」，用 rather than 表「而非」。

解答：

People normally worship god in the same form of their forefathers. There is certain value in old traditions. Frugality usually is the rule rather than the exception.

補充說明：

關於 rather than 的用法，這裡有二點需要說明。第一，當 rather than 用作 and not 的意思時，rather 是副詞，而 than 是連接詞，其後跟原形動詞，例如：I decided to phone my sister rather than visit her. 這裡的 visit 是從 to visit 演變而來，與 to phone 乃對稱平行。這種用法與

sooner than 的用法相同，例如： I would go to the market and do shopping sooner than stay with him. 第二，當 rather than 用作 instead of 或 to the exclusion of 的意思時， 一般視作系詞片語，例如在 Rather than buying a sports car, I bought a sedan 一句中，rather than 之後用動名詞。在用 rather than 時需注意保持句子的對稱與平行，例如在 I bought a sedan rather than a sports car 一句中，sedan 及 sports car 屬對稱平行。又需注意的是，當 rather than 置於主動詞之前，則其後需用動名詞，例如： The heated arguments among the board members, rather than ending the discussion, only prolonged the meeting，或如： The heated arguments among the board members, rather than ending the discussion, prolong the meeting. 在這二個例子中，如按上述對稱平行的原則，照理 rather than 之後分別應用過去式或現在式，但習慣上是用動名詞， 反之，rather than 如置於主動詞之後，除可跟原形動詞外，也可用其他動詞時式，例如： The heated arguments among the board members only prolonged the meeting rather than ended the discussion. 在此例中，rather than 先後的動詞時式屬對稱平行。

2)　將上面三句依本節所討論的方法連成一小段。

解析：

本題需先依文意決定何者為主題句，何者為細節。根據文意，第二句應為主題句，1）及 3）句分別屬二個例示來舉證。

解答：

There is certain value in old traditions. As a case in point, frugality usually is the rule rather than the exception. As another case in point, people normally worship god in the same form of their forefathers.

補充說明：

這裡我們又用了二個轉折詞 a case in point 及 another case in point 使

文句銜接流暢。

習題三

A) 下面二段來自第 4.1 節中習題五的解答，指出其文意的伸展是採用何種方法。

（一）用前置法：3）The media industry of this tiny African country is almost non-existent. 1）In this tiny African country there are a total of two cable TV companies with less than 10 cable channels. 2）Cable TV reaches only 7 percent of the population, which is the lowest anywhere in Africa. 4）This tiny African country has 15 magazine publishers that produce 27 titles annually. 5）There are three major book publishers that published over 4000 textbooks last year. 6）This is a figure that falls little short of its total number of students enrolled in schools.

（二）用後置法：1）In this tiny African country there are a total of two cable TV companies with less than 10 cable channels. 2）Cable TV reaches only 7 percent of the population, which is the lowest anywhere in Africa. 4）This tiny African country has 15 magazine publishers that produce 27 titles annually. 5）There are three major book publishers that published over 4000 textbooks last year. 6）This is a figure that falls little short of its total number of students enrolled in schools. 3）The media industry of this tiny African country is almost non-existent.

解析：

從主題句及段落的型式來著手作內容分析。

解答：

本段的內容，不論主題句為前置或後置，皆靠各種統計數字來例舉而

伸展文意。

補充說明：

這裡，如果我們將主題句看作是總綱的話，那末解答（一）的文意是由總綱演繹到細節，而解答（二）的文意是由細節歸納到總綱。關於歸納法及演繹法的用法，請參第 4.3.4 節。

B） 將上面二段用第 4.2 各節所討論的方法來改進。

解析：

在解答（一）中，1）句的 in this tiny African country 是贅文可省略，因為這意思在主題句中可看出。2）句中的 which 子句可用同位語的寫法，以破折號來表達而改寫成 Cable TV reaches only 7 percent of the population – the lowest anywhere in Africa. 4）句的主詞可用代名詞 it 來表達，同時也可依第 4.2.3 節的討論，使用與前句文意有引申關係的轉折詞 in addition，如此可使文意銜接流暢而寫成 In addition, it has 15 magazine publishers that produce 27 titles annually. 同理，我們也可在 5）句之前使用相同性質的轉折詞 and，而 5）句與 6）句文意有密切相關，因此可以設法連成一句，這裡我們也用同位語的寫法，以破折號來表達而寫成 And there are three major book publishers that published over 4000 textbooks last year – a figure that falls little short of its total number of students enrolled in schools. 此外，在解答（二）中的 3）句，另可用與前句文意有總結關係的轉折詞 in short.

解答：

解答（一）經修正後的全文應是：

3） The media industry of this tiny African country is almost non-existent. 1） There are a total of two cable TV companies with less than 10 cable channels. 2） Cable TV reaches only 7 percent of the population – the lowest anywhere in Africa. 4） In addition, it has 15 magazine publishers

that produce 27 titles annually. 5）And there are three major book publishers that published over 4000 textbooks last year－6）a figure that falls little short of its total number of students enrolled in schools.

解答（二）經修正後的全文應是：

1）In this tiny African country there are a total of two cable TV companies with less than 10 cable channels. 2)Cable TV reaches only 7 percent of the population－the lowest anywhere in Africa. 4）In addition, it has 15 magazine publishers that produce 27 titles annually. 5）And there are three major book publishers that published over 4000 textbooks last year－6）a figure that falls little short of its total number of students enrolled in schools. In short, the media industry of this tiny African country is almost non-existent.

補充說明：

對本題的來龍去脈，我們需要作一扼要的說明。

第一， 本題原文是依「全民英檢」的題型出題，最初出現在第 2.2.2 節的綜合習題一中，該習題透過逐句解析，將重點置於詞語的搭配，句構的妥善使用及中譯英的基本方法。

第二， 原文又出現在第 4.1 節的習題五中，該習題重點在於練習段落的型式，同時進一步用省略的方法來求文句的靈活使用。

第三， 在本節中，重點在使用第 4.2 節的方法來求聯句的圓通及根據本節的討論來探討應用何種方法以求文意的周密。

以上從遣詞，造句及成段三方面，概略的剖析了應試此類題型時應注意的地方，同時也介紹了如何用本書所討論的技巧來應試。本章其他各節本文及習題，另有很多類似這樣的範例供讀者反復練習作文的技巧，希望透過這種方法來破解這類題型，好使讀者在應試時能取得理想的分數。

習題四

斟酌第 4.1 節習題六的英文初稿，試用本節所討論的方法加以改進。

4.3.3 比照與比喻

　　有時我們可用事義並舉的方法來著重同類事物的並比
（comparison），或使用雙比奇偶的方法來著重不同事物的對照
（contrast），在使用（並）比（對）照的過程中應注意幾點。第一，
比「同」與比「異」需清晰不允含糊。第二，相比的二類事物，需
以相當的份量在文中分析，以免偏執。第三，可從「種」（genus or
class）比「類」（specifics），也可從「類」比「種」。例如一段比較
中、西菜（種）的文字，可從不同燒菜法（類）來討論，或是從每
一種燒法（類）來說明中、西菜（種）的不同，前者的方法可用下
圖一來表示，後者的方法可用下圖二來表示。

I） 中菜	I） 炒
a） 炒	a） 中菜
b） 燜	b） 西菜
c） 燉	II）燜
II） 西菜	a） 中菜
a） 炒	b） 西菜
b） 燜	III）燉
c） 燉	a） 中菜
	b） 西菜

　圖一：由種比類　　　　圖二：由類比種

我們用第 4.1 節，習題三的前二段來說明如何比照。

Perhaps Mr. Bean is among the organizers of the Jubilee Pageant
that will parade past Buckingham Palace tomorrow to mark the
Queen's 50 years on the throne. Certainly somebody must have a

dark, bizarre sense of humour. How else to explain that the procession will be led by 50 Hells Angels?

Murderers? Shippers of cocaine? Perish the thought. These are *nice* Hells Angels – respectable ones. Quite different from the scum found in Canada and Scandinavia, where scores of bikers have died in Angels' turf wars over the years. This we know because the palace has been solemnly assured that none of the riders slated to rumble past has a criminal background. Rather, their gleaming Harley Davidsons will be a paean to Britain's "cultural diversity," the Jubilee's theme. Right.

這二段究竟是並比還是對照表明得很清楚，文中將 bad Hells Angels 與 nice Hells Angels 來並比，在第二段中以相當的份量來討論，其所用的方法是從「種」（bad and nice Hells Angels）來比「類」（即 bad Hells Angels 有犯罪的各種行為，而 nice Hells Angles 無犯罪的記錄），屬上面圖一的結構，文意是透過相反相成的方法組合而成。

　　有時我們也可用比喻的方法來申述主旨。比喻與比照不同，比照著重在比較，而比喻則著重在類推。一般而言，比喻有三個要素，分別是喻體，喻詞及喻本（亦稱本體）。例如在 Days are short like any dream 一句中，days 是喻體，like 是喻詞，dream 是喻本。比喻須具備二個條件，第一，喻體與喻本須指二個不同的事物，如上例的 days 與 dream 所示，第二，在喻體與喻本間指出一共同的現象，例如上例的 days 與 dream 二者間指出一短暫（short）的現象。比喻有明喻（simile）及隱喻（metaphor）二種，例如上例的意思明顯，故屬明喻。但有時比喻的含義隱微而不易看出，例如在 I sometimes suspect that when I am headed east, my critical faculties are retarded almost to the vanishing point, like a frog's heartbeat in winter 一句中，是用青蛙冬眠背後所隱藏心跳減緩的意思來形容自己思維的遲鈍，這種比喻稱隱喻。使用比喻的好處是以「推物寓言」的方式使文意鮮明生動。例如在 At night, in the still evening when the afterglow lit the water, the motors whined about one's ears like mosquitoes 一句中，作者將從遠處水面上不斷傳來的馬達聲，唯妙唯肖地描寫成蚊子掠耳的嗡嗡聲。

使用比喻也可收寓抽象於具體的功效。例如在 Most of people think of peace as a state of Nothing Bad Happening, or Nothing Much Happening 一句中，將「無壞事」（Nothing Bad Happening）及「無事」（Nothing Much Happening）二個具體的事實來形容一個抽象的概念 peace，代表了人們企求和平，因此希望 Nothing Bad Happening，也代表了人們憧憬和平的恃久，故而希望 Nothing Much Happening。再如在下例中：

> We hear much of visions, and I trust we shall continue to have visions and dream of dreams of a fairer future for the race. But visions are one thing and visionaries are another, and the mechanical appliances of the rhetorician designed to give a picture of a present which does not exist and of a future which no man can predict are as unreal and short-lived as the steam or canvas clouds, the angels suspended on wires, and the artificial lights of the stage.
>
> Henry Cabot Lodge, "Let Us Beware How We Palter with Our Independence"（A speech read on August 12, 1919, to the U.S. Senate.）

作者用 steam, canvas clouds, angels suspended on wires 以及 artificial lights of the stage 的本質來比喻 mechanical appliances of the rhetorician，增進讀者對此種 mechanical appliances of the

rhetorician 的印象，如此以不同的形象突出喻意，使文意相互呼應，自然成文。

比照是轉義（trope）用法的一種，轉義另可有反語法（irony），例如莎士比亞中的 Hamlet 曾說 I humbly thank you. 這一句，表面上表示衷心致謝，實際上，作為一個王子的，鮮有如此謙虛的心胸。轉義也有用舉偶法（synecdoche）來表達的，例如用 Hercules 來表孔武有力的人。此外，轉義也有用換喻法（metonymy）來表達的，例如在 The pen is mightier than the sword 一成語中，以 pen 喻 power of literature，以 sword 喻 force.

在作文時，如能偶而插入一個恰當的轉義，不但能使文意生動，而且也可使讀者更易接受文中的論點，在應試時可爭取一些印象分數。

本節第一及第二兩個習題不難但很費時，讀者在做每個習題時，不妨分二個步驟去做，先做中譯英，然後再做聯句的圓通及文意的周密，這樣就不會感到有太大的壓力。

習題一

指出下段是用何種方法來表達文意，並將原文譯成英文。

1）一般而言，英文的文體有二種。2）一為在大多數寫與講的情形下所使用的文體，這種文體稱為通用英語。3）另一為針對少數對象所使用的著作中而採用的文體。這種文體稱為正規英語。4）每一種文體有其一己的特點。5）通用英語所用的字彙較具體，且為一般讀者所熟習。6）正規英語中使用從不同學術領域而來的抽象字彙。7）通用英語的句子相對上較短且其句構不涉及複雜的插句。8）在正規英語中，句子傾向長句，且其句構常涉及平行結構的使用。9）通用英語的文體比較隨便，而句構及用字的嚴謹選擇是正規英語的特色。

解析：

本題需從二個步驟著手。第一步是根據本節的討論來分析本段是用何種方法使文意脈絡貫通，第二步是中翻英。

第一步： 文意如何脈絡貫通

解答：

根據文意我們知道，本段是使用事義並舉的方法來寫成的。重點是在比「異」，是將二「種」不同的文體（即通用英語及正規英語）根據用字及句構（二個不同的「類」）來對照相比，是採用圖二的方法來伸展文意。

第二步： 中翻英。

1) 一般而言，英文的文體有二種。

解析：

用 style 表「文體」。

解答：

Generally speaking there are two types of style in English.

2) 一為在大多數寫與講的情形下所使用的文體，這種文體稱為通用英語。

解析：

用片語 general English 表「通用英語」，注意從句構看，「這種文體 …」應該用 which 子句來成句。

解答：

One is used in most writing and speaking situations, which is called general English.

3) 另一為針對少數對象所使用的著作中而採用的文體，這種文體稱為正規英語。

解析：

用 restricted 與 groups 相搭配表「少數對象」，片語 formal English 表「正規英語」。注意從句構看，「針對少數對象所使用的著作」應該用 that 子句來成句。

解答：

The other is found in books that are intended for use in restricted groups, which is called formal English.

4) 每一種文體有其一己的特點。

解析：

用 trait 表「特點」。

解答：

Each style has its own traits.

5) 通用英語所用的字彙較具體，且為一般讀者所熟習。

解析：

用 vocabulary 表「字彙」，concrete 表「具體」，用 common 與 readers 相搭配表「一般讀者」。

解答：

In general English the vocabulary used is likely to be concrete and familiar to common readers.

6) 正規英語中使用從不同學術領域而來的抽象字彙。

解析：

用 derive 表「從...而來」，其後需與 from 相搭配，用片語 scholarly field 表「學術領域」，片語 abstract term 表「抽象字彙」。注意從句構看，「從不同學術領域而來的抽象字彙」應該用 that 子句來成句。

解答：

The vocabulary of formal English has many abstract terms that are derived from different scholarly fields.

補充說明：

注意 scholarly 此處是形容詞而非副詞。

7)　通用英語的句子相對上較短且其句構不涉及複雜的插句。

解析：

用 involve 表「涉及」，用 elaborate 表「複雜」，以 interrupting 與 clause 相搭配表「插句」。

解答：

Sentences in general English are relatively short and their structure involves no elaborate interrupting clauses.

8)　在正規英語中，句子傾向長句，且其句構常涉及平行結構的使用。

解析：

用 tend 表「傾向」其後需與 to be 相搭配，以 parallel 與 pattern 相搭配表「平行結構」。

解答：

Sentences in formal English tend to be long and their structure involves the frequent use of parallel patterns.

9)　通用英語的文體比較隨便，而句構及用字的嚴謹選擇是正規英語的特色。

解析：

用 casual 表「隨便」，以 deliberate 與 choice 相搭配表「嚴謹選擇」，用 characterize 表「特色」。

解答：

The style of general English is casual, and deliberate choice of sentence structure as well as words characterizes formal English.

補充說明：

注意 as well as 與此處動詞的身數無關。

全段英文的初步解答如下：

1）Generally speaking there are two types of style in English. 2）One is used in most writing and speaking situations, which is called general English. 3）The other is found in books that are intended for use in restricted groups, which is called formal English. 4）Each style has its own traits. 5）In general English the vocabulary used is likely to be concrete and familiar to common readers. 6）The vocabulary of formal English has many abstract terms that are derived from different scholarly fields. 7）Sentences in general English are relatively short, and their structure involves no elaborate interrupting clauses. 8）Sentences in formal English tend to be long and their structure involves the frequent use of parallel patterns. 9）The style of general English is casual, and deliberate choice of sentence structure as well as words characterizes formal English.

　　上面初步的解答，應另從聯句圓通的立場來改善。1）句是主題句，但沒有清楚說明那二種文體，這違反了主題句須分明（clarity）的要求，因此不妨改寫成 Generally speaking there are two types of style in English： general English and formal English. 根據這主題句，2）及 3）兩句需作相應的調整，我們試將此二句合寫成一複合句 The former is used in most writing and speaking situations and the latter is found in works intended for use in restricted groups. 此處 the former 及 the latter 是第 4.2.3 節中所介紹的一系列用法，同時將 that are intended 用省略法改寫成 intended. 從 4）句到 9）句，我們可依文意斟酌使用不同的轉折詞，在 6）句可插入 however，同時將 that are derived from 省略改寫成 derived from. 在 7）句中可插入 in addition，在 8）句中可使用 but，同時在 9）句中使用 in short 作總結. 修正後的全文如下：

1）Generally speaking there are two types of style in English： general English and formal English. 2）The former is used in most writing and speaking situations, and 3）the latter is found in works intended for use in restricted groups. 4）Each style has its own traits. 5）In general English the vocabulary used is likely to be concrete and familiar to common readers. 6）However, the vocabulary of formal English has many abstract terms derived from different scholarly fields. 7）In addition, sentences in general English are relatively short and their structure involves no elaborate interrupting clauses. 8）But sentences in formal English tend to be long and their structure involves the frequent use of parallel patterns. 9）In short, the style of general English is casual, and deliberate choice of sentence structure as well as words characterizes formal English.

習題二

指出下段用何種方法表達文意，並將原文譯成英文。

1）偏見好像生活一樣永不靜止，而驕傲常隨意一揮使真理變成偏見。2）由此緣由，我們必須避免因驕傲而使真理及偏見混淆不清。3）偏見是一己的，內在的，而真理是共同的，常存的。4）偏見是個人的直覺，而真理是群族的信仰。5）偏見或能成為信仰，就像群族允或有偏見。6）偏見及真理二者並無永久的關係。7）一旦信仰成為偏見，它即失去真確性。8）當群族選擇偏見時，將以犧牲真理作代價。

解析：

本題也需從二個步驟著手。第一步是根據本節的討論來分析本段

全民英檢
中高級作文指南

是用何種方法使文意脈絡貫通,第二步是中翻英。

第一步:文意如何脈絡貫通

解答:

根據文意可以知道,本段是用雙比奇偶的方法寫成,重點是在對照偏見與真理的不同,是以圖一的方法來伸展文意。

第二步:中翻英

1)偏見好像生活一樣永不靜止,而驕傲常隨意一揮使真理變成偏見。

解析:

用 never 與 static 相搭配表「永不靜止」,用片語 a simple touch 表「隨意一揮」,用 bring 表「使變成」其後需與 into 相搭配。從句構看,本句需用并列句。

解答:

Bias, like life, is never static and pride often brings truth into bias with a simple touch.

2)由此緣由,我們必須避免因驕傲而使真理及偏見混淆不清。

解析:

用 reason 表「緣由」,其前需與 for 相搭配,用 confuse 表「混淆不清」,其後需與 with 相搭配。從句構看,「使真理及偏見混淆不清」需用 that 子句來成句。

解答:

For this reason it is necessary for us to avoid pride that confuses bias with truth.

3)偏見是一己的,內在的,而真理是共同的,常存的。

解析:

用 individual 表「一己的」,用 innate 表「內在的」,用 common 表「共同的」,用 lasting 表「常存的」。從句構看,本句宜用表 while 的複合句。

352

解答：

Bias is individual and innate while truth is common and lasting.

4）偏見是個人的直覺，而真理是群族的信仰。

解析：

用 instinct 表「直覺」。從句構看，本句需用并列句。

解答：

Bias is the instinct of an individual and truth is the belief of a group.

5）偏見或能成為信仰，就像群族允或有偏見。

解析：

用 just as 表「就像」。

解答：

Bias may become a belief; just as a group my have bias.

補充說明：

此并列句是用分號來替代 and，是一個常見的方法。

6）偏見及真理二者並無永久的關係。

解析：

用 permanent 與 relationship 相搭配表「永久的關係」。

解答：

There can be no permanent relationship between bias and truth.

7）一旦信仰成為偏見，它即失去真確性。

解析：

用 as soon as 表「一旦」，cease 表「失去」。

解答：

As soon as a belief becomes a bias, it ceases to be true.

8）當群族選擇偏見時，將以犧牲真理作代價。

解析：

用 adopt 表「選擇」，用 cost（作名詞）表「犧牲之代價」，注意此處需用片語 at the cost of 相搭配。從句構看，本句宜用表 when 的複合句。

解答：

When a group adopts a bias, it does so at the cost of truth.

補充說明：

此處 group 是一個集體名詞，故動詞用單數，如果 group 是指其各構成份子時，其動詞需用複數，例如： The group are divided on the issue of centralization.

全段英文的初步解答如下：

1）Bias, like life, is never static and pride often brings truth into bias with a simple touch. 2）For this reason it is necessary for us to avoid pride that confuses bias with truth. 3）Bias is individual and innate while truth is common and lasting. 4）Bias is the instinct of an individual and truth is the belief of a group. 5）Bias may become a belief; just as a group my have bias. 6）There can be no permanent relationship between bias and truth. 7）As soon as a belief becomes a bias, it ceases to be true. 8）When a group adopts a bias, it does so at the cost of truth.

上面初步的解答，另應從文句圓通的立場來改善。3）及 4）兩句中的 bias 及 truth 是重複，因此 4）句可用 the former 及 the latter，同時，4）句也可用省略法改寫成 The former is the instinct of an individual and the latter, the belief of a group. 6）句的語氣需用轉折詞來變化，同時 bias 及 truth 可用 them 來取代而改寫成 But there can be no permanent relationship between them. 7）句實際上是解釋 6）句的意思，因此 6）7）二句可改寫成 But there can be no permanent relationship between them, for as soon as a belief becomes a bias, it ceases to be true. 修正後的全文如下：

1）Bias, like life, is never static and pride often brings truth into bias with a simple touch. 2）For this reason it is necessary for us to avoid pride that confuses bias with truth. 3）Bias is individual and innate while truth is common and lasting. 4）The former is the instinct of an individual and the latter, the belief of a group. 5）Bias may become a belief; just as a group my have bias. 6）But, there can be no permanent relationship between them, 7）for as soon as a belief becomes a bias, it ceases to be true. 8）When a group adopts a bias, it does so at the cost of truth.

習題三

下段摘自一篇書評，試舉出是用何種方法來控引情理。

DeLillo writes precision sentences. Each grim surmise and silly development comes slipcased in its own deluxe handcrafted paragraph. In one of this book's wintry aphorisms, a woman tells Packer, "Talent is more erotic when it's wasted." If that's true, this may be the sexiest book of the year.

Time（April 21, 2003）, at 60.

本段第三句中的 talent 是喻體，wasted talent 是喻本，而 erotic 是喻詞，作者在最後一句中用 the sexiest book 來影射 DeLillo 是個 wasted talent，這段是用暗喻的方法寫成。

習題四

　　斟酌第 4.1 節習題六的英文初稿，試用本節所討論的方法加以改進。

4.3.4 分析與界定

　　分析有二種，一是順著總綱討論各項細節，一是由各項細節回

歸到總綱。前者稱演繹，後者稱歸納。採用演繹的方法，整段的結構猶如一座金字塔，總綱是塔頂，各項細節的內容為塔基，而歸納法的整段結構猶如一座倒金字塔，從各項細節的文意而延伸到總綱。不論採演繹法或歸納法，在伸展文意時，每一步要交代清楚以及酌情作附加說明，務求層次分明，脈絡清晰，這樣才能使全段文意連貫通順。我們用下面一個例子來說明。

1）Grammar, usage, and mechanics establish the ground rules of writing, circumscribing what you are free to do. 2）Within them, you may select various strategies and work out those strategies in your own words, sentences, and paragraphs. 3）The ground rules, however, are relatively inflexible. 4）Of course you can choose to break them – just as a base runner can cut directly from the first base to third. 5）But if he does, he is out. 6）And if you choose to write ungrammatically, or to pay no attention to the usage or mechanics, readers will rule you out.

Thomas S. Kane, *The Oxford Guide to Writing：A Rhetoric and Handbook for College Students* （Oxford, Oxford University Press, 1983）, at 17.

這一段的文意，先須根據上節聯句圓通的原則來分析。為便於解釋起見，此段各句的相互關係可用下列方法來表示：

1）句 = topic sentence （General rules of writing are governed by three factors, i.e., grammar, usage, and mechanics.）

2）句 = development of topic sentence （Writing strategies are to be applied within these three factors.）

3）句 = use of contradiction （Grammar rules of writing are inflexible.）

4）句 = use of comparison （writing vis-à-vis baseball game）.

5）句 = link to 4）句 （consequences of breaking rules of baseball game）.

6）句 = link to 5）句及回復到 1）句（consequences of breaking ground rules of writing）.

在這段中，1）句是全段的總綱，2）句到 6）句是引申總綱的細節。全段使用幾種不同的方法來使各句前顧後應，例如 3）句中的 inflexible 與 5）及 6）兩句中的 out 是字義相通的用法，2）及 4）兩句中的 them 是以代名詞指 1）句中的 ground rules of writing. 全段中分別用在句首的 however, of course, but, and 等轉折詞，皆是用來導引讀者的路標。

根據以上內容的分析，本段各句的排列組合可由下圖來表達其架構：

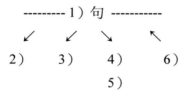

根據上圖，我們可從切題及全段的起承轉合二點來說明如何使用分析法。

從切題來討論，每一句皆直接或間接緊扣主題。2）句中的 within them 指 1）句中的三個因素，3）句用同義字眼（ground rules）與 1）句相承，4）句中的 them 述及 1）句中的 ground rules of writing，5）句述及 4）句中違背 baseball rules 一點，6）句用否定語氣來回復到主旨。從起承轉合來看，這一段是採取演繹的方法寫成。1）句是主題句，其中所涉及的三個因素在 2）句中用 within them 來交代清楚，而 3）句用轉折語氣（however）來引申說明主題句中所談到的 ground rules of writing 之無伸縮性。4）句用 of course 來與（3）句文意直接

相連，並用 them（代名詞）間接與 1）句中的 ground rules of writing 相承，同時用 baseball game 作比較，為以下二句作鋪墊，5）句用轉折詞 but 與 4）句文意相連，來附加說明違背 baseball rules 的後果。6）句又用轉折詞 and 與 5）句文意相通，同時用否定語氣（ungrammatical, pay no attention to usage and mechanics）來回復總結到 1）句的主旨。全段脈絡清晰，佈局妥貼工穩。

　　這一段透過演繹法，使用圓通的文句使全段連貫有序，利用周密的文意使全文連貫通順，於是整個一段成為一嚴謹的整體。

　　我們再用下段作例子來說明歸納法的寫法。

　　1）They visited a Nazi concentration camp. 2）In the open field rows upon rows of wooden cells were aligned like match boxes. 3）Each cell was bare except for a few used beds. 4）One side wall was dominated by the regulation of the place written in simple words. 5）Well inside the campsite they came upon an execution room. 6）Inside, thousands upon thousands of innocent souls once disappeared on mass. 7）They were dazed and terrified, recalling the hideous casualties imposed upon those helpless Jews who were poisoned to death in groups here.

這段文意也可先根據聯句圓通的道理來分析，而各句間的相互關係可用下列方法來表示：

1）句 = indication of the place visited（Nazi concentration camp）.

2）句 = description of the place visited（cells aligned like match boxes）.

3）句 = description of the inside of each cell（used beds）.

4）句 = description of the inside of each cell again（regulation posted on side wall）.

5）句 = description of the place visited again（the execution room）.

358

6）句 = description of what had happened inside the execution room（innocent souls disappeared）.

7）句 = topic sentence（dazed feelings caused by the hideous casualties imposed upon Jews）.

　　這一段，主要是透過字義相通的方法，使各句前後照應，例如 3）句中的 cell（牢房）述及 2）句中的 cell，另與 4）句相關，皆述及牢房內部的情形，5）句中的營地（campsite）與 1）句的集中營相遙對，由遠及近與 6）句共同描寫行刑室（execution room），以上各句皆屬細節，7）句是經由上述各細節後所衍生的感受，是全段的總綱。

　　根據以上內容的分析，本段各句的排列組合可由下圖來表達其架構：

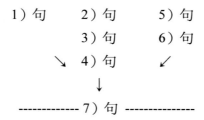

```
        1）句      2）句      5）句

                   3）句      6）句

          ↘        4）句      ↙

                    ↓

 ------------ 7）句 ---------------
```

　　根據上圖，我們可從切題及全段的起承轉合二點來說明如何使用分析法。從切題看，1）句的集中營，2）到 4）各句的描寫牢房，及 5）、6）二句描寫行刑室的情形，皆直接與 7）句中所表的感受有關。從起承轉合看，這一段是採取歸納的方法寫成。全段文意由近及遠層層搖曳而出，先寫所訪問的地方（1）句）為以下各句作鋪墊，從 2）句到 6）句筆法徐疾變化有致，其中 2）句到 4）句描寫牢房，5）、6）二句描寫行刑室，高潮迭起，7）句因景生情，用作結尾，使全段成一有機的整體。

　　有時為了便於讀者了解起見，我們也可用界定（definition）的

方法來闡明解釋主旨。界定的方法很多，最普通的方法是參照字典中的定義（dictionary definition）。另一種方法是從語源學（etymology）的立場來求一個觀念的含蘊。再一種方法是從分類（classification）的觀察來界定，著重在考究各觀念或事物的特徵（attribute）是否相同來界定屬那一種類。我們用 Stephen Leacock 對 humuor 所下的定義來作說明。

> Humour may be defined as the kindly contemplation of the incongruities of life and the artistic expression thereof. I think this the best I know because I wrote it myself. I don't like any others nearly as well. Students of writing will do well to pause at the word *kindly* and ponder it well. The very essence of humour is that it must be kindly. "Good jests," said King Charles the Second, that most humorous and kindly king who saved monarchy in England, "ought to bite like lambs, not dogs; they should cut, not wound." The minute they begin to bite and wound that is not humour. That is satire and as it gets more and more satirical the humour dries out of it, leaving only the snarl and rasp of sarcasm.
>
> *How to Write* (New York, N.Y., Dodd, Mead, 1943), at 213-214.

這一段是使用分類的方法來界定 humour 的意義，指出其特徵具「友善性」，同時借助比照法（詳參第 4.3.3 節）與 satire 二者來對照，指出後者的特徵具「傷害性」（wound），這樣使二者涇渭分明，凡入傷害性者屬 satire，凡入友善性者屬 humour。此外在界定的過程中，用「羊齧」及「狗噬」作比喻來說明 humour 的本質是「割」（cut）而非「傷」，同時作者又用了一個字義相通的方法將 jest 來說明 humour。

本章詳細討論了如何求段落圓通及周密的各種方法，在此須另外

說明一點的是，一段精彩的文章，除了要講究段落的型式，聯句的圓通及文意的周密外，更重要的是全段的文思，對陶鈞文思要講求順一己的情致來導引文辭，畢竟方式的講究應為「膚葉」，段落的內容才是「骨髓」。因此，當我們在綜合使用各種不同的方法時，要以文思控制文意，以文意來駕馭方式。至於如何做到選擇適當的方法以突顯文意的功夫，則需我們平常多閱讀佳作，多練習作文，以及多作比較，這樣在應試時才能應付自如，寫出一段文采並茂的佳作。

　　本節習題不難但很費時，讀者在做每個習題時，不妨分二個步驟去做，先做中譯英，然後再做聯句的圓通及文意的周密，這樣就不會有太大的壓力。

習題一

將下段譯成英文，並依本節所討論的方法寫成一段。

1） 教育意謂著學習的過程及成果本身二者。

2） 教育傳授實用技能及正當思考的模式。

3） 教育的過程教導市民涉及有關決策的思考藝術。

4） 市民必須自我教育用以曉得如何解決疑難及如何思考。

5） 教育的成果不在於學位而在於解決疑難之能力。

6） 教育的成果能使市民獲得做決策的智慧。

7） 就一般市民言，教育對其人生有雙重貢獻。

8） 曉得如何解決疑難及如何思考二者之結合構成一個有教養的市民。

9） 教育是塑造智力追求的一種手段，這種追求突出通才教育的主要目的。

10） 教育是獲取解決疑難技能的一種方式，這種技能現代市民必須具有。

　　這習題有二個要求，即中譯英及改寫成一段。全題須分三個步

驟來做。第一步是將每句譯成英文。第二步是分析各句之間的相互關係，決定何者為主旨，何者為主旨的延伸，這一步著重在內容分析。第三步是根據內容分析的結果點出全段的架構來寫成一段，這一步著重在文意的周密及聯句的圓通，後二步是針對如何寫成一段嚴謹的整體文章而設。

第一步：中譯英

1）　教育意謂著學習的過程及成果本身二者。

解析：

用 imply 表「意謂」，用片語 process of learning 表「學習的過程」，用 product 表「成果」，用 both ...and 表「二者」。

解答：

Education implies both the process of learning and the product itself.

2）　教育傳授實用技能及正當思考的模式。

解析：

用 convey 表「傳授」，以 practical 與 skill 相搭配表「實用技能」，以 proper 與 thinking 相搭配表「正當思考」。

解答：

Education conveys practical skills and a model of proper thinking.

補充說明：

這裡不能用 practicable，其與 practical 之不同可從下例看出，We can rely on a practical skill to make a living, but it is not practicable for us to learn all practical skills. 此處 practicable 解作「切不切實際」。

3）　教育的過程教導市民涉及有關決策的思考藝術。

解析：

用片語 process of education 表「教育的過程」，decision-making 表「決策」，用 associate 表「涉及有關」其後需與 with 相搭配。從句構看，

「涉及有關決策」需用一 that 子句來成句。

解答：

The process of education teaches citizens the art of thinking that is associated with decision-making.

4）　市民必須自我教育用以曉得如何解決疑難及如何思考。

解析：

用 trouble-shoot 表「解決疑難」。不妨將「曉得如何解決疑難及如何思考」用不定詞來表達。

解答：

To know how to trouble-shoot and how to think are what citizens should educate themselves.

補充說明：

這一句是由下句改寫而成：

Citizens should educate themselves to know how to trouble-shoot and how to think. 原答案是用置換的方法來特出「如何解決疑難」及「如何思考」。

5）　教育的成果不在於學位而在於解決疑難之能力。

解析：

用 outcome 表「成果」，以 academic 與 degree 相搭配表「學位」。

解答：

The outcome of education is not academic degree but the ability of trouble-shooting.

6）　教育的成果能使市民獲得做決策的智慧。

解析：

用 acquire 表「獲得」，以 make 與 decision 相搭配表「做決策」。

解答：

The outcome of education enables citizens to acquire the wisdom of making decisions.

7) 就一般市民言，教育對其人生有雙重貢獻。

解析：

用 twofold 表「雙重」，contribution 表「貢獻」其後需與 to 相搭配。

解答：

For ordinary citizens education makes a twofold contribution to their life.

8) 曉得如何解決疑難及如何思考二者之結合構成一個有教養的市民。

解析：

用 combination 表「結合」，constitute 表「構成」，片語 an educated citizen 表「一個有教養的市民」。

解答：

The combination of how to trouble-shoot and how to think constitutes an educated citizen.

9) 教育是塑造智力追求的一種手段，這種追求突出通才教育的主要目的。

解析：

用 shape（作動詞）表「塑造」，以 intellectual 與 pursuit 相搭配表「智力追求」，用 characterize 表「突出」，片語 liberal education 表「通才教育」。從句構看，「這種追求突出通才教育的主要目的」需用一 that 子句來成句。

解答：

Education is a means to the shaping of intellectual pursuit that characterizes the main purpose of a liberal education.

10）教育是獲取解決疑難技能的一種方式，這種技能現代市民必須具有。

解析：

用 way 表「方式」。從句構看，「這種技能現代市民必須具有」需用一 that 子句來成句。

解答：

Education is a way to acquire trouble-shooting skills that modern citizens must have.

第二步：內容分析

解析：

為便於了解起見，此段各文句之間的相互關係可以用下列的方式來表達：

2）句 = topic sentence（Education conveys practical skills and a model of proper thinking.）

7）句 = exemplification of the main theme（Education makes a twofold contribution to a citizen's life.）

10）句= first contribution (to acquire trouble-shooting skills).

9）句= second contribution（a means of shaping intellectual pursuit）. 注意 10）、9）二句乃是 7）句的延伸。

1）句= 10）及 9）二句的結論並為下面 5），6）及 3）三句作張本（Education is a process of learning and a product itself.）

5）句 = first product (the ability of trouble-shooting).

6）句 = second product (to acquire the wisdom of making decision).

3）句 = process of education（to teach the art of thinking）. 注意 5）、6）及 3）三句是 1）句的延伸。

4）句 = reinforcement of the main theme（Trouble-shooting skills and proper thinking are what citizens should educate themselves.）

8）句 = conclusion of the main theme （i.e., what constitutes an educated citizen.）

第三步：文意的周密及聯句的圓通

解析：

根據第二步的內容分析，本段各句的組合可由下圖來表達其架構：

$$
2) 句 \rightarrow 7) 句 \quad
\begin{array}{c} 10) 句 \\ \\ 9) 句 \end{array}
\rightarrow 1) 句 \rightarrow 6) 句
\begin{array}{c} 5) 句 \\ \\ 3) 句 \end{array}
\rightarrow 4) 句 \rightarrow 8) 句
$$

↑ ——————————————————————— ↑

我們可從切題及文意的起承轉合二點來討論文意的周密。

A) 切題：

我們從上圖曉得，每一句皆與主旨 2）句）有關，這是說 7）句用 twofold contribution 來與 topic sentence 中的 practical skills 及 model of proper thinking 相應，作引申下面文意的句眼，10）及 9）二句引申 7）句所提的 twofold contribution（problem-solving skills 及 the shaping of intellectual pursuit），1）句一方面綜合 10）及 9）二句的意思，另一方面為 5）、6）及 3）各句作張本，而 5）、6）及 3）各句的文意仍與主旨有關。4）句重申 trouble-shooting skills 及 proper thinking 之重要。8）句迴環往復到主旨。這段文意的切題可從每句皆直接或間接緊扣主旨中看出。

B) 文意的起承轉合：

這一段文意順序漸進的用演繹法寫成，先提主旨（2）句），點明議題，再引申主旨的二點（7）句），接著 10）、9）二句用作細節來申述 7）句的文意，然後轉門（1）句）將文意用二種不同的觀點來進一步申述（即 5）、6）及 3）各句）。4）句是後收歸正再由 8）句回到主旨，使全段結構嚴謹緊湊。值得注意的是，本段

的主題句簡潔（僅十個字），具概括扼要的特性，提供全段文意待放的機會，使作者認為全段重要的意思都包括在內無所遺漏。根據上面的解析，我們初步的解答是：

（2）Education conveys practical skills and a model of proper thinking.（7）For ordinary citizens education makes a twofold contribution to their life.（10）Education is a way to acquire trouble-shooting skills that modern citizens must have.（9）Education is a means to the shaping of intellectual pursuit that characterizes the main purpose of a liberal education.（1）Education implies both the process of learning and the product itself.（5）The outcome of education is not academic degree but the ability of trouble-shooting.

（6）The outcome of education enables citizens to acquire the wisdom of making decisions.（3）The process of education teaches citizens the art of thinking that is associated with decision-making.

（4）To know how to trouble-shoot and how to think are what citizens should educate themselves.（8）The combination of how to trouble-shoot and how to think constitutes an educated citizen.

上面的初步解答仍可從句構的靈活使用及文句圓通的觀點來改善如下。

A) 第 10）及 9）二句既然是 7）句的延伸，那末我們可將這三句改寫成一句，使三句文意成一整體。我們可用二種不同的方法來改寫，一是用破折號，一是用轉折詞：

For ordinary citizens education makes a twofold contribution to their life – a way to acquire problem-solving skills that modern citizens must have and a means to the shaping of intellectual pursuit that characterizes the main purpose of a liberal education. 此處破折號是

採同位語的方法來解釋 a twofold contribution。關於這一點請參第 4.2.2 節。另一種寫法可用下句來表達：

For ordinary citizens education makes a twofold contribution to their life. On the one hand, education is a way to acquire problem-solving skills that modern citizens must have. On the other hand, education is a means to the shaping of intellectual pursuit that characterizes the main purpose of a liberal education. 這是使用轉折詞使文句圓通，關於這一點請參第 4.2.3 節。

B) 在 1）句中可加表重複關係的轉折詞 in this sense，置於主詞之後。

C) 同理，5）及 6）二句意義相關，可用省略法改寫成一整句。

The outcome of education, not academic degree, but the ability of trouble-shooting, enables citizens to acquire the wisdom of making decisions. 這句中二個省略後的短音節（not academic degree 及 but the ability of trouble-shooting）可收加重語氣的功效。

D) 在 3）句前可加表時間關係的轉折詞 at the same time, 同時可用省略法改寫成：

At the same time the process of education teaches citizens the art of thinking associated with decision-making.

E) 在 4）句前可加表結果關係的轉折詞 therefore。

F) 8）句中的 how to trouble-shoot 及 how to think 是述及 4）句的意思，因此可用 the two 來替代。

根據上面的各點分析，修正後的解答應是：

（2）Education conveys practical skills and a model of proper thinking. （7）For ordinary citizens education makes a twofold contribution to their life –（10）a way to acquire trouble-shooting skills that modern citizens must have and （9）a means to the shaping of intellectual pursuit that characterizes the main purpose of a liberal education. [或（7）For ordinary citizens education makes a twofold contribution to their life.（10）On the one hand, education is a way to acquire trouble-shooting skills that modern citizens must have.（9）On the other hand, education is a means to the shaping of intellectual pursuit that characterizes the main purpose of a liberal education.]（1）Education, in this sense, implies both the process of learning and the product itself. The outcome of education,（5）not academic degree, but the ability of trouble-shooting,（6）enables citizens to acquire the wisdom of making decisions.（3）At the same time the process of education teaches citizens the art of thinking associated with decision-making.（4）Therefore, to know how to trouble-shoot and how to think are what citizens should educate themselves.（8）The combination of the two constitutes an educated citizen.

　　讀者不妨比較初步答案及修正後的答案，不難發現後者文句圓通，妥善運用了各種路標使文意流暢自然便於了解。

習題二

將下段譯成英文，並依本節所討論的方法寫成一段。

1）一個強烈的海嘯毀夷了整個鄉村。

2）海嘯毀壞力的影響，在很多運氣不佳的村民心中，留下了茫茫感。

3）海嘯毀了他所有的財產及奪走了他的親戚。

4）海嘯使他生命遭受挫折，一無所有。

5）一位中年男士，骨瘦如柴，臉色蒼白。

6）一位中年男士，不知何故，沿著荒蕪的街道蹣跚而行。

　　這習題有二個要求，即中譯英及改寫成一段。全題也須分三個步驟來做。第一步是將每句譯成英文。第二步是分析各句之間的相

互關係，決定何者為主旨，何者為主旨的延伸，這一步著重在內容的分析。第三步是根據內容分析的結果點出全段的架構來寫成一段，這一步著重在文意的周密及聯句的圓通，後二步是針對如何寫成一段嚴謹的整體文章而設。

第一步：中譯英

1）　一個強烈的海嘯毀夷了整個鄉村。

解析

用 tsunami 表「海嘯」，用 obliterate 表「毀夷」。

解答：

A strong tsunami obliterated the entire village.

2）　海嘯毀壞力的影響，在很多運氣不佳的村民心中，留下了茫茫感。

解析

用 impact 表「影響」，devastation 表「毀壞力」，ill-starred 表「運氣不佳」，用片語 a sense of hollowness 表「茫茫感」。

解答：

The impact of tsunami's devastation left a sense of hollowness in the minds of many ill-starred villagers.

3）　海嘯毀了他所有的財產及奪走了他的親戚。

解析：

用 destroy 表「毀」，用 take 與 away 相搭配表「奪走」。

解答：

The tsunami destroyed all his properties and took his relatives away from him.

4）　海嘯使他生命遭受挫折，一無所有。

解析：

用 pull 與 down 相搭配表「受挫折」，用片語 everything to zero 表「一無所有」，此片語用破折號表同位語來寫比較容易（詳參第 4.2.2 節）。

解答：

The tsunami pulled down his life – everything to zero.

補充說明：

此處破折號用來加重語氣（請參第 3.3.6 節）。

5）　一位中年男士，骨瘦如柴，臉色蒼白。

解析：

用 gaunt 表「骨瘦如柴」。

解答：

A middle-aged man was gaunt and pale.

6）　一位中年男士，不知何故，沿著荒蕪的街道蹣跚而行。

解析：

用 hobble 表「蹣跚而行」，其後須與 along 相搭配，以 ruined 與 streets 相搭配表「荒蕪的街道」，以 without 與 explanation 相搭配表「不知何故」。

解答：

A middle-aged man hobbled along the ruined streets without explanation.

第二步：內容分析

解析：

這一段的文意在說明海嘯對中年男士所產生的影響，為便於了解起見，我們將這段中各文句的相互關係用下列方式來表達：

1）句 = beginning sentence（A strong tsunami obliterated the entire village.）

2）句 = the effects of tsunami in general（upon ill-starred villagers）.

5）句 = description of a middle-aged man（gaunt and pale）.

6）句 = description of what he did（hobbling along the ruined streets）.

3）句 = the effects of tsunami in particular（loss of properties and relatives to the middle-aged man）.

4）句 = topic sentence（The tsunami pulled down his life.）

　　這一段分別用字義相同及字義相通的方法來使各句前後照應，例如1）、2）、3）及4）各句皆用海嘯一字使各句文意相銜接，而6）句中用同義字 ruined 與海嘯相應，此外3）、4）、5）及6）各句皆用代名詞來述及中年人，1）、2）、5）、6）及3）各句皆屬海嘯所造成災害的細節，而 4）句是總結海嘯對一特定人（中年人）所產生的影響，是屬主題句（即總綱）。

第三步：文意的周密及聯句的圓通

　　根據第二步的內容分析，本段各句的組合可由下圖來表達其架構：

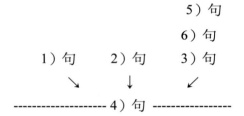

　　根據上圖，我們可從切題及文意的起承轉合二點來作解答。從切題看，2）句由1）句領起，描寫文中所提的強烈海嘯對一般不幸的村民所生的影響，而5）句、6）句及3）句是描寫強烈海嘯對一特定人所生的影響，而以 4）句作總結。從文意的起承轉合看，這一段文意是採取歸納法寫成。1）句是起調，領起以下各句，使各句層層向前推展，2）句交代清楚強烈海嘯的一般後果，進而用5）句、6）句及3）句鋪陳敘寫中年男士的蹇運另作說明，而 4）句乃包含全段描摹的意蘊，為全段在細節描寫中作文意的總結。值得注意的是，本段的主題句（4）句）簡潔，僅九個字，同時用破折號來加強

語氣。

根據上面的解析，我們初步的解答是：

1）A strong tsunami obliterated the entire village. 2）The impact of the tsunami's devastation left a sense of hollowness in the minds of many ill-starred villagers. 5）A middle-aged man was gaunt and pale. 6）A middle-aged man hobbled along the ruined streets without explanation. 3）The tsunami destroyed all his properties and took his relatives away from him. 4）The tsunami pulled down his life – everything to zero.

　　上面的初步解答仍可從句構的靈活使用及聯句圓通的二個觀點來改善。5）及6）二句文意相密，故可用 who 子句改寫成一複合句，即 A middle-aged man, who was gaunt and pale, hobbled along the ruined streets without explanation. 而這複合句又可用省略法改寫成一同位語，A middle-aged man, gaunt and pale, hobbled along the ruined streets without explanation. 2）句的 tsunami 述及 1）句的 tsunami，故可用代名詞（it）來取代。同樣 4）句中的 tsunami 述及 3）句中的 tsunami，故也可用代名詞（it）來取代。但需注意的是，3）句中的 tsunami 不宜用 it 取代，因為這樣可能引起指 5）句及 6）句描寫中年男士蹣跚而行的事，如此文意就不通了。根據以上各點，修正後的解答應是：

1）A strong tsunami obliterated the entire village. 2）The impact of tsunami left a sense of hollowness in the minds of many ill-starred villagers. 5）A middle-aged man, gaunt and pale, 6）hobbled along the ruined streets without explanation. 3）The tsunami destroyed all his properties and took his relatives away from him. 4）It pulled down his life – everything to zero.

習題三

I) 根據文意為下段設計一個英文主題句,同時指出文意是用何種方法來引申。

II) 試將其內容譯成英文。

畫是藝術的媒介,也是藝術的作品。畫是一種視覺圖案,由此圖案畫家使用比口頭表示更生動地來表達自己。受正確了解的畫述及評論家及畫家二者的觀點。這種觀點的關係是畫家的意見與評論家的意見二者相因而成。 這種關係導致來自二個不同意見的和諧。 評論家並非複製一張畫的意義。評論家是更客觀但並非偏狹地去發現一張畫的真正意義。畫是評論家及畫家二者溝通的最佳方式之一。

第 I)題解答

這段文意是用一張畫的功用作出發點來界定畫的意義,因此可用 What is a painting? 作主題句。其文意是用界定的方法來伸展,主題句以疑問句的形式來表達。

第 II)題

解析:

這一小題須分二個步驟去做,第一步是中譯英,第二步是根據聯句的圓通及文意的周密來成段。

第一步:中譯英

1) 何謂畫?

解析:

這句是指"畫是什麼?"

解答:

What is a painting?

2) 畫是藝術的媒介,也是藝術的作品。

解析：

用 medium 表「媒介」。

解答：

A painting is the medium of an art as well as a work of art.

3）　畫是一種視覺圖案，由此圖案畫家使用比口頭表示更生動地來表達自己。

解析：

用 visual 與 device 相搭配表「視覺圖案」，以 verbal 與 expression 相搭配表「口頭表示」，以 communicate 表「表達」。注意，從句構看，「由此圖案…」需用 which 子句來表達，同時用尺度比的方法來成句（詳參第 3.3.4 節）。

解答：

A painting is a visual device through which a painter may communicate himself more vividly than his own verbal expressions.

4）　受正確了解的畫述及評論家及畫家二者的觀點。

解析：

用 understand 表「了解」，用 relate 表「述及」，以 the critic 表「評論家」，佣 idea 表「觀點」。注意，從句構看，「受正確了解的畫」需用 that 子句來表達。

解答：

Paintings that are properly understood relate the ideas of a painter to the ideas of a critic.

5）　這種觀點的關係是畫家的意見與評論家的意見二者相因而成。

解析：

用 combine 表「相因」，其後需與 with 相搭配。

解答：

全民英檢
中高級作文指南

Such a relationship of ideas combines the view of the painter with the view of the critic.

6) 這種關係導致來自二個不同意見的和諧。

解析：

用 lead 表「導致」，其後需與 to 相搭配。用 harmony 表「和諧」。

解答：

Such a relationship leads to a harmony out of two individual views.

7) 評論家並非複製一張畫的意義。

解析：

用 duplicate 表「複製」。

解答：

A critic does not duplicate the meaning of a painting.

8) 評論家是更客觀但並非偏狹地去發現一張畫的真正意義。

解析：

用 objectively 表「客觀地」，以 narrow-mindedly 表「偏狹地」，用 discover 表「發現」。用 more ... but less 表「更 ... 但非」。注意，在文法上，這裡的 more 與 less 是用作副詞，二者用 but 相連結，而不是比較級的使用。

解答：

A critic discovers more objectively but less narrow-mindedly the true meaning of a painting.

9) 畫是評論家及畫家二者溝通的最佳方式之一。

解析：

用片語 a means of communication 表「溝通的方式」。

解答：

Paitinings are one of the best means of communication between a critic

376

and a painter.

根據以上的譯文，我們初步的解答是：

1）What is a painting? 2）A painting is the medium of an art as well as a work of art. 3）A painting is a visual device through which a painter may communicate himself more vividly than his own verbal expressions. 4）Paintings that are properly understood relate the ideas of a painter to the ideas of a critic. 5）Such a relationship of ideas combines the view of the painter with the view of the critic. 6）Such a relationship leads to a harmony out of two individual views. 7）A critic does not duplicate the meaning of a painting. 8）A critic discovers more objectively but less narrow-mindedly the true meaning of a painting. 9）Paitinings are one of the best means of communication between a critic and a painter.

第二步：文意的周密與聯句的圓通

解析：

為便於分析起見，我們將此段各句的相互關係用下列方式來表達：

1）句 = topic sentence（What is a painting?）

2）句 = definition of a painting – main theme（Painting is the medium of an art and a work of art.）

3）句 = exemplification of the main theme（Painting is a visual device used by a painter to communicate himself.）

4）句 = development of the main theme（A painting relates the ideas of a painter to those of a critic.）為 5）句作張本。

5）句 = exemplification of the above（Such a relationship combines the view of a painter with the view of a critic.）領起 6）句的結論。

6）句 = conclusion of the above relationship（a harmony of two individual views）.

7）句 = contrast（A critic does not duplicate the meaning of a painting.）
　　　將評論家及畫家之角色相較，為下句作鋪墊。

8）句 = development of the above（A critic discovers the true meaning of a painting.）

9）句 = conclusion of the whole paragraph（Paintings are one of the best means of communication between a critic and a painter.）

　　全段共九句，除 5）及 6）二句外，其他各句皆用第 4.2.1 節中字義相同的方法來求各文句的圓通，亦即皆用 painting，而 2）句的 painting 與 1）句的 painting 是用頂真法寫成，至於 5）及 6）二句雖未直接提到 painting 一字，但其文意間接與 painting 有關。
根據以上的分析，本段各句文意的組合可由下圖來表達其架構。

　　　　　　　　　　　　　4）句　　　　　　7）句
1）句 → 2）句 → 3）句 → 5）句 → 6）句→ 8）句 → 9）句
　　　　↑ ＿＿＿＿＿＿＿＿＿＿＿＿＿＿＿＿＿＿＿＿＿ ↑

我們從上圖曉得，1）句是起調，領起以下各句，2）句是 1）句的解答，是對「畫」所採的定義。3）句是從畫家的立場來說明畫的功用，4）句是「畫」功用的延伸，關係到畫家及評論家二者的觀念。5）句是 4）句的延伸，而 6）句是 4）及 5）二句的結論。7）句轉變語氣來說明評論家及畫家的不同，8）句是 7）句的引申，就一張畫的真正意義說明評論家的角色何在，9）句回旋往復到 2）句的定義。

　　從以上的內容分析，對這段文意的切題，可從每句皆直接或間接涉及 painting 的定義（2）句）有關中看出。從文意的起承轉合而言，這一段文意順序漸進，套用演繹的方法，對「畫」作一定義。起調 1）句點明是用界定的方法來伸展文意，2）句為主旨，為以下各句緊扣議題，層層向前推展，3）句以跳接之筆引申畫對畫家的功

用，4）句一闔一開，逆入評論家與畫家間的情隨意切，5）句補充4）句的文意，6）句作4）及5）二句的總結，7）句用轉折的筆法點明評論家與畫家的不同，8）句引申說明 7）句的意義，9）句是結尾，跌宕回復到2）句的主旨。

　　上面的初步解答仍可再從句構的靈活使用及聯句圓通的二個觀點來改善。3）句的主詞（painting）與2）句的主詞相同，故可採第4.2.2 節的方法，用 it 來取代，4）句可用省略法改寫成 Paintings properly understood relate the ideas of a painter to those of a critic. 5）句中用了二個 the view, 故第二個 the view 可用 that 來替代，而改寫成 Such a relationship of ideas combines the view of a painter with that of a critic. 這裡 4）句中的 relate 與 5）句的 relationship 是詞類互用的使用法。須注意的是，這二句的關係緊密，因此可改寫成一整句，同時可依第 4.2.2 節所討論的方法，用 the former 指 the painter，用 the latter 指 the critic，使這二句改寫成 Paintings properly understood relate the ideas of a painter to those of a critic, combining the view of the former with that of the latter. 6）句中的 such a relationship of ideas 述及 5）句中的主詞，故可用 it 來替代，同時 6）句為 4）及 5）二句的總結，故在句前可用轉折詞 as a result。 7）句根據文意是屬轉換語氣，因此可用轉折詞 but 使文意流暢，而將這一句改寫成 But a critic does not duplicate the meaning of a painting. 7）及 8）二句文意密切，故 8）句前可考慮用 instead 而將這一句改寫成 Instead, a critic discovers more objectively but less narrow-mindedly the true meaning of a painting. 9）句是結論，故可考慮用 in short 而將這一句改寫成 In short , paintings are one of the best means of communication between a critic and a painter. 根據以上各點，修正後的解答應是：

1）What is a painting? 2）A painting is the medium of an art as well as a work of art. 3）It is a visual device through which a painter may communicate himself more vividly than his own verbal expressions. 4）Paintings properly understood relate the ideas of a painter to those of a critic. 5）Such a relationship of ideas combines the view of the painter with that of the critic. [或者 4]Paintings properly understood relate the ideas of a painter to those of a critic, 5]combining the view of the former with that of the latter.] 6）As a result, it leads to a harmony out of two individual views. 7）But a critic does not duplicate the meaning of a painting. 8）Instead, a critic discovers more objectively but less narrow-mindedly the true meaning of a painting. 9）In short, paintings are one of the best means of communication between a critic and a painter.

　　本段使用了不同的路標，包括頂真法，代名詞，同義字及轉折詞，使文句圓通及文意易於了解。

習題四

　　我們對如何求文意周密，已做了很多習題，現在不妨用這些方法來改進自己作的英文第二稿。首先對主題句再斟酌一下。我們雖已根據簡潔，分明及切題的要求定奪了一個主題句，但需更進一步使主題句另具概括扼要的特性，這一點是我們在做本節習題一時發現的訣竅，所以要這樣做，為的是能提供我們在作文時文意待放的機會，否則在應試時，難免因主題狹窄而窒息思路，使文思無法發揮。在此不妨依此觀點將主題句重新再推敲一下，這樣將有助於我們有更多發揮文思的空間。

　　其次，再針對內容，確定一下此稿是採何種方法來求文意的周密，然後根據這方法來推敲一下是否妥善運用了這方法，譬如，所採用的是分析法時，那末不論是由總綱到細節，或由細節到總綱，都需研究一下層次是否分明，脈絡是否相承。然後將此稿作一詳細

的內容分析，審查各句組合排列的相互關係，建立起全段文意的合理架構，照此架構再從切題及起承轉合作出發點來審稿。

　　從切題言，中文原稿雖曾做過去蕪存菁的功夫（見第 4.1 節，習題六，第一步），但經過上述內容的分析及幾次從聯句圓通的觀點修改後，內容或仍有所不妥的地方需再度改善，在此，凡對主旨有所遺漏的地方需另行起句詳細說明，而與主旨僅具間接關係的句子也須加以補充說明，用以充實，而與主旨不符的地方則應予刪除。從起承轉合的角度來看，注意文意的伸展是否脈絡清晰，而整段的佈局是否妥貼工穩。相信經過這樣的修正，這最後一稿的內容非但緊扣主旨，同時結構嚴整緊湊，達到全段文意連貫通順而成一整體的要求，如此才能算是定稿。

　　讀者不妨將第一稿及此最後一稿互作比較，看看最後一稿不論從聯句的圓通及文意的周密講是否比第一稿高明。

　　不過，由於我們要求中文原稿有 400 字之多，這英文最後一稿的字數或許超出通常段落應有的字數，對這樣的長稿我們應該設法改寫成數段，關於這一點我們將在下節中討論。

4.4　章篇之結構

　　中高級「全民英檢」引導寫作的部份，祇要求考生寫一段 150-180 字左右的文章，根據字數，這要求僅及於段落而不涉及章篇。但大凡作文皆由句成段，由段成章，各段有其表主旨的文眼，每段的文眼靠緊扣全篇的主旨作導引而順勢發展，凡意盡乃成一段，意窮遂成一章。一方面，從各句的首尾圓通求全段文意的周密，另一方面，由各段的條貫統序而求全章的總義一體，因此我們在此另闢一節討論章篇的結構，作為本章的結尾。

　　如果段落是子句的化身，那末章篇是段落的縮影，表主旨的段

落是章篇的起段，每章以起段領起，點明全篇的題意，由破題而達放，總寫全章，使全篇中腹的內容自然流行。起段通常用直接方法來表達，例如羅斯福總統在要求國會對日宣戰的演講中，使用一個日期，作為珍珠港事件的歷史意義，來引申為何要向日本宣戰的原因，全篇演講辭的起段是：

> Yesterday, December 7, 1941 – a date which will live in infamy – the United States of America was suddenly and deliberately attacked by naval and air forces of the empire of Japan.

為求內容的完整一致，章篇也講究段落間的起承轉合，使各段環結緊密，文意流暢，以便導引讀者循文生意。最簡單而常用的方法是採用表順序的字眼，如 one reason, another reason 以及用數字及字母，諸如 first（firstly 或 in the first place）, second（secondly）, third（thirdly）或 1）、2）、3）…以及 a）、b）、c）…等。下例是一個典型的列示法：

> One reason why we find it so hard to know our own likings is because we are so little accustomed to try; we have our likings found for us in respect of by far the greater number of the matters that concern us; thus we have grown all our limbs on the strength of the likings of our ancestors and adopt these without question.
>
> Another reason is that, except in mere matters of eating and drinking, people do not realize the importance of finding out what it is that gives them pleasure if, that is to say, they would make themselves as comfortable here as they reasonably can. Very few, however, seem to care greatly whether they are comfortable or not….
>
> Samuel Butler, *On Knowing What Gives Us Pleasure*

英文中有很多字彙及片語常用作表段落間的邏輯關係，例如

and, but, consequently, finally, for example, for instance, furthermore, however, in contrast, in other words, in short, moreover, on the other hand, therefore 等。這些字彙及片語可用作連接先後二段的路標，如下例所示：

It is not yet known whether a computer has its own consciousness, and it would be hard to find out about this. When you walk into one of those great halls now built for the huge machines, and stand listening, it is easy to imagine that the faint, distant noises are the sound of thinking, and the turning of the spools gives them the look of wild creatures rolling their eyes in the effort to concentrate, choking with information. But real thinking, and dreaming, are other matters.

On the other hand, the evidences of something like an *unconscious*, equivalent to ours, are all around, in every mail. As extensions of the human brain, they have been construed with the same property of error, spontaneous, uncontrolled, and rich in possibilities.

Lewis Thomas, *The Err Is Human*

　　有時我們也可使用聯珠體的方法來謀求段落間的起承轉合，這種方法是使後段的起句採用前段末句的主要字彙，使先後二段的文意相互陪隨呼應，我們用下面的例子來作說明。

To convince doubters that the lands had been justly divided, [the Greek philosophers] took it upon themselves to prove the measurements rational as well as reasonable, by abstract argument. Hence the theorems of Pythagoras and Euclid. Reason gets out of hand once it deals with abstraction.

Abstract reasoning under the name of 'philosophy' became a new

sport for the leisured classes of Greece, and was applied not only to mathematics and physics, but to metaphysics.

Robert Graves, The Case for Xanthippe

在上例中，表前段末句的主要字彙 reason 及 abstraction 為後段的首句所使用（abstract reasoning），充作二段「承上起下」的過度，使文意緊密結合。

另一種段落起承轉合的方法是在前段的末提出一個問題，而在下段以回答此問題作引申，下面摘自一篇書評的二段即為「設問舉答」的一例：

.... Clearly their expectations were gratified, and they have brought to the task of recording the results the blend of charm and thoroughness already evinced in their nursery rhyme collections. Their 400-page book takes the reader right into the heart of the child country. What does he find there?

Leaving aside games（to be the subject of a second volume later）, the mass of sayings and customs here presented refers to almost every aspect of the unofficial social life of childhood between the ages six and fourteen. It is made up of rhymes, parodies, jokes, riddles, nicknames and repartee, together with more practical formulae of promise, barter, friendship, fortune and superstition, and a miscellaneous collection of calendar customs, pranks, and such expertise as the use of lean bacon rashers to deaden caning ....

Philip Larkin, The Savage Seventh

再一種方法是使後段的首句綜合前段的意思，然後再從另一角度來討論一個課題，例如本書第 4.3.4 節中最後一段，首先綜結以上各段的內容（即「本章詳細討論了如何求段落圓通及周密的各種方

法」），然後再提出一個應注意的地方，來更進一步的討論此課題，這是一個典型的「承先啟後」的用法。

使用段落起承轉合的目的是在使前後二段的文意層次分明，蟬聯成一體。在作文時不必拘泥於一體，不妨依文意使用以上所討論的各種方法，使似斷實續的文意，相抱相扣的連接在一起。

每篇文章都有結尾，結尾要呼應篇首，與起段看似成為兩截，但文意卻從起段經中腹一直貫注到底，使全文成首尾一體來卒章顯旨，總束全章。

習題一

指出本書第 3.3.3 節中前四段是採用何種起承轉合的方法。

解析：

該節第一段舉例解釋「詞類互用」的意義，其次三段開始皆用「詞類互用」的字眼來推衍文意。

解答：

這是使用聯珠體的方法來求各段文意的陪隨呼應。

習題二

指出本書第 1.1 節中，談及遣詞應注意的地方，是採用何種起承轉合的方法。

解析：

該節中有關遣詞應注意的地方，是採用「第一個」，「第二個」，「另一個」等分別來說明。

解答：

這是使用列示法來引申。

習題三

將您自己做的英文最後一稿,用本節所討論的方法改寫成數段。

解析:

這裡需注意幾點。第一,採用一個適合原稿文意的邏輯關係(諸如,前因後果,時間先後等)來分段。第二,分段後,每段仍需根據聯句的圓通及文意的周密來潤稿,例如在新的段落中酌情另加一個有關的主題句。第三,分段後要注意各段落間應使用何種起承轉合的方法,使全文文意脈絡相通,這裡我們要做到「句句相儷,段段相銜」的要求。

習題四

在您當地出版的英文報紙上找幾篇社論,仔細閱讀一遍,曉得詳細的內容後,按本節所討論的方法來指出各段文意是如何緊密結合的。

後記

　　讀者如依本書所討論的內容逐章逐節的做習題，那末在做完所有的習題之後，相信對本書所介紹的各種作文技巧已有相當程度的認識。但是運用不同的作文技巧，就猶如練十八般武藝一般，雖招招精通但無實際對招的經驗仍是枉然。所謂「操千曲而後曉聲」，意思無非是指要多多練習，才能熟能生巧。培養英文的作文能力也是如此，需要讀者在現有的基礎上常常且持續的練習才能致功。

　　在自修的過程中，讀者難免有應使用何種參考書的問題發生。下面將我個人認為可值得參考的幾本專著，介紹給讀者。

1)　Aarts, Bas, *English Syntax and Argumentation* (New York, N.Y.: St. Martins Press, 1997).

　　這本書的內容與很多傳統句法書在見解上不盡相同。讀者需先了解其內容及其特殊用詞，然後才能了解如何應用在造句上。這本書各節皆附習題供讀者練習。本書所採用的八字構圖，大多來自這本書的 x-bar syntax 的觀念。本書雖然不止一處利用八字構圖來分析隸屬關係以明瞭文句的結構，但對八字構圖本身並無詳細介紹，讀者如想對八字構圖作進一步的認識，不妨在閱讀此書之前另參考 Stageberg, Norman C., *An Introductory English Grammar*, 3rd ed. (New York, N.Y.: Holt, Rinehart and Winston, 1977)，其中第 19 章對 x-bar syntax 有詳細的介紹，並帶習題及解答。根據我手頭的資料，這本書最近一版是第五版，出版於 2000 年。

2)　Curme, George O., *A Grammar of the English Language* (Essex, Conn.: Verbatim, 1977).

這部書有二本，第一本講文法 (Parts of Speech)，第二本講句法 (Syntax)。這是一部鉅著，作者在第二本中引經據典的來說明各種句法的使用。國內坊間有很多「英語正則」一類的書，其內容皆可在此部書中找到權威性的解釋。

3) Huddleston, Rodney, *Introduction to the Grammar of English* (London: Cambridge University Press, 1984).

這本書雖自稱為「英文文法緒論」，但其內容是針對大專程度的學生而寫，因此讀者須具基本的文法常識才能將此書的內容融會貫通。

4) Quirk, Randolph, et al., *A Grammar of Contemporary English* (New York, N.Y., American Press, 1972).

這本書的內容非常齊備，除逐章討論詞性及分析句式外，另附語調 (intonation) 及標點符號的使用。讀者初讀這本書時，或許不易抓住大綱。對句式變化一點，不妨利用本書各章的內容作出發點與此書對照閱讀，相信這樣會比較容易抓住重點。而讀者將來如果對英文寫作有興趣的話，不妨買一本置於案頭以作平時的參考。根據我手頭的資料，這本書最近一版修定版於 1980 年出版。

此外，以下幾本書的內容及重點雖然不盡相同，但對英文的正確用法皆有舉例詳細說明，可常常放在手頭以作簡便參考之用。

1) *The American Heritage Book of English Usage: A Practical and Authoritative Guide to Contemporary English* (Boston, N.Y.: Houghton Mifflin, 1996).

這本書對文法，寫作風格 (style)，選字，疑難發音的字，以及字的構成 (word formation) 等皆有詳細的解釋，對每一個有爭

論的用法，皆經由其 Usage Panel 的成員投票，取多數意見來供讀者參考。本書在第 3.3.1 節中所列舉被動語態在何種情形下使用以及多處在補充說明中所採用的用法，皆以此書為依據。

2) *The New Fowler's Modern English Usage,* rev. 3rd ed. (Oxford, Oxford University Press, 2004).

這是一本廣受讀者歡迎的參考書。當初在 1927 年出版時，其標題為 *A Dictionary of Modern English Usage*。自初版至今，幾經修訂及再版，最近一版是第三版修訂版。作者 Fowler Henry Watson (1858-1933) 著作等身，本身是個權威。這本書對英語的正確用法逐條分析，提供讀者很多寶貴的看法，而作者用字的簡賅及句法的精煉是該書的另一特點。

3) Partridge, Eric, *Usage and Abuse: A Guide to Good English,* New edition (New York, N.Y.: Norton, 1995)

這本書曾由 Book-of-the-Month-Club 推薦過，重點在討論於作文及演講時，如何選字，及如何避免不當用字。這第二版是由 Janet Whitcut 主編，添了很多新的資料，為本書生色不少。

國家圖書館出版品預行編目

全民英檢中高級作文指南 / 唐清世著. -- 一版

. -- 臺北市：秀威資訊科技, 2006〔民 95〕
面； 公分. -- （語言文學類；PF0014）

ISBN 978-986-7080-46-72（精裝）

1. 英國語言 - 作文

805.17   95008705

 社會科學類　PF0014

全民英檢

作　　者 / 唐清世
發 行 人 / 宋政坤
執行編輯 / 李坤城
圖文排版 / 劉逸倩
封面設計 / 羅季芬
數位轉譯 / 徐真玉　沈裕閔
銷售發行 / 林怡君
網路服務 / 徐國晉
出版印製 / 秀威資訊科技股份有限公司
　　　　　台北市內湖區瑞光路 583 巷 25 號 1 樓
　　　　　電話：02-2657-9211　　　傳真：02-2657-9106
　　　　　E-mail：service@showwe.com.tw
經 銷 商 / 紅螞蟻圖書有限公司
　　　　　台北市內湖區舊宗路二段 121 巷 28、32 號 4 樓
　　　　　電話：02-2795-3656　　　傳真：02-2795-4100
　　　　　http://www.e-redant.com

2006 年 7 月 BOD 再刷
定價：470 元

讀　者　回　函　卡

感謝您購買本書，為提升服務品質，煩請填寫以下問卷，收到您的寶貴意見後，我們會仔細收藏記錄並回贈紀念品，謝謝！

1.您購買的書名：＿＿＿＿＿＿＿＿＿＿＿＿＿＿＿＿＿＿＿＿

2.您從何得知本書的消息？

　　□網路書店　　□部落格　　□資料庫搜尋　　□書訊　　□電子報　　□書店

　　□平面媒體　　□ 朋友推薦　　□網站推薦 □其他＿＿＿＿＿＿

3.您對本書的評價：(請填代號　1.非常滿意 2.滿意 3.尚可 4.再改進)

　　封面設計＿＿＿　版面編排＿＿＿　內容＿＿＿　文/譯筆＿＿＿　價格＿＿＿

4.讀完書後您覺得：

　　□很有收獲　　□有收獲　　□收獲不多　　□沒收獲

5.您會推薦本書給朋友嗎？

　　□會　□不會，為什麼？＿＿＿＿＿＿＿＿＿＿＿＿＿＿＿＿＿＿＿＿＿

6.其他寶貴的意見：＿＿＿＿＿＿＿＿＿＿＿＿＿＿＿＿＿＿＿＿

＿＿＿＿＿＿＿＿＿＿＿＿＿＿＿＿＿＿＿＿＿＿＿＿＿＿＿＿＿＿

＿＿＿＿＿＿＿＿＿＿＿＿＿＿＿＿＿＿＿＿＿＿＿＿＿＿＿＿＿＿

＿＿＿＿＿＿＿＿＿＿＿＿＿＿＿＿＿＿＿＿＿＿＿＿＿＿＿＿＿＿

讀者基本資料

姓名：＿＿＿＿＿＿＿＿＿＿　年齡：＿＿＿＿　性別：□女 □男

聯絡電話：＿＿＿＿＿＿＿＿　E-mail：＿＿＿＿＿＿＿＿＿＿

地址：＿＿＿＿＿＿＿＿＿＿＿＿＿＿＿＿＿＿＿＿＿＿＿＿＿＿

學歷：□高中(含)以下　　□高中　　□專科學校　　□大學

　　　□研究所(含)以上 □其他＿＿＿＿＿＿＿＿

職業：□製造業 □金融業 □資訊業 □軍警 □傳播業 □自由業

　　　□服務業 □公務員 □教職　　□學生 □其他＿＿＿＿＿＿

To：114

台北市內湖區瑞光路 583 巷 25 號 1 樓

秀威資訊科技股份有限公司　　　收

寄件人姓名：

寄件人地址：□□□

(請沿線對摺寄回,謝謝!)

秀威與 BOD

BOD（Books On Demand）是數位出版的大趨勢，秀威資訊率先運用 POD 數位印刷設備來生產書籍，並提供作者全程數位出版服務，致使書籍產銷零庫存，知識傳承不絕版，目前已開闢以下書系：

一、BOD 學術著作—專業論述的閱讀延伸
二、BOD 個人著作—分享生命的心路歷程
三、BOD 旅遊著作—個人深度旅遊文學創作
四、BOD 大陸學者—大陸專業學者學術出版
五、POD 獨家經銷—數位產製的代發行書籍

BOD 秀威網路書店：www.showwe.com.tw
政府出版品網路書店：www.govbooks.com.tw

永不絕版的故事・自己寫・永不休止的音符・自己唱